NEW YORK TIMES BESTSELLING AUTHOR

NICHOLAS SANSBURY SMITH
AND ANTHONY J. MELCHIORRI

WILD LANDS

THE NEW FRONTIER BOOK 2

aethonbooks.com

To the readers of the Trackers and New Frontier universe. Thank you for continuing to track and hunt with Raven and Creek. We are thrilled so many of you are enjoying their adventures!

"It was a hard land, and it bred hard men to hard ways." – Louis L'Amour

RECAP OF NEW FRONTIER BOOK 1: WILD FIRE

OVER TWO YEARS HAVE PASSED SINCE NORTH KOREA launched an EMP attack that crippled the United States of America. While much of the country has been on the long road to recovery, the land stretching between the Rocky Mountains to Sierra Nevada has been mired in chaos. Gangs and militias rule veritable fiefdoms where the law of the US Federal Government is nearly impossible to enforce. This stretch of dangerous terrain has been dubbed the New Frontier.

Marine Recon veteran and professional tracker Raven Spears deployed extensively in the New Frontier to track down missing people. Colorado Rangers Sheriff Lindsey Plymouth reorganized the previously all-volunteer Rangers into a formidable defensive force with the task of securing Colorado's shaky borders. And Steel Runner Iron Team Lead Calvin Jackson has been running ramped-up security for the armored trains that deliver vital goods across the country.

Raven, Calvin, and Lindsey worked together to protect an important shipment of medical supplies through Colorado.

Unfortunately, the train was attacked and derailed in

Utah. The cargo was stolen and most of the security forces defending it killed, but the raiders responsible weren't the only danger plaguing the New Frontier. A new bioengineered disease called Wild Fire emerged. USAMRIID was sent at the behest of Secretary of Defense Charlize Montgomery to help contain the rapidly spreading epidemic.

While dealing with this biological threat, Raven and Calvin worked with the Colorado Rangers to track down the criminals behind the train attack. Intel from USAMRIID and Lindsey led them to discover a terrorist cell known as the Reapers. These evil men were responsible for orchestrating violence and deploying Wild Fire across the New Frontier.

In their quest to stop this rogue group, Calvin and Raven were taken prisoner by a disgruntled man running a vigilante group from the Navajo Nation named Eddy Nez. They barely escaped, but not before severely wounding Eddy.

All of these events occurred during a turbulent election year. With President Diego doing what he can to maintain a sense of stability, firebrand challenger Senator Patrick Shelby seeks to take his place in the Oval Office. The ongoing campaign season tied Diego's hands and restricted some of his aid to the New Frontier for fears of compromising electoral optics. Despite a lack of support, the Colorado Rangers and their allies managed to stop the Reapers. But even with the splinter group of Iranian extremist terrorists eradicated, new enemies arise in the vacuum of power. Between these new hostile groups and Wild Fire still raging through the region, the New Frontier has become more wild and dangerous than ever before. Raven, Lindsey, and Calvin will be faced with more tough decisions to try and save their homes from bloodshed.

Welcome back to the New Frontier ... war is on the horizon.

THE WARM LATE AFTERNOON SUN BLANKETED RAVEN Spears in a comforting embrace as he stepped out into the front yard of his cabin. He breathed in the scent of sunbaked ponderosa pines and crisp mountain air. The fragrant aromas were joined by the gaminess of soil from a fresh rain and the smoky hint of a nearby campfire.

A nearby stream burbled with the whisper of wind through leaves in a quiet natural symphony. His bare feet crushed the gentle leaves of grass poking up from the twigs and pebbles.

Today was the epitome of peaceful.

He felt relaxed, but there was always the lingering horror of the past two years in the back of his mind. The death and losses had piled up.

For that reason, he was glad he wasn't alone. His sister, Sandra, was with him staring at a small fire burning next to the sweat lodge adjacent to his cabin. Her dark hair was swept back in a ponytail, and she wore a mask of concentration as if deep in thought.

Skinny eight-year-old Allie bent down next to the orange

flames, stoking a burning log heating a hanging pot. She was a miniature spitting image of her mother.

Raven's one-eyed Akita, Creek, wagged his tail, tongue hanging out. He looked happily back and forth between his human family members.

"Careful!" Sandra chided Allie as Raven approached. "Don't burn yourself."

"I'm fine, Mom," Allie said. "Geez."

Sandra looked to Raven. "You know she's stubborn as a wild horse. I blame you for that."

Raven held up his hands in a mock defensive gesture. "She's your daughter, Sis."

"Yeah, but I think she's spent too much time with you."

"Yup," Allie said with a chuckle. "I'm stubborn like Raven."

Raven gave Allie a mischievous grin as he knelt next to her. "I'm really stubborn?"

He watched her use a large ladle to stir the *wohanpi* soup while raising a brow.

"Are you seriously asking me that?" she asked. "Mom says you're more stubborn than an angry mule on a hot summer day."

Raven laughed and then took in a whiff of the salty aroma from the meat and vegetables. "Smells great."

His stomach growled again in hunger.

"You fasted, didn't you?" Sandra looked at him with concern.

"It's part of the ceremony, Sis. Relax."

"Relax? I know it's been a few weeks, but your body is still recovering from... all of that. You need to eat."

She gestured toward the mountains. Clearly, she was referring to Raven's last mission in the New Frontier with

Steel Runner Calvin Jackson. But she didn't want to go into details in front of Allie.

Creek whined next to him as if he agreed with Sandra.

"As soon as we finish the ceremony, I'll eat," Raven promised. "Besides, I'm good now. I'm feeling healthy. Shoot, even Calvin looks like he's ready to join the SEALs again. And you saw him after his stint in the hospital."

Sandra huffed. "Look, you both took a beating. Calvin's lucky he's had time to do physical therapy. And his lungs... you know I'm not supposed to be telling you this stuff anyway."

"Eh, Calvin already told me. He's almost back to normal. Point is, I can handle some fasting." Then he gave Allie a sideways glance. "Just so you know... fasting is better than what people used to do."

"What's that?" Allie asked.

Sandra eyed Raven.

"You don't want me to tell her?" he asked.

Sandra scoffed. "Ah, fine. Go on. She's seen worse."

Allie leaned toward him, intrigue painted over her features.

"They—" Raven began.

Before he could continue, the sound of tires biting over gravel interrupted them. He stood, reaching instinctively for the hatchet sheathed on his utility belt.

His world was one of danger, especially with the collapse of the United States. It was impossible to shake the instincts he'd honed to keep himself alive and protect those he loved.

Sandra seemed to notice and put a hand on his shoulder. "Just our guests."

"Yeah..." Raven said.

Creek ran toward the rust-pocked red Buick parking on the drive. Out from the driver's seat came gray-haired, leather-skinned Joanne Lithgow, beaming. Every wrinkle in her face seemed to smile. Her happiness was contagious.

The passenger door opened, and Joanne's sixteen-year-old granddaughter, Lara, got out. Her skin was a shade darker than Joanne's and she had a nearly black ponytail, imbued by her half-Sioux heritage.

Allie ran up to Lara and hugged her.

"She's looking so much healthier," Sandra said quietly to Raven. "Her spirit is glowing."

Raven smiled.

They exchanged greetings and embraces with Lara and Joanne.

Sandra, Allie, and Raven had known them for almost a month now. So much had happened since, it felt like a lifetime.

When Joanne gave Raven a hug, she looked up at him with crystal blue eyes.

"Lara told me all about the Sun Dance Ceremony," Joanne said. "I understand that non-Native American individuals usually don't—or aren't allowed to attend these ceremonies—so I'm honored to be here."

"You're Lara's family," Raven said. "We wouldn't have it any other way."

Sandra gave Joanne's hand a light squeeze. "For that matter, you're practically *our* family now. We're all just happy to celebrate this with some good people."

Raven had the group gather around a twelve-foot wooden pole he'd planted in his yard.

"This is the central pole," he explained. "I didn't exactly have time to construct the whole lodge that should go with it."

Lara shrugged. "Not every tribe did anyway."

"You've been reading up on the ceremony?" Raven asked.

"As much as I can. The Estes Park Library has a lot of good books to borrow."

Raven looked up at the pole. "Then maybe you can tell Allie what people did around the pole."

Lara took a step back, her foot breaking a twig. "We're not going to actually do it, are we?"

Raven gave her a comforting smile. "No, we're not."

"What? What aren't we going to do?" Allie glanced between the two of them.

Joanne appeared just as confused.

"Just tell us already!" Allie said, throwing her hands up dramatically in the air.

Sandra rolled her eyes. "Might as well explain all the gruesome details. I'll go light the sage."

As Raven motioned for the others to gather closer to the pole, Sandra gathered a few smudge pots and began setting them out around a circular perimeter.

"The traditional Sun Ceremony varies between tribes," Raven said. "One similarity between many is self-mortification."

"What's that mean?" Allie asked.

Sandra started lighting the smudge pots. Creek followed her, sniffing at each. The air filled with the aroma of sage.

"It means they used to hurt themselves," Lara said. "People would put skewers through their chest or back." She pointed to the pole. "Then they'd tie themselves to the pole with leather strips and move or dance around it until they were exhausted."

Allie had a hand over her mouth.

"The US government made the Sun Ceremony illegal for a while because of it," Lara continued. "But people kept practicing it anyway. Right, Raven?"

"Indeed we did," he replied.

Allie folded her arms over her chest. "Lots of stubborn people like you, Uncle Raven. See?"

"Our culture would never have survived if we weren't stubborn." Raven looked to Sandra. "We're stubborn because we're fighters."

His sister gave a prideful nod.

"I apologize, but why would people want to hurt themselves like this?" Joanne asked.

"Well, today, a lot of people simply fast, like I did," Raven said. "We make small sacrifices like that to remind ourselves of how lucky we are to be alive. It also shows that we can and will heal from that temporary pain."

"Sacrifice is necessary for healing," Sandra said. "At least, that's the idea."

Raven nodded. "Normally, the Sun Dance Ceremony is conducted at the beginning of the summer. It welcomes a new season, and it also shows gratitude for everything that allows us to survive, from food to shelter."

"It seems very fitting for these times," Joanne said.

Sandra returned to their circle after lighting the last smudge pot. Creek settled on his haunches next to her.

"Sister, you want to lead us?" Raven asked.

"Sure." Sandra kicked off the ceremony using a drum she'd brought from her home. Then Raven led Allie and Lara in a series of songs and dances with a chant. Their voices carried as the afternoon slowly turned to evening. The first threads of orange sky simmered up from the western mountains as the sun set. Sandra joined Raven, Allie, and Lara as they danced in circles around the central pole.

Joanne watched with a respectful gaze, quiet and observant.

While they danced, Raven's thoughts swirled to Colorado

Rangers Larry Yoon, Juan Molina, and all the others that had lost their lives to stop the Reapers and the spread of the Wild Fire plague. The only good news was that the Reapers appeared to have acted alone as a rogue group of terrorists hailing from Iran.

There was no evidence any of them were left in the United States. The international community had acted swiftly to investigate the matter on the diplomatic stage to ensure Iran wasn't actually culpable.

Whatever those investigations amounted to be, it didn't matter.

The Wild Fire was still in the New Frontier killing people. Raven had a feeling many, many more lives would fall before Wild Fire was stopped. Those thoughts were why a day or so without food seemed like a needed sacrifice. One he could easily afford when so many others had already paid the ultimate price.

This ceremony was for the deceased as much as for the living.

He concluded the ceremony with a whistle, motioning for them all to find seats back near the fire. The flames had long since settled into the gentle glow of orange embers.

A few bubbles popped in the soup.

Raven took a large ladle and pulled a sample of the soup up to his nose. He took in a big whiff. "I think it's ready."

"Great," Joanne said. "I'll go get all the extra bowls. Lara, can you help?"

"I will too," Allie said.

The three of them made their way to Joanne's Buick.

Raven and Sandra watched them go.

"It feels good to have a little normalcy like this," she said. "Working in the clinics all day, with all these Wild Fire patients, it still feels like the apocalypse."

"You think things are getting any better since we at least have a cure?" Raven asked.

"It's going to be a while before we can really tell," Sandra replied. "And we still need more of that cure. Just like you said about the ceremony, this is the beginning of our healing process. We've been told the government is working on producing enough of the cure to stop Wild Fire."

The girls and Joanne returned with stacks of big plastic bowls with lids and boxes to carry them. Raven and Sandra helped, forming a human assembly line. They put lids on the bowls and stacked them in larger boxes.

It took a good fifteen minutes to finish dishing out the soup.

Creek licked his lips as he stared at the pot.

"Sorry, boy, first things first," Raven said.

He gave Lara an especially wide smile. During some particularly dark times, she had brought him a bowl of the soup before to thank him for saving her from the New Frontier.

Now they would be serving it to dozens of people who had been displaced from the violent Badlands and were staying at the Estes Park Refugee Center

"This is why we do the Sun Dance Ceremony." Raven loaded a box of soup bowls into the Buick's trunk. "We honor the life we were given and use it to help others."

"And you've done more than your fair share of helping around here," Joanne said. "If it weren't for people like you, I wouldn't have Lara back." Then she turned to Sandra. "You've taken her under your wing at the clinic, and I can't thank you enough for that either."

"Oh, trust me, we're lucky to have a young woman like Lara helping us," Sandra said.

Raven closed the trunk as the girls got into the Buick, and he started for his Jeep.

Even though he was still hungry, he couldn't help but feel full. Full of hope. Full of optimism. Full of spirit from the ceremony.

The New Frontier would heal. And someday, when Allie was an adult, she would raise a family in a country that had once again found peace.

Sometimes all it took was handing out bowls of warm, nutritious soup to hungry, desperate families. Other times, it took leaps of heroism, like how Yoon and Molina had fought to their dying breaths.

Raven hoped it would be more of the former and not the latter.

But he was prepared to fight if it came down to it.

He was always ready for a fight.

———

Eddy "Ahiga" Nez sat atop his black mare, Yanaba.

Yanaba meant "She Meets Her Enemy" in Navajo—and she was about to make good on that in due time.

He itched at the bandages covering the burn wounds on his face.

Eventually, they would stop oozing under the gauze and heal. The scars would remain, but that did not bother Eddy. He cared more about the scars inflicted on his people, his tribe, and the whole of the New Frontier by the United States government. Psychological and societal wounds that had not ever been allowed to properly heal.

Not since the government had forced his people—and people like his—to abandon their lands and march, sometimes to their deaths, with false promises of safe and bountiful reservations to live on.

He had spent his life trying to change the fate of his people and was even making headway.

Until he met the man responsible for the scars on his face.

Every time he looked in a mirror, he thought of Raven Spears, the traitor that shared Native blood.

Tonight, he would let the anger burning through his veins fuel him. This was the next phase of his plan to take back what belonged to his people.

After all, his new nickname, Ahiga, meant "he fights."

Fighting was what he did. Fighting was what he was born to do. It was the only way to save his people and preserve their way of life.

In the pale moonlight filtering between the pine trees, he could see the faces of his men. Men that shared his vision. Their faces were dark with shadows and paint. Only the whites of their eyes seemed to show.

Warpaint wasn't common among Navajo traditions. But they weren't just Navajo.

They were the Rattlesnakes.

Thirty of the loyal warriors had followed him here to this lookout above Eagle, Colorado. On horses of their own, they carried rifles of all types. Molotov cocktails and other home-made explosives were secured to tactical harnesses and belts.

These warriors had defected from the Navajo Nation for the same reason he had. They were tired of fruitless peace talks and negotiations. Tired of bowing down to governments and peoples that didn't recognize or respect their strength.

Eddy had even recruited allies from other tribes. Men who wanted the same thing he did. Freedom from their oppressors.

Men like Robert Cosey. Eddy's second-in-command.

"We're almost ready, Ahiga," he said.

The thirty-four-year-old Apache had brought a group of his men to join Eddy's forces in the early days after the Great Reversal.

Eddy glanced over at the tall, lean warrior saddled on a brown-and-white stallion. He had a black band painted over his eyes and white streaks down his face. A long snake tattoo curled around his left arm. His face was weathered by the sun, and a long scar traced over his cheek. He was almost a head taller than Eddy, his body covered in roping muscles.

A stone ball club hung from his hip, and he wore a slung AK-47.

Eddy nodded after a beat, then adjusted the strap of his weapon, an M4 hanging over his shoulder.

He was holding a pair of binoculars to his eyes. Then he lowered them and passed them to Eddy. "The Union forces are moving into positions."

He directed them toward a creek winding between the mountains on either side of the valley. In the moonlight, Eddy thought he saw movement from more of their allies—another group of fighters hellbent on stopping the government and their henchmen.

Eddy didn't like the fact that some of these men didn't have Native blood. But he was a realistic leader. In the past, many of his ancestors had doomed themselves by going at it alone. They were brave, but ultimately lost their war.

As a student of history, Eddy long ago realized to win against the US, he would need troops and weapons. When the Great Reversal happened, he had been granted an opportunity he had never anticipated. He did not want to waste it.

To win this fight, he had started recruiting non-Native American militias and organizations into what became known as the Rattlesnake Union.

Another thirty men had assembled tonight under their banner.

There were many more Union forces throughout the New Frontier, ready for what Eddy called Operation White Buffalo, a campaign to reshape these lands.

Eddy scoped their target, nearly two hundred feet down the gentle slope.

He didn't need night vision. The glaring white lights illuminating the area gave away his enemies' positions.

Soldiers wearing the uniforms of the Civilian Volunteer Recovery Task Force patrolled along a chain-link gate set up on the road leading to the Eagle Recovery Site. A large building with pipes snaking in and out of it thrummed behind them. That was the biomass plant.

The entire base was surrounded by an electric fence. Almost all the security forces were positioned near the two-story building that had once been a three-bedroom home by the front gate. This was the facility's security center. The gate itself consisted of a corrugated metal panel that slid on motors.

Tonight, a pair of men stood guard in each of two wooden towers flanking the gate. Four men patrolled directly behind the gate. Another five or so should be in the security center.

Elsewhere in the facility were three more patrol teams of two men. All those teams were supposed to converge on the security center for a shift change at around three in the morning.

From intel Eddy had gathered, he knew it had been cobbled together from scavenged equipment from the nearby destroyed plant in Gypsum. It was intended to provide power to some of the nearby New Frontier communities.

Past it was the water treatment plant that had taken two years to restore. Beyond that, a golf resort had been converted to a massive solar farm. The huge panels were everywhere.

The US had spent an inordinate sum of money in these efforts. All of it was part of a concerted effort to take back the New Frontier for themselves.

"The men are ready," Robert confirmed as he gripped the handle of his club. "Let's paint the streets with their blood."

"Yes, no more waiting," said another Apache named Simon Kitcheyan. He was one of Robert's most vicious warriors, though he was nowhere near as big. He had a clear disdain for authority and about as much patience as a coyote salivating over bacon.

While Eddy wasn't a fan of the man's rash behavior, Kitcheyan and Robert were tools he needed for war.

"Patience. We wait for the shift change," Eddy said.

Kitcheyan gave a harumph and spat on the ground. The man was like a rabid dog biting at his restraints, ready to be let loose.

Eddy remained calm and took in the view. Lifting his watch, he saw the shift change was due fifteen minutes ago. Had the enemy somehow gotten wind of this attack?

The thought did give him pause.

He could certainly launch an attack now, but he wanted the base's security forces as concentrated as possible. His goal was to deliver a single devastating blow and give the enemy as little time to respond as possible.

"What if they saw us?" Kitcheyan said. Even from a few feet away, Eddy could smell alcohol on the man's breath. "We should strike now, before they hit us!"

He took a couple steps down the slope, raising his rifle.

"Patience before vengeance," Eddy said, trying to remain calm. "It's the rabid wolf that gets killed first."

"And the rabid wolf that *kills* first," Kitcheyan added.

"How do we reshape the New Frontier if we're dead

because we could not wait fifteen more minutes?" Eddy asked.

That fifteen minutes came and passed.

Then twenty-five minutes.

Eddy's heart beat faster in anticipation. He didn't want Kitcheyan to be right. He truly believed there was a time for cold calculation and another for unbridled ferocity.

The road to victory was paved with knowing which was the right choice in the moment.

Finally, the rumble of a truck engine echoed in the valley.

Patience had been the right call.

Eddy signaled for his men to slowly advance from their positions. Kitcheyan joined the ranks of the other Rattlesnakes on the slope.

Headlights speared up from a road down the northern side of the valley.

The truck rumbled up to the front gate that was already open.

Eddy thought of Raven Spears, anger rushing through his chest. He held up a hand, then dropped it and kicked Yanaba hard in the haunches. She rocketed forward, hooves sending up a shower of gravel and dirt.

Eddy used his radio to call his allies waiting near the gate. "Charge!"

Union forces rose from their hiding spots on the opposite side of the road leading to the gate. All thirty men were on foot, storming the gate and towers with rifles and shotguns. The blasts of gunfire became almost deafening as they tore into the enemy.

The Rattlesnakes began firing as they closed in. Salvo after salvo tore into the enemy's defensive positions.

The security personnel hadn't been ready for this two-pronged attack. With the lights near the gate, Eddy could see them retreating from the security center, seeking positions deeper in the Recovery Site.

Eddy and Yanaba galloped down the hillside, closing in on the gate.

Already three dead security personnel were sprawled across the road on the other side. Eddy counted seven other enemy troops running for the cover of buildings.

"Get them!" Eddy said.

Robert let out a shriek, then urged his horse on faster. Kitcheyan and the other Apache warriors followed.

In seconds, Robert caught up to the closest guard. He cranked back his stone ball club, then slammed it hard into the back of the guard's neck just under his helmet.

An audible crack snapped from the impact. The man crumpled, instantly paralyzed. Kitcheyan let out a diabolical laugh as he threw a hatchet that struck another soldier in the spine.

Robert flung himself off his horse onto another fleeing guard. They hit the ground in a jumble of tangled limbs and skidded to a stop.

Eddy twisted in the saddle with his rifle as the man rolled on top of Robert. The enemy raised a knife, ready to tear into Robert. Eddy fired his rifle into the chest of the soldier before he could stab the Apache man.

That left four more men.

Eddy pulled on Yanaba's reins, slowing. He lifted his rifle and sighted up a guard firing from the shelter of a forklift near the biomass plant. Eddy waited until his horse was stopped, then sighted up the soldier's head and fired three shots.

One of them connected, blowing off part of his skull in the moonlight.

Most of the other Rattlesnakes charged ahead, firing from their saddles with Kitcheyan at the lead. He leapt off his horse with an axe in hand and landed on a soldier. In seconds, he scalped the guard, leaving the man screaming in pain.

The remaining security personnel fell under the onslaught within moments.

"Secure the rest of the site!" Eddy shouted. "Take any workers prisoner. Then torch it all!"

A few men tossed Molotov cocktails at the forklift and some crates stacked next to the biomass plant. Others used hatchets and other weapons to bust the windows into the building. Men rushed into the buildings, screaming war cries.

Flames suddenly roared from inside the biomass plant and the water treatment facility. Embers caught on nearby trees, turning the place into an inferno.

The sight of so much fire evoked the anger ingrained in Eddy after Raven's attack.

He stared at the destruction as another group of Rattlesnakes rode their horses between the solar panels. They battered the panels or tossed homemade explosives between them. Low booms thudded out.

Victory was almost assuredly his.

Eddy turned Yanaba around to trot back toward the security gate.

On his way, he passed by Robert's first victim. The man was still lying on the ground. A low moan escaped him as blood pooled around his head.

Eddy raised his rifle, said a silent prayer, and shot the man. Death was still worth respecting, even if it was the death of his enemy.

Not far away, Robert was clubbing another victim. Blood and bone splashed up from the blows.

"Robert!" Eddy called. "With me!"

The warrior, drenched in blood, climbed back up onto his

horse. Together they returned to the security center. Flames licked out from the busted windows.

The soldiers fighting for the Rattlesnake Union gathered around the gate wore black fatigues and leather jackets. They represented one of the militias that had joined the Union six months ago: the Skulls.

All turned toward Eddy when he approached.

"The rest of the forces are with staff inside the buildings," Robert said.

"I want as many non-hostile hostages as possible," he replied.

The man glared for a long moment before finally nodding. Then he disappeared into the mess of buildings to join the rest of the Rattlesnakes burning the place down and gathering prisoners.

The leader of the Skulls, a bald man named Shupert with a dark beard and leather jacket, looked up at Eddy from under a helmet. He had an AR variant in his gloved hands, and a skull tattooed on his face.

"Like shooting fish in a barrel," he said.

"It won't always be this easy, but tonight was a great victory," Eddy said. "Tonight, we begin the march to free these lands."

The hoots and hollers of the Rattlesnakes filled the air, drowning out the random screams of staff trapped inside the buildings.

Robert and a group of warriors began to drag over the staff they had captured. They forced the enemies to their knees and smacked the people that begged for their lives.

Eddy paced in front of them.

"Please, please, I have kids," said one of the men.

"We're just workers," another guy said.

"Relax, we aren't going to kill you... yet," Eddy said. "Cooperate and you might be saved."

That silenced them, and he motioned for the prisoners to be taken away. Then he turned back to the gathering troops.

"Your gold will be delivered before the week is over," Eddy said to cheers.

Shupert smiled a big shit-eating grin. "The Steel Runners and their precious Angel Line couldn't deliver supplies as quickly as you, Eddy."

"The Steel Runners, Angel Line, and everyone outside the New Frontier will learn to fear us," Robert said. "None of them will be delivering anything through here again."

"We will—" Eddy began.

The crack of glass burst from the burning security center. A man in a mottled CVRTF uniform lunged from a second-story window, right out over the electric fence near the gate. He landed among some bushes and started limping toward the stream. He held one of his arms as if he'd been wounded.

A few men raised their rifles, but Eddy held up a hand.

"I'll run him down," Robert said.

"No, let him go," Eddy said. "Let him tell the story of what happened here. We need people to be afraid of us. Fear is our best weapon."

He secured his rifle over his back and turned his horse. Then he started toward the northwest corner of the facility. It was an empty metal warehouse in the middle of construction without a roof. On one of the corrugated steel walls, he used a can of spray paint to draw a large white buffalo.

It was a sacred symbol. A sign of hope, it promised the coming of good times and prosperity.

For Eddy, there was no greater hope than reconquering this land and returning it to the people who deserved it. He turned Yanaba back toward the other burning buildings as the flames climbed ever higher. The morning sun was just beginning to stretch over the horizon, turning the dark skies a pale blue.

Yes, for the people who lived in the New Frontier, the future would be filled with better times. Operation White Buffalo had truly begun.

2

COLORADO RANGERS SHERIFF LINDSEY PLYMOUTH drove her beloved white Ford Bronco down I-70. The open windows let in the crisp, early morning mountain air that blasted her and her passengers. UK Royal Marine Lieutenant George Blair sat in the front passenger seat. In the back was one of Lindsey's most loyal Rangers, Corporal John Rogers.

The sun had just broken over the horizon. This was her favorite part of the day. Quiet. Calm. Hopefully, it would remain that way.

They were on a routine drive to check on some nearby checkpoints along the border of the New Frontier. Every now and then, Lindsey liked to personally inspect them to make sure all was well. Given I-70 was still the major thoroughfare through Colorado, this was the most important road connecting them to the Western states—and if Lindsey was successful, it would eventually serve to reunite the communities in the New Frontier.

A George Strait song played from the old CD player. The sound wasn't the greatest. Some of the speakers were a bit crackly, but for once, in all the hell that surrounded her, it was nice to hear the classic innocence of "Check Yes or No."

For a moment, she got lost in Strait's lyrics regaling the purity of grade school romance.

"I will never understand this dreadful mumbling that Americans pass off as music," Lieutenant Blair said with a smirk. His thin mustache twitched as he spoke with his North London accent, sounding somewhere between Hugh Grant and Michael Caine to Lindsey's ears. "It's an assault to human decency."

"You know, I was actually beginning to enjoy it," Lindsey said.

"Nah, Sheriff, we need to play some *real* American music," Rogers said from the back seat. "Get me some Skynyrd or Zeppelin."

"Led Zeppelin is British," Blair said.

Rogers leaned forward in his seat. The guy had a buzzcut, but with the tattoos on his neck and peeking out of his sleeves, he looked like he'd be better suited with long hair like an 80s metal rockstar. "And who influenced them?" Rogers said. "Muddy Waters and Skip James. American blues, brother."

"You know, I was enjoying a nice song and these mountains, then you two had to open your mouths and talk," Lindsey said.

"I was merely trying to start a conversation." Blair let out a slight chuckle, stretching his left arm.

His cast had just been removed yesterday.

Lindsey turned the radio down. She was used to his good-natured ribbing—and more than ready to give it back. "The doctors said you should still be taking it easy back in Fort Golden. I've got half a mind to turn around and leave you there."

"Absolutely not. I'm out here to measure the Rangers'

progress on behalf of the Foreign Advisory Council. I take that job quite seriously." He spoke with a dry sort of biting sarcasm that Lindsey had come to appreciate.

"As part of that assignment, I'd appreciate it if you didn't criticize my music. After all, we're in the US of A and you're going to enjoy some good old American culture."

"Damn right he is!" Rogers said. "Look, man, you got to let me play some of my own songs on the guitar. You'd dig them. I admit I got inspired by a couple of these Brit bands, but trust me, when I say I can shred on the guitar, I mean it."

"Oh, you fancy yourself a new Hendrix?" Blair asked.

"Didn't claim to be a god, man," Rogers said, leaning back.

Lindsey looked through the rearview mirror to catch him looking longingly out at the mountains.

"Got to say, I always dreamed of playing at Red Rocks," Rogers said. "All this crap in the New Frontier has really ruined my music career aspirations."

"I'd say your guitar playing ruined your aspirations," Lindsey said with a laugh.

Blair chuckled.

"Ah, you guys are just jealous." Rogers still smiled when he said it. "You wish you could rip a solo that makes people's hair stand on end."

Lindsey let out a slight laugh. It felt good to laugh like that, even if just for a second. It momentarily pushed away the dark thoughts swirling at the back of her mind.

Of course, no matter how she distracted herself, she would never really forget the Rangers or Steel Runners that had lost their lives. So many had fought bravely to protect the Angel Line, then on the search to find and stop the Reapers.

All the while, the engineered Wild Fire plague was still spreading between people in the Badlands.

Yes, there was a lot of darkness out there. To mentally

endure it, she thought back to what her old mentor, Estes Park Police Chief Marcus Colton, would say: *When the night is dark as hell, you got to light a fire to keep you alive until morning. Whatever happens, rain or snow, you never let that fire go out. It'll keep you warm and give you something to fight for.*

She clung to that fire in her soul, never letting it go out. The one that told her there was a chance, with the help of people like Blair, she might live until the next morning.

"Weather's turning out nice," Rogers finally said again from the backseat. "I got high hopes for today."

"I like peaceful days," Blair said. "It makes me think this is working. The more days we have where the situation is under control, the easier it is to convince the other FAC members we're making progress. And of course, the easier it is to convince them to increase their support."

"Things are working," Lindsey said, nodding. "Restoring power and clean water has been helpful. It's expensive, but if it stops the people in the Badlands from attacking our supply lines, then I'm all for it. I'd rather spend millions of dollars rebuilding power plants and water treatment centers than bury another Ranger."

"A campaign of hearts and minds," Rogers said. "My dudes, this is just what we need."

A checkpoint ahead pulled Lindsey back to reality. In front of the barriers were a group of four Rangers. Chain-link fences topped with razor-wire traced the boundary on either side of the gate, leading toward the mountains and away from I-70.

Two Humvees were parked nearby. Guards were stationed in the machine gun turret of each.

"Everything looks tiptop here still," Blair said.

To their left, the wind whipped against a large white tent. It was surrounded by more chain-link fences. Two ambulances were parked beside it. The few people right outside the tent wore full biohazard suits.

Lindsey rolled her window down as a redhaired man in his early twenties approached. His nametape read LEVY. She showed her ID, even though he no doubt knew she was sheriff.

"How is the new quarantine camp?" Lindsey asked.

Levy looked over his shoulder, then sighed when turning back to the Bronco. "Sheriff, I won't lie. It filled up pretty fast. We had another six people trying to cross the border last night. That makes about twenty waiting out their quarantine in this tent alone."

"Any Wild Fire symptoms?"

"Not yet."

"Are you all ready in case someone does waltz in here showing symptoms?"

"We have our masks, meds, and medics ready at all times, ma'am. You've kept us well-equipped, so I'm not too worried."

Lindsey wanted to say, "I am," but bit her tongue. Instead, she simply said, "Glad to hear it. Don't hesitate to call my office if you need anything."

"I appreciate that, Sheriff."

Lindsey continued toward the gate that the guards were already opening.

One of the men dipped his helmet at her as she passed through.

"Backup's ready to join you, ma'am," he called.

A tan SUV with the bronze badge logo of the Rangers had been parked alongside the road. Four Rangers were in the SUV, including one medic that she knew well. They would provide help should her routine inspections turn sour.

Lindsey accelerated down the mostly empty interstate with the SUV following.

They flew past broken down cars and trucks lining the ditches. Nearly all their wheels were gone, and everything else of value had been stripped away.

Occasionally, they passed a torn backpack or a suitcase filled with sodden clothing discarded between the vehicles.

Lindsey tried not to think of the stories of loss and failed escapes behind each item. She joined Blair in watching their surroundings for threats.

Even with his mostly recovered injury from the Reapers, he was vigilant as ever. A sudden buzz on Lindsey's radio sounded.

"Sheriff, this is Corporal Nuke. Do you copy?" the voice called. His voice twinged in panic.

Bradley "Nuke" Giang was one of her recon scouts. The son of Vietnamese immigrants, he had studied nuclear engineering and worked with the Department of Energy in Grand Junction before the Collapse. Moving to Colorado had given him a love of the mountains, rock climbing, hiking, and backcountry skiing.

It had also given him an opportunity to volunteer with the Colorado Search & Rescue Association. He was a vital part of Lindsey's scouting teams.

Which meant if he sounded worried about something, it was serious.

Lindsey scooped up her radio. "Nuke, I copy."

"Sheriff, something happened to Eagle. They're not responding to any calls. I'm headed toward it right now from White River National Forest to the southwest."

"How long have they not been responding?"

"The guard shift that normally checks in failed to, and when I called, no one answered." There was a pause. "I can see big plumes of black smoke between the peaks. I'm headed in to investigate."

"Copy, Nuke. Be careful. I'm on my way."

Lindsey pressed the pedal to the floor, all thoughts of a peaceful morning erased. "Rogers, call the I-70 checkpoint for backup. We need people up there immediately."

As Rogers began coordinating reinforcements, Lindsey tried hailing the Eagle Recovery Site.

"Eagle, this is Sheriff Plymouth. Do you copy?"

No response.

A sour feeling welled up in her stomach.

She tried calling again as they sped past the mountains on either side of the interstate. She tried to see if she could see smoke, but from their vantage on the highway, she had a limited view of the sky.

"Eagle, does anyone copy? Over."

Still, nothing.

They came around a long bend on their way to Vail. She could just see the first gray wisps of smoke on the wind.

While she studied the smoke, Blair suddenly shouted.

"Look! There!"

Lindsey followed his finger. She slammed on the brakes and pulled toward the side of the road.

A lone man limped right past a charred school bus. There was a car on the side of the highway, its hood smoking about a half-mile away. It looked like this man had crashed the car, then come stumbling down this way for help.

The arms of his khaki jacket had been torn off, and his pants were torn. From this distance, he practically looked like a zombie.

Maybe he had an advanced Wild Fire infection.

"Put on your mask," Lindsey said to Blair. "Rogers, cover us."

Blair was already grabbing their medical protection supplies from the back seat. They donned their gas masks, then stepped out. Lindsey strapped an M4 over her back, and Blair carried his 9mm Marine-issued L131A1 pistol.

The limping man had a pistol holstered on his belt. Lindsey wasn't sure if he was dangerous, but she wouldn't take too many chances with him.

"Stop right there," Lindsey said forcefully.

The man kept on stumbling toward her.

"Sir, please stay where you are!" Lindsey said, raising her voice.

The man looked up at her with a bloody face that was also coated in grime or soot. He opened his mouth to say something, but then fell forward to his knees on the pavement.

"Rogers, get the medkit!" Lindsey called back.

Rogers rushed toward her with a med kit under his arm. He wore a gas mask like hers. She signaled for the other men to keep a lookout for a potential ambush in case this was a trap.

"Help..." the man mumbled. "I need..."

She approached him carefully, stopping just short of ten feet. The man looked up at her again.

It was then she noticed why his sleeves had been torn off. One had been wrapped tightly around his upper arm, the other around his leg.

She still wasn't sure if this was a setup—or if this guy had Wild Fire. With all the soot and blood, it was too hard to see any lesions or other telltale symptoms.

"Please," he muttered.

The man looked up to meet Lindsey's eyes.

She lowered her rifle slightly and examined his wounds. They looked like gashes from glass or something sharp.

Reaching down, she took her canteen off her belt and tossed it toward the man. He reached for it and started gulping greedily.

Rogers sidled up beside her. "Sheriff..."

"Go ahead, help him," Lindsey said.

When he finished drinking, he wiped his mouth.

"I'm with... I'm with the CVRTF."

The CVRTF was the Civilian Volunteer Recovery Task Force, a group of individuals who were putting their engineering, technology, construction, or other skills to use helping repair the United States' infrastructure.

"I was at Eagle. We were... We were attacked.... maybe a few hours ago... I don't know," he said. "Didn't have a radio on me when I escaped. Sheriff, these men came charging down the hill on horses. I ran, then took that car... but my head hurts now. I got in a crash and..."

"Hold on, we're going to get you help," Lindsey said. He was clearly suffering a concussion. She hoped he could hold it together to give her the information she wanted. "But I need to know what's going on. These men with horses... Who were they?"

He groaned as the medic began to check his wounds.

"Who were they?" she entreated.

The worker glanced back to her and mumbled out something about a snake.

A knot twisted painfully in her gut.

The Rattlesnakes.

The splinter group led by Eddy Nez from the Navajo Nation.

If they had attacked Eagle...

She turned to Blair and Rogers. "Get back in the Bronco. Call Raven Spears. We've got to get to Eagle."

———

Raven drove his Jeep up I-70 between the sun-drenched slopes. Creek sat in the passenger seat with his head out the window. Wind rustled over his coat.

Seeing the joy something simple like this brought to his dog made Raven smile. But his own joy was erased when his radio blared with a message from Sheriff Plymouth.

"Raven, there's been an attack at Eagle. Do you copy?"

He grabbed the radio from his dash. "Copy, yeah. What do you mean an attack?"

Raven felt the final warm bit of joy ripped away and replaced with cold dread as she explained everything.

Only a few days after they had defeated the Reapers and already they had new enemies to contend with.

The Rattlesnakes.

"Creek, sit," he said.

Raven did a U-turn and then mashed the pedal down. He thought of how Eddy and the Rattlesnakes had taken him captive at Montezuma Creek. It was there Raven smashed Eddy with a kerosene lamp in order to escape.

For the next hour, Raven sped toward Eagle, his heart hammering. His hope for peace was starting to look like another dream.

He finally pulled off the interstate and drove through Eagle. The town itself had been mostly destroyed in the Collapse. Blackened ruins of buildings lay in heaps. Pipes stuck up from the ground next to the fallen remains of a house.

Despite the devastation of the town, this site had been chosen for its strategic location to host the Eagle Recovery Site.

Now it was burning again.

Raven followed the road toward the drifting columns of

black smoke. The smell of burned plastic and wood filled the car, growing stronger the closer he got.

As he crested a hill, he got his first good view of the valley.

The gate to the facility below was wide open. Only a few timbers remained from what appeared to be watchtowers. Smoke fingered from the windows of the large biomass plant just beyond.

Four Ranger trucks were parked around the gate. Eight men stood guard, aiming their weapons in Raven's direction until they evidently recognized him. Then they waved Raven into the facility.

Once he got inside, he pulled up next to Lindsey's Bronco.

He grabbed his utility belt with hatchets and his Sig Sauer P365, then strapped his suppressed M4 over his back. Before getting out of the Jeep, he snagged his gas mask and slipped it over his head, not yet pulling it down completely.

Creek got out, sniffing the air.

Lindsey was headed from the biomass plant his way. Some of her red hair had fallen loose from under her sheriff's hat. She tucked it away as she joined Raven.

Soot was smeared across her khaki pants and shirt.

Blair wasn't far away, dressed in his Royal Marine combat uniform. Another Ranger followed them. Raven recognized his tattoos and the bandages he wore to cover his earlobe gauges when he was on duty. Corporal Rogers, the wannabe rockstar.

"Thanks for getting here so quickly," Lindsey said. "It's... it's a mess here."

"The hell happened..." Raven said.

"You don't need the mask," Rogers remarked.

"No infected?" he asked.

"No one's alive to be infected."

A leaden weight settled in Raven. He closed his eyes a moment, thinking of all the men and women who'd worked up here.

"How many...?" Raven started.

"We have a total of twenty-two deceased," Lindsey said. "More—about sixteen—may still be missing."

"Taken prisoner?"

"Maybe. We're still combing the area. Follow me."

She seemed to be holding it together, but Raven could tell she was disturbed. He followed her and Blair to the biomass plant and the water treatment center with Creek trotting after them.

The dog let out a quiet whine as they passed a wide green tarp. On it lay twelve bodies covered with white sheets.

The smell of death and barbecued flesh made Raven's eyes water.

Ahead, near the fields of solar panels, an excavator had its arm stuck straight out in the air. From its bucket hung two bodies strung up by their necks. Three Rangers worked to get them down.

While they walked, he scanned the ground. He noted the hoofprints in the dirt and crushed grass. Boot prints were everywhere.

Streaks of blood and bits of flesh covered parts of the sidewalk and pavement where it appeared someone had dragged bodies.

"The Rattlesnakes did this?" Raven asked. "I didn't realize they had so much firepower."

"We recovered one witness that says it was them," Lindsey said, still marching forward.

"Is this man... still alive?"

"He's in the ICU back in Golden."

"We have people waiting for the doctors to give us permission to ask him more questions," Blair said.

"Ok. Let's wait and see." Raven noticed they were following a particular set of hoofprints. "Do you have any idea where the Rattlesnakes went?"

"We've got scouts scouring the area," Lindsey said.

Raven raised a brow. The Rangers were good, but not all of them knew the mountains like he did. "You got scouts out there? Or do you need me to go right now?"

"Nuke is already out searching for traces of the enemy," Lindsey said.

Raven nodded. The guy was skilled at his job. From the few times Raven had run into Nuke, he knew the man had spent hundreds of hours training and even rescuing people off these mountains. "That's a relief."

"The enemy hightailed it like bats out of hell after the slaughter," Rogers said. "Don't know if even Nuke will find much."

"Son of a..." Raven muttered. He couldn't believe what he was seeing. As he walked through the macabre scene, he thought back to Montezuma Creek, recalling a map and talk of plans Eddy had for the New Frontier.

"This must have been part of his vision," Raven said.

Lindsey turned back as they walked between lines of trees. "Vision?"

"Eddy was talking about taking over parts of the New Frontier when he captured us. I remember him saying he was going to use us as hostages for something."

"Hostages to attack this place?" Blair scratched at his mustache. "It hardly seems like they needed hostages to get into and out of this area."

The lines of trees gave way to a wide parking lot. Next to the lot were a few unfinished warehouses.

"Eddy's people left that. Do you know what it means?" Lindsey pointed across the parking lot toward the side of one of the unfinished warehouses.

A crudely spray-painted white buffalo head with curled horns took up most of one wall. Streaks of paint dripped down from the wall, giving it an almost ghoulish appearance.

"Does this have any significance to Eddy's Navajo origins?" Blair asked.

"Significance, yes." Raven walked toward the warehouse with Creek padding along beside him. "A white buffalo is a sacred symbol to many Plains Indians."

He paused at the edge of the parking lot, a shiver tracing his spine. He turned toward the trees covering the slopes just outside the facility.

"What is it?" Lindsey asked.

Raven took in the entire scene, unsure.

"Sam, what are you thinking?"

"I don't know," he replied. "This symbol is so sacred in Native American traditions, it's difficult to understand why Eddy would associate it with this massacre."

"Maybe he's forsaken his culture and traditions," Blair offered.

"And his tribe," Raven agreed, but that still didn't feel quite right.

"Can you tell me what the deal is with this white buffalo then?" Rogers asked.

Creek sat on his haunches, pressing himself closer to Raven.

"The legend is different depending on the tribe, but I can give you one version," he said. "The Sioux were camping in the summer, generations ago. People were starving. They couldn't find anything to hunt.

"They sent two young men to look for food. They explored the Black Hills of South Dakota, seeking game." A cool wind rushed past Raven, carrying the scent of burned flesh and hair. "They encountered a beautiful young woman dressed all in white. She told them to return to their people and let them know she was coming.

"When she returned to the Lakota Sioux people, she brought a sacred pipe. The people shared it with her. She taught them everything about the world. All its mysteries. How nature and mankind and the beyond are connected. She told them how to act and how they should live. Before she left, she morphed into a white buffalo calf, then disappeared entirely. Not long after she vanished, a herd of buffalo surrounded the starving camp."

"So a white buffalo is a *good* sign?" Lindsey clarified.

"That's what most people believed. White buffalos are the most sacred living thing because of how rare they are."

"They actually exist, then?" Blair asked.

Raven nodded. "Every once in a while, they're observed in a normal herd of buffalo. Their birth symbolizes a future full of good luck and hope."

"Highly prophetic, then," Blair said. "Which begs the question why Eddy would use this symbol."

"Maybe Eddy thinks he's the white buffalo," Lindsey said. "Maybe he's a narcissist who believes he's the harbinger of prosperity in the New Frontier."

"Hey, man, that makes sense," Rogers said. "You said that the Sioux were starving before they saw the white buffalo. That fits with the past two years of suffering. He thinks that somehow all that is about to change."

"So I know I'm saying what we're all thinking, but then this attack is just the beginning of something bigger," Blair said.

"Yes, and we need to figure out what pronto," Raven said. "Before he can kill more people..."

Lindsey shook her head as she took in the damaged buildings.

"He's already set us back two full years. We put so much manpower and money into this Recovery Site," she said. "Manpower and money that we desperately need. It's going to take even longer now to return clean water and power to these lands. I don't know what kind of abundance and prosperity Eddy expects if he's just going to destroy the good we're doing."

"To me, it seems like the message he's sending is clear," Blair said. "He doesn't want us out here trying to make these lands better for the United States. He wants to keep them wild for his people to make their own."

3

Lindsey sat at her desk in her Fort Golden office with a cup of coffee. No matter how many times she'd showered in the past day, she could still smell the scent of burned flesh.

She couldn't tell if it was clinging to her hair and skin—or if it was just a terrible memory etched into her brain.

Maybe the smell wasn't real, but what happened in Eagle sure as hell was. Soon, she would visit the families of the Rangers lost in the Eagle attack.

She thought also of the CVRTF members and Rangers.

Twenty-four people dead. Another fifteen missing. All those lives needlessly lost.

Sure, they had almost a thousand people working for the Rangers. But stretched out between the prisons, Fort Golden, checkpoints, scouting duties, and general posts within Front Range communities, that didn't turn out to be a lot. Sitting in her office felt like she wasn't doing anything for them, but she was here because she needed to be. Thirty minutes after sitting at her desk, the satellite phone rang.

"Sheriff Plymouth," she answered.

The voice of Secretary of Defense Charlize Montgomery replied. "Lindsey, my God, I'm so sorry to hear about what happened."

"Thank you, Madam Secretary. It's been a huge shock to us. Just another cruel reminder there are more threats out here."

Lindsey took another sip of coffee. Its warmth didn't do anything to stop the chill of worry deep in her core.

"I spoke with President Tso of the Navajo Nation like you requested," Charlize went on. "After that day Raven visited Montezuma Creek, President Tso lost all contact with Eddy Nez and the Rattlesnakes. He was unaware of many of their activities."

"I hope he's not trying to pull one over on us."

"I believe him when he says that he had no idea just how power hungry and violent Eddy's people were getting. They acted entirely on their own. Tso vowed he'd do whatever possible to help find Eddy."

"So that means he doesn't know where they might be right now?"

"Not yet. He's having his people conduct an internal investigation. Most importantly, he's also sending one of his best Navajo Police Detectives, who also happens to be a close confidante of Tso. He'll help your team with whatever they need."

"That's great. Do you know who it is?"

"A detective named Jay Wauneka. Apparently, he and Eddy used to serve as Navajo Nation Police Officers. They even grew up together."

"But they aren't friends now."

"No, but I can understand if you're skeptical. Either Jay is going to be a big asset, or he is going to be a problem."

"I'll keep a close eye on him, and while I'm grateful, we

need a lot more help than one of Eddy's former friends... can I be honest?"

"Of course."

Lindsey swallowed, recalling the devastating scene from Eagle. "What I saw at the attack site was bad, Madame Secretary. The Rattlesnakes had a lot of men. They were clearly very organized."

The line was quiet for a few painful seconds.

"I understand, but President Diego is trying to maintain control of the borders and the coasts," Charlize said. "Food supplies are constantly in flux. People are going hungry and getting restless across the country. We're having a hell of a time dealing with those problems. As it stands, Diego believes the Rangers and the international peacekeeping forces you have from your Foreign Advisory Council's command should be enough."

"Perhaps you can inform him that Fort Golden's prison is full. We're struggling to maintain peace at the quarantine zones at our border checkpoints, and with the attacks on the rail lines, the Angel Line isn't sending supplies out to the New Frontier anymore. We're on the brink and the Rattlesnakes just sent us over the edge."

"Diego's got faith in you and your people. I do as well."

Lindsey hesitated.

"Is there something else?" Charlize asked.

"You told me I can be honest, and that compels me to believe this has to do with the election. I get it, I do. If I were POTUS, I wouldn't want everything happening out here to hit the news too, but we were close to—"

"Lindsey."

"Yes?"

"You're right, and while it seems like Diego is ignoring

this, I assure you that he isn't. That's why you and I are talking now."

"I see."

"We're very focused on the Wild Fire plague, supporting USAMRIID's mission, and keeping our allies from fleeing." Charlize let out an uncharacteristic sigh. "Everyone is spooked by the disease. They want to start pulling people back. They're even considering slowing aid shipments to prevent its spread."

"What? We *need* that aid. As much as I hate to admit it, we need the FAC."

"I know. Diego and I are doing what we can to ensure our allies will continue helping."

"Thank you. But, speaking freely, ma'am, how much *is* the election impacting Diego's decisions?"

"Truthfully, of course, the elections are always on our minds. Right now, Diego is ahead in the polls against Senator Patrick Shelby. But Shelby has been aggressively campaigning. He's taking advantage of the violence in the cities and using that to impugn Diego. We don't want to add more fuel to the fire."

"I see," Lindsey said.

"If we let this bubble over in the New Frontier, I'm afraid that's exactly what we'll be doing. You know that foreign aid you said you needed?"

"Of course."

"Shelby is saying that it's precisely the foreign aid that's been holding the US back, along with this incessant worrying about the New Frontier. He's taking an approach that would isolate our allies. He wants to send them all back so Americans aren't relying on aid to rebuild. Instead, he thinks we should be focusing on using all our own resources and companies to foster our economic growth."

"That's ridiculous."

"I know. This is why we've got to do everything in our power to keep Diego at the helm. Some of his choices might be slightly abrasive to your goals, but I assure you, Shelby's proposals would be downright destructive."

"I see."

"For now, I need you to continue doing this with what you've got. You and the Rangers have pulled off miracles and I know you will continue to support USAMRIID. Part of that will be stopping the Rattlesnakes with Jay's help. You've got this, Lindsey."

"I won't let you down."

"I know. Call anytime. I'm always here to help."

"Thank you. It means the world. Honest."

When the call ended and before Jay arrived, Lindsey's first order of business was to see how USAMRIID's mission was going, just like Diego wanted.

Minutes later, she was in the passenger seat of her deputy's lifted pickup truck headed around Denver. Cody Palmer had his signature aviator shades on. His sleeves were rolled up to reveal arms inked with bald eagles and a menagerie of red, white, and blue that would make Uncle Sam jealous.

Whispers of the Eagles' "Desperado" came from the speakers. The volume was turned down low enough Lindsey could barely hear the music.

"Did the meeting with the Secretary of Defense go okay, ma'am?" Palmer asked.

"Depends on what you mean by okay," Lindsey said. "The president essentially is patting us on the back while refusing to send more personnel. Shelby's got him too scared to do anything drastic."

Palmer shook his head as he turned the truck down

another road. They passed the broken skyline that used to be downtown Denver. Scaffolds traced up and down buildings with a couple cranes hanging high above.

"This election year, nonsense has really got the president acting like a softy," Palmer said. "It's like most of the country has their heads buried in the sand instead of facing what's brewing out here."

"Yeah, but Charlize did tell me trouble's brewing in all parts of the country. Maybe we got the Wild Fire and Rattlesnakes, but even she thinks that the security situation is getting tougher across America. People are starving. Allies are getting scared. Aid is slowing."

"Guess it's a perfect storm. Still, I wish Diego would do *something* out here."

"Wishes don't change minds," Lindsey said. "I'm afraid we're mostly on our own, which is how it's been for a while."

Palmer navigated the potholes like a pro by twisting the wheel with calculated precision. Lindsey watched the mostly abandoned suburbs go by, thinking about new and existing threats.

"We're here," Palmer said.

She snapped from her thoughts and saw a massive rectangular building on the outskirts of Centennial at the southwestern edge of Denver. That was their target.

This area was once a hub of industrial activity consisting of factories, manufacturing plants, and other businesses. Now it was mostly a ghost town. The only structure still active was the Regeneraid Therapeutics building.

Palmer pulled into a parking lot alive with work. Forklifts carted supplies from truck trailers in the loading dock into the building. CVRTF and USAMRIID personnel filed in and out of the glass doors at the front carrying in supplies from smaller trucks.

Lindsey squeezed through the workers with Palmer. Inside, they were greeted with sounds of hammering and whining drills. She and Palmer walked down the corridor until they heard a familiar voice booming orders.

"Yes, yes, those all need to go into the bioreactor room! Careful you do not dent them! And do not crimp those tubes! We cannot risk compromising any system."

In between the sea of people moving down the hall, Lindsey spotted the whisps of gray hair above Doctor Wheeler's bushy gray eyebrows. He waved when he spotted her.

"Doctor," she said.

"Sheriff."

"Looks like things are moving along."

"Well, it may look that way." Wheeler adjusted his black-rimmed glasses. "But all this work might be for nothing. Come with me."

Lindsey didn't like the sounds of that.

Wheeler guided her and Palmer away from the crowds.

They made it into a massive room with huge silver cylinders. Thin gas lines ran in parallel with larger tubes along the ceiling.

"I heard about the Eagle attack," Wheeler said. "I know your plate is already full, so I'll make this quick."

Lindsey nodded, dipping her sheriff's hat. "So what's the problem?"

"Despite all our research, we've only found a single cure to the Wild Fire," Wheeler said. "It's the bacteriocin the Reapers left behind. We've code-named the cure Commander."

"Oh, like after the aircraft that puts out forest fires?" Palmer asked.

"Correct," Wheeler said. "The problem is that this bacteriocin is not produced in many locations. There are minor production facilities in China, Germany and the UK."

Lindsey guessed where Wheeler was going with this. "But they can't supply enough for us?"

"Also correct," Wheeler said. "I'm sure you've been briefed, but with our allies getting nervous about the Wild Fire situation, I do not want to rely on foreign aid. I want to produce these Commander drugs at home. Even more important, with the state of things around the country, it's particularly important to reduce the need for transporting this drug from the coasts."

"It's going to be hard enough keeping the New Frontier secure. I don't want to rely on lengthy shipments vulnerable to attack."

"Glad we're on the same page." Wheeler gestured to the huge steel drums. "Here's where I need your help. Commander is a toxic peptide that can only be produced by a specific bacterium. We cannot simply replicate that peptide on our own. But these bioreactors can grow literal tons of that bacteria. The bacteria will produce the Commander peptide, which we can harvest from the culture liquid flowing through the reactors. First, though, we need the bacteria."

Lindsey was beginning to piece everything together, though she wasn't sure she completely understood all the science. "I take it these bacteria aren't easy to find if you're asking for our help. Where can we get it?"

Wheeler took out his smartphone and showed Lindsey a map of Southern California. "There's a lab at UCLA that was working with these bacteria prior to the Collapse. I already reached out. They still have samples in cold storage."

"And you want *us* to go get them?" Lindsey asked.

"I do." Wheeler's expression got serious.

"Why not send some of your own people?"

"Oh, I am. Plus, I've got people standing by in California to assist. But this mission is critical to our success. I want to know the people who retrieve the bacteria care about our mission as much as I do and they have the ability to get the job done. I trust you. I know you have a dog in this fight, so to speak."

"I *am* the dog in this fight, but I'm stretched thin again."

"I know, but you dealt with the Reapers. I'm sure you can handle these Rattlesnakes."

He smiled. "Besides, you have a knack for cutting through bureaucracy and red tape to get things done. Very valuable skills."

"I do my best."

"She *is* the best," Palmer said.

"So will you help ensure the absolutely vital delivery of these bacteria or will this all be for nothing?" Wheeler turned and looked at the building.

"Give me a minute," Lindsey said.

She walked to the side with Palmer so they could speak in private.

"The walls are closing in," she said.

"Yeah, tell me about it," Palmer replied.

"We need more people..."

"There is one."

Lindsey raised a brow at Palmer. "Who?"

"Calvin Jackson. He's an expert at logistics and defense of high-value cargo. Maybe him and some of his Steel Runners can help."

"It's a lot to ask of them."

"True... but it's not like they got any trains to ride right now."

Lindsey thought about it another minute as she surveyed the work in the distance.

"Okay, round 'em up and go with them, Palmer," she said. "I need you to make sure the bacteria get back here safely."

Palmer nodded. "You can count on me, Sheriff."

———

Navy SEAL veteran and Steel Runner Iron Lead Calvin Jackson gritted his teeth. He propped his elbows and knees on a mat in the physical therapy room of the Estes Park Medical Clinic. Keeping his lower back straight, he focused on keeping his muscles tight, doing his best to ignore the heat in his lumbar region as he held a plank position.

"Good, good, you're holding it longer and longer each session," his physical therapist, Tamber Stone, said. She glanced up at the clock on the wall. "Same time in two days?"

Calvin sighed as he stood and picked up the mat. "I think I can handle my exercises on my own again."

Tamber smiled as she wrote something on her notepad. "You've made a hell of a lot of progress, sure. But I like to make sure we're on the right path before I set you loose."

"Doc, I'm good. Trust me."

"Calvin, you spent a week and half in the hospital just recovering from the plague. We're only a couple weeks out from you being released from the hospital. Your wounds have mostly healed from the beating you took in Moab, but you need to build up strength again. You've gone through a lot."

"And I've made more progress than any of your other patients, haven't I?"

She tapped her pen on her notepad. "You're not wrong. But even an ex-Navy SEAL isn't invincible. You said yourself, you've had that back injury since your helicopter accident. Battlefield injuries like that don't just go away through force of will. We've got to manage the pain through PT."

Calvin gave her a dismissive wave. "I've heard it all before."

"Then you know how important it is."

An elderly woman came into the PT room using a cane. She gave Calvin and Tamber a big smile.

"Next appointment's here," Tamber said. "You're free for now."

Calvin left the room. The pain in his lower back was a shadow of its former fiery agony. And for the most part, the bruised ribs and the lacerations all over his skin no longer bothered him. His lungs had finally recovered from the Wild Fire.

But while PT might help with the battlefield injuries, it wouldn't fix everything.

About a month ago, he had watched his closest friend, Steve "Mouse" Gomez, die after a terrible attack on the Angel Line train they'd been assigned to defend.

His blood warmed his face at the memories, overcoming the pain. He still saw the horrifying explosion that took Mouse, along with the images of the Reapers sifting through the wreckage and executing his comrades.

The agonized voices of dying Steel Runners echoed in his mind. Anger started to fill Calvin. His pulse drummed heavily in his ears. His fingers curled into fists.

Mouse's oft-repeated motto played through Calvin's thoughts: *It's just a mind game.*

He had to fight back the emotion. Had to calm himself. Because none of his useless anger would help him avenge their deaths or ensure their sacrifices weren't in vain.

Instead, he headed down the corridor to the clinic's entrance, ready to get back to his volunteer work at the Estes Park Refugee Center. He stopped when he heard feet pounding behind him. He turned to see Deputy Cody Palmer running toward him.

"Cal! Hold up!" Palmer said.

Calvin paused in the corridor, stepping out of the way of a doctor pushing a man in a wheelchair past.

Palmer caught up. "Sorry to bust in here like this, but I didn't want to miss you. I was asking around for you, and Anna told me you were in PT."

Anna was one of Calvin's trusted Steel Runners. She had been spending her time in Estes Park while recovering from her own injuries helping out at the nearby Refugee Center.

"Just got done with it. What's up, Palmer?"

"There's been a development. Calvin, I won't sugarcoat a turd and call it a donut, so I want to be frank with you. We need your help."

"I'm not sure I can help with anything," Calvin said. "As much as I want to, I've got to figure out a way to San Diego to go help some people that are like family to me."

"Now, I haven't spent much time in Cali," Palmer said, "and truth be told, it never was my favorite state, but I'm pretty sure LA is only a short drive from San Diego."

"Yeah. What are you going on about?"

"Well, under Sheriff Plymouth's direction, I'm organizing an airlift mission to and from LA. We've got to pick up a high-value asset from a UCLA lab. We could use your help organizing security. Frankly put, we don't got a lot of our own men we can afford to send."

"That all sounds well and good," Calvin said, "but I want to get to San Diego and *stay* there."

"Oh, if you want to stay in SoCal after, that's your prerogative. We can get you a ride down to San Diego if you help us get the cargo to and from UCLA."

"Shoot, Palmer, if you get me to LA, you don't need to get me a ride. I'll walk to San Diego."

"Does that mean you're in?"

Calvin clapped Palmer on the shoulder. "I'm ready to get my sorry ass to California, you bet. But I don't speak for the rest of the Runners. I've got to go talk to them."

"Thanks, Cal," Palmer said. "We're going to need to move out in a hurry, so as soon as you can, get yourself and any Runners that want to help down to Buckley. I'll have more info for you guys when you get there."

Calvin wasted no time in heading to the Refugee Center. He walked past downtown filled with stores, restaurants, and hotels. Many of the businesses had been turned into apartments and temporary homes for those who lived on the outskirts of Estes Park.

The power hadn't been reliably restored to most rural areas, so people preferred congregating in places like this where they could work together to protect and repair the community.

The Refugee Center was one such place. Calvin walked toward Lake Estes. He could see the green-roofed cabin-like buildings that made up the Estes Park Resort, the complex that had been converted into the Refugee Center.

One his way to the three-story building, he saw a couple of familiar faces at one of the pavilions beside the concrete path alongside the lake. Three people were seated at a picnic table.

First was Leo "Boston" Barnes. A short brown beard covered his chin. Stocky and muscular, he sat on the edge of the picnic table. A cigarette between his fingers glowed with each puff. Bits of gray flecked his hair.

"Calvin, wicked good to see you, my man. You want a

fricking smoke or what, chief?" Boston said with an accent that immediately explained his nickname.

"I'm good, but thanks."

Calvin took a seat at the table. Next to Boston was Anna. Chin-length brown hair framed her face. She wore a dirty White Sox cap.

"The both of you too good for a smoke, then?" Boston said.

"There are enough things trying to kill me out here," Anna said. "I don't need to add lung cancer to the list. Plan on growing old with my sister and nieces back out east, ya know?"

"You going to head east soon?" Calvin asked, sitting at the picnic table. "You're looking healthy and fit again."

Anna had been one of the many injured in the Angel Line attack. She turned her attention to the lake. A few ducks quacked as they flew over the water nearby then landed with a splash.

"Not quite yet," Anna said. "Got work to be done out here. And I'm not leaving Colorado for good until *all* our Runners can."

Calvin smiled at that. "I appreciate that. You still wearing Travis's hat, huh?"

Anna tapped on the White Sox cap. "I miss that man. Sure, Travis could be annoying. What with his constant bitching and thinking he was going to be America's next great billionaire by losing his money at every poker table he saw... but I kind of liked that surly dude."

"Me too. The hat looks better on you, though."

"It'd look a lot better if you guys were talking about the Red Sox instead of the White," Boston said. "Fricking shame if you ask me."

"Ah, nobody asked you," Calvin said with a chuckle.

"Chicago beats Boston any day of the week. 'Course the Orioles were always better, in my opinion. But I got a question for you two. What do you think about the West Coast?"

"You kidding me, man? You guys really going to ask me?" Boston asked.

Calvin held up his hands defensively. "Shouldn't have asked. Here's the deal, last I checked, we got twenty Runners that have been released from the hospital."

"You got it right," Anna said. "Still got another six in recovery. Guys and gals that I'm not sure are getting out anytime soon."

Calvin looked back out at the ducks for a second. Some of the Runners had lost limbs in the train attack that had stranded them all here. But they were still the lucky ones. They were the ones that had come here in stretchers instead of body bags.

"Well, I just got a job from Golden," Calvin continued.

"You mean the Ranger boys?" Boston asked.

Calvin nodded. "They want us to help them recover some key ingredients to manufacture the cure to Wild Fire."

"Ah, chief, that's a wicked big deal. But why us? They aren't sending their own?"

Calvin shrugged. "Can't. Got too much going around here. I'm going. And after I do this job, I'm planning on staying out West."

"Take care of Mouse's family?" Anna guessed.

"You got it. I ain't going to leave them high and dry."

"Shit, chief," Boston said. "You go, I go. Anna and I can round up the others. No one's gonna want to sit this out."

Anna didn't look so certain. She took the White Sox cap off and toyed with the brim.

"Something up, Sister?" Calvin asked.

"Cal, I didn't know when or how to tell you this, but I'm

planning on giving up running. I wasn't keen on doing the transport thing again. No more rails for me."

"I get it," Calvin said. "I wouldn't fault a single one of you if you wanted to stay here in Estes Park and take it easy for the rest of your lives. God knows you deserve it."

"I can tell there's a 'but'," Anna said.

"One last mission," Calvin said. "One last run. It's just a couple days. We go into LA, pick up the goods, then get them back on the plane to get here. I just want to reiterate: We're talking the ingredients the eggheads in USAMRIID need to stop Wild Fire. I wouldn't ask if it wasn't important, you dig?"

Anna paused a second, staring out at the lake. "All right. For Travis."

"Thanks, Anna," Calvin said. "You guys seen Ortiz or Marino lately?"

Boston used a thumb to indicate the Refugee Center behind them. "Both of 'em are on shift with us. The rest of 'em are scattered around town. R&R, you know?"

"Good. Have Ortiz and Marino help us gather the team. We got twenty people that can help save thousands, maybe tens of thousands, of lives. Trust me when I say this is worth it. Then if you guys choose not to run steel again, I won't come begging for help. Deal?"

"Deal," Anna said.

Boston huffed a breath full of smoke. "Fo sho."

"Great," Calvin said. "I've got to work out logistics and make a call to Mouse's family. But I'll see you guys soon."

As soon as Boston and Anna left, Calvin used a sat phone he had borrowed from the Refugee Center to dial Maureen's restored landline number. She picked up after only a few rings.

"Calvin," she answered.

"How are you and the kids?"

"Raquel and Frankie are... I don't know," she said. "I'm not sure they really believe Steve is gone. They're used to him being away for work, and I think... I think in a sad way, it just isn't real for them."

Calvin again didn't know what to say, so he apologized, again.

"I'm so sorry, Maureen."

"It's not your fault, Calvin."

But it *was* his fault. He had failed Mouse. Failed the Angel Line and his Steel Runners.

"Calvin..." she said after a pause.

"Yeah, I'm here."

"Really. It's not your fault, and we're all glad you're alive."

Calvin closed his eyes, and then let out an exhale away from the phone. He was alive, Mouse was dead, and the Angel Line was gone.

His mission from Palmer was to help get the ingredients for the Wild Fire cure. But his new mission in life was to help Maureen and her kids.

"What's the situation like around San Diego?" Calvin said. "Are you and the kids safe?"

The line remained silent for a few seconds. Worry coiled in his gut.

"It's getting worse every day," Maureen said. "But I guess that's the story around the country."

"Look, remember how I told you before I'd take a car and drive all the way there if I have to just so I can see you guys."

"No, Calvin. You'd be risking your life. It isn't safe to drive across the New Frontier. Not with the crime and disease."

"Well, there's no need anymore."

"How's that, Cal?"

"I've got a ride." He started walking along the path around

the lake again. The ducks took off, flapping and flying into the blue sky. "I'm going to get an airlift out there. I'll see you and the kids soon. I promise."

It looked like he got the excuse he needed to skip that last PT appointment after all.

4

RAVEN STOOD IN THE TALL GRASS WITH HIS ARMS FOLDED across his chest with Creek next to him. He smiled as Allie pulled back the string on Lara's bow. The teenager watched the younger girl aim at a target Raven had set up on his sister's property.

Allie pulled back the string just like Raven had taught her, elbow high, past her ear.

"Okay," he said. "Looks good."

His niece let the arrow fly. It zipped right into a bush next to the target.

"Nice try," Lara said.

The young woman gave Allie a pat on the back. Allie gently lowered the homemade bow.

"I can't do it," Allie said with a frown.

"Yes, you can," Lara said. "You just need to focus more."

Raven didn't say anything. Lara was doing a good job training Allie. And he planned on letting her continue to do so. It was a good confidence builder for Lara, and truthfully, Raven was happy to see her taking on this responsibility.

Lara and Allie retrieved the arrow and returned to the

shooting line. The sun was beginning to drop behind the mountains to their west. The sky had already darkened and shadows filled the forest.

They wouldn't have much more time to practice, but Allie seemed determined to hit that target.

Allie nocked the arrow, pulled back, aimed, and let it fly.

The arrow got closer this time, but lanced into a nearby tree instead of the target.

"Dang it!" Allie said.

"Why don't you take another step closer?" Lara asked.

"No way," Allie said. "You didn't, and you still hit the target."

"Yes, but I've been shooting this bow for years. Skill takes time."

Raven smiled slightly at that.

The young woman had truly broken out of her shell after he'd helped her escape the mountains and the New Frontier. It was amazing what the love of her grandmother, a welcoming community like Estes Park, and some warm food could do in a month.

Of course, Lara's spirit of determination and plucky attitude had no small part to play in her journey.

"What am I doing wrong?" Allie asked.

Lara looked back to Raven, his cue to step in. He walked over and lowered his arms.

"You've got to keep your arm still," he instructed. "Even when you let go of the string, keep that bow arm straight out."

"I'm trying," Allie said. "It isn't easy, though."

"Lara, go ahead and show her again," Raven said.

She took her own bow and nocked an arrow. It was hard to believe that a tool like that had kept the young woman alive in a terrible situation and now was being used to teach Allie in the safety of Sandra's yard.

Lara drew the string back, closed one eye, then let it go.

The end of the arrow slammed into the center of the target. Lara lowered the bow with a grin.

"Very nice," Raven said.

"Every time." Allie threw up a hand in mock exasperation. "I don't even need a bull's eye. I just want to hit the target."

"You'll get there," Lara said. "I promise."

She coached Allie on how to draw the arrow back again. Using a soothing voice and gentle touch, she showed Allie where her elbow on her nocking arm should be and how to better control her bow arm.

"Try again," Lara said.

Allie did as she was instructed and let the string go. The arrow cut through the air. This time, it hit the target with a solid thwack, landing cleanly in the seven-point ring.

Allie lowered her bow. "I actually got it!"

Raven held out his hand for a high-five. "Great job!"

She bypassed it completely and instead threw her arms around his waist in a hug. He pulled her in close and couldn't help the smile crossing his face.

When Allie pulled away, she gave Lara a big hug.

"Thank you, guys!" Allie said. "I promise I'm going to keep getting better."

"I have no doubt," Raven said.

He relished seeing her smile. She was practically like a daughter to him. He felt what he believed to be the joy of a parent.

Before the Collapse, he hadn't really considered being a parent. He'd been too focused on his own needs.

Now, even if he did find someone to love and start a family with, he wasn't sure if it was a good idea. Especially when he considered all he saw at Eagle, it was hard to believe bringing a child into this world was the right thing to do. The dangers of the New Frontier, the instability of the United States, and the ravages of the Wild Fire were terrible enough. He couldn't imagine trying to protect a child's innocence from all that.

That was a worry for another day, though.

He shook those thoughts from his mind and focused on his niece and Lara. They continued practicing for another good fifteen minutes before Sandra's car rolled up into the driveway.

"Mom's home!" Allie said. "I'm going to show her what I've learned."

Sandra stepped out of the vehicle still wearing scrubs from the clinic. She looked exhausted and overworked but managed a smile. Raven could tell it was forced.

Allie ran to greet her, telling her all about her archery skills, before returning to the yard to show those skills off.

Sandra watched, but Raven saw her mind wasn't in it. She wore the same nearly blank expression she had adopted as a kid when their father came home drunk and yelling. It was like she flipped a switch that turned off all her emotions.

At first, he feared she was pissed at him for letting Allie use the bow.

But the more he studied Sandra's expression, the more he realized there was something else going on.

"Hey, Lara, do you mind helping out Allie a bit more?" Raven asked. "I want to talk to Sandra for a moment."

Lara seemed to sense his worry. "Sure."

"Creek, you stay with them and help," Raven said to the dog. "Listen to all Creek's advice, okay, Allie?"

The girl laughed, shaking her head as Raven led Sandra to her front porch, out of earshot of the girls.

"Bad shift?" Raven asked.

Sandra's expression seemed to deflate. "I thought when they found a cure for Wild Fire, things would get better. But they aren't. We're getting more and more patients. We're going to be working double-shifts soon, and I'm still trying to help at the Refugee Center. Everyone's already exhausted."

"Damn..."

"There's talk that the schools might not reopen at the end of summer either, and I'll still have to work. I don't know what I'm going to do about Allie..."

She looked at Raven like she expected him to volunteer to watch his niece.

"I'll do what I can," he said. "But I've still got to make a living."

"I know you've got to help Lindsey. You've got work to do in the New Frontier."

Raven frowned. "I'm sorry, Sis. It's true, though. We have no idea what the Rattlesnakes are planning. All we know is we need to stop them."

"You told me, sure. But she's got the Rangers and the FAC..."

"Yeah, but if the rumors are true, I'm not sure how long the FAC is gonna be around."

"We might lose them?"

Raven shrugged. He grabbed the railing of the porch and looked at Allie and Lara. His mind returned to his earlier thoughts about protecting his niece.

Staying home to watch her was one way to do it, but the real work was done out there. In the New Frontier.

He sighed as his eyes shifted to the mountains. "Someone's got to stop the assholes in the Badlands from leaking into the Front Range communities. I've got to be one of those someones."

"Did you see that, Mom?" Allie shouted.

Sandra raised a hand like she had. "Yeah, good job!"

Allie turned back to the target and prepared another shot while Sandra looked back to Raven.

"You know, it's because Eddy and his type are in the New Frontier that I'm actually glad you two are teaching Allie how to use a bow," she said.

"Really?" Raven asked.

"I'm afraid she's going to need to know how to use weapons like that far too soon."

"Not if I can help it." Raven watched the girls retrieving their arrows. "That's why I've got to keep fighting."

Sandra put her hand on the side of Raven's arm and gave it a squeeze. She didn't say anything else, but Raven still had one thing left on his mind. A dream maybe, but he was going to give everything he had to make it a reality.

"We'll find peace someday," he said. "I feel it in my heart, Sis."

———

Two days had passed since the Rattlesnakes led the victory at the Eagle Recovery Site. Victory had tasted sweet to Eddy at the time. But this was only the beginning for his vision.

He didn't let himself or his men celebrate too long.

They had work to do.

He sauntered between the cluster of four-story brown buildings that made up Telluride Ski Resort's Mountain Village. Frozen ski lifts led up and down the mountain. Climbing up the slopes without them wasn't easy. This was precisely why it had made a good temporary camp for their constantly moving headquarters.

Like his ancestors, Eddy never made any specific location home for long. He had to stay one step ahead of his enemies.

The tree that dug in its roots eventually got cut down. The tumbleweed that traveled across the desert escaped such a fate.

His force of over two hundred Rattlesnakes was spread throughout the New Frontier. He had augmented his Rattlesnakes with militias, tribes, and other communities representing nearly another seven hundred fighters through his Rattlesnake Union—assuming they all agreed to go to war with him.

And tonight, he hoped to recruit even more.

"I don't know anything!" a voice bellowed.

Eddy turned the corner to see six of his Rattlesnakes guarding the old-fashioned stocks they'd constructed in the Village Park next to the old Telluride Conference Center. Kitcheyan was among them, watching Robert stalk between the prisoners.

There were ten of them that had their heads and arms locked into place in the stocks. Another six were shackled in metal chains to a light post nearby.

Robert held his stone ball club above one of the men in the stockades that wore a blood stained CVRTF jacket. "Tell me about the foreigners. Tell me how many of them are still helping the feds."

The man sobbed. "I don't know anything!"

Mucus and blood dripped down the man's thick brown beard as his bloodshot eyes flitted from Robert to Kitcheyan.

"Crack his skull open," Kitcheyan said, lifting his flask and laughing.

"No, no, please!" the man yelled.

"Look at me, not him!" Robert shouted. He brought the club down on the prisoner's fingers, smashing one to pulp.

The audible crack was followed by a ghoulish scream of pain.

Kitcheyan laughed some more. To Eddy, it was one thing to dole out pain. It was another to treat it as a joke.

He stepped closer, but his presence did little to rein the Apache back in.

"I'm telling you everything I know!" the prisoner stammered. "The Chinese are talking about pulling their aid workers and engineers. The British, Canadians, and Mexicans are worried about Wild Fire. Even the UN is considering leaving the New Frontier. Are you happy? Is that what you want to know?"

Robert cocked the club back. "I won't be happy until these people leave us alone!"

He cracked his club against the man's other hand to another scream of pain.

"Robert," Eddy said calmly.

He turned and wiped his club on his pant leg, leaving bloodstains, as he walked over to Eddy.

"The CVRTF guys aren't saying much, Ahiga," Robert explained.

"Perhaps they don't know much." Eddy scrutinized them as he walked past the prisoners. Four had blood dripping down their heads and were unconscious. Another three quietly cried and moaned in pain. The rest kept their gaze on the ground, terrified to make eye contact.

"Give me a rundown on who we've got so far," Eddy said.

Robert twirled his club.

"Ten are CVRTF. Guards, engineers. We also have three Rangers."

"The last three?" Eddy asked.

"Chinese."

"Peacekeepers?" Eddy glanced over his shoulder back at the men.

"No. More engineers."

The sounds of motorcycles and truck engines echoed in the distance.

"Sounds like the Union council reps are on their way," Eddy said. "Let's get to the bonfire. You and Kitcheyan can finish with the questioning later."

Robert gave the prisoners one last glaring look before following the order. Kitcheyan's grin remained as they walked away. Eddy led them around the park's pond.

As the sun began to drop behind the mountains, the flicker of a fire drew Eddy in. He inhaled the familiar scent of burning ash with hints of hickory. They followed a stone pathway between buildings toward the bonfire. The low thump of drums resonated.

"What did you learn from the Chinese?" Eddy asked.

"Not too much," Robert replied. "They were assigned to help the other *wašíču* rebuild the water treatment plants. That's all."

Wašíču was a word derived from the Lakota and Dakota people to refer to non-indigenous peoples. It literally meant "he who takes fat," signifying the way foreigners had long since robbed the indigenous people of their lands and resources.

While neither Eddy nor Robert had an ounce of Dakota or Lakota Sioux in them, Eddy found the name fitting enough.

"Should we get rid of them when we're done, Ahiga?" Kitcheyan asked.

"Don't kill them," Eddy said. "They might be useful, and we don't want to draw the Chinese back into the New Frontier."

"Ah, you're right," Robert said with a firm nod. "Always thinking about future repercussions. I like that."

"It's the only way to victory."

The drumbeats were getting louder, and the glow of the

fire brighter. Those engines Eddy had heard before grew closer.

They stepped around another corner as the drumming swelled.

"Maybe we can even do more to encourage these foreigners to abandon our country by using these prisoners. Without them, who will control these lands?"

"Us."

The sight of the brilliant, high flames licking at the sky made Eddy pause. Drummers and dancers circling the fire glowed, making them look like spirits.

Eddy bit back the storm of emotions that came every time he saw flames.

The scars Raven had left him with extended deep into his psyche. Never before had he been afraid of fire. Now, thanks to Raven, he'd developed some kind of phobia. A phobia he vowed to conquer.

Every time he saw fire, he couldn't help but think of Raven swinging the kerosene lantern that smashed into his face. The pain of the fires licking across his flesh were spirits that haunted him every living second.

He refused to let anyone, not even Robert, realize this.

Even as his chest tightened, he strode toward the fire. He let his body's response to the threat of fire sublimate into vengeful rage and righteousness.

The white buffalo is coming, Eddy said to himself. *Soon we'll be prosperous again. Free again.*

He centered his mind on those thoughts to calm himself, listening to the drummers and

accompanying vocals.

Already, a couple dozen local militia leaders, mayors, and governors—all self-appointed leaders of various New Frontier communities—had arrived. Many of them represented small organizations and groups—sometimes as few as five or six warriors. Other times, a hundred or more.

The last couple of vehicles rolled to a stop in the nearby parking lot. Men and women in camouflage gear got out. Weapons were strapped across their backs. They strode toward the fire, eyes glued to the display of dancers, singers, and drummers.

Some of this powwow had been taken from tradition. Other parts were for show.

These non-First Nation people were so easily entertained by the powwow. He saw it in their faces. That plus their cocky arrogance. How important they seemed to think they were, being invited to this supposedly sacred meeting. They were all so stupid, so simple.

He fingered the handle of the tomahawk secured to his belt. He wanted to cleave it right through the skull of every sorry wannabe militia or community leader here. That would ensure no one would stand against him.

But he refrained. What they might lack in sophistication and wit, they made up for in numbers. The one resource he needed was the one resource they had in ample supply: manpower.

When the last of the militia leaders sat, Eddy held up a fist. His men fell silent. The dancers vanished back into the darkness shrouding their surroundings.

With the sun finally set, only the fire cast light around the circle. He held out his hands, and in a booming voice, yelled, "Brothers and sisters of the New Frontier, I, Eddy Nez, Leader of the Rattlesnakes, welcome you into the fold of the Union!"

A few voices murmured from the crowd. He took a moment to take in the people before him. There were a good fifty men and women gathered here tonight in addition to the fifty Rattlesnakes here.

"The federal government took my people's lands long ago. Back in 1864, my people endured what you might have heard called the Long Walk. We were driven off our lands. Our crops were burned, settlements destroyed, and warriors hunted down like dogs. The Navajo Nation had no choice but to walk to the Bosque Redondo Reservation at Fort Sumner, in New Mexico. Our children and our elders died in those years. Women, too, and almost an entire generation of men."

His heart burned at the thought of their plight.

"The feds starved us, then gave us barren soil to bury our dead and told us where we had to live. They took everything we knew and loved. That's our story." Again, he pointed to the Union leaders. "They are coming back to the New Frontier to do the same thing to you. So I ask you, who here is coward enough to stand by while they take everything?"

No one said anything.

"Each of you represents a community of rugged individuals who have survived the New Frontier." Eddy paced around the fire. The heat of it warmed his wounds, and that tightness returned to his chest, but he again ignored it. "Your story may be different than my people's. You may have a different relationship to the government. A different history. But when the Great Reversal came, all of you made the same choice I did.

"You could have given up and crawled back to the protection of the United States government in fear when the electricity stopped. Instead, you all have chosen to build lives in spite of the hardships we have collectively endured these past two years. We are not weak. We did not come sniveling back to the government for handouts. We've worked hard to build communities and protect our people. You have earned every-thing you've reaped. None of us want the United States' Federal Government to come in here and try to take that away from us."

A few cheers came from the crowd. He noted Shupert was among them, representing the Skulls. The man still seemed high off their victory in Eagle.

"Two nights ago, I kicked off a campaign to take back what's ours by destroying the Eagle Recovery Site," Eddy went on. "This marks the beginning of our conquest. We will fight to preserve the freedoms that our Creator gave us."

This time, more people clapped and hooted.

Eddy eyed the stalwarts who still seemed skeptical. He had paid off every one of these people at one time or another. His men had also politicked with them to garner support for the Union. But some were still dubious.

"I don't want to be your king," he continued. "What I want is for my people and yours"—he thumped his chest—"to be free from tyranny. To take back and keep the lands they call the New Frontier."

Then he pointed to the people seated on logs around him. "We all want the freedom to live where we want, to travel where we want, to make our homes where we want, without someone telling us where we can and cannot do those things. We want the government to stop interfering with lands that are rightfully ours."

He circled the fire, trying to meet every person's eye as he went.

Silence reigned except for the crackle of the fire.

"Who here would let the government beat us into the ground and tell us we've been living our lives wrong?"

Again, silence.

He nodded at Robert, who was standing off to the side of

the circle. Robert disappeared briefly into a neighboring hotel building.

"Some of you have already agreed to campaign with me, to give blood to our campaign, so that future generations can be free," Eddy said. "So that we can protect our children's rights to these lands. And to protect their children's rights. We want a better future for them, and we cannot do it alone."

Robert returned with twelve men lugging wooden chests. They set the chests down.

"Together, we will conquer the New Frontier," Eddy said. "We will push out the foreigners and the feds. We will make these lands wild and free again."

Now more people cheered. Eddy reveled in their applause for a few seconds before one man yelled out, "What about the Wild Fire?"

A man in his early thirties stepped forward. His face was clean shaven, and he appeared fit, dressed in a snug leather jacket and jeans. He was thin and average-height with a face that looked closer to an action movie star than a man who called the Badlands home.

"What about the sickness that plagues our people and threatens any campaign, ordained by our Creator or not?" the man asked, standing.

Eddy remembered his name.

Ryan Lincoln, the leader of the Liberty Militia.

Sure, his words sounded smooth, and he carried himself with confidence, but Eddy had spent enough time to recognize a bilker when he saw one.

Still, Eddy wanted this man on his side.

Lincoln had an entire community of four hundred people in Southwest Colorado. He had at least a hundred men of fighting age and ability that Eddy hoped would fall in line with the Rattlesnakes. They had even had weapons from raiding a National Guard outpost at the beginning of the Collapse.

Lincoln and his people were a powerful weapon to have in the Union, indeed.

"What about the disease?" Eddy asked.

"I've seen the sickness spread, destroying God's good people," Lincoln said. "Despite all His blessings, our people are suffering. Why are we supposed to refuse the government's help when they might help us heal the sick?"

Eddy tried not to let his rage flow. He despised Lincoln and his charlatan ways. The man pretended to be godly but was concerned mostly with maintaining control over his people. It would be easier to put a bullet through Lincoln's head—and more satisfying.

Still, Eddy was forced to do things he didn't like to achieve the goals he'd set out for his people.

He motioned to one of his men. They opened one of the chests. It was filled with boxes of bacteriocin that his people had raided from an old Reapers' depot the Colorado Rangers hadn't discovered.

"I have medicine," he said. "Everyone who works with us will be treated."

"My people trust God," Lincoln said. "How can they trust you?"

"How can you trust the feds?" Eddy asked. "Ask yourself, when their USAMRIID teams come rambling through the New Frontier, what motive do they have for saving us? When they offer help, do you think it's out of kindness?"

He paused a moment to let Lincoln dwell on it.

"Far from it," Eddy said. "They want to poison us like rats."

"Trust is fine," a man named Williams said. He had to be older than forty based on the creases around his eyes, but he was built like a rhino. He represented a force of seventy Comanche tribe members who had defected from their tribe like Eddy had his. Normally quiet and reserved, Williams was one of the last individuals Eddy had convinced to attend tonight's powwow. "Trust doesn't feed our people. It doesn't shoot out our guns either."

Eddy motioned for his men to open the other chests. Some were filled with ammunition. Others with silver and gold in bullions and jewelry. He knew the types of men he'd invited to tonight's powwow. They were easily inspired by one thing, and it wasn't words.

As soon as the chests opened, a Rattlesnake brought a torch over to reveal the contents. Hushed conversations broke out.

"You won't have to worry about bullets or food if you fight with me," Eddy said.

The white buffalo will *come,* he thought to himself.

Some of the Union men started to wander over the chests to see the goods Eddy was offering. He motioned for his guards to close them.

Williams nodded, seeming satisfied.

"If you work with the Rattlesnake Union, then know there is plenty more where that came from."

"I can vouch for him!" Shupert shouted. "Eddy Nez is a true warrior! He led the charge at Eagle and did not shy away from bloodshed. Not only that, but he will reward us all well."

"There is plenty of silver, gold, ammo, and anything else you desire for those that remain loyal to the Rattlesnake Union," Eddy explained. "However, if anyone crosses the Rattlesnakes or our allies..."

Eddy nodded toward Robert. The huge man shone a flashlight onto the side of a nearby hotel to illuminate a wall that had been basking in shadows.

Four bodies dangled from windows.

"Days ago, I found these men in my ranks trying to sneak from our organization and warn the Navajo Nation of our mission," Eddy said. "I gave them mercy by killing them swiftly, but that mercy won't be extended to all..."

The drums tapped in the distance, startling some of the bikers and other people. The music started to burgeon, and Eddy raised a hand. The dancers once again circled the fire, singing and chanting.

"The wašíču in our lands think that we are rodents to be squashed," Eddy said. "But together, we will prove to them we are not vermin. We are wolves!"

5

LINDSEY SAW A MAN DRESSED IN THE HIDE OF A WHITE buffalo with obsidian horns. She had only seen pictures of the man, but she recognized him well enough.

Eddy Nez.

He raised a tomahawk high into the air, let out a howl, then threw it at Lindsey. It whistled through the air. Time slowed. It was as if she could hear every whirl, every thump of the blade through the sand grains caught in the wind.

That sound quickly morphed from a slashing wail to a staccato ring.

The blade was only inches from her face when she opened her eyes to the familiar darkness of her bedroom. Blankets curled around her. A fan blew from a corner.

She was at home.

In Golden.

Alive.

And yet, her chest heaved from the nightmare.

She put a hand on her sternum, feeling the rapid rise and fall of her ribs. Then she noticed the green light blinking on her ringing satellite phone next to her bed. She snatched it up.

"Sheriff Plymouth here," she said.

"Sheriff," huffed Doctor Wheeler. "Something's happened. I need your help."

"Slow down, Doctor," Lindsey said.

"One of my teams in the New Frontier ran into trouble."

"Which team?" Lindsey slipped out of bed and searched for her khaki pants, pulling them up and buckling them.

"The team near a town called... Henley... no, no, that's not right. Herney?"

"Heeney," Lindsey said. "Near Green Mountain Reservoir. That would be Uniform-Mike-Charlie. Team three. What happened?"

"They were delivering Commander meds and documenting Wild Fire infections. Someone started shooting at them."

Lindsey was already buttoning up a shirt. She'd woken from one nightmare right back into another.

"Any idea who, Doctor?" she asked.

Her first thoughts went to the Rattlesnakes.

"I don't know, but the team is at the Boulder Medical Center now," Wheeler said.

"I'm on it."

She ended the call and started strapping on her utility belt with her loaded Glock 22.

As she started downstairs, she called Palmer.

"I know you're leaving for UCLA in just a few hours," she said, "but I've got to get up to Boulder."

She quickly told him everything.

"I can stay back in Colorado," Palmer said. "Calvin's got a team of twenty Steel Runners ready to go. They can take care of the bacteria transport."

"No, Calvin's staying in San Diego after he gets the goods

airborne. Doctor Wheeler and I want someone we trust on that mission all the way through."

"Then what else can I do, ma'am?"

"Jay Wauneka was supposed to arrive last night. Did he?" she asked, leaving her condo.

"He did. I had a couple of our Rangers set him up in one of the bunk rooms at Fort Golden. You want to bring him to Boulder?"

"I might as well." Lindsey got into her Bronco and started the engine. "The earlier we involve him, the more help he can be."

"Earlier's always better than later. It's what I always say."

Lindsey reversed out of the drive and started down the street. "Don't recall hearing you say that ever, Palmer."

"I started today, ma'am."

"Well, then, make sure Jay is ready immediately. Then just focus on preparing for your UCLA mission."

"Good luck."

She hung up. The next call was to Raven.

"What do you got for me, Lindsey? Not another appearance of the white buffalo, I hope."

"No." She didn't add, *not yet.* "I'm headed to Boulder. A USAMRIID team was hit in the New Frontier. Could be Eddy's doing. I want to gather as much intel as possible. I'd appreciate if you come."

"I can do that."

"Second part of that is you're going to meet the guy Tso sent. Jay Wauneka. He just arrived, and I'd like to get him as involved as possible into our investigations."

"Who?"

"Jay Wauneka. He's from the Navajo Nation."

"Ugh..."

Lindsey didn't give Raven a chance to argue. "I'll see you in Boulder in about an hour."

As soon as she made it to Fort Golden, she got her first view of a man that had to be Jay. He was waiting for her outside the gates with a rifle slung over a light brown leather jacket. Leather cowboy boots peeked out of black jeans.

Lindsey pulled up in front of him and rolled down her window.

A thin black beard traced the man's stern jawline. His expression was serious and solemn, with long straight black hair trailing down his neck.

"Sheriff Plymouth," he said.

"Jay Wauneka."

"Yes." He flashed Lindsey a Navajo Nation Police ID card and badge.

"Hop in," Lindsey said.

Jay opened the passenger side door and reached out to shake her hand.

"Thanks for coming," she said. "I'm glad to have your help."

"Happy to be here.... I mean, not happy about the circumstances, but I'll do anything to help the Navajo Nation people." He shook his head wearily. "President Tso told me everything about Eagle, the white buffalo, and that man you rescued who mentioned the snakes."

"Yeah?" Lindsey asked as they drove down the road.

"I think your suspicions are correct. This has Eddy written all over it. Or I should say 'Ahiga,' as his men started calling him back when he formed the Rattlesnakes."

"What's that mean?"

"'He fights.' And that's exactly what Eddy does. Fights. Since he was a kid. I mean, I worked with Eddy when he was on the Navajo National Police force with me. But I never really liked him. Bad apple, you know?"

"I'm fully aware, but keep talking. I need to know more about him, especially recent news."

"Okay." Jay brushed a strand of hair from his face "Last we heard from the Rattlesnakes was they had some delusions of grandeur that they would protect *all* the New Frontier again. Eddy even alluded to a conquest. That's when Tso had a heart-to-heart, as you might call it. And as you may have guessed, it did not end well. Eddy fled and went dark. We never heard from him for a year. Figured maybe he got killed by one of those militias in the Badlands."

"Wish that were true."

"He gives our people a bad name," Jay explained. "There are hundreds of thousands of us, but Eddy and a few hundred nuts are going to ruin our reputation. Trust me when I say I want to take him down, as much for your people as for mine."

Lindsey and Jay chatted on the remaining thirty minutes of their drive, but Jay didn't know much about Eddy's whereabouts since Raven had run into him at Montezuma Creek. He did seem just as eager as she was to find him.

The early morning sun warmed the horizon as they made their way into Boulder.

After she parked and started toward the front entrance of the medical center with Jay, she spotted Raven near some nurses taking a smoke break.

Raven smiled, striding toward Lindsey. He met her in a hug.

"Good to see you're all right," he said. "You doing okay after... after Eagle?"

Lindsey dipped her sheriff's hat as she pulled away. "About as good as I can, you know?"

Raven gripped her hand. "I know. Trust me, I know."

Then he turned toward Jay. "So you're the guy Tso sent up to help?"

"My reputation precedes me," Jay replied.

They shook hands, introducing each other.

"Jay's known Eddy for a long time, so if you got questions, he might be able to help," Lindsey said.

"Long time, eh?" Raven raised an eyebrow. "You buds with him?"

"Used to be. When we were young," Jay said with that same calm voice he'd used since Lindsey met him. "Now, no. No fricking way."

"Man, I'm looking forward to picking your brain on that asshole."

"And I'm looking forward to what you guys come up with." Lindsey jerked her chin toward the entrance. "For now, I want you two to take notes on everything the USAMRIID team has to say. See how this might fit into Eddy's motives and, if this does involve Eddy, I want to have clues on where he's gone."

They entered a lobby bustling with patients and nurses. They were immediately directed to put on personal protective equipment. Once they'd donned all the usual gloves, masks, and gowns, a nurse led them to the room of one of the USAM-RIID medical technicians.

Lindsey approached the bedside of a woman in her late twenties. Her hair was a tangled mess of blond, and she had a sheet pulled up to her neck. IV tubes snaked down toward an arm wrapped in bandages. Her eyes were bloodshot, maybe from exhaustion or from crying. A combination of both probably.

"You must be the sheriff," the woman said, her voice scratchy. "Doctor Wheeler told me to expect you. I'm Maryam. And these guys? They're Rangers?"

"Not quite," Lindsey said. "But they're going to help me figure out who did this to you guys. Can you tell me what happened?"

Maryam nodded, wincing. A wet sheen formed in her eyes. "These people that attacked us... they killed five of the USAMRIID team and ran the rest of us off. All we were doing was trying to help."

"Can you tell us who these attackers were?" Raven asked. "Were the guys on horses? Maybe you've heard of the Rattlesnakes."

Maryam's eyelids drooped. She was clearly exhausted. "Just a group of men and women from Heeney. Normal people. They looked like civilians."

"You're sure?" Jay asked. "This sounds like something Eddy's people would do."

"Positive. They were just a bunch of people that lived in Heeney. We offered them medicine last night. We told them we could help anyone in their town suffering from Wild Fire. And then..."

Maryam started to sob.

"It's okay." Lindsey placed a hand gently on the woman's shoulder. "You're safe now."

"I'm more concerned about the people who are sick," Maryam continued. "They're just going to keep spreading this disease. We just want to help the families who were suffering. I saw some of those kids, Sheriff. They're going to die if they don't let us help."

"Jesus," Raven said. "Do you know why they ran you off?"

Maryam glanced over. "When we first made contact with the townspeople, I was talking to a mother of two kids," she explained. "Her name's Eileen Graves. She wanted me to help her kids, but some of their men had just returned from somewhere out near Ouray saying they weren't supposed to trust us."

"Ouray ring a bell?" Raven asked Jay.

The Navajo detective shrugged. "I got nothing. Certainly not on my radar."

Lindsey started jotting notes on a notepad. "Maryam, do you know what's in Ouray?"

"Eileen told me something about snakes being down there. I don't know what she meant."

"And *there* it is," Jay said.

"The Rattlesnakes," Lindsey said. "Eddy's gang."

"All I know is Eileen said these men were telling the whole town to turn down any government help," Maryam continued. "She warned us we should leave, but we wanted to help and…"

Maryam's lips began trembling.

"It's gonna be okay," Lindsey said again. "You're safe here, but we need your help. Can you think of any other information that might be helpful?"

"I'm sorry. That's all I know."

Lindsey left a business card on a nightstand by her bed. "Here's my direct number at Fort Golden. You can of course tell Doctor Wheeler if you think of anything else, but feel free to call me directly. I know he's busy."

The woman managed a nod.

"Thank you, Maryam," Lindsey said. "You've been very helpful."

They spoke to a few more USAMRIID team members. A couple of the medics had IV tubes tracing from arms bandaged to cover bullet wounds. Another had her leg in a cast, her femur broken from a nasty hit. It was propped up on her bed.

One man had bandages covering his chest from shrapnel

splintering into his flesh from stray bullets hitting their vehicle.

And while all had suffered during the attack, none knew anything more than Maryam.

"So all we got is that some Rattlesnakes *might've* been in Ouray," Raven said.

"It just doesn't make sense," Jay said. "As far as I know, none of our people have been in Ouray for the past two years. I have no idea what Eddy would be doing there."

Lindsey sighed, looking out at the mountains. "I wish we had more. If the Rattlesnakes are telling New Frontier civilians to shoot our people, this situation is just going to get worse. We have to stop the Rattlesnakes."

"Absolutely." Jay toyed with the badge he wore on his chest. "One thing I can tell you about Eddy is that he is a diehard believer in what he thinks the Navajo Nation people deserve. If he really is on some kind of warpath, it's not going to end until we end him. But he also inspires vicious loyalty through fear and respect. His people will likely die to defend him. He's charismatic like that. So we got to be careful going after him. He's dangerous, and so are his comrades."

What Lindsey had seen at Eagle confirmed this was true. She looked to Raven, who had narrowly escaped Eddy and his forces a few weeks earlier.

"So what, we going to send a big force into Ouray to take him down?" Raven asked.

"We don't know for sure he's even there," Jay said. "If you send too many people and make it obvious we've got a lead, he's going to go right back into hiding. Like I said, his people will give everything to protect him. Plus, there's a good chance if you send Rangers marching right into Ouray, even if Eddy isn't there, your guys aren't coming home."

Lindsey took a deep breath. "So we need a recon team.

Someone who can do this quietly. I've got people scouting the mountains, but my guys aren't spies. They can't just meld into a place like Ouray. Do you think...?"

"I'll go with Creek," Raven said. "I'll let you know what I find out there."

"You aren't going alone," Jay said. "I know Eddy. I know his people. Let me go with."

"Jay, you mind if I have a moment alone with Raven?" Lindsey asked.

They waited until Jay was back at the Bronco.

"What do you think of him?" Raven asked in a low voice.

"I don't know yet... He's eager to help. I trust Tso of course. And Jay seems sincere. But I haven't known him for long. I like to think I'm a good judge of character. Ultimately, it's your call."

"I trust your gut, Lindsey," Raven said. "All the same, I'll keep a close eye on him. I could use someone that knows the Nation, Eddy, and the Rattlesnakes, because I sure as hell don't."

"Okay. While you guys do that, I'm going to see if we can get what's left of our allies' peacekeeping forces to help defend the USAMRIID teams. We need to get medicine to these people. But, Raven, please, please be safe."

Raven nodded. "You be safe too."

"Always."

———

Palmer stood on the tarmac inside Buckley Air Force base. The infamous massive white golf balls towered over several of the buildings. From what he knew, those things were called radomes and protected sensitive satellite equipment. He wasn't sure they were working anymore—not much at

Buckley AFB really was—but their resemblance to golf balls reminded Palmer of the days before the Collapse.

Days when America still stood tall and proud.

Days when he could hit the links in morning, then visit one of Denver's many breweries in the afternoon for a few mugs of local craft brews. American made. Not some of that cheap swill they imported by the boatload or those snooty foreign beers that cost twenty bucks a six-pack.

Screw that.

The most prominent reminder of the America he knew was the line of fighter aircraft in the hangars. Buckley's primary mission had been supporting air-to-air or air-to-ground fighters.

Most of those fighters had been disabled by the EMP attack. Many were still being repaired. The money and resources required to repair those aircraft were hard to come by.

Fortunately, they had access to one particular aircraft for this mission. USAMRIID's own CH-47J Chinook.

The massive dual-rotor helicopter had enlarged fuel tanks to support long-range trips.

After all, they needed a hell of a lot of gas. There weren't many friendly places to land between here and the coast.

Steel Runners loaded crates of ammunition and weapons into the Chinook from their SUVs.

Once they arrived in LA, California National Guardsmen would provide additional ground transport and security support.

All this to defend the precious microscopic cargo they hoped to bring back to Colorado.

But bringing back cargo wasn't all they were going to do. They had an equally important delivery.

Palmer joined Calvin, who was near the open rear ramp

of the Chinook. The man stood near a wooden casket placed on a riser. His dark skin glimmered under the heat of the late summer sun. An American flag was draped over the coffin.

Four other Steel Runners Palmer didn't know well were beside the coffin.

At Palmer's approach, Calvin wiped his eyes with the back of his hand. "I know we're in a hurry, but thanks for giving us a moment with Mouse."

Palmer tipped his cowboy hat. "It's the least I can do, sir."

Calvin stood for a moment longer with his hand on the casket. "You're finally going home, brother." Then Calvin stepped away from the coffin. "Palmer, I've got four teams of Runners that will be working with us under my command. I want you to meet the team leads. This is Anna."

A woman in a White Sox cap gave him a nod.

"Boston," Calvin gestured to a muscular man.

"Good to meet you, Palmer," Boston said with a characteristic accent. "I used to despise coppers like you. A guy that looked like you threw me in the slammer for a couple years."

Palmer's shock must've showed on his face.

"No harm, no foul," Boston said. "I made right with my God and the state. Did my time. Planned to do good things when I got out, then the Collapse hit. Running Steel gave me another way to pay for my sins."

"Uh, glad to hear it." Palmer wasn't sure how else to respond to the guy. He was an odd duck, that was for sure.

He turned to the last two Steel Runners.

One was a tall, thin woman with blond hair in a pixie cut. She held out a hand to Palmer. "Rosanna Marino. Originally from the Pacific Northwest. Seattle. Still trying to get used to all this sun in Colorado."

Palmer smiled.

A man with a cowboy hat extended a calloused hand. He

wore a silver necklace with a cross and had a belt buckle with a coyote on it. "Alberto Ortiz. New Mexico. Left during the Collapse when it all went to shit. I'd like to move back home when Albuquerque is safe again, so it's my honor to be on this mission, sir."

"Thank you all for joining in," Palmer said. "I'm sure Calvin told you just how important this is. We wouldn't be able to do it without you."

"No shit," Boston said with a grin. "Nobody gets nothing done in this country without the Steel Runners."

When the rest of the ammunition and weapons were loaded, Palmer helped Calvin and his four team leaders place Mouse's coffin inside. They secured it on the metal rails before finding a couple of empty red jump seats on the bulkhead.

The space was tight.

Nearly the whole deck was filled with equipment. That included two crates Doctor Wheeler's team had prepared with portable cold storage tanks to transport the bacteria.

"Not exactly first class," Calvin said as a crew chief raised the rear ramp. "You good?"

"I flew some budget airlines pre-Collapse with even less leg room," Palmer said. "I'm not gonna complain."

In minutes, the big chopper lifted from the ground. The heavy thump of the rotors reverberated in the hold, shaking up Palmer's spine. Many of the Steel Runners seated around him and Calvin had closed their eyes and fallen asleep the moment they took to the air.

Not Calvin. The man's gaze was fixed on Mouse's casket. Boston, Ortiz, Anna, and Marino had remained awake too.

"I always heard that people in the armed forces were good at snagging some shuteye whenever they could, but that's downright impressive," Palmer said, leaning toward Calvin.

"You've got to," Calvin said. "You never knew when the mission might change. Suddenly, that easy three-hour op you thought was going to be done by nightfall is a twenty-four-hour, entrenched gun battle from hell."

"You think that our in-and-out pickup in LA is going to be like that?"

"I got a briefing from the National Guard about what we can expect," Calvin said. "Sounds like there are occasional riots and protests, but they think our ride from the airport to UCLA and back isn't in a particularly hot zone. So, hopefully, it's smooth rails."

Boston huffed. "They always say that. Until suddenly they're wrong."

"Ah, what do you know, Boston?" Ortiz asked. "You never served."

"Oh, he served," Marino said with a smile. "In prison."

Boston laughed. "Come on, you guys. They got me because I beat up a guy who was threatening my sister. You all would've done the same. Cops had it in for me."

"And why's that?" Marino asked.

Boston grinned. "I didn't keep the best company back then. Ah, hell, they probably had good reason to keep their eye on me and my boys. But I'm over that stuff. I'm not running with that crowd anymore. I'm running with you guys."

"Cut him some slack," Anna said. "When we're up shit creek without a paddle, I'll take Boston on my side."

"What's your story?" Palmer asked Marino. "How'd you end up coming down from Seattle to running steel? Seattle's supposed to be safe now."

Marino laughed. "No place is really safe anymore. Look, before the Collapse, I was planning on a big trip to Southeast Asia. Thailand, Cambodia, Vietnam. Get my head right."

"From what?" Palmer asked.

"I was a homicide detective. Seattle PD. Just got off a case where I'd seen a mom and her two kids killed. Not just any killing. I'll spare you the details, but suffice to say, I needed a sabbatical."

"And then the Collapse happened," Ortiz added.

"Then the Collapse happened," Marino repeated. "Suddenly, they were looking for people to protect cargo, and if I wasn't going to see the world, I figured I might as well see my country and work my ass off protecting it at the same time."

"Okay, so tell me this," Palmer said. "You guys have seen a lot of the country. Is it as bad as Diego claims? You think he really can't afford to send more people our way or is it just politicians being politicians because of the election in November?"

"Yeah, everything's pretty much a big heaping pile of dog shit," Boston said.

"And he'd know," Marino said. "On account of being from a big heaping pile of dog shit city."

"You take that back, Sister!" Boston sounded angry, but he was grinning.

"Seriously, though, he's right," Calvin said. "It might seem like we got a lot of troops protecting us out there. But think about it this way. You got what? A thousand-odd Rangers working between Fort Golden and out on patrol and doing recon, right?"

Palmer dipped his hat. "That's about right."

"Sounds like a lot," Calvin continued, "but then you realize your Rangers gotta cover over one hundred thousand square miles of land."

"True enough," Palmer said. "Plus, our prisons are already overflowing."

"Ain't easy, especially when you're dealing with mountains and forests and all those nooks and crannies where the bad assholes like to hide," Ortiz added.

"It's a mess out there," Anna added. "In every town, people are so hungry, they chase the trains for food, hoping we'll drop something for them."

"People are so desperate, they might rush us, even without weapons," Ortiz said. "Sure, we get attacked the most in the New Frontier, but the Steel Runners have experienced casualties on just about every inch of the rails."

"You guys had an important job, and you're still not getting support," Palmer said. "Doesn't that make you question Diego's motives?"

"You bet it does," Calvin said. "But we're the ones that are supposed to be protecting the rails. That was the whole reason for the creation of the Steel Runners, you get what I mean? There wasn't supposed to be reinforcements for us because *we're* the reinforcements."

Their banter continued on for a little while until one by one the other Steel Runners dozed off. Palmer must've too because the next thing he heard was the pilot over the intercom.

"We're approaching Los Angeles AFB. Twenty minutes until landing."

Palmer peered out the closest window.

The city was a spiderweb of black and gray roads stretching between buildings. Threads of traffic wound through the city and the suburbs.

"Looks almost normal," Palmer remarked to Calvin.

"Wait until we get closer," Calvin replied.

As they did, those buildings that looked normal from above were covered in black scorch marks. Towering offices and apartments were missing windows. Debris had fallen at their feet like scree.

Wrecked cars lined the streets, allowing only narrow paths for traffic.

Soon they swooped over the perimeter fences of the AFB. People pressed up against those fences, reaching through the chain-link at the soldiers and airmen working beyond.

"See?" Calvin said. "Not so pretty up close. This is why Diego's hands are tied."

In minutes, they were on the tarmac. Three transport trucks and four Humvees raced to meet them as the rear ramp lowered.

A group of Honor Guard Marines from the AFB entered and loaded Mouse's casket into a Humvee. A tear rolled out of Calvin's eye before he wiped it away.

As soon as the coffin was loaded, Calvin, Palmer, and the Steel Runner team leads were taken by a pair of National Guard soldiers to a hangar. Between a pair of HH60G Pave Hawks, a man with the face of a bulldog and the stature to match welcomed them to a set of crates, tables, and a projector screen he was using as a temporary command post.

"Welcome to California," he said. "I'm Captain Ronald Schwimmer. I know we don't have much time, so let's get right to business. I've been told you men and women are some of the best at making sure precious cargo gets to its destination safely."

"Born and bred for it," Boston said.

"Something like that," Calvin said. He immediately strode over to the table and studied the maps of Los Angeles sprawled across it. "I've already worked out a couple of routes."

The civilian crowd outside the base was growing louder, their voices carrying even into the hangar.

"With people this angry, I don't want to leave anything to chance," Calvin continued. "I have a feeling, whether we like it or not, we'll be attracting attention. So I've brought four teams of Steel Runners. We'll split them up into four Humvees. You got enough for that?"

"I can scrounge them up," Schwimmer replied. "I've got twelve Guardsmen I can loan you too. Plus the two MTV trucks for transporting all the scientific cargo."

"Perfect," Calvin said. He traced his finger across the maps, and Palmer took notes on everything the Steel Runner said. "We'll shoot for a direct route between UCLA and this AFB. This will be designated our primary evacuation route, Echo-Romeo-One."

Again, he indicated two more routes.

"These are Echo-Romeo-Two and Three. I want you to allocate six of your people in two-man teams to these buildings."

He gestured to the map again, pointing out specific blocks.

"They'll be the ones keeping an eye on civilian activity in the streets, calling out potential dangers, protestors, whatever might be headed our way."

"Consider it done," Schwimmer said. "Anything else?"

"We've got guns and bullets," Calvin said. "But what we don't have are nonlethals for crowd control. I don't exactly want to be firing at our own people if things get out of hand."

"I've already got everything from flashbangs to rubber bullets." Schwimmer used a hand to indicate a couple of crates near the entrance to the hangar. "Next thing we need to do is get to UCLA and get those bacteria samples."

"We're ready for the drive," Palmer said. "I'll be heading to UCLA with the four Steel Runner teams. After we get to UCLA, Calvin's got to head south to deliver some other precious cargo to San Diego."

"So we've heard," Schwimmer said. "The Honor Guard will be ready for your departure, Calvin."

"Thank you, sir," Calvin said.

"Arrangements have already been made for Gomez's funeral in two days," Schwimmer said. "We'll need that time to prepare all the scientific equipment at UCLA anyway. As long as you're back to help us get to the AFB before then, we'll be good and you can stay in California. From the sounds of it, the future of the New Frontier—and maybe the US—depend on this cargo."

6

RAVEN HAD SPENT THE PAST DAY AND A HALF CAUTIOUSLY traveling through the mountains with Jay and Creek. They'd spent most of that time getting to know each other. Raven felt a little better after having learned about Jay's career in the Navajo Nation Police Department and his role as a detective. The man had personally been tapped to lead several high-profile investigations, including missing persons and murders following the days of the Collapse.

And according to Jay, he'd solved all of them.

Hopefully, Eddy's location was another investigation Jay could solve.

They had safely parked Raven's Jeep about a five-hour straight hike from Ouray outside a town called Ridgway. From there, they'd snuck through the woods, taking long winding paths to scout the area. Their five-hour hike turned into a ten-hour excursion.

But if the Rattlesnakes were in fact out here, Raven would rather be tedious and slow than end up at the wrong end of a gun barrel.

Jay swept his gaze back and forth over the darkened landscape, from the rocky slopes covered in trees to a nearby gurgling stream. Dried brush, boulders, and craggy outcroppings provided cover.

From Raven's calculations, they were finally about twenty minutes outside of Ouray now. He had his crossbow in hand as Creek prowled next to him. Jay cradled a suppressed M4 carbine the Rangers had lent him.

As they followed the stream down a slight slope, Jay suddenly held up a fist. He motioned for Raven to seek cover behind a clutch of trees.

Raven dropped to his knees in the grass, listening for what had grabbed Jay's attention.

He could hardly hear anything except for a light breeze rustling through leaves.

For a few minutes, he sat still as a statue, his eyes glued to the road past the trees.

Then he heard it. The steady thump of boots on asphalt. Four men stalked up the road.

Each carried an assault rifle with tactical lights attached to their gun barrels. As they got closer, Raven noticed they wore cowboy hats, plaid shirts, and jeans. They might as well have come from working on a ranch.

Raven and Creek waited in silence as the four men continued down the road. Jay had pressed himself flat against a boulder.

When the man finally signaled the coast was clear, Raven came out from the trees with Creek.

"Good eyes and ears," Raven whispered to Jay as they continued on.

"Not good. Just well-trained."

As they neared Ouray, laughter and booming voices echoed against the rocky walls of the surrounding valley. They paused at a ridgeline overlooking the town.

The place looked straight out of the Wild West. Two-story brick and wood buildings lined Main Street. Flickering light spilled from nearly all the establishments. Horses were tied up in front of saloons, and people milled about the streets.

"Didn't expect this place to be so busy," Jay said.

"Maybe it's because Eddy and his Rattlesnakes made this his new home," Raven guessed.

"I don't know. Eddy never liked to make anywhere his home for long." Jay turned to Raven after a second. "If we're going in, it's probably best to use some assumed identities."

"Wait, you want to go down there?"

"Why? You want to sit up here and watch? The party's in those saloons. Not up here."

"To start... yeah. If we waltz down there and Eddy sees us—"

"Just waltz down there? Eddy knows who we both are." Jay stared at Raven for a beat. "You think I'm stupid?"

"I'm starting to worry about it," Raven said.

Jay laughed. "You got to grow some balls like me."

"I think you got balls, but there's a difference between balls and arrogance," Raven said. "Trust me, I used to *waltz* into places too, but times have changed."

Jay frowned. "You do think I'm stupid, then."

"No."

"All right, let me tell you my plan before you make your judgment." He pulled his bandana up around his face. "We wear these, say we're bounty hunters to anyone that asks, and go find some drunk to tell us where Eddy is."

"You trust a drunk?" Raven asked.

"I don't trust anyone. Never have."

"Spoken like a true cop."

"I've worked with a lot of scum over the years. You lose

your rose-tinted glasses real quick when you work drug busts and homicides."

Raven recalled his run-ins with the law back in his troubled days. He had never liked law enforcement much, and believed he was targeted unfairly. But he had also learned to respect them and work with them.

He thought of Chief Marcus Colton, who had gone from foe to friend.

And a good friend to the end, Raven thought.

"Still, you want info from a drunk?" Raven asked.

"They're usually the most willing to talk," Jay said. "So, you good with my plan?"

Raven thought on it a moment. He was used to working on his own. Working with Calvin had been an exception that proved worthwhile, but even then, he had known Calvin longer, even if it was brief. Calvin had proven himself a worthy comrade.

Jay might be a talented detective, but Raven was the tracker. He had been in these mountains for the past two years.

This was his territory.

"I'm good with your plan," Raven said, "but only if you let me lead."

Jay paused, seeming to scrutinize Raven for a second. "All right. I'll follow. It's your mission, boss."

Raven pulled up his shemagh scarf to conceal his features. They snuck down the slope and toward town, Creek bounding after them.

As soon as they were close to Main Street, they came out of the shadows and joined the throngs of people. Raven guessed a good half of them seemed drunk, stumbling between five different saloons.

Blending in might not be as hard as he thought. People

here wore everything from plaid shirts, jeans, hats, and boots that made them seem like they'd just come from a rodeo to camouflage uniforms and even second-hand Army helmets that gave them a decidedly militant appearance.

Jay started toward a saloon when a hooting crowd near the end of the street drew his attention.

A gallows had been constructed next to a store selling firearms and ammunition. Two men hung from ropes, already limp and dead. Signs hung around their necks.

Raven squinted to make out the rough handwriting on the signs.

Thief.

It appeared another thief was about to get hung for the same crime, but this was a woman. Thin, gaunt, and terrified.

She had something tied around her mouth that muffled her pleas.

Raven followed Jay but watched out of the corner of his eye.

An executioner stood next to a lever, waiting for the order. A guard ripped the muffle from her mouth.

"Please, my children were hungry!" she screamed.

The crowd booed and hissed.

A man with a white goatee stepped up on the stage, holding a hand up for silence. Everyone immediately went quiet.

The way this guy commanded attention, he was obviously a local leader. The wrinkles across his face appeared even deeper with the fire from nearby lanterns flicking over him. A gleaming belt buckle shaped like a lion, visible from even where Raven stood at the back of the crowd. It told Raven all they needed to know about what this man thought about himself.

"You should've joined up with the Ouray Militia, then," the man said.

"I will!" she promised. "I will! I'll even work for the Rattle—"

The leader gave a nod, and the executioner pulled the lever. The platform dropped and she fell. But the rope didn't snap her neck. She hung there, kicking, and straining.

Most people watched in silence, some even turning away, but a few cheered. The man with the belt buckle watched. Raven swore a slight smile crossed his face.

Then the man addressed the crowd. He thumped his chest. "Let it be known that, as your mayor, I do not take kindly to criminals in this community." He pointed to the mountains. "What you do beyond Ouray is your business, but when you are in our town, you follow our laws."

So that was who he was, Raven realized. The mayor.

"It's downright barbaric out here," Jay said.

"What did you expect?" Raven said. "Come on."

He led the way, wondering if Jay was starting to regret his 'plan.'

Together they walked as confidently as they could through the dispersing crowd. No one gave them so much as a second glance, even with Creek at their heels. They weren't the only ones wearing masks or walking around with weapons.

Raven stopped at the saloon. The sign above it read Saddle and Spurs. Boisterous conversation roiled from the place. Creek followed them in.

As soon as the three of them pushed through the wooden swinging doors to get in, Raven was met by a wall of sound and the scent of body odor. He took a few steps on the sticky floor that seemed like it hadn't seen a mop since the Collapse.

Raven wasn't sure if this was the kind of place where a

bouncer would make him check his weapons in at the door. But judging by the rifles and crossbows slung over patrons' backs or handguns holstered at their side, it looked like he would be fine.

A woman played the piano in the corner as people circled around tables for card games. Others were seated at the bar, clinking frothy mugs of beer together under the light of lanterns and chandeliers filled with candles.

A staircase led to a walkway that lined the second floor. Women in lingerie posed next to doorways as lascivious men stared up at them.

"Recognize anyone?" Raven asked Jay as they moved into the center of the crowded bar.

Jay swept the room. "No. No one I recognize from the Rattlesnakes or the Nation."

"You think the Rattlesnakes aren't here, then?"

"Didn't say that," Jay said. "There are plenty of people in the Nation I wouldn't recognize. Rattlesnakes included. We should still ask around."

Raven gestured to the middle-aged, blonde-haired woman behind the bar for two drinks. She gave him a sly smile back, filled up two mugs, and handed them over.

"How are you paying?" she asked.

That caught Raven off-guard. "Cash, of course."

The woman laughed. "Fed bucks?"

"Are fed bucks what you call dollars?"

The woman smiled and nodded. "No good here, honey. You new to town?"

"Matter of fact, we are." Jay lowered his handkerchief to take a sip, then put a small silver coin on the bar. "You accept that?"

"That'll buy you drinks and some time upstairs with the ladies if you want."

"Hmm." Jay toyed with the coin. "I didn't catch your name."

She smiled, flicking back some of her long hair. "It's Lily, honey. Like the flower."

"And you are more beautiful than one," Jay said.

Raven was surprised to hear Jay laying it on this thick.

"You can butter me up all you want, but those drinks aren't going to be free," she said.

"Course not. I'm a gentleman, and I always pay my way," he said. "So, do your ladies get a lot of visitors?"

Lily nodded. "They do. But they'll treat you as if you're the only one."

"Hmm." Jay turned around and whispered in a low voice as Lily went off to deal with another patron. "I think I might be interested in time with the ladies."

"The hell, man? We're here to search for Eddy. Or are you thinking with your dick instead of your head?"

"Both," Jay said, giving Raven a ridiculous grin of pearly white teeth.

The dude had the definition of a million-dollar smile.

"You're going to have to explain how time with the ladies are both," Raven said. "Unless you think one of the ladies works for Eddy. I, on the other hand, think we should be looking for his men..."

Jay shrugged a shoulder. "I'm guessing we can spend all day looking for them, and we're not going to see them. If I know one thing about Eddy, it's that he's good at covering his tracks. How do you think he went so long without Tso or any of us realizing he had some scheme to defect from the Nation?"

"I say we go to another saloon and keep looking."

"Give me one shot here," Jay said. He pointed up at the ladies. "When men are in the middle of a good time up there, in my experience, they have a habit of letting important intelligence slip. You remember the CIA director *himself* was caught a few years before the Collapse saying shit to his mistress."

Raven cocked a brow then tilted his head. "Fair point."

"If I know Eddy, he's not going to be found out in the open. He won't just roll into a bar like this unless he's surrounded by his army. And I haven't seen any signs of his army yet. So if he is nearby, it's better we get some real solid leads to work off. You know what I mean?"

"I guess, man. But what if you go up there and bump uglies with some lady and she doesn't know anything? We're wasting time."

Jay gave Raven that mischievous smile again. "Well, I wouldn't call it time wasted... I'm pretty sure I paid enough you could rock your socks off too if you want. Maybe we'll both get lucky in multiple ways."

Raven held up a hand. "Nah, man. I'm good. You do you. But it better be worthwhile."

"It will be."

Jay went and talked with Lily, who pointed him upstairs. Raven watched him speak to a couple of the women. Jay locked arms with one, then they disappeared into their room.

Creek looked up at him as if he disapproved of Jay's actions. Raven simply ordered another drink, trying not to get nervous. He didn't have to wait long.

Twenty minutes later, just as he finished his drink, Jay came striding down the stairs. He pulled up his belt at the bottom and grinned at Raven from ear to ear.

Creek got up with Raven and met him outside where they could talk in private. They found an alley around the side of the building filled with trash.

"Well?" Raven asked.

"Got a good workout in," Jay said.

"And?"

"Yeah, our friend's people were here. Kept the women up there busy."

"They still in town somewhere?"

Jay shook his head. "No. They never really spent much time here. Just passing through. My, uh, *friend* wasn't sure where they went off to. She said the Rattlesnakes are like that. They pop in unexpectedly, then leave almost as quickly."

"They coming back? Maybe we could stake the place out."

Jay shrugged. "Could be. Might be back in a week. Might never be back. They're not predictable."

"Not very helpful."

"Not that, but she did give me a lead. Someone who knows more about Eddy."

"Yeah?"

Jay stopped and made sure no one was close to them to hear.

"There's this guy named David Singer," he said in a low voice. "She told me where he lives. A couple weeks ago, he comes in here pissed off, spitting curses left and right, drunk. Spent some time with my lady friend. David told her he was going to kill Eddy. That he hates Eddy. That he's got a plan to take Eddy out, in fact."

"Sounds like someone we could use."

"My thought exactly. I even know where to find the guy."

"Good, good. But just in case, any other leads? Anyone else we can ask?"

Jay shook his head. "Unlikely. She says people are scared of Eddy. No one talks about them if they don't have to. This was the first and only guy she heard talking so openly about disliking Eddy to her. She said if we go around asking about

Eddy, we're liable to end up like those poor souls we saw at the hanging."

"Then let's go pay this David a visit."

———

Lindsey drove her dusty Bronco back out into the New Frontier with Blair in the passenger seat. Corporal Rangers Nuke and Rogers sat in the backseat. The clock on her dash had just hit ten in the morning. Walls of evergreen framed the highway.

Today, she was too stressed to listen to George Strait. Instead, she had the windows open, listening to the wind rush by.

"Raven's supposed to call now, is he not?" Blair asked.

"He is," Lindsey replied. "They should've made it into Ouray last night. Unless..."

"Everything I've seen from that guy, I'm sure he's okay," Nuke said. "He knows the mountains and the people in them better than I do... and if a nuclear engineer from Illinois can survive out there, you can bet your ass Raven can."

"Amen to that," Rogers said. "Guy's a rockstar in the wilderness."

Lindsey appreciated their encouraging words. But she still couldn't help worrying until Raven called and confirmed that everything was going alright in Ouray.

In front of them, a 1980s green Chevrolet Blazer led their small four-vehicle convoy. The bronze star-and-badge logo of the Colorado Rangers was painted on the side doors, occasionally visible when they took bends in the road. Four of Lindsey's Rangers were inside.

Behind them followed a Royal Marines' Land Rover Wolf filled with four of Blair's men.

Bringing up the rear of the convoy was an older Stewart and Stevenson cargo truck. A canvas top sheltered the bed where a five-man USAMRIID team carried medical supplies and Commander pills. Two additional crew members rode in the cab.

The cargo truck's diesel engine bellowed each time they took a slight incline. Its six big rubber tires spit loose gravel and mud over the neglected roadways. They'd already made one brief stop to a three-cabin community. A recon Ranger had reported three families living there days prior, but no one was around when they'd arrived.

She hoped the next destination would be different.

After the previous attack on the USAMRIID crew, Lindsey wanted to personally escort this team. It would give her a chance to see what was going on and report to the FAC so they could hopefully bolster their support for the convoys.

They were headed to Elkhorn Ranch tucked away between Highway 9 and 131, off Trough Road. It wasn't an easy place to get to, but a refugee with Wild Fire at the Golden Medical Clinic told one of Lindsey's Rangers that the community was suffering from the disease.

Her sat phone rang. Immediately, she picked it up. It was from Raven's number. A cool wave of relief washed over her.

"Got an update for me?" she asked, picking the phone up.

"We might have a potential contact," Raven said.

"Does this contact know where Eddy is?"

"Not sure."

"What do you mean?"

Lindsey took another bend in the road, heading down Trough Road past rocky slopes with only a few sparse trees.

"We've been staking out his place, but haven't seen him yet," Raven said.

"You sure it's not a trap?"

"No."

"Be careful, Sam. If this guy stinks like a pile of shit..."

"Then there's a good chance he is. I'm watching where I step. Don't worry, Lindsey."

"Easy for you to say." Lindsey followed the Blazer down another gravel road. "Keep me updated and let me know if you need help."

"I appreciate it, but we're good for now. We don't want to tip off Eddy. I'll do my best to keep in touch."

They ended the call as the convoy followed a road that went up and down like a natural roller coaster. Soon she spotted a clearing lined with a wooden fence.

Six cabins and a couple of barns lay beyond. A timber watchtower with a corrugated steel roof had been constructed above a humble wooden gate. Someone appeared to be perched in it with a rifle.

"All units, caution," Lindsey said over her radio. "Ready your weapons, but do not make any open signs of aggression."

The sounds of Rogers and Nuke preparing their weapons clicked from the back seat. They slowly pulled up to the front of the Elkhorn Ranch compound.

Lindsey put on a gas mask and stepped out of the vehicle. She stayed behind her open door for shelter. Nuke and Rogers each took up a shooting position behind the Bronco.

The Blazer disgorged another four Rangers.

The man looking down from the watchtower was mostly concealed in the shade. Lindsey couldn't make out his features except to see he wore what looked like jeans and a plaid shirt. He held a rifle, but it wasn't pointed at her or her men.

"I'm Sheriff Lindsey Plymouth with the Colorado Rangers," Lindsey shouted. "We heard there are some people here who might be sick, and we've come to help."

"Bullshit!" the man yelled. "You've come to take us all in like livestock to slaughter."

"No, sir, that's not true at all. We're here to help."

The man shouldered his rifle and aimed it at the ground in front of her Bronco. "We don't want your help."

Lindsey ducked back slightly and held up her hand to ensure her people didn't fire. Blair glanced over at Lindsey, but she couldn't make out his features behind his mask.

"Sir, we can just leave the meds for your people with instructions if you'd like," Lindsey said. "We don't have to even go into your compound. Can you tell me how many sick people you have so we know how much medicine to leave?"

The man stepped forward toward the sunlight, revealing his face. Oozing lesions marred his skin, giving him a bulbous appearance. He coughed before speaking again.

"We don't want that poison! Now get the hell out of here before I put a hole in your pretty little face!"

He fired a shot that kicked into the dirt just in front of the Bronco.

"Okay, we get the point!" Lindsey shouted. She gave the signal to retreat and climbed back into her vehicle. The other trucks followed her away from the compound to Trough Road.

"That man was bloody mad," Blair said. "He was sick and *still* refused aid."

"They don't trust us," Nuke said. "Every place I've been to out here has it out for the government. It's just getting worse."

"Insanity," Rogers said. "We can't help them if they don't let us. They got to learn to trust us."

Lindsey turned the wheel as they took a turn past a screen of trees. "It's a shame, but I won't risk our lives to try and earn that trust. We can't save everyone."

Lindsey radioed for the Royal Marines to take the lead in their Wolf. The SUV was more protected from rounds than her Bronco or the Blazer her men were driving.

They spent the rest of the morning trying to visit three more compounds and camps. Each had active Wild Fire infections, and each time, the people inside refused help.

"We're never going to be able to stamp out Wild Fire if these people don't let us give them the treatment," Nuke said.

"Shoot, man, just let them all get sick and die," Rogers said.

"I would be lying if I said my superiors didn't feel similarly," Blair said.

"Even if that was our strategy, Doctor Wheeler tells me we risk the disease exploding and spreading worse than it already has," Lindsey said. "We have to stomp it out here."

Nuke spoke up again. "Plus, imagine if we gave it time to mutate or evolve. I don't want Wild Fire turning into something even worse because we let it fester for a year or two in the New Frontier."

"You think that would really happen?" Rogers asked.

"I don't know," Nuke said. "I mean, biology isn't my scientific specialty, but I sure don't want to risk it happening. You know?"

"I'm with you, Nuke," Lindsey said. "We're going to try one last community today. I'm hoping we finally get lucky. Maybe they'll be receptive."

They slowed as they came up to an intersection mired with broken down vehicles.

"Careful here," Lindsey called to the men. "This is a perfect chokepoint for an ambush."

The Wolf continued in the lead, winding between the charcoaled SUVs and the blackened chassis of smaller cars that were still clogging the ditches and in some cases, the roadway. Lindsey followed the Wolf in her Bronco. Behind her was the Blazer, and the USAMRIID truck was in the back.

They headed toward a bridge over the Colorado River. The bridge was a mere six feet from the frothy waters overflowing from a recent thunderstorm.

The four-vehicle convoy stopped and scoped for contacts.

"Anyone got eyes?" Lindsey called over the radio.

"Mike One, copy," called the driver of the Marine's Wolf. "Nothing here."

Then came the reply from the USAMRIID truck. "Uniform One, negative."

"Good," Lindsey said. "Proceed with caution."

The Wolf began pushing across the bridge.

Before it even made it ten feet onto the fifty-foot-long bridge, blinding light flashed from the middle. Concrete gave way as a cloud of gray dust billowed up. Slabs of the bridge started to slide into the river.

"What the fuck was that?" Rogers yelled from the backseat.

"I didn't see a rocket!" Nuke said.

"IED!" Blair said. "Watch for an ambush!"

Lindsey threw the Bronco into reverse. Its tires squealed as they shot backward from the broken bridge, the Blazer and the USAMRIID truck doing the same.

The USAMRIID truck rammed into one of the burned-out sedans, pushing it backward and clearing a way for the Blazer and Lindsey's Bronco.

But the Wolf didn't make it.

The crumbling bridge gave way, and the Land Rover shuddered forward. It fell a couple of yards with the rest of the debris into the water with a tremendous splash. When the water and dust subsided, the Wolf was left partially submerged amid the rapids.

"No!" Blair yelled.

Lindsey slammed the car into park as he leapt out.

"Blair, get back here!" she shouted.

The Marine bolted toward the edge of the bridge as Lindsey cursed.

"All Romeos and Uniforms, secure a perimeter immediately!" she said into her radio. "We need to get those Marines out of the river!"

The Rangers and armed USAMRIID personnel flooded out of their vehicles with shouldered weapons.

"Who's got eyes?" she yelled.

"There!" Nuke was looking through his scope, pointing up the hills at Cottonwood Peak.

Before she could give an order, gunfire cracked out all around her, lancing into the trees nearly four hundred yards away. They had very little chance of hitting the enemy, especially when Lindsey saw a shape flit up the side of the mountain, disappearing into the woods.

But the Marines stranded in the Wolf needed the cover fire so they didn't get picked off.

"Romeos, stay on the defensive," Lindsey said. "Uniforms, I need help with the Marines!"

Lindsey rushed down the rocky bank of the Colorado. Nuke and Rogers ran at her heels.

Rubble from the bridge filled the water, creating a dam. Water eddied and swirled around the concrete chunks. Churning waves splashed violently against the side of the partially submerged Wolf. Concrete debris locked its doors in place.

"Nuke, Rogers, cover us!" she called.

The two Rangers dropped into firing positions between the trees and rocks. Nuke scoped the peaks with his rifle.

That vehicle would be the Marines' tomb if Lindsey

didn't act fast. She began wading into the freezing water. Blair came in after. Three USAMRIID medics came pushing in through the frigid waters with them.

Lindsey climbed up the back of the Wolf. She started banging on the rear windshield. For a moment, she didn't see any movement inside. She worried that all the Marines had been knocked unconscious. Water was gushing in between the edges of the dented and bent doors.

"Son of—" she turned to Blair. "We've got to break this window!"

She unstrapped her rifle and slammed the stock of it against the glass. Spiderwebs of cracks spread from the impact. Blair took out his sidearm and bashed the windshield with the handle.

Together they hammered at the glass. Water continued to slosh inside the vehicle. Suddenly, she saw movement inside. A pair of Marines were hammering at the glass from the Wolf's interior.

The three medics piled up around her, ready to help. But there wouldn't be anyone to help if they didn't hurry.

"Bloody hell!" Blair yelled. He slammed his pistol against the window again.

This time, the toughened glass finally burst in crystalline pebbles.

"Hurry!" Lindsey said as a couple of the USAMRIID medics stood near the rear windshield, waiting to help the Marines.

Two of the Marines unstrapped an unconscious Marine from his seat. Another helped them hand the injured colleague out to the waiting medics through the rear windshield.

One by one, they guided them to shore. Medics checked the conscious Marines over for injuries. One medic performed

CPR on the fourth until the man woke up coughing and spitting out water.

Blair bent down with Lindsey to help a dazed Marine. He seemed to have suffered a concussion and his steps were unsteady. They guided him over the rocky shore and behind a tree for cover.

"Anyone got eyes?" Lindsey called out.

"Nothing," Nuke said.

"No more movement at all," Rogers agreed.

It seemed whoever had laid the ambush was gone or watching.

Blair grumbled as he checked his men, then went back to Lindsey. "We're lucky they are alive. I'm going to have to report this to my commanding officer."

Lindsey held up a hand. "You do that, and you could get pulled out of here."

"We just lost our Wolf, and almost lost everyone inside, Sheriff." Blair shook his head. "I've seen a lot of death out here. Lost some good blokes under my command."

"I know, but things are getting better."

"Are they? We got a disease burning through a violent local population that are refusing help and trying to kill us." He walked away to check on his people again.

Lindsey heaved a sigh. She stared up at the mountains. Goosebumps prickled up her arms from the water evaporating from the sun's heat.

Blair was right. Things weren't getting better. She couldn't keep pretending like they were, even with the Reapers gone.

Another group had already replaced them. Not just that; the locals didn't trust her, didn't want help, and were trying to kill the people out here trying to render aid.

But if the Wild Fire went unchecked, it would devour the New Frontier and beyond. They needed a new plan.

They were losing the support of the FAC, and President Diego wasn't going to do shit. She was down good men too. Men like Molina, Yoon, and so many others.

And Raven was out there playing with fire, as usual.

Somehow, she had to find new allies. Friends were running scarce in a land of enemies.

7

A COOL SEA BREEZE CURLED AROUND CALVIN AS HE GOT out of the Humvee that had taken him down to Fort Rose-crans National Cemetery. The driver, California National Guardsman Private Milo Browning, was going to be Calvin and the Gomezes' ride back home after the funeral.

"I've still got to take you back up to LA tonight," Browning said, "and I really don't want to hurry you, sir, but it's best if we get there before midnight, you know? Things get dicey the later it gets."

"Yeah, I hear you," Calvin said.

"I'm really sorry, sir. Not trying to be rude. Just the way things are here."

"Don't worry yourself. I understand. Trust me."

The Pacific Ocean glinted with whitecaps reflecting sunlight. White tombstones stretched before him over a rolling green hillside at Fort Rosecrans National Cemetery. Amid the tombstones, Calvin saw figures milling around one of the newest tombstones.

First, he spotted a military chaplain. Next to him were two older gentlemen—maybe in their seventies—who were serving as the two-man uniformed military detail. Each wore their dress blues.

Before them sat a handful of metal folding chairs. Maureen Gomez sat in one of those chairs. She was staring at the newest tombstone at the cemetery as she snuggled with her five-year-old son Frankie and seven-year-old daughter Raquel. The children were leaning on the edges of their seats to be close with their mother.

The boy had the same big ears as Mouse and those same friendly brown eyes. Raquel had a softer, gentler version of Mouse's square jaw and twinkling smile that reminded Calvin of Mouse's mischievous grin.

Calvin approached the gravesite, treading lightly, anxious. Almost as anxious as the moments before a battle. In some ways, he felt the same dread.

His eyes flitted to the small cross engraved in the tombstone for Petty Officer First Class Steve "Mouse" Gomez. An American flag was draped over the casket in front of it.

He took in a deep breath and then finished the walk to Maureen and the kids.

"Calvin," she said when she heard him come up behind her.

"Hi, Maureen," Calvin said gingerly.

She stood and immediately wrapped her arms around him. "Oh, Calvin."

Burying her face against his shoulder, she began to sob. Warm tears soaked into Calvin's uniform. Raquel and Frankie joined the embrace and he put his hands on their backs.

"I'm so, so sorry about Steve," he said.

Maureen cried for a few minutes. Calvin shed a tear and tried to hold it together, but it was more difficult than he'd imagined now that he was with Maureen and her kids.

The chaplain looked at Calvin and the Gomezes when they finally took their seats. "Shall we begin?"

Maureen nodded somberly.

"I welcome you to today's Memorial Ceremony in honor of the life and service of Petty Officer First Class Steve Gomez. Please stand for the invocation."

Maureen stood, shaking slightly. The kids held her hands. Raquel, standing between Calvin and Maureen, slipped her other small hand into Calvin's.

"Heavenly Father, today is no easy day. We come here grieving the loss of our dear brother, husband, and father, Steve Gomez..."

Maureen cried as the Father went on with the invocation. Calvin himself could hardly hear the words. He was too overcome by memories of Mouse, his best friend and comrade. As the chaplain continued, inviting them to sit again, Calvin looked over at Raquel.

Her lip quivered, and she squeezed her mother's and Calvin's hands so tightly, her little knuckles were going white.

The chaplain continued with a memorial meditation, reflecting on Mouse's life. He relayed memories that Maureen must've shared with him before the service along with regaling them with Mouse's service records. The chaplain continued with the benediction and after the "amen."

Then he began one of the hardest parts of a military funeral in Calvin's eyes. The Last Roll Call.

"Chief Petty Officer Jackson," the chaplain called, serving as an officer.

"Here," Calvin called in his deepest, rumbling voice.

"Petty Officer First Class Gomez."

Silence reigned for three long seconds.

"Petty Officer First Class Gomez."

More silence. Maureen let out a sob. Frankie cried, and Calvin swallowed the hard lump in his throat.

"Petty Officer First Class Steve Gomez."

One of the uniformed service detail members called out, "Present arms."

The other lifted a bugle and began playing "Taps."

When it was done, the two older men folded the American flag from Mouse's coffin. One knelt in front of Maureen with it, holding it out to her.

"On behalf of the President of the United States, the United States Navy, and a grateful nation, please accept this flag as a symbol of our appreciation for your loved one's honorable and faithful service."

With the ceremony concluded, the chaplain left with the two other men. Calvin thought he heard one of them say they still had another four ceremonies to perform. Today was indeed no easy day.

Calvin gave Maureen and the kids a final chance to say goodbye for now to Mouse. He waited as they stood by the casket for nearly half an hour, speaking between each other, until he joined them again.

He didn't want to rush them. But it was time to go.

Especially now that the sun was beginning its fiery descent to the horizon. Darkness would come soon after and it was best to be off the streets by then.

He walked over to her and placed a gentle hand on her shoulder but didn't say anything. She nodded in understanding.

"My dad was a great man, wasn't he?" Raquel asked.

"The best," Calvin said.

"Is my dad a hero?" Frankie asked, glancing up.

"No question about it," Calvin said. "He was one of the

bravest heroes I've ever met. That's why your dad gets to rest here."

"He's just resting?"

Calvin leaned down to the boy who didn't seem to quite understand. "Yes, he's resting."

"I don't want him to rest," Frankie said. "I want to see him again."

"I know, baby, so do I." Maureen pulled Frankie close as he sobbed.

The orange sunset split the horizon over the ocean. Calvin took in a deep breath.

Mouse had loved the water. Calvin remembered visiting them and coming to the beach with Raquel when she was just two years old. He could still see big old Mouse lumbering into the ocean. He held Raquel's hands in his, walking behind her and helping her splash in the water as it rolled over the soft yellow sand.

Maureen, pregnant with Frankie at the time, had warned Mouse that Raquel wouldn't like the cold water. Then a particularly violent wave rolled toward shore, surprising even Mouse. It washed right into Raquel, knocking her on her diapered butt, even as Mouse kept his grip on her little hands.

Calvin had thought Raquel would wail in fright.

Instead, the girl let out the biggest, heartiest laugh he'd ever heard from a two-year-old. That laugh sounded frighteningly like her father's when he turned around to face Maureen and Calvin with a shit-eating grin plastered across his face.

Moments like that would eventually help Calvin look on the past with joy, even though right now all he felt was sadness. He knew someday he would come back here and smile at the memories. This was a wonderful place to lay his best friend.

"Your father will always be with you," Calvin said to Frankie. "You can come visit him and talk to him here. He'll listen."

Maureen wiped a tear from her face. She took Calvin's hand as he started to lead them back toward the Humvee. She looked out the window one last time as they wound through the treelined road back toward San Diego. Their driver, Browning, kept a careful eye on the road.

While normal traffic inched through the streets, Calvin noticed the hungry eyes from people sheltering in doorways or in the tents around parks. Hastily constructed shanty towns filled alleyways and golf courses. They even blocked off some of the smaller streets between office buildings and apartments that had once been bustling with carefree individuals.

Calvin looked over to see Frankie and Raquel nestled against their mother. Both stared out the window, their eyes now dry but distant.

He looked away to see brake lights flaring in the dusk ahead.

A horn blared.

The Humvee slowed to nearly a stop.

"What's going on?" Calvin asked as calmly as possible. He leaned forward and looked through the windshield to see what had caused them to stop.

Cars were stopped in the streets, their headlights glaring. People walked past them on the sidewalks. To Calvin, it sure seemed like a *lot* of people. Maybe twenty, thirty all headed the opposite direction they were going.

His hand slid toward his holstered sidearm.

Browning turned toward them. "A bit of a traffic jam, I think."

"That's all?" Calvin asked.

Browning shrugged. "We're in San Diego. Happens all

the time."

Calvin studied the slog of vehicles ahead. He didn't like it. Not as the sky continued to darken. He'd hoped they would make it home before night enveloped the city, especially given that only half the streetlights seemed to work.

Taking his hand away from his pistol, he tried to center himself.

After a career spent searching his surroundings for enemies, it was nearly impossible to pretend like everything was okay now.

Calvin looked at the park to their right. Tents and haphazardly constructed shelters filled it. An alley crossed to their left, but it was clogged with trash and even more tents.

Loud voices began to sound from in front of them. A clatter of footsteps and metal banging against metal rang out.

"This looks like a cluster..." Calvin whispered. He leaned toward Browning. "Any chance you can find another way?"

"Is something wrong?" Raquel asked.

"No, everything's fine, sweetie," Maureen replied.

"I think we should go," Calvin said, this time more urgently.

"It's probably just a protest or something," Browning said. "With all the reduced rations, it happens frequently."

Maureen turned for a better view, clearly anxious now.

People started to flood down the street. They carried signs painted with all kinds of messages.

"We're starving!"

"Food is a human right!"

"They're killing us!"

The people chanted as they moved toward the Humvee. Some carried metal bats and pipes. Most appeared unarmed, but all it took was a couple of belligerent delinquents with weapons to turn things violent quickly.

If they didn't move soon, the Humvee would be surrounded.

Caught in the middle of a protest. Shit.

Calvin worried it might quickly turn into a riot. He leaned forward to get a better view through the windshield, seeing more and more people flooding into the streets. Some were running. His hand went back to his pistol. He grimaced from the movement. His back hurt, and while the pain was something he was used to fighting through, he worried it would mess with his senses.

"You need to get us out of here," Calvin said, doing his best to keep his voice low. He didn't want to scare the children. "Now."

"Yeah," Browning agreed. He put the vehicle in reverse.

Screaming came from a few cars ahead. Calvin saw a man with a baseball bat take out a headlight of a honking car.

The driver got out of the car and appeared to yell something. The other man swung the bat right into his stomach, knocking the driver to his knees.

"Shit," Calvin grumbled. "We need to move, man."

"I know," Browning said defensively.

He turned the wheel, peeled off the street, and drove through the park, tires digging through grass and soil. They raced past the crowd and between the tents, dodging bystanders, some of them throwing trash or whatever they could find at the vehicle.

A bottle hit a window.

Maureen reached out to both kids. "It's going to be okay. We're fine. We're fine. Just stay down."

As they accelerated away, Calvin watched through the rear windshield as the protesters surrounded the other cars. He thought he saw a few pin down the guy with the bat and take away his weapon.

Then a gunshot cracked somewhere between the buildings.

The kids cried out and Maureen pulled them tighter.

Browning got them to a clear road a few minutes later.

"Almost there," Browning said.

Calvin's heart never settled until they started winding through the more peaceful and quieter neighborhood where the Gomezes lived. Night had settled by the time they reached the shady residential blocks.

"We'll be home soon," Maureen told the kids.

Home, Calvin thought.

He saw more tents ahead. People walked along the pothole-ridden street. Some of those wandering around were probably good people that were going through tough times like most Americans. But some could also be desperate enough to kill for a warm supper.

San Diego was in worse shape than he expected.

But then again, most places were bad out there. That was why he had come to look after Maureen and her kids. Take care of them now that Mouse was gone. Doing that here was going to be hard. He needed a job for that.

His mind drifted as they drove, even while he tried to stay focused on more threats in the road. It reminded him of the train rides, when his mind would wander, but he would watch for threats.

There had to be a place out there that was safe. A place where they could start over. Thing is, that would mean leaving their father, who they had just buried. And he had just promised them they could visit him anytime they liked.

But was risking their lives worth that?

Calvin shook his head wearily.

"Here we are," said Browning. He pulled into a driveway.

The one-story beige house was covered in vinyl siding.

And graffiti tags marred that siding, just like many of the houses down the street. Calvin spotted a couple of men lingering near a lamppost about a block away. They glanced suspiciously at the Humvee.

What was happening to this once peaceful neighborhood?

Calvin didn't like leaving them, but he had to get back to the AFB in LA to finish his job.

He got out of the Humvee and walked Maureen and the kids up to the house.

"I'll be back as soon as I can," he said. "Okay?"

"You have to leave already?" Frankie asked.

"He has work," Maureen said. "Now say goodbye to Calvin."

Raquel looked down at the ground while Frankie frowned.

"Come on now," Maureen said.

"It's okay," Calvin said. He bent down in front of the kids. "I'll be back, and I'm going to make sure you stay safe. I promise, okay?"

Both kids looked at him and nodded.

He hugged them in turn and then hugged Maureen.

"We'll be okay here," she said. "Don't worry."

Calvin hesitated another moment before returning to the truck. He hated leaving them, but he had a promise to uphold. Then he would be back to work on his promise to Mouse.

———

Eddy's chest swelled with pride as he walked among the line of twenty Rattlesnakes toward the edge of Pioneer Lookout Point. In the pale moonlight, he could just see the snaking Gunnison River below. Its surface reflected the stars.

The precipice looked out over steep valley walls lined in

trees and bushes clinging to slopes of rock. Twelve people were lined up on their knees in front of the cliff with their hands tied behind their backs.

Just two hours ago, the Skulls militia, led by Shupert, captured these federal government and foreign aid workers near Crested Butte. The loyal militia had not only helped bring him success at Eagle, but they were proving to be valuable tools of war. They were a necessary evil to ensure the Rattlesnake Union had the power they needed to conquer the New Frontier.

Shupert stood beside the prisoners in a loose-fitting leather jacket. The skeletal black tattoo covering his face made him look diabolical in the moonlight.

The four men beside him sported identical tattoos. A couple wore t-shirts with short sleeves that showed off the human bones inked on their flesh. Each bone tattooed on their body represented a person they had killed.

Eddy didn't condone the way they memorialized their violent acts. Death, even of your enemies, was not something to brag about with a tattoo.

But they had proven their worth in the Rattlesnake Union. Eddy would reluctantly accept their strange habits.

Eddy outstretched a hand toward the Skull's leader. "Good job, Shupert. First you succeed in Eagle, and now this."

Shupert shook his hand. "I told you, the Skulls are nothing if not loyal to the Rattlesnakes. We caught these USAMRIID people trying to peddle their garbage to some of our people."

Eddy looked down at the ranks of men and women in US Army combat uniforms. Their rifles lay in a pile next to them where Robert stood. He held his stone ball club like he was ready to start swinging it.

Kitcheyan was next to him, a fiendish grin painted across his face. He looked like he was ready to spill the prisoners' blood.

"They're all USAMRIID?" Eddy walked down the line. "Doesn't look like it."

He stopped in front of four men with the blue band around their upper arms representing the United Nations.

"Is that a problem?" Shupert asked.

Eddy smiled. "No, it's even better than expected. These people could be useful. Maybe they'll give us leverage to convince the UN peacekeepers to withdraw from the New Frontier."

A few prisoners tried to yell out against their cloth gags.

Robert raised his club eagerly. "Shut your traps or I'll shut them for you."

"Yeah, you guys wouldn't like that," Kitcheyan said. He took a swig from his flask and then wiped his mouth off.

"I'll take it from here," Eddy said to Shupert. He turned to start questioning the prisoners, but heard a throat being cleared.

"Uh, Eddy," a voice followed.

He turned to Shupert.

"What?" Eddy asked.

"Well, you promised that for our loyalty, you would provide rewards like in Eagle." Shupert took a step toward Eddy. "I brought these guys in. We even lost one of our own in the shootout, so I expect—"

"You worried I'm not a man of my word?" Eddy interrupted.

Shupert shook his head, then his eyes flitted to the ranks of Rattlesnakes behind Eddy. They went to Robert next, who tapped the stone ball of his club against his palm.

"No, I'm just letting you know what happened," Shupert

said. "I'm a patient man."

"Good, because I was beginning to think you wanted something this second," Eddy replied. "There is still work to be done."

He moved up to Shupert until they were face to face. Nervous beads of sweat rolled down his forehead. They traced over his tattoo and glimmered in the moonlight.

From the man's expression, Eddy could tell the Skull was fully subservient and feared the Rattlesnakes.

Good.

Fear would keep this disgrace of a man from doing something stupid.

Eddy enjoyed the power he held. The foreboding intensity of raw fear. This was exactly what would keep people listening to his every word.

But fear alone wasn't enough to keep a man in power.

In a land as tumultuous as the New Frontier, terror would last for only so long until someone else rose to challenge him.

Fear had to be used hand-in-hand with payments, but he wasn't going to just be handing out gold, silver, and ammo like it was candy.

He wanted his soldiers to prove their loyalty over time.

"I've got another mission for you," Eddy said. "You'll be heading north, close to Rocky Mountain National Park. Stick close to your radio over the next couple days. The militia from Silverton will join you."

Shupert's brow furrowed.

"What?" Eddy asked.

"I heard the guys in Silverton had second thoughts. Their sheriff doesn't want them to go anymore."

Eddy snorted. "Loyalty being tested already."

"Slimy bastards if you ask me," Shupert said.

For a minute, Eddy wondered if the man was lying to him.

Maybe he wanted more silver for himself.

"I'll send a scout to confirm their intent," Eddy said.

"If this is true, I'll skin the traitors alive," Robert said.

"That's the least that will be done," Kitcheyan said.

"No," Eddy snapped. "I will deal with it."

He waved Shupert off, watching as the man retreated toward where the other vehicles were parked. He left on a dirt bike with the other four Skulls following, their noisy motorcycles whining into the night.

After giving himself a moment to breathe, Eddy then walked up and down the ranks of USAMRIID and UN personnel that were lined up next to the cliff. Their frightened eyes followed his every movement.

"Welcome to the *real* New Frontier." Eddy paused in the middle of the group. "This land is no longer the United States, despite what you were led to believe."

He indicated the warriors behind him with a wave of his hand. "This land is and always will be *our* land."

Several of the prisoners nodded vehemently as if they were ready to agree with anything Eddy said. One of them was a woman from the UN.

Eddy knelt in front of her. He put a finger on her chin and forced her to look into his eyes.

"I could let you go to spread this message," he said. "The only problem is I've already made that message clear, and still, here you wašíču are. Maybe I need to send a different message."

"A very different message." Robert cocked his club back, aiming it at the head of one of the USAMRIID medics. The prisoner wriggled on his knees, backing up slightly until his boots were just over the precipice.

"I suppose that depends on what you all tell me." Eddy gestured for Robert to lower the club for now.

One of the USAMRIID members tried to speak against his gag. Eddy nodded, and Robert removed the gag.

"We're just trying to help," the man said, worry filling his face. "We're not trying to take over your land. We're just trying to deliver—"

Robert kicked the prisoner square in the chest. He landed just inches from the side of the edge.

"You don't talk until we tell you to talk," Robert said.

Kitcheyan let out a chuckle.

Eddy crouched in front of the USAMRIID man.

"What's your name?" he asked.

"Stuart... Stuart Johnson."

"All right, Stuart. I'm going to ask you some questions. I want clear answers. If you don't give them to me, then you will need to sprout wings because you're going over that cliff. Understand?"

Stuart swallowed hard as he nodded.

"Good," Eddy said. "Truthfully, I don't like killing people. I just want my people to have what they deserve. What's rightfully theirs. What was taken by the US government years ago. I assume you're familiar with the way my people have historically been treated."

"I get it, I really do. What happened back then was wrong."

"Back then?" Eddy stood. "It's not just back then. You don't understand, clearly. You're doing the same thing those people did. You're encroaching on our lands today."

Robert cranked back his club.

"No, no, wait, please, we'll leave," Stuart said.

The other prisoners also nodded.

Robert twirled his club and walked down the line.

"I can give you information," Stuart said. "Things that can help you."

Eddy folded his arms over his chest. "Speak."

"Well, I work for Doctor Wheeler," Stuart continued. "He's in charge of the USAMRIID operation in Denver. He and the Rangers' Sheriff, Lindsey Plymouth, are trying to produce more Commander to stop the Wild Fire."

Stuart spilled every detail he knew about the pharmaceutical plant Wheeler was using. Where it was located. How long they thought it would take to get up and running. How much Commander they thought they could produce.

"This is all interesting," Eddy said. "But I need more. I assume the attack on Eagle didn't go unnoticed."

"No, sir, it did not."

"How are the Rangers going to respond?"

Stuart was quiet for a moment, pressing his lips together. "I... I..."

A sobbing woman at the other end of the line of prisoners suddenly shot to her feet. She started running along the cliff's edge with her hands still tied behind her back.

"Kitcheyan, stop her," Eddy said.

The Apache man took off running with his axe out. He suddenly cocked his arm back.

"No!" Eddy yelled.

But it was too late. The axe flew through the air and hit her in the back between the shoulder blades. She stumbled, tried to reach over her shoulders while screaming in agony. Turning, she stared at Eddy with a horrified look, then stumbled a few steps before tumbling over the edge of the cliff.

The other prisoners whimpered and blubbered against their gags.

Eddy walked away from Stuart over to Kitcheyan.

"I said *stop* her," Eddy said.

"I did stop her," Kitcheyan said.

Eddy slapped the grin off Kitcheyan's face, forcing the

Apache back a foot. Kitcheyan brought his hands up into fists, but Robert ran over with his club to protect Eddy.

Pulling his knife out, Eddy motioned for Robert to get back to the prisoners. He didn't need protecting.

"You want to fight me," Eddy said. "Go ahead. See if you can gut me before I have your stomach dragging in the dirt."

Kitcheyan seemed to think on it, his face bright red with anger, and his chest heaving.

"Come on!" Eddy shouted. "Do it, or back the fuck down and stop acting like an uncivilized barbarian."

Kitcheyan backed down.

"Give me your flask," Eddy said.

"What?" Kitcheyan said.

"You heard me."

Kitcheyan fished it out of his pocket and handed it over. Eddy tossed it over the cliff.

"Your behavior improves or you will need wings too," Eddy said.

Then he turned back to the prisoners. They were all staring at the ground, afraid to meet his gaze.

"The more we kill, the angrier our enemy will get," Eddy explained, lowering his voice. "There will be a time to fight, but right now, we build our army and hold hostages—alive—to use for negotiations in the future. Do you understand?"

Kitcheyan, his face still red, finally bobbed his head.

"Good," Eddy said. He walked over and patted Kitcheyan's arm. "The time to unleash your vengeance will come. Save it for when I need you the most."

"Hey, Ahiga!" Robert called. He was standing and grinning in front of a woman with matted down hair in a USAMRIID shirt. "Looks like some of these people have even more intel for us."

Intrigued, Eddy walked back over with Kitcheyan.

"What information do you have for us?" Eddy asked the woman.

She looked up, her eyes filled with pure terror. "I... will you... will you let us go if I help?"

"It depends on how helpful you are," Eddy said.

The woman's lips trembled a moment before she answered. "The Rangers have patrols searching for you."

Eddy laughed. "I know that. Why do you think no one's cooperated with your people? Why do you think they're having trouble finding me?" He sneered at her, bending closer. "Because everyone who betrays us know that death is the only outcome. And everyone who is loyal will die to protect us."

"But... it's not just the Rangers now," she said. "I mean, we talked with the Rangers. We were working with them recently."

"You're telling me things I already know again," Eddy said.

"I mean, the Rangers... they said the sheriff sent out someone else to find out where you are. To protect us from you."

"Someone else?" Eddy asked. "And who would that be?"

"A tracker that's worked closely with us before. Raven."

"Raven Spears?"

"Yes, that's it. The name. He's with some man from the Navajo Nation."

"Who?"

"I really don't know."

Eddy turned back to Robert. "Tell the militia leaders to keep an eye out for two Native Americans searching for me." Then he grinned, looking back at Kitcheyan. "It looks like that day of vengeance might be coming even sooner than I'd hoped."

8

Banks of white lights illuminated Spaulding Field at UCLA. Palmer and the USAMRIID team were using the expansive former football practice field to stage the convoy that would take them back to the AFB. Then all they'd have to do was fly home.

Two medium tactical vehicle (MTV) trucks idled with a pair of Humvees parked in front and behind them. California National Guardsmen manned the M249s on each of the turrets.

In addition to the Guardsmen, Calvin's Steel Runners were spread out between the Humvees, and the trucks.

It was quite impressive from where Palmer stood, but he knew as soon as they left this area, they would be targets for raiders. In a perfect world, they would have used air support, but they couldn't land a Chinook here.

Too many haphazardly constructed structures, buildings, and abandoned vehicles were scattered around campus to allow for a helicopter to safely land anywhere nearby. Not only that, but command had decided it was too risky to fly the supplies in something that could attract too much attention and be shot down over downtown LA.

That meant taking the roads was the best and only option. From the UCLA campus, the convoy would navigate between the buildings and wreckage downtown. The journey would take an hour, assuming they didn't run into trouble.

The rumble of a Humvee engine announced the arrival of their latest addition to the convoy. The vehicle parked, and Calvin stepped out.

Palmer waved as he came over. He wanted to ask how the funeral went, but that sounded stupid. All funerals were tough.

"I'm sorry about Mouse, sir," he said instead. "I hope the family's doing okay."

"About as okay as can be expected."

"They will be better once you're with them," Palmer said. "Sooner we get this done, sooner you can go back down and see 'em."

"Let's do it." Calvin walked by his side, talking as they moved. "I was planning on riding in the rearguard Humvee with Anna's team. Mind joining me back there to help coordinate our defensive efforts?"

"Sure," Palmer said.

In moments, they were loaded up into the Humvee.

Palmer took the front passenger seat. Calvin sat in the back with Anna.

"Our driver is Private Marta Ramirez," she said.

Ramirez gave them all a nod.

Anna indicated the man poking his head out the turret. "Private Zeunik is on the gun."

"Howdy, folks," the shorter, tawny man said.

"Boston, Ortiz, Marino," Calvin called into his radio. "All good in your Humvees?"

"Ready to ride," Ortiz called back.

"You bet, chief," Boston said.

"Yes, sir. We're ready," Marino replied.

Calvin pressed the button on the radio again. "All call signs, roll out."

The convoy started out of the campus through LA's streets under the cover of the night.

While the less savory types tended to lurk outside at these late hours, the traffic was also far sparser. That allowed for a speedier getaway if they needed.

"Palmer, I want to warn you," Calvin said, "I knew the situation here would be bad, but we ran into a protest earlier. It might be worse than I even expected downtown."

"Don't worry, sir," Ramirez said, glancing over her shoulder. "If we run into trouble, I'll run you right out of it."

"I appreciate that, Private," Calvin said.

"We've taken all the precautions you noted," Palmer said as they carried on through the streets. "We've got Guardsmen positioned in pairs throughout our route. They're going to be watching for danger. Everyone's equipped with nonlethal arms in case we run into problems with civilians."

"Good," Calvin said.

They made their way between towering vacant office and apartment buildings, many with broken windows. The convoy skirted around potholes and the random broken-down vehicle. Some were bullet-pocked and left where they were shot up by thieves.

As Palmer watched out the window, he saw the shapes of what appeared to be a couple dead bodies down an alley.

"Is that normal?" Palmer asked Ramirez, trying to subtly nod toward the bodies.

"Unfortunately," Ramirez replied. "We just don't have

the resources to constantly search the city for bodies unless someone specifically reports them."

"We're going to call those ones in, right?" Anna asked.

Ramirez picked up the radio to do just that.

Palmer wasn't much for superstitions, but he didn't think the sight of corpses at the beginning of a mission was ever a sign of good luck.

"Guardians Alpha," Calvin said over his radio, "convoy is approaching your position now. Sector still clear?"

"Still clear," a National Guard soldier called back.

"How we looking up front, Ortiz?" Calvin asked.

"Coast is wide open," Ortiz replied.

"Anything behind us?" Calvin asked the gunner.

Zeunik continued roving the machine gun back and forth. "Don't see anything unusual. Just some curious eyes from the buildings."

Palmer definitely didn't like hearing that.

"Spotters?" he asked.

"Perhaps," Ramirez said.

The eerie sensation of being watched unnerved Palmer. Kind of like that time he'd gone for a long run in the foothills only to realize about halfway through a mountain lion was stalking him.

The hair on the back of his neck stood straight, his pulse racing. He certainly didn't consider himself a coward, but this felt like sitting in a barrel with fish waiting to be popped full of lead.

"Guardian Bravo, Convoy Lead here. You got eyes on anything suspicious?" Calvin called.

"We're keeping an eye on a few civilian groups, but right now, they're off-route," another spotter in a building called. "You're clear to proceed."

The convoy continued past construction equipment

caked in a thick layer of dust. Excavators and front loaders sat in front of a chain-link fence marked with orange warning signs. Behind that fence was a building with half its front façade collapsed.

"Convoy Lead, Guardian Bravo here. Route is no longer clear. Recommending you proceed to alternative escape route, Echo-Romeo-Two."

"Shit," Ramirez said.

"Thought you said all this looked normal."

"Things change," Ramirez said.

She cranked hard on the wheel to follow the convoy at an intersection. They turned northward to another street.

"Convoy Lead, Guardian Bravo again," a panicked voice called. "You need to proceed to alternative route Echo-Romeo-Three immediately! Echo-Romeo-Two is being block-aded as we speak. People are flooding out of all the nearby buildings!"

"Copy that," Calvin replied. "Ramirez, get us out of here!"

"Son of a..." Ramirez started. "Zeunik, you better stay frosty up there!"

"I am!" the gunner shouted down.

Palmer tightened his grip on the rifle, eyes staring at the window. He didn't see anything but empty cars and curious onlookers so far. But he couldn't stop feeling that they were headed right into danger.

Ramirez turned the Humvee around, and they proceeded southward with the rest of the convoy. This time, they raced across an intersection filled with trash. The Humvee crunched over something, and Palmer winced.

"If Echo-Romeo-Three's compromised, we don't have another alternative," Ramirez said.

"I don't like that," Palmer said.

"We'll figure something out," Calvin said. Then he called on the radio. "Ortiz, you see another way out of this from up front? We can take an alley or—"

The flash of fire bloomed in front of them. Black smoke billowed up.

"What was that?" Anna asked.

"We got rioters!" Ortiz called over the radio. Marino's voice came in next. "We're seeing potential hostiles converge on our location. They're tossing Molotov cocktails."

Another burst of flame erupted in front of the convoy. The fire raged behind the silhouettes of people a few blocks away rushing toward the lead truck.

"Guardian Bravo here to Convoy Lead. There doesn't appear to be a way out. You've got civilians closing in on every side. I just... I just don't see how to get past them. They're flooding out of buildings and... just everywhere."

A gunshot boomed from somewhere. Palmer pulled back the charging handle on his rifle.

"We got armed civilians," Ortiz called.

"Guardian Bravo here. I can confirm armed civilian sightings. I count... Jesus, maybe a hundred encircling your positions."

"Damn it!" Ramirez slammed her hands on the driving wheel. "They probably think we have food or something."

"Guardian Bravo, Convoy Lead here again. I'm going to need you to try making contact with the group," Calvin said. "Say we don't have resources for them. We don't have goods."

"We'll try," Guardian Bravo said.

There was a moment of silence on the radio.

The roar of the crowd grew closer. More shapes flashed between the flames. Palmer heard Guardian Bravo's voice booming over a megaphone, telling the crowds to disperse.

From what little Palmer could see, the incoming horde of

people were now just a block away from the lead Humvee and closing in quickly.

Anna cursed as she looked out the window of the back seat. Palmer saw why a moment later.

Behind them, several blocks past the Humvee at the rear of the convoy, more people ran down the street, illuminated by the few working streetlamps.

Ramirez backed up slightly so they could see to their left and right. People were also storming down those blocks.

Gunshots cracked from a block north. Right where the two men on the Guardian Bravo team were located.

"Guardian Bravo here again. They're not listening!"

"What do we do?" Ramirez asked as the Humvee's engine idled.

Zeunik swiveled back and forth above them. "I can fire a warning shot."

"Fire on American citizens?" Palmer asked. "Won't that make things way worse?"

"We might not have a choice, but I'm going to try to avoid it at all costs," Calvin said. He leaned forward from the back seat. "Look, I've been in this situation before, and Palmer's got the right idea. We open fire, we invite violence. Even if we make it out, a full-blown panicked riot could leave dozens of US citizens dead. We have to deploy nonlethal measures first. Tear gas to our north and south. See if it drives them away."

Calvin relayed the order to his other Steel Runners.

Seconds later, the throaty thumps of grenade launchers came from both ends of the convoy. White gas drifted through the city streets.

The crowds broke into chaos. Some retreated through the haze, disappearing down other streets.

But more continued pressing on.

"Rubber bullets," Calvin said.

Palmer could see the pain on the man's face ordering this assault on his fellow countrymen. He felt the same. He would die to protect his American brothers and sisters; he just hadn't expected he'd have to fight against them.

The deputy handed a shotgun up to Zeunik. The man launched a few rubber buckshot rounds at the crowd.

That only seemed to anger them. They surged forward, advancing between the trash and stalled vehicles clogging the streets.

"It's not working," Anna said.

At the same time, small amounts of the tear gas were seeping into the Humvee. Palmer could feel his eyes getting scratchy. Mucus ran from his nose.

The crowds began to close in. Someone threw a Molotov cocktail at their Humvee. It burst against the rear windshield, glass and flames spreading everywhere.

"Ah, crap!" Zeunik said, dropping into the car.

Flames danced across his jacket. Palmer helped swat them out. The man was panting when they were done.

"I'm about to light these assholes up," Zeunik said.

"No!" Palmer shouted. "You heard Calvin."

Zeunik secured the hatch shut right before another Molotov cocktail smashed against the Humvee.

Marino's voice came over the radio. "They're throwing Molotov cocktails directly at us!"

Then came Boston. "Bricks and rocks and shit too! We got to do something!"

"Can we get the Guards' helicopters in here or something?" Anna asked.

"No," Calvin said. "They can't make it through these buildings. LZ's too hot. And if we do that, we'd have to abandon all this science cargo in those MTVs."

Palmer racked his mind for a second. He came up with a

risky idea. "Hey, we think they want food, right? We want them off our backs, we give it to them."

He told Calvin his idea.

"God, I hope it works," Calvin said. He called the AFB and told them their proposed plan.

Civilians began to crowd around the Humvee. They hammered on the windows, battering the bulletproof glass.

Someone took a bat to the side of the Humvee. They hit the window over and over.

Cracks started to spiderweb through the glass. The Humvees were strong as hell, but eventually, they'd give.

Sweat beaded down Palmer's forehead. They just needed to hold out a bit longer.

Then came the distant thump of helicopters.

"Come on, baby," Palmer said. "Come on."

Four Black Hawks raced high over downtown. They had their side doors open, illuminated by their onboard cabin lights.

A voice boomed from the megaphones attached to one of the choppers. "Rioters, if you want food, desist from these activities and back away from the road!"

People began pushing the Humvee from both sides, rocking it as if to flip it. A few heads turned toward the chopper.

Then one of the choppers lowered a crate secured in its utility net. Another chopper shone a spotlight on the crate.

"Stop at once!" the voice boomed over the loudspeakers again. "We're providing food! But supplies will be limited."

Several of the rioters stopped rocking the Humvee and turned from it. They began running toward the lowering crate nearly three blocks straight north.

As those people ran, more and more peeled away.

No one wanted to be the last to reach the promised provisions.

Ortiz called over the radio. "We've got an opening up front!"

"Go, go, go!" Calvin shouted.

The convoy took off again, barreling through the streets past the racing civilians. They carried on until they reached clearer streets, far from the persistent thump of the chopper engines.

Silence reigned in the group until they spotted the walls around the Los Angeles AFB.

"They bought it," Calvin said. "Nice thinking, Palmer."

"Yeah," Ramirez said. "Last thing I wanted to do was reward that behavior with actual food. Dropping empty crates in the street. Perfect distraction."

"Of course, we won't be able to pull another trick like that," Zeunik said. "Going to have to think of something different next time."

"Hey, at least we're all safe and alive *this* time," Anna said.

They made it out of Los Angeles without further incident, but the adrenaline didn't subside for Calvin. Everything he saw out here confirmed San Diego was worse than he had thought.

He watched the roads for a few more minutes before turning to Palmer.

"You got room on the way back to Colorado?" Calvin asked.

Palmer grinned. "Change of heart? You miss the mountains already?"

"I'm thinking they might be safer for the Gomezes, to be honest."

"Yeah, I'd say so."

"You got room for all of us? Maybe set them up in the Refugee Center back in Estes?"

"You bet; the more the merrier," Palmer said.

"Thanks." Calvin took out a borrowed sat phone and dialed Maureen.

"Hello?" she answered.

"Maureen, it's Calvin. The kids still up?"

"Yeah, why... is everything okay?"

"Yes, go ask them how they feel about taking a little vacation to the Rocky Mountains."

———

Raven trekked through the woods southeast of Ouray with Creek. Somewhere about a hundred meters ahead, Jay was scouting through clusters of evergreens to make sure no one was set to ambush them.

Lindsey had called him the day before, telling him about the USAMRIID team that had disappeared. They'd gone missing almost three hours away from here, somewhere around Creste Butte.

It wasn't close, but it made Raven nervous about where Eddy's forces might be and what they were up to.

Between staking out the house Jay's lady friend had sent them to, he and Jay had taken turns trying to search for the Rattlesnakes in the nearby area.

So far, they hadn't seen any evidence of the group. There were plenty of hard-looking assholes out here, though. They didn't find anyone else willing to talk to them. Everyone seemed to be a threat or were just too scared to talk anyway.

Without another lead and people getting more suspicious, they had no choice but to circle back around the house where David was supposed to be.

"Guess we're going to see if you actually got something other than herpes from that lady," Raven said to Jay. "A day of watching David's place, and we haven't seen evidence anyone lives there. I'm not feeling confident."

The detective guided them through the trees and toward a clearing where the cabin was located.

Like before, it seemed empty. No lights on the inside. No recent tracks on the path in front of the house. It sat alone in the clearing looking as if nothing but mice and insects called it home.

At the edge of the clearing, Jay and Raven both crouched. Creek continued through the brush to sniff for enemies while the men scoped the area.

The old one-story cabin was in bad shape like most structures out here. Soggy cardboard had been taped up over broken windows. Hard to believe anyone would *want* to call this place home.

"Lovely little cabin," Raven whispered. "I bet David got tired of this shithole and left."

They waited a few minutes. A few turned into thirty. Then an hour until, finally, they heard someone crunching through the dirt and gravel across the clearing.

Raven tried to contain his excitement. Was David finally returning to his place?

A man walked toward the cabin with something in his hand. He brought it up to his lips and then lit a match. The brief flare of light illuminated a long, drawn face with a rough, unkempt red beard.

Over his back, he had three rabbits tied up on a rope.

So that was where he'd been. Searching for food.

"Is that David?" Raven asked.

"My lady friend told me he had a red beard nastier than a

mule deer's ass," he said. "That's got to be him. You cover me. I'm going in to check him out before he gets inside."

Before Raven could protest, Jay was moving.

The guy was gutsy, that was for sure.

Jay trekked through the trees and broke out into the clearing. He walked hurriedly across the path.

David saw Jay, then froze, dropping his cigarette and the rabbits. He quickly reached for a pistol at his side.

Jay held up his hands. "Hey, just want to talk."

Raven brought up his rifle just in case he needed to take a long shot. He held up the scope, centering on the man. David continued inching toward his cabin, his hand firmly on his pistol now.

It was too far for Raven to hear anything, but Jay said something else and David finally stopped. They stood in the middle of the clearing for several minutes. From what Raven could tell, they were both fairly calm and speaking quietly.

Suddenly, the man moved past his cabin and motioned for Jay to follow. They disappeared past the cabin, and Raven lost sight of them.

What was this guy's game?

"Shit," Raven said. He raised his rifle and stood as the pair vanished around the back of the cabin.

He whistled for Creek and waited for the dog to come trotting over. Then they made their way around the clearing to get a better vantage. He switched to his crossbow again as he moved around the corner of the cabin.

They came to an overgrown field of grass that bordered another patch of forest. In the moonlight, Raven spotted Jay and the man walking into the woods.

Raven and Creek stalked them for a good twenty minutes. He kept an eye out for other followers and sent the Akita on a security sweep searching for hostiles.

The trail took them to a gurgling stream that Raven remembered from a map as Portland Creek. He heard voices along the bank to his right and followed them to a shed. A pair of kayaks leaned up against its side.

"You can come out now," Jay called.

Slowly, Raven walked over with his bow still up. Under the awning of the small boat house and shed, Jay stood with David. Closer up, the man reeked of body odor. Dirt covered his face, and Raven detected alcohol.

Maybe his absence wasn't just a hunting trip. The guy looked like he'd just woken up from a bender.

"This is my friend," Jay said, gesturing to Raven. "We're all good here."

Raven nodded and lowered his bow, trusting Creek would sniff out other people.

"This is indeed David Singer," Jay said. "David knows all about the Rattlesnakes, isn't that right?"

The man nodded. He used a hand to indicate the cliffs in the distance. "Eddy and his people killed my brother up there. Dumped his body in this here creek. I found him not too far from here."

"I'm sorry," Raven said.

The man scoffed. "I don't want pity. I want the Rattlesnakes stopped." He looked around as if the trees might have eyes. "Eddy's killed a lot of people in these parts. Anyone that doesn't support his cause—especially the vocal ones—find themselves six feet under really quickly."

"You know where Eddy is?" Raven asked.

"He's like a ghost, just wandering these mountains. Last I heard, he was camped out at Montezuma Creek, but that was two, maybe three weeks ago."

"Yeah, we know he's gone now." Raven looked to Jay. This wasn't new information. "I'm assuming you got a better lead."

"Hear him out," Jay said.

"Okay, go on," Raven said.

"I was gonna kill Eddy myself," David said, "but shit, things have changed."

"Changed how?" Raven asked.

"For starters, the Rattlesnakes aren't just a lone group of half-crazed vigilantes anymore." David stared at the running water, then shook his head. "Eddy's recruited native tribes, militias, independent communities, everyone he can. He's building a fricking army."

"What? How?"

"Silver. Ammo. Medicine. Anything and everything he stole over the past two years."

"So he has been planning this?" Raven looked back to Jay. "You didn't mention any of this before. Did you know about this?"

"Hell no, man. Eddy went rogue a while ago. That's a huge part of why we aren't friends anymore."

"You were friends with him?" David's voice quaked in anger.

"Long time ago," Jay admitted. "He's changed. Got some kind of evil inside of him that took root and grew deep."

David huffed. "Evil is an understatement. He's like a cult leader. People fall under his spell. Even Pernell Clayton, the mayor of Ouray. You seen him?"

"That the guy that does the town hangings?" Raven asked.

"Yup, the mayor gets off on people dying," David said. "He's a bad dude, but shit, I'd take him over Eddy. Most people in town are either scared of Eddy or in league with the Rattlesnakes. But no one knows anything really about Eddy or what he's up to. Except for Clayton."

"Why Clayton?" Jay asked.

"I'm pretty sure Clayton is one of the bigwigs working for

Eddy now. He leads the Ouray militia, which, from what I heard, is going to join up with Eddy for whatever they're planning. I've personally seen Eddy go in and out of his compound."

"His compound?" Raven asked.

"Yes, it's at the northwest part of town, about a half-mile into the mountains. You got a map of the area?"

Raven nodded and pulled one out of his pack.

David pointed to a spot on the map. "It's basically a fortress. He rarely comes into town, except for executions. Just sticks to the area around his compound. If anyone knows where Eddy is, it's Clayton."

"There's got to be someone else. Someone we can get to easier."

"Maybe, but chances are they can't be trusted," David said. "Plus they aren't going to know what Clayton knows. The guy must be a big deal if Eddy talks with him, you know."

"I like to expend all my options," Jay said.

"You go asking around for Eddy, and you're gonna get killed."

How about sleeping around? Raven thought, resisting the urge to chide Jay.

He had David circle the area where the compound was located.

"Thanks," he said.

"I don't need your thanks," David said. "You can thank me by killing Eddy. It's what I been wanting to do for a while now. It's why I've been trying to figure out what he and Clayton got going on."

"I get it," Raven said. "This goes without saying, but you can't tell anyone you met with us."

"I don't even know your names."

"And we're going to keep it that way," Jay said. "We'll make sure your brother is avenged."

David nodded. "I hope so. If you guys aren't careful, you'll end up just like him. Now I'm going to pretend like I didn't see you and get back home. Time for me to start a rabbit stew. Got it?"

Raven stepped aside to let the man go. David trudged down the bank of the stream and then into the forest.

"You really trust him to tell no one?" Raven asked.

"Not sure what reason he would have to betray us," Jay said. "Unless he was lying about everything."

"That's a pretty good reason to betray us, but I didn't get that from him."

"Me either."

"I guess we stake out the mayor's place to see if David's intel is right." Raven gestured to the spot on his map outside the mayor's compound. "That's a lot of ground to cover, so let's split up. We'll meet up periodically just to check in."

Raven met back up with Creek and started through the forest. He listened to the groaning limbs of tree branches and the peaceful wind. It almost seemed relaxing, but any sense of peace was going to be short-lived. Eddy had apparently built an army that sounded more dangerous than anyone had suspected, and he had the resources to feed that army. Clearly, Eddy and his army were hellbent on taking over the New Frontier.

-9-

LINDSEY STOOD ON THE EDGE OF A WIDE COVERED DECK overlooking Lake Estes at the aptly. She thought back to when the resort was home to wide-eyed tourists admiring the surrounding mountains. Now, in the face of so much pain and destruction, they needed the complex more than ever as their primary Refugee Center.

Soon they would be getting more refugees if Raven was right.

According to him, a war was coming. She still had a hard time believing the Rattlesnakes had created a massive army, but based on what she had seen at the Eagle Recovery Site, it was no doubt the truth.

Raven had explained the intel late last night. He hadn't had any luck finding Eddy but hoped staking out the Ouray mayor's compound would lead to actionable intel on his whereabouts.

If they could cut the head off the snake, maybe it was still possible to stop this war before it really started.

Then again, maybe Eddy wasn't the cause of their troubles. Maybe he was just a symptom.

Eddy had convinced so many people to follow him. All the while, Lindsey was short on manpower. Not to mention the New Frontier locals were becoming more and more violent. Every time her people made contact, they got yelled at, shot at, or worse.

In her mind's eye, she couldn't help seeing the Land Rover Wolf full of Royal Marines crash into the river again.

They'd been lucky that the situation hadn't been worse.

All the same, Blair's warning that their foreign allies were growing increasingly frustrated wore on her.

She needed new tactics. New allies.

New ways to involve the members of her Foreign Advisory Council in the rebuilding and security efforts without driving them away.

Today, she was going to do just that.

She joined the four members of her Foreign Advisory Council waiting for her on a deck near the entrance.

"Thank you all for joining us up here," she said as she looked at them in turn.

Lieutenant Cui Tiankai of China wore his familiar, neatly pressed green uniform. Lieutenant Delphine Piard, representing Canada, stared at Lindsey with blue eyes that radiated ferocious intensity. Captain Juan Martinez from Mexico had youthful round features belied only by the slight wrinkles near his eyes and the gray hairs peeking out from his cap. Blair waited patiently beside them beneath the cloudy sky.

"This past week has been enormously difficult," she said. "You've all seen the reports. You know one USAMRIID team was attacked. You know another is MIA somewhere in the southwestern quadrant of the state. Rest assured, we're doing everything we can to find these men and women."

"It was UN personnel that went missing with that USAMRIID team this time," Martinez said, hand pressed against his chest. "But how long until it's my people? Or Piard's?"

"We've already lost more men than I can count." Tiankai bowed his head.

"I'm truly sorry," Lindsey said. "I realize you've made enormous sacrifices in our struggle. I don't want any of these losses to be in vain. That's why we must continue to fight."

A gentle wind blew through the trees lining the lake.

"My government is worried that this is going to be an uncontrollable active hot zone," Martinez said. "They're talking about retreating from active sites of conflict. Which seems to be most of the United States at this point."

"We're being told to shift over fifty percent of our military personnel away from the New Frontier," Piard said, "especially with the resistance the people out there are showing to your USAMRIID teams."

"I'm facing the same protests from my superiors," Tiankai said. "I want to help, Sheriff, but between the burgeoning wave of Wild Fire and these unprovoked attacks, my superiors strongly disagree that it's worth the effort."

There it was, exactly what Lindsey had feared.

"The worst thing we can do right now is retreat from this situation," she said. "That is why I asked you to meet here. I want to show you how your personnel can avoid coming under direct threats with the enemy to getting more involved in the hearts and minds campaign. Changing the way inhabitants of the New Frontier see us is crucial to our victory, and I think that starts here at one of our refugee centers. "

The FAC members seemed pleased enough with that. She felt like she'd at least earned enough respect and trust, especially over the past couple of weeks, to encourage their support.

Today, she wanted to give them another reason.

Her sat phone buzzed, and she checked it. Palmer had sent her a message. He was just a couple minutes away now.

Perfect timing.

She led the FAC to the front of the resort.

Under the porte-cochere, Aaron Huff waited for them. He was a portly man with a cheerful contagious smile. A paisley tie hung from his neck, loosened slightly to deal with the summer heat.

With him came two Rangers that Lindsey had assigned to help protect the center. Flannery, a once-avid backpacker, and Thomas, a retired Fort Collins police officer who'd rejoined the service as a Ranger. Where Thomas looked like a clean-cut older gentleman, Flannery was tattooed and wore her hair in braids, testament to her more hippie ways.

Huff strode toward the group with Rangers in tow, making quick introductions.

"Mister Huff is the director of operations for the Estes Park Refugee Center," Lindsey said. "He's been working to provide a home and purpose for every person that leaves the New Frontier, hoping to rejoin the United States for a better life. Flannery and Thomas have been helping keep this place secure."

"Pleased to meet you all," he said.

"I assume Wild Fire has made your job very difficult," Tiankai said.

"Not as much as you'd think," Huff said. "The USAM-RIID have done an excellent job ensuring that all the refugees we get are free of Wild Fire."

"We screen them extensively before bringing them in here," Flannery said. "And of course they go through quarantine first."

Thomas nodded along.

"We also have a close relationship with Estes Park

Medical Clinic to ensure anyone who might be sick is immediately treated," Huff explained. "So long as Doctor Wheeler's team can start producing more of those meds, I'm confident our mission can continue successfully."

"How many refugees are you currently handling?" Piard asked.

"We're dealing with an inflow of anywhere from five to fifteen a day," Thomas said in a low voice.

"They don't all stay here, though," Huff added. "We try to spread them through other centers throughout the state."

"And how's this helping tame the New Frontier?" Martinez asked.

"Hearts and minds, like Lindsey always says," Flannery said. "The people we bring into these centers offer valuable intel on what their communities are like. Plus, the refugees often have families and friends they've left behind."

"So you want to use them to appeal to the rest of their community," Tiankai said matter-of-factly.

"We believe it will help," Lindsey said. "We hope to shift tactics to focus more on these personal connections, leveraging them to convince communities to allow us to help them. Instead of rolling into a town looking like we're going to invade, we'll come in as peaceful non-governmental groups providing support and assistance. Most importantly, we'll be bringing goodwill ambassadors on these missions."

Huff gestured back at the Refugee Center. "We have over sixty people staying at just this facility. Already twenty have volunteered to travel with us and try to recruit more of their communities to accept our help."

"Impressive," Martinez said. "How do you envision us taking part in this?"

Lindsey rubbed her hands together. "Well, here's the deal. We need vehicles to support these efforts. We also need more fuel and supplies. The unfortunate truth is that though we'll try the peaceful approach, no one here is foolish enough to believe we don't need armed support. There will still be some communities that resist or meet our peaceful ambassadors with the threat of violence. We'll always need armed reinforcements ready to respond, backup, or at least evacuate our community ambassadors. That's where you all come in."

The members of the FAC all looked uncertain.

At that moment, a black SUV rolled up the drive and onto the center's parking lot. It pulled to a stop by the end of a row of sedans, trucks, and SUVs.

"Ah, just in time," she said.

The FAC turned as Palmer got out of the SUV and jogged over. Four Steel Runners were with him. They left the vehicle to head inside.

"Deputy Palmer and the Steel Runners are freshly back from California where they were able to extract the ingredients needed to help produce the cure to Wild Fire," Lindsey said.

Palmer nodded. "It wasn't easy, but we did it."

"A win," Lindsey said. "With the help of our Steel Runners."

"Yes, indeed, Sheriff."

"Good news," said Martinez.

The other FAC members seemed pleased as well.

"Let your superiors know, and then tell them about my request," Lindsey said. "We need your support to help contain this outbreak."

"What is President Diego doing?" Piard asked.

It was a damn good question.

"Why can't he send more vehicles and people?" Tiankai asked.

"He has already sent USAAMRIID to help, with vehicles

and troops," Lindsey said. "The Secretary of Defense is scrounging up what she can to help. We should have more information soon, but the reality is we have problems all across the US demanding Diego's attention and personnel."

"You should have seen LA," Palmer said. "Freaking nightmare."

"I've heard stories from my counterparts out east," Martinez said.

"We can't give up now," Lindsey said. "I'm going to let Huff, Thomas, and Flannery explain more about the Refugee Center and other ways you all can support its mission. I truly believe there are more opportunities to curb the violence in the New Frontier and stop the Wild Fire. I hope you'll support these endeavors as we evolve our efforts. Now I must take off to deal with some other issues."

The FAC crowded around Huff, peppering the man with questions as Lindsey made her way toward the parking lot.

Palmer led her back to the SUV where she let out a sigh.

"Back just in time, thank you," she said to Palmer. "So it was really that bad?"

"You have no idea, ma'am." He replied. "But Wheeler seemed happy enough with everything we brought back. Said he could start culturing it immediately, whatever that means."

"It means we've got a real hope of fighting the Wild Fire."

Another trio of SUVs rolled into the lot. This was the rest of the group coming back from the mission.

Calvin got out of the first SUV. Lindsey saw a few other Steel Runners she recognized head into the Refugee Center. But Calvin strode straight over to Lindsey instead of joining them.

"Sheriff," he said. "As Palmer probably warned you, I didn't come back alone." He opened the rear passenger door. A young boy and girl got out with his help, followed by a blond woman who looked to be their mother. "This is Maureen Gomez and her son Frankie and daughter Raquel."

"Pleased to meet you all," Lindsey said. She thought about offering her condolences about their father, but the kids seemed excited to be here. She didn't want to ruin it.

"I heard there's snow in the mountains," Frankie said. "I've never seen snow."

Lindsey grinned. "There's a little left on the highest mountains, but just you wait and see when the winter rolls around. You'll have more than enough of it."

"We're staying that long?" Frankie asked.

"We'll see," Maureen said.

Raquel held her by the side, peering up sheepishly.

"Well, we better find a place for you all to stay," Lindsey said.

"I've already got a request in with Director Huff," Palmer said. "He's got a room ready."

"Excellent. Let's check it out."

Lindsey waved for the family to follow her. Calvin joined them.

They made their way into the facility, where they saw another pair of familiar faces. Sandra Spears and Lara Lithgow were volunteering extra hours to do medical checks on the people here and provide warm meals.

For a moment, Lindsey relished in this reunion of so many people who shared her vision of a better Colorado. Despite the horrible ambushes over the past couple of days, and the threat of a new war, she thought they might actually have a chance. Maybe this shift in her tactics would protect the New Frontier—and the people of her beloved state.

She just hoped the FAC would stick around to help.

She wasn't sure they would survive without them.

Raven had spent the past day and a half doing recon around Mayor Clayton's compound outside of Ouray. He was perched in a fence of pine trees on a bluff with Creek. Night had fallen over the fortress below and the moon gave Raven enough light to survey the defenses around the compound. He had to take his time to avoid being spotted by the routine patrols around the area.

He wished Lindsey was out here with a Ranger squad, but he was basically on his own with Jay. It was about time for the two of them to meet up again and trade notes.

Raven started walking through the woods toward the rendezvous point as he considered the recent call from Lindsey. She had updated him about the attack on her USAMRIID escort and also how the team that had gone missing near Crested Butte still hadn't been found.

Things were getting worse by the day.

There were only four USAMRIID teams—twenty medical staff and technicians—left to deliver the meds the New Frontier communities desperately needed. The rest of the USAMRIID team was staying put at the Regeneraid facilities.

Lindsey had reassured Raven they were going to try a new strategy to protect those invaluable teams, but there was still no telling when the Rattlesnakes or some other group might attack them. These teams needed to be able to deliver the Commander meds to the people of the New Frontier. Their intel, based off refugees coming into the Front Range, put the number of infected into the thousands.

The disease was exploding out here. They had to find Eddy before it was too late.

Raven couldn't stand waiting around while his allies were

in danger. He needed intel from Mayor Clayton. The man seemed to be the only one that might know where Eddy was and why he was raising an army.

Still, it wasn't going to be easy getting to Clayton.

Raven paused and raised his scope back to the compound. A six-foot concrete wall surrounded a three story mansion. Old-fashioned spires on either end made it look as if it had been constructed long before asphalt and concrete highways traced through the mountains.

At each corner, wooden watchtowers had been constructed. Each was about fifteen feet tall with a single guard.

Raven could see the one closest to him clearly.

A bearded man leaned back in a folding chair and lit a cigarette. He had a scoped rifle propped up against the short knee-high wall tracing the top of the tower.

Over the past thirty-six hours, Raven had only seen a single vehicle enter the facility. It had been an old black Mercedes Benz straight from the 1960s. The Mercedes had driven straight through the open gate and into the compound's four-car garage.

He hadn't had a chance to see its occupants. Since then, the vehicle hadn't left.

Creek nestled up to Raven. He stroked the dog.

"Patience, boy," he said.

The dog let out a low whine.

A warning.

Raven strained his ears, picking up the crunch of boots traipsing through the forest below. One of Clayton's routine guard patrols was drawing near again. They came just under Raven's lookout once every two hours, almost on the dot.

The guard patrols were predictable. But they were still

thorough, canvassing almost all the forest around the compound.

With so many of them, he hadn't found a good way to get into the compound without running into at least a few of Clayton's stooges.

The footsteps came closer.

Raven pressed himself lower against the rock and dirt, hiding behind the bushes. Creek lay beside him.

Fighting their way into Clayton's place was a losing proposition. He had no plans of going full Rambo with so much backup ready to descend on intruders. Especially when he wasn't sure if Jay was at the rendezvous point.

So unless Clayton left those walls, there was little chance of confronting the man.

It seemed David's intel, even if it was correct, wasn't going to help.

The guards grew even closer, walking just below the precipice where Raven was. He held his breath, listening as they finally passed.

Then a pair of headlights far in the distance grabbed Raven's attention.

Slowly as he could, he got up for a look. The vehicle curved up the road straight toward the compound.

Raven's heart beat in anticipation, wondering who these people might be.

Maybe if he was lucky, it would be Eddy. That would be the evidence he needed to call hell down on this place.

The vehicle stopped at the front gate to the compound. Spotlights shone from the two nearest watchtowers, illuminating a rusty white sprinter van.

It didn't look like a vehicle Eddy would be driving in, but then again, the Rattlesnake was full of surprises.

As the guards patrolling near Raven marched deeper into

the forest, Raven got up and watched the van enter the facility. Spotlights traced it past the mansion's gardens and up to the entrance.

He expected armed men to pile out of the vehicle.

Instead, when the rear door opened, three women got out. He raised his scope, zooming in to find these were escorts in scant clothing. Judging by how quickly the van was waved into the compound, this was not their first visit.

Raven guessed the prostitutes also had a better idea of what lay inside the compound than he could ever get watching from the woods for another week.

"We got to move, buddy," he whispered to Creek.

They crept through the woods until he neared the rendezvous point area where Jay was supposed to be. There was no sign of the man among the boulders or fallen trees. No footprints. No sounds.

He scanned the darkness. Creek stuck his nose in the air, sniffing. The dog went down on his forelegs and let out a soft growl.

Raven turned the direction Creek was facing just in time to see Jay emerge silently from between the trees.

"Sorry, I had to be sure it was you," Jay whispered.

"Shoot, man, we've been meeting up several times over the past day and a half. You know it's me." Raven shook his head. "You about scared the piss out of me."

"That's an image."

Raven quickly told him his conclusions on the prostitutes. "If we can get back to Saddle and Spurs, maybe Lily will help us."

"After the money I spent at that place, I have no doubt."

Raven shook his head. "Guess we'll find out. Come on."

They snuck back to Ouray, arriving at just before four in the morning.

The town was quiet. Most of the drunks had already gone home or passed out in the street. Just a couple lights from saloons and a three-story hotel remained on.

With Creek at their heels, Raven and Jay crept through the side streets and alleys until they made it to Saddle and Spurs. They hid behind the rusted chassis of an old Toyota in the alley.

They didn't wait long before the door swung open.

Raven snuck a look at a tall woman with straight black hair striding out in knee-high boots.

"Night," she said.

As she walked to the main street, Raven pushed up his shemagh scarf to cover his features. Then he slipped toward the door before it closed. Jay had his bandana back over his face as Raven opened the door gently. He slipped inside with Jay and Creek.

Lily was counting coins at a cash register.

"You forget your bag again, Charity?" she asked without looking up.

"Nah, but you didn't forget about me, did you?" Jay asked. He closed the door behind him, locking it. Creek prowled around the bar after Raven.

Lily looked at them in turn.

"You boys again?" Lily asked. "Bar's closed and the ladies have all gone home for some well-deserved rest. I'd advise you both to go home as well."

"No can do," Jay said, slipping onto a bar stool. "We got some questions."

"Questions?" she asked. "Those will cost you."

Jay fished out a small silver coin and dropped it on the bar top. "What do you think of Mayor Clayton?"

Lily's face flushed, a scowl flickering over her features before she got control of it. Raven could tell she was talking through gritted teeth when she said, "He's a perfectly fine mayor."

Raven made a mental note of that.

"Interesting," Jay said. "Thing is, we saw your girls going to the mayor's compound. I didn't realize you can order delivery from here."

"Clayton has a... special arrangement," Lily answered.

"I see," Raven said. "Seems like your girls might know a thing or two about getting into his place. Maybe even getting access to Clayton."

Lily leaned over the bar. "And what kind of business would you two have with Clayton?"

"The mayor's got some information that's pretty important to us," Jay said. "We noticed he doesn't come into town much except to kill people. So not much opportunity to talk."

"We just want to get into the compound. Can you tell us how or not?" Raven asked.

Lily propped her elbows on the bartop. "You guys have a death wish." She let out a long breath. "I do send my girls up to the mayor. He won't come down here for them."

Raven noticed her nostrils twitch again when she talked about the mayor. Her words dripped with venom. He could almost feel the heat rising from the woman as if she was fighting back anger.

"You really don't like the guy," he said.

She opened her mouth as if to argue.

"No use denying it," Raven said. "I can tell."

Creek whined next to him.

"Look, even he agrees."

She paused as if thinking over her next words. "He has my son. Mark."

Ah, there it was. The leverage Raven had been looking for.

"Why's he got your son?" Jay asked.

Lily hesitated.

"You don't know who you're messing with or who he works for," she whispered. "And I don't want any part of whatever you got planned to get yourself killed."

"Maybe we can help you," Raven said.

"How? You going to break into his compound and get my son back?"

Jay and Raven exchanged a glance. They both knew getting into the compound like some kind of insane SWAT team wasn't going to work, but maybe there was another way to talk to Clayton and force some info out of him. Maybe they could trick the guy into coming out into the open, nab him when he was most vulnerable.

They were hoping Lily had that answer.

Lily played with the silver coin Jay had dropped on the counter.

"You want the truth?" she asked. "Clayton likes playing rough with his women. Rough in a way I don't like. When I tried to tell him I wouldn't be sending any more of my girls up there, he had his men come down here and take my son, Markie. Told me if he couldn't have his girls, I couldn't have Markie."

A wet sheen formed over her eyes, her bottom lip trembling. "So I've been sending them up and he *still* hasn't let me see Mark again. The boy's just six. I have no idea what Clayton is doing with him. He needs me."

Lily paused, wiping a tear from her eye.

"Mark isn't the first kid that Clayton stole from town. Hell, he ain't the first person Clayton stole. People that go up there have a habit of never coming back."

"Jesus," Raven said. "This guy sounds like a dirtbag."

Jay spat on the floor. "Asshole. You know what he does to people?"

"He's a really big fucking asshole," Lily said, choking back the tears. "But I don't got any idea what he's doing in that fortress of his besides treating my girls like shit."

"So can you help us?" Raven asked.

"If Clayton catches you guys and you rat me out, he'll kill me," she said. "Mark too."

Raven understood her fear, but he was confident that wouldn't happen. "If you can help us get in contact with the mayor, we will help you get your son back."

"You're making big promises that I have no faith you can keep."

"I know we're asking a lot, but what have you got to lose? All we want is an idea—any idea—about how we can get access to the mayor and even bring him to justice. Worst case scenario, you never see me, my friend, or my dog again. Best case, we get what we want and *maybe* you get your son back. What do you say?"

Lily pursed her lips, looking like she was just going to tell them to get the hell out for a moment.

Then she looked down at the coin. "Clayton loves to hunt. But like I said, he doesn't leave his compound much."

"How's this helpful?" Jay asked.

"Well, I'll tell you, honey. He uses my girls as a warmup for his hunts. Tells them it gets the testosterone flowing, so he can focus the next day."

"What the hell does he hunt up here?" Raven asked. "I haven't seen hardly a single wild animal in the area worth hunting."

"True enough," Lily said. "Clayton takes it easy. My girls say he keeps his game in the compound, then releases it. It's not even really a hunt. He never seems to have to go far. But he always has a hunt the day after a night with the girls."

"What kind of game should we be looking for?" Raven asked.

Lily shrugged. "Don't know. Might be deer or wolves or just some stupid goats. Couldn't tell you. But what I can say is that if you want access to Clayton, that's the best way. Otherwise, you got to wait for him to come to town again for an execution."

"Our whole goal is to prevent more people from getting unfairly executed," Jay said. "Looks like we're going out to hunt the hunter."

10

Calvin walked side by side with Maureen up the tree-lined trail around picturesque Bear Lake in Rocky Mountain National Park. Sandra Spears had told them that it was one of her favorite easy hikes in the park.

Being here, he could easily see why. The views were gorgeous. The lake was crystal clear, to the point he could see fish swimming, and the foliage was a breathtaking wash of color.

Since it was well within the safe zone past the borders, Calvin judged it would be okay to take the kids. He hoped the jaunt would take their mind off losing their father.

The hike was an easy one for the kids, and for Calvin. His muscles still felt weak from his bout with the plague. Though the doctors assured him he'd make a full recovery, he didn't yet feel one hundred percent. The usual back pain throbbed in his fused vertebrae, a persistent reminder of past battles. Getting out into nature like this seemed to help settle his body and mind. His physical therapist had even approved of the outing.

Just like the kids, he needed this.

"It smells so different here." Raquel lifted her nose into the air, sniffing, her eyes closed. "It's clean! Almost like when we do the laundry!"

Maureen let out a soft chuckle.

"I like seeing the snow." Frankie pointed up to the white-capped mountains in the distance. They peaked above the trees circling the emerald water of Bear Lake. "Is that where we're hiking today? Could we go sledding?"

"That's a little far, but wait until winter," Calvin said. "The snow will come to you."

"That would be *so* cool," Frankie said.

He and Raquel started to walk ahead, chattering incessantly with each other about all the great things they would do in Colorado.

"I was worried they would miss home, but I think this change will be good for them," Maureen said. She looked up to the sky. "Steve is looking down right now feeling the same."

"I have no doubt he is," Calvin said. "Look, I know you guys always loved San Diego, so I'm sorry I dragged you out here and away from where we buried Steve."

"*Steve* loved San Diego," Maureen said. "I was there because I loved Steve. Really, I'm a Midwest girl at heart. This isn't exactly the cornfields of Iowa, but the mountains will do. Trust me."

A couple of blackbirds pecked at the soil ahead.

"Let's catch 'em!" Frankie said, egging his sister on.

They darted after the creatures, but the birds flapped away. Raquel changed course down to the lake shore.

"Don't go too far!" Maureen said. "Stay where I can see you!"

Frankie followed Raquel to the water, where she picked up a rock.

"Let's skip a few," she said.

Calvin and Maureen watched until the children got bored. They started back on the path, jogging ahead.

"Wait up," Calvin called.

"I'm sorry," Maureen said, shaking her head. "They're as wild as Steve."

Calvin cracked a smile, thinking of some of the things Mouse had done over the years.

"That's one thing that scares me," Maureen said. "I worry I won't raise them right without Steve, especially in this new dangerous world."

Calvin understood her fear. Although he didn't want to overstep, he felt now was a good time to tell her something.

"Mouse stood by me through thick and thin, Maureen," he said. "I promised I'd help look after you guys, and that's exactly what I'm going to do. Make sure you and the family are safe."

"Thank you. It means a lot. I do feel better being out here with you."

"Truth is, there's danger here, just like there is in San Diego. I mean, for that matter, as a Steel Runner, I haven't seen a part of the United States that I think *is* completely safe."

"All the same, I feel better knowing at least one of Steve's SEAL swim buddies is going to be looking out for us up here. Plus, you've got other Steel Runners working at the Refugee Center where we're staying. How many of them?"

"We had about thirty Steel Runners stay behind in Colorado."

"And they're doing okay? I mean, they're all the ones that were injured in the attacks on the Angel Line, right?"

"Most are doing pretty well. About twenty are working again. Anna and the gang really seem to like their new assignments around the Refugee Center and providing security for Estes Park."

"I don't blame them. It does seem more peaceful up here." Maureen picked up her pace. "I've met a lot of good people. The whole Spears family is great, and Sheriff Plymouth is a no-nonsense leader that gets stuff done. I haven't worked beside these people for long, but I'd put my faith in them."

Maureen smiled as her eyes glimmered again.

"I'm sorry," she said. "I promised myself I'd stop crying. At least for the kids, but..."

"You're a strong woman, Maureen. But just because you're strong doesn't mean you can't grieve."

She nodded, dabbing at her eyes again. In an instant, she went from crying to laughing at Raquel and Frankie. The kids had picked up two dead branches and were engaged in a mock swordfight.

"You sure you want to stick around and help?" Maureen asked.

Calvin chuckled as they followed the children. They continued up a trail, running now with their branches.

Doing his best to keep up, Calvin jogged after them. Needles climbed through his spine. The last mission had really screwed with his back, but he wouldn't let it screw with protecting Mouse's family.

"There's a campsite up here!" Frankie called, setting down his fake saber. "Do you think we can stay overnight here?"

The pain subsided as adrenaline rushed through Calvin. All the alarms built into him from years of training and service rang in his mind. He hurried after the kids, seeing them at the edge of a massive boulder, gawking at something.

"They were cooking something," Raquel said. "Can you smell it? It's kind of weird."

As Calvin drew closer, he got a hint of exactly what she was talking about.

Grilled meat and barbecue had been a staple of family gatherings growing up. This sure smelled like charcoaled meat, but it was unlike any barbecue Calvin had ever had.

A sinking feeling began to twist in his gut.

"Go back to your mother, please," Calvin said, trying not to alarm the children with his tone. "I think she saw some fish in the lake. Thought I even saw one of them jumping."

"I don't want to watch the fish," Frankie said. "I want to camp!"

"Yeah, why can't we campout here?" Raquel asked. "These people are."

"Come here," Maureen said.

The kids went over to her. She retreated a few feet with her arms around them.

Calvin curved around the boulder where they were looking, moving his hand to his pistol grip.

Sure enough, someone had set out a sleeping bag under a lean-to. A rucksack lay next to it. In front of it all was a small bonfire with blackened skewered meat. The fire had since burned out. A couple of embers were still orange.

"Maureen, you mind taking the kids back to the lake?" Calvin asked.

He felt the worry rising in his chest and gave her a stern look that he hoped conveyed his seriousness.

She got the message, pulling the kids back toward the lake.

Calvin stepped closer to the campfire.

The meat on the skewer looked unfamiliar. It was too big to be from a small animal like a squirrel or rabbit. He didn't see the remains of a deer anywhere nearby either. But he noticed that the rucksack was seeping liquid. Its fabric was stained dark.

Heart hammering, he stepped up to the sack.

At the same time, he searched the woods, looking to see if anyone was watching from between the tree trunks. He drew his pistol slowly.

Boot prints were everywhere leading up another trail to the west.

Whoever had left this tent had either gone on the hunt or got spooked when the kids discovered their camp.

When Calvin got up to the rucksack, he used one hand to pull it open. He nearly gagged at the sight.

Inside was a rotten deer carcass in black clotted blood. Half the meat had been hacked off most of it, leaving bone and ragged flesh.

He nearly retched as he drew away from the bag, rushing from the camp and toward the Gomezes. The meat looked worse than roadkill. Whoever had scavenged this and was eating it was truly desperate.

Desperate people did desperate things, especially when they saw seemingly healthy and well-fed people like Calvin and the Gomezes.

"We need to get moving," Calvin said. "Now."

"But—" Frankie said.

"Whoever was at that campsite is not a good person."

He picked up Raquel in one arm, holding his handgun with the other. Maureen scooped up Frankie.

"We're going to race back to the trailhead," Calvin said, starting forward. "But we want to be quiet. Very quiet."

"I can do that." Raquel pressed her lips closely tightly.

"Good job," Calvin said.

He started to rush Maureen and the kids back down the

trail. But before he made it far, he heard footsteps crashing through the forest.

"Wait, wait, wait!" someone yelled.

Two men came galloping out of the shadow of the tree cover, straight for the trail. Setting down Raquel, Calvin stepped in front of her.

"Stop right there!" he said, wheeling the weapon up on them.

The men paused, their hands in the air. One was a fifty-year-old man whose face was gaunt with hunger. His clothes were soiled and dirty. Beside him was a man in his early thirties, just as emaciated and covered in mud. Even between the grime, Calvin could see festering pocks covering the men's flesh.

They were sick with Wild Fire.

The older man had a rifle in his hand. It wasn't pointed at Calvin or the kids. Yet.

"Put down your weapon," Calvin said.

"We just want help," the older man said, before coughing. "We're sick."

"I can see that. We can get you medicine and—"

The younger man threw his hands into the air, clearly irate. "We ain't taking any of that poison! The Rattlesnakes warned us what would happen. Are you another of 'em? A stooge coming to take us in? That why you're out here?"

The older man stepped forward. "We're hungry. Haven't eaten good food since our community kicked us out. That's the kind of help we want."

"I told you," Calvin said. "Put your weapon down, and we'll talk."

"What's wrong with them, Mom?" Raquel asked from behind Calvin.

Calvin said nothing. He just kept his pistol trained on the

guy with the weapon. It seemed their feverish minds were driving them mad. They weren't thinking rationally.

"Maureen, get the kids moving," Calvin said, whispering to her. He never took his eyes off the two men. He heard footsteps starting to recede as Maureen started back down the path.

"Buddy, did you hear what I said?" Calvin asked the older man. He started to back away, hoping these guys would just stay put.

"I'm hungry," the younger man said. "You got anything in your pack? Or maybe the kids have something? Tell them to come back."

"No," Calvin growled. "Back the hell up."

"Give me that pack!" the older man shouted.

Calvin was going to do it, but there was no time. The guy lifted his rifle and Calvin was forced to pull the trigger twice. The rounds blasted into the man's chest, sending him sprawling backward into the leaves and grass.

Birds squawked and exploded into the sky.

The second man took off running, and Calvin let him go.

Then he looked at the dead man sprawled on the ground. and the man's eyes staring blankly at the sky.

"I'm sorry, man, fuck," Calvin muttered. He turned and sprinted to catch up to Maureen and the kids. Maureen didn't ask questions and hugged the sobbing kids tightly.

"It's okay," he said. "Don't worry. Everything's okay again."

Calvin scooped up Raquel again, then led them toward the parking lot where they'd left an old Ford sedan that Huff had lent them for the day.

All the while, he scanned their surroundings looking for any sign of movement from the other guy just in case he returned or if he had friends.

Calvin would die before he let men like that get Maureen and the kids sick—or worse.

They ran down the damp soil and through the trees. Every snapping branch and breeze rustling through the forest made Calvin spin on his heels.

He would need to tell the Rangers about this too.

He feared what today's incident meant for the security of Estes Park.

As they drew closer to the Ford, he realized that his goal of protecting Mouse's family was going to be far more difficult than he'd realized. He just hoped bringing them to Colorado hadn't been a mistake.

————

Raven wasn't sure if this was going to work, but the information Lily had provided about the hunt was their best chance of capturing Mayor Clayton. Then they could interrogate him about where Eddy was and what in the hell the Rattlesnakes and their army had planned for the New Frontier.

It was going to be dangerous, but Raven had a plan to make Clayton talk and then making sure it didn't get back to Eddy. Mostly that involved tying the mayor up and getting them the hell out of there. From what little Raven and Jay had witnessed, Clayton deserved to be living in a jail cell, not the grandiose compound he'd constructed for himself. Getting him back to Fort Golden and into Lindsey's custody might do a lot to bringing peace to this part of the New Frontier.

Soon that plan would unfold in the river valley below.

Raven and Creek perched on a steep slope near an old rundown mine equipment building nestled in the trees. They were a good four or five hundred yards up from the valley floor. Jay was only a few hundred yards away to the east in his own hidden spot.

In the middle of the valley, Cascade Creek meandered through the rocky terrain.

Clouds and shadow from the rock walls made it difficult to see some of the valley, but Raven used his binoculars to sweep the landscape. Most of it was covered in trees all the way to the compound's gates. He didn't see much movement except for a few birds rising on updrafts. Occasionally, he saw what might have been an animal slinking through the foliage, but it was impossible to get a good glimpse for long.

There was one point where he thought he saw the silhouette of a man sprinting through the shadow. But when he looked again, he saw nothing. Figured it was his eyes playing tricks on him.

He started to grow frustrated. Maybe this hunt wasn't going to happen. Maybe it was postponed. Maybe he should just give up his plan to bring the mayor in and continue out of this shitty town to try and find Eddy.

Then they would be back at square one. Stuck with no leads and out on their own, trying to track down the most dangerous man in the New Frontier.

He was about ready to call it all off when he noticed Creek standing still, his tail frozen, ears perked. Then he heard what got the Akita's attention. The bark of dogs came from somewhere in the trees below.

Human voices suddenly boomed through the valley, echoing off the rocky slopes.

Raven caught flashes of movement. Multiple men and horses, it looked like. The hunting party. Finally. They were following the creek to the east.

He ran to where Jay was, then motioned for him to follow.

They both started running at a hunch down the slope toward the water, closing in on their targets. Creek ran after them.

Five foxhounds bounded through the stream, splashing and barking. Their tails stuck straight up behind them. Raven knew the specially bred and trained dogs locked onto one scent at a time.

He and Jay hid behind the screen of leaves and tree trunks as the hunting party drew near. So long as they stayed still and didn't spook the animals, they would carry on after their quarry.

Sure enough, the dogs powered past.

Soon the clatter of hooves sounded.

They finally got their first real good look at their targets.

Six men on horses appeared through the trees.

Most of them wore jeans, boots, hats, and button-up shirts that made them look like they'd grown up on a ranch. They had lassos secured to their saddles and rifles over their backs.

The man leading the party group wore a big gold belt buckle shaped like a lion. He had a white goatee and cheeks colored red from rosacea.

Mayor Clayton. Raven recognized him from the execution when he entered Ouray.

"Almost got him!" he yelled. "First round's on me if one of you gets 'em first."

They galloped past Jay and Raven. The pair waited a second to see to make sure no one else followed.

Raven gestured that they should go after Clayton. He, Jay, and Creek crept through the woods as they followed the pounding of hooves and yells of the men. They stalked through the trees, staying distant but maintaining a view of the hunting party.

A sudden animalistic shriek came from ahead, echoing off the valley's slopes.

"We got 'em!" Clayton boomed.

Raven and Jay rushed through the dense green bushes to catch up.

While Clayton was focused on his quarry, this would be the perfect time to ambush him.

With any luck, they could get all six men to lower their weapons. It shouldn't be too hard to convince them when Jay and Raven had their guns pointed at the men's backs.

In a matter of minutes, they found Clayton's hunting party circled around their quarry between a thicket of trees near the running water. The fox hounds brayed and barked viciously at whatever they had cornered.

Raven had Creek go low and prowl around to the north. They hid in a dense copse of sagebrush and windswept limber pine. Jay headed east, finding his own cover not far away.

Clayton had dismounted from his horse. The other five men were still atop theirs.

Water rushing around his boots, the mayor held one end of his lasso rope. The rope stretched toward whatever he'd caught on the side of another boulder.

"Couldn't run for long, could you?" Clayton said to his quarry.

To Raven's surprise, a man's voice answered. "Please, don't! I told you everything. I swear!"

Raven felt a cold pang in his gut.

Clayton wasn't hunting animals.

He was hunting people.

After they got what they wanted from Clayton, this man was definitely going away for a very long time.

The mayor yanked back the lasso, pulling a person toward him over the rocks of the shallow creek. The fox hounds followed, growling at the bearded man in Clayton's custody.

Long, bloody wounds scraped up and down the man's

shirtless chest and back as if he'd been whipped and beaten. Raven recognized the man's frightened features and his characteristic red beard.

David Singer. The guy that had lost his brother to the Rattlesnakes. The man who had initially told them about Clayton.

Raven's heart beat faster.

If he told these guys about Raven and Jay looking for Eddy, then their mission was compromised and they were in extreme danger.

Raven looked for Jay but no longer saw him in his position.

Cursing under his breath, Raven slowly raised his crossbow as Clayton pulled David across the stream. The prisoner wailed in agony as the lasso tightened around his chest, pinning his arms to his side. Fox hounds growled at David, their hackles raised.

"You didn't tell me *everything*," Clayton said. "Who were these guys asking about me and Eddy, huh?"

"I told you. I don't know. I never saw their faces. They wore bandanas and—"

Clayton yanked on the lasso, pulling David back down. His head thwacked against a rock. Blood mixed in with the clear creek water. One of the dogs snapped at him.

Raven looked for Jay again, but still didn't see him.

Had he run off?

Maybe you should do the same thing… Raven thought.

Before he could come up with a plan, gunshots cracked to the east.

One of the men walking out into the stream toward David jerked from impacts of bullets to the back. The horses kicked up in fear, bucking two of the other men out of the saddles.

Clayton dove to the ground behind his horse, yelling

something into a walkie-talkie. The dogs scattered, retreating toward the other men on horses.

More gunshots came from the forest, and Raven finally saw Jay behind the trigger. He started charging through the brush, firing shots that sparked against rocks.

Return fire forced him behind a tree, the bullets slamming against the bark.

Now, with the horses in the way, Raven didn't have a good shot on Clayton.

Instead, he aimed at one of Clayton's men, then let a bolt fly. The arrow lanced straight through the man's neck.

That left four men, including Clayton.

Raven ducked back into the brush. He crawled for a new position as return fire slammed into where he'd been moments ago.

Damn it, Jay, Raven thought.

Jay had let his anger get the better of him. But Raven couldn't blame him for that; he used to do the exact same thing.

"Let's go!" Clayton leaped up onto his horse and gave it a kick to the flanks. His surviving two comrades started running toward the horses.

Jay fired another salvo. One of those rounds caught a man in the back, sending him crashing into the water. A man with the limp threw himself onto his horse and galloped away, along with a goon with a prominent birthmark across his face. They lay flat on their horses as they disappeared around a curve in the creek. The hunting dogs hightailed it after them.

Jay ran down to check on David, who thrashed in the water.

Raven stood from his position, watching the horsemen gallop through the woods.

"I have to stop them," Raven said. "You help David. I'll go after them."

Raven whistled for Creek. The dog bolted ahead, keeping to cover just like Raven had trained him.

Things had quickly spiraled into a dangerous situation.

As Raven ran, he considered breaking off the chase. But this might be his best chance to stop the mayor, bring him to justice, and figure out what was going on with the Rattlesnakes.

If the mayor got back to his compound and told them about this, it was over. All their efforts and time in Ouray would be for nothing, and Eddy would know about Jay and Raven.

He caught glimpses of the horses through the trees.

They had slowed somewhat as the trail grew more dangerous and winding, the trees denser and rocks sharper.

Then came the sound of more pounding hooves. Through the evergreens, Raven caught sight of several new men on horses racing toward where Raven had left Jay and David.

Oh, no.

Raven hoped for Jay's sake the man was already running to safety with David.

Clayton was only a couple dozen yards away and slowing. They were only about a half-mile to the compound.

"Help! Now!" Clayton bellowed.

The sudden sound of more horse hooves filled the valley.

What the fu—?

Another five armed men on horses rushed past Clayton, heading straight along the creek. They roved their gazes over the brush.

Raven was forced to run south, away from Clayton.

As the men on horses rode to head off anyone pursuing

Clayton, another group raced down from the southern slope toward Raven.

Shit, shit, shit.

Raven didn't have a clear exit route. Not with all these men closing in.

"I got footprints!" one yelled.

Running so hard after Clayton, of course Raven hadn't had time to cover his tracks.

He began creeping slower through the forest, hoping he could find somewhere to hide.

Maybe he could shelter in the old mining equipment building he had been at earlier. He just had to shake these guys first.

But either way, he wouldn't risk Creek's life. He pointed up the slope toward the building nearly a half-mile away and whispered to Creek, "Go, boy."

The dog whined, refusing at first to leave Raven's side as the men circled closer on their horses.

"Go," Raven whispered more fiercely. "Hide!"

The dog took off, shooting low through the thickets of trees and brush.

"I think I see movement," a man yelled, turning his horse toward where Creek had run. The man started in that direction.

Oh, hell no, Raven thought. He shouldered his rifle and fired. The man slumped out of his saddle and hit the damp soil, the horse rearing up and kicking at the air.

Raven began running again.

There was no hope of catching Clayton now.

But maybe he could still escape. At least he'd protected Creek.

The four remaining horsemen looped around the area where Raven was.

They formed a tightening perimeter, closing in on Raven. This was clearly not their first time hunting humans. They formed a dragnet that looked nearly inescapable. The only way Raven would get past was if he could fly or fight his way out.

Fuck.

He got up and started sprinting, trying to get away as quietly as he could.

But before he made it a dozen yards, he heard a voice booming from behind him. "There he is!"

Raven glanced back for a fraction of a second. Just in time to see the lasso whipping toward him. A rope tightened around his chest and arms, yanking him off his feet. He fell back against the soil and rocks, pain ricocheting through his body. The men on horses began circling around him. Hooves kicked up dirt, men's voices hooting and hollering around Raven.

In a matter of seconds, he had gone from being the hunter to being the hunted.

And now, he was caught.

11

EDDY RODE YANABA INTO THE TOWN OF SILVERTON, Colorado at a gentle trot with Robert beside him on his brown-and-white stallion. Earlier, he'd received information from a couple of messengers.

First, the good news: the Rangers were still looking around Crested Butte helplessly looking for the USAMRIID team. They had no idea Eddy had taken them nearly three hours driving distance to the southwest.

Second, the bad: another messenger had returned from Silverton. He had confirmed Shupert's claims about the town's decision to leave the Rattlesnake Union's campaign.

A line of fifteen Rattlesnakes on horses followed them up Greene Street in the middle of the small town. At the end of their convoy were a couple of horses with saddlebags full of supplies.

The noise of all their hoof-steps clattering against the asphalt echoed against the two-story wood buildings. People watched furtively from some of the windows.

He ignored them.

They weren't his concern.

The people inside the Silverton City Hall were.

The two-story red-stone building had decorative ionic columns above an oakwood front door.

Eddy paused in front of it. "This is it."

He made a hand gesture to his Rattlesnakes, and they formed a perimeter around the building, unstrapping their weapons.

"Sheriff Bruner should be in there," he continued. "Bring him and his people out."

Robert dismounted his horse. Five of the Rattlesnakes followed.

Eddy waited calmly.

A couple of screams came from inside followed by a gunshot. Then more screams.

While Eddy waited, he gestured toward a few of his men beside the two horses with their packed saddlebags. The men took off the saddlebags and placed them beside Yanaba.

Eddy dismounted the horse at the sound of another gunshot from within the town hall.

Finally, Robert emerged.

Blood covered the front of his shirt. He carried his revolver in one hand. In the other, he dragged a man by the collar. Blood ran from the prisoner's broken nose and into a thick mustache.

The other Rattlesnakes brought out a line of eight men, all with their hands up.

Dressed in jeans and collared shirts, the prisoners stood in a line in front of the city hall. Robert dragged his charge to the middle of the line and yanked the guy up to his knees.

The man wore a silver star on his chest and a defiant expression, despite his busted nose and cracked lip.

Eddy stepped toward him. "Sheriff Bruner, I really was hoping the rumors weren't true."

"Just give me a chance to explain," Bruner said.

Robert kicked him in the back. The sheriff fell forward, but then Robert yanked him back up by a tuft of his hair.

"Explain why you're refusing to send all your men of fighting age north to join the Skulls outside Rocky Mountain National Park?" Eddy asked. "That was the deal you agreed to, a deal that is imperative for the success of Operation White Buffalo."

"We don't have the men, and frankly..." Bruner let his words trail.

"Speak, Sheriff."

"I'm in between a rock and a hard place here, Eddy, with all due respect. I heard what happened to those medical folks, and I got the vision to see what it all means."

Eddy took a step back to give the sheriff some space, hoping it would help him feel safer to speak his mind. He wanted to know what the man had to say.

"More people you kill and kidnap, the more the government is going to notice," Bruner said. "That puts the Union and all of us that want to live out here free at risk."

"Go on."

"How can we be free if the president sends the army to stop you and your allies? That's exactly what will happen."

"Do you not trust me?"

Bruner looked at Eddy like he was crazy.

"I've planned for this since the Collapse, and now is the time to take back what was ours, to make this land truly free again."

He took a step back toward Bruner.

"All it takes for evil to prevail is for good men to do nothing." Eddy let one of his favorite paraphrased quotes sink in for a second. "You and I both want freedom. We want to protect the New Frontier. We can't let evil men come in here to make us prisoners in our own lands. Standing by and doing nothing"—Eddy pointed at the city hall—"or hiding in your office doing nothing, you might as well be working for the other side."

Eddy turned to make sure all the townspeople now gathering on their front porches or looking out the windows down the street could hear.

"Sheriff Bruner, you might as well be selling out the good people of Silverton," Eddy boomed.

He knelt in front of Bruner as Robert held the guy's face up. Blood dribbled from Bruner's mouth.

"I'm not an unreasonable man," Eddy said. "I understand I'm asking a lot, but unless we have full cooperation from everyone in these lands, we'll never hold off the wašíču tyrants."

"I understand," Bruner said.

"Do you?"

"Yes, I'll send my people."

"It's too late for that," Eddy said. He gave Kitcheyan a nod. The Apache didn't smirk or smile like he might have in the past. Today, he was all business.

Pulling out his knife, he came up to Bruner. He pressed the blade toward Bruner's neck.

"Please, I'll send them! I promise."

"I believe you will," Eddy said, "but I don't just want people who do what I ask. I want people who are loyal. People who *believe* in this cause."

He bent down and plucked the silver star from Bruner's chest.

Bruner bent his head low in submission.

"A demotion isn't enough," Eddy said. "This man will just betray us again when he gets the chance. Kitcheyan."

Kitcheyan sliced the blade across Bruner's neck before the

man could protest again. Blood pumped from the slit in Bruner's throat as his hands grasped uselessly at the wound. People watching from the shelter of the buildings down the street retreated inside or closed their shutters.

Others who had nowhere to hide gasped, slowly backing away as if that would protect them.

Eddy turned and addressed the people and the men still standing in a line. "I'm looking for someone who is unafraid to do what is necessary to defend these lands. Someone who is not afraid to help send the tyrants back to their own lands. Is there such a man here?"

A redheaded man at the end of the line stepped forward.

"I'll do it," he said in a shaky voice. "I'll take over."

Eddy went over to scrutinize this man face to face. The redheaded guy flinched, his lips trembling.

"No," Eddy said. "You speak from fear. Not fidelity. There is nothing wrong with fear, but giving in to fear is not the mark of a leader. Is there anyone who will show me your people deserve the rewards we're giving them?"

Eddy stepped away to another man that stepped out from the line of prisoners.

A thick brown beard hung down to his chest, and his face was shaded by a leather ten-gallon hat. "I can't say I agree with all your tactics." The man glanced at Bruner. "But I didn't agree with the sheriff for breaking the deal. I told him that."

Eddy faced this man.

"I am here for the people of Silverton, first and foremost. If that means heading north to fight beside your people, so be it," he said.

"What do you think, Robert?" Eddy asked.

Robert traced his fingers over his knife blade, then flicked some of the blood off. He pressed his blood-covered fingers over the volunteer's chin, moving the guys' face back and forth like he was a doctor examining a patient.

The man grimaced, but he didn't wince or back away.

"Seems like he's not completely full of shit," Robert said.

"Good." Eddy held out a hand. "Good to meet you..."

"Grant. Grant Holston."

"Grant Holston." Eddy gripped his hand tight, and Holston returned the same tough handshake.

"Grant Holston, do you have a family?"

"I do," Holston said. "I—"

He paused, evidently realizing that might be a mistake.

"We're just talking, man-to-man," Eddy said. "I've got an ex-wife and son back in Window Rock, so trust me, I know that when you fight for family, you're willing to do anything."

Holston nodded. "I've got a wife, two sons, and a daughter."

"And they will be rewarded for your loyalty," Eddy said. He didn't make any threats, because why would he need to at this point? This man knew the score.

People knew what would happen to them and their family if they failed to live up to their side of a deal.

Eddy handed the star over. "Congratulations, Sheriff Holston."

Holston nodded back.

Whistling, Eddy gestured to the saddlebags on the ground by Yanaba. His men opened them, revealing the ammunition and food inside.

"We've brought some extra supplies just to show how much I appreciate the people of Silverton," Eddy said.

With his work in Silverton done, Eddy led his men back up the scenic Million Dollar Highway toward Telluride.

Robert rode along beside him as they passed towering ponderosa pines and wide patches of verdant brush. The mountains surrounding them spiked up and down like the back of an enormous dragon.

"We can't let any hint of rebellion or defection take hold in our ranks," Eddy said calmly.

"Agreed. It was good that our men caught a whiff of Bruner's treason before we let it rot the whole town," Robert replied. "Things could have gotten worse than refusing orders. Bruner could have told the Colorado Rangers of our plan."

"All the more reason to keep our actual plans close to the vest. No Union leader should be privy to *everything* we discuss. There are simply too many leaks in a land this big."

"Very true."

"Our message should be clear now that Bruner is gone. Loyalty, or Kitcheyan."

Eddy looked back at the Apache man. He rode his horse stoically, his eyes on the forest, his chest and shoulders puffed up with pride.

"You knocked him down a peg on that cliff," Robert said.

Eddy turned back to his comrade. "It was that or knock him over the edge. Truth is, we need Kitcheyan on the battlefield, and I need you for everything *off* the battlefield."

"How do you mean?"

"Victory isn't just about killing your opponent. It's about winning the people's spirits as well. We have to make sure the Union believes in what we're fighting for like we do. We have to make sure they know we have their backs if they have ours. That we'll all stand against the wašíču not as separate tribes or militias, but as a united people."

Robert nodded with no hesitation.

He was fiercely loyal just like Kitcheyan was fiercely brutal. Both men had tools that Eddy utilized differently.

They continued silently for a few minutes until Eddy's radio began to buzz.

"Rattlesnake One here," he answered.

"Rattlesnake One, this is Outpost Alpha," one of his Rattlesnakes replied.

Outpost Alpha was the codename for the current camp in Telluride.

"We've got news about Raven Spears and another Native American man that were looking for you," the Rattlesnake said.

"What news?" Eddy asked.

"We think they've been captured."

Eddy's heart kicked. "When? Where? And who is this other man?"

"Several hours ago in Ouray. Mayor Clayton has a man we believe to be Raven and another named Jay Wauneka."

Eddy pulled up on the reins of his horse, stopping it in its tracks.

"Wauneka?" he said over the radio.

"Yes."

"You know him, Ahiga?" Robert asked.

Eddy couldn't believe his ears. The Navajo detective and him went way back.

"He was an old friend," Eddy said.

"Now an enemy?"

"A traitor, like Spears."

It pained Eddy to hear this. Back when they were both working for the Navajo Police Department, Jay had believed in protecting the Navajo people. Now it seemed Jay had been bought and paid for by the wašíču.

This wasn't a huge surprise. Jay had long ago distanced himself from Eddy when he tried to recruit Jay to the Rattlesnakes. Jay wasn't the only Navajo that had declined.

"What do you want to do?" Robert asked.

The chance at getting back at Raven had Eddy practically salivating, but he had to act with strategy and patience. The temptation of doing exactly the opposite with Raven was almost too great to resist.

Of course, he had other plans to execute. Other missions that had to be carried out at the same time. This would call for some tough choices.

"Is the Skull militia in position?" Eddy asked.

"They're outside Rocky Mountain National Park as we speak," Robert said. "Their scouts have been scouring the park for the past couple days."

"Good. Tell them the attack is still on. They will continue as planned without the men of Silverton. Thanks to Bruner's delay, the Silverton militia won't make it up there in time. So I don't want the Skulls waiting around. We'll make a detour to Ouray before joining up with them after their mission."

"You got it." Robert dropped back to make the call.

Eddy twisted in his saddle to the other Rattlesnakes.

"Change of plans," he called back. "We got an important date with some old friends in Ouray. Let's ride!"

———

Lindsey stepped out of her Bronco in the busy parking lot of the Regeneraid facility. Construction equipment buzzed around the complex. Box trucks were still being unloaded, and people went in and out of the front entrance with crates.

The place was a hive of activity. It gave her confidence that this place would be up-and-running again soon.

She made a call on her radio while crossing the parking lot.

"Palmer here," answered the deputy.

"Palmer, what's the status of the FAC?"

"Got my ears perked and eyes peeled, Sheriff, but so far, no word if they are sticking around or not. I'll keep you updated."

"And Calvin? Did he agree to help advise security around Estes Park?"

"He said he'd be absolutely grateful to do so," Palmer said. "His words, not mine, in fact. Seems like the perfect fit for him since he wants to stick close to the Gomezes, I believe."

"Even better. For the time being, stay up there to help Calvin learn the ropes with the Rangers assigned to the area. I don't know who's responsible for that camp of Wild Fire victims Calvin found, but we need to be absolutely vigilant."

"You've got it, ma'am," Palmer said. "Rangers are currently patrolling the area, but we don't have any leads yet. We don't know what community those guys came from, but we haven't seen anyone else out there."

She ended the call as she strode into the Regeneraid building and made her way to a second-floor conference room.

Doctor Wheeler was already there with Lieutenant Blair.

"Good to see you both," she said as she slumped into a seat at the head of the table.

Blair was sipping tea from a Styrofoam cup. Wheeler had his hands wrapped around a bottle of water.

Behind Wheeler's seat, an expansive glass window looked out over the bioreactor room. People in white lab coats and goggles flitted between the equipment. The hum and thump of machinery resonated softly into the conference room.

"I'm happy to see things in working order around here," Lindsey said. "At least, it seems like it's in working order, right?"

"Yes," Wheeler replied. "The bacteria from UCLA are taking to our bioreactors very well. It'll only be a few weeks before we're producing quantities of the Commander bacteriocin for testing, then manufacturing purposes."

"Weeks." Blair sighed. "That means weeks of holding back the flow of Wild Fire victims."

"On the scale of pharmaceutical development, weeks is an extraordinarily short period of time," Wheeler said.

"Weeks might be short on a scientific scale, but that's practically an eternity in a landscape that's in the middle of what might well be described as a simmering war," Blair said.

"I'm well aware," Wheeler said. "I lost an entire team out there. People that I cannot replace. People with friends and families and... I mean, I'm feeling the pressure too, Lieutenant. I know what's at stake."

"Trust me, we'll talk about all of this soon." Lindsey checked her watch, then nodded at the phone in the middle of the table. "Let's not keep the Secretary waiting."

In seconds, they had Secretary Charlize Montgomery on a conference call with them.

Wheeler was the first to begin. "Ma'am, we've got good and bad news. Which first?"

"Let's get the good news out of the way, so we can focus on solutions to the bad."

"Thanks to Lindsey's team, we're ramping up our production process," Wheeler said. He updated her quickly on what he'd just told Lindsey and Blair. "Soon we'll be producing the cure to Wild Fire at rates sufficient to eradicate the disease."

"Excellent," Charlize said. "President Diego will be pleased to hear this too. Any more good news?"

Lindsey steepled her fingers together, pausing a moment. "I'm afraid that's the best we've got. I assume you saw my report about the USAMRIID teams."

"I have. It's unfortunate," Charlize said.

"Unfortunate," Wheeler scoffed below his breath.

"Any progress on finding what happened to them?" asked Charlize.

"No idea yet, but with everything going on, it's hard not to suspect the Rattlesnakes. We've been scouring the New Frontier with teams, including Raven and Jay, but so far, Eddy seems to be off the grid," Lindsey said. "The local populations are protecting him. He's built up an apparently enormous following that is simultaneously terrified of him and also willing to die rather than betray him."

"Not good." Charlize exhaled audibly. "We need to find out his location and exactly how many soldiers have rallied to his side."

"Raven and Jay might have a lead in Ouray," Lindsey said. "They believe the mayor might know something. If all goes well, they'll have some idea where Eddy is in the next couple of days."

"I hope so," Charlize said. "The president is increasingly worried about the situation, but things are a mess everywhere. With the loss of so many trains, our supply chains have been crushed. Food riots are popping up in cities that were stable months ago. The entire country is suddenly at risk of major violence."

Lindsey had heard this story before, but Charlize seemed even more worried now. Like she was in a car going a hundred miles-per-hour and the brakes had just failed.

"Worse, with the election just around the corner, Senator Shelby's gaining in the polls," Charlize continued. "He's harping on these failures even as Diego is trying to reshuffle what few troops we have available to gain control. It's getting bad faster than we expected. Lieutenant Blair can probably tell you his compatriots are retreating from especially violent cities because of the casualties they're suffering."

Blair nodded somberly.

"He's told me, yes," Lindsey said. She couldn't help but think of Blair taking his troops out of the New Frontier after they were attacked. "We're missing them in the field."

"To deal with their withdrawal, we're having to reassign our own troops," Charlize explained. "More and more of our armed forces are playing the role of law enforcement officers and crowd control. We're doing everything we can to prevent this from bubbling over into a disaster that consumes the entire country."

"All due respect, but Wild Fire is also a risk of bubbling over into a disaster that spreads not just in the US, but across the oceans," Wheeler said.

"Which is why Diego has sent you, Doctor Wheeler, and the USAMRIID teams," Charlize explained.

Wheeler folded his arms across his chest.

"I'm not a tactician, but we can't afford to lose more USAMRIID teams trying to deliver meds," Wheeler said. "If Lindsey's plans *don't* work and we can't control the Wild Fire spread, we're headed face-first into another disaster. One Shelby could easily capitalize on."

"It's certainly something we've been thinking about and... Look, I'm not trying to push my politics and election concerns on you, Lindsey," Charlize said, "so I apologize if what I said came out that way. My career has always been about defending the United States, ever since I was in the Air Force. That duty comes first and foremost. That being said, if we're absolutely desperate, I can try finding new ways to convince Diego to send more manpower your way. I can package it as a deal that will help with the election efforts."

"Anything to sweeten the deal, sure," Lindsey said.

"I'm afraid we might need that help sooner than expected," Wheeler added. "The hospitals are beginning to reach peak capacity. We're going to need more people just to take care of the patients."

"Maybe that's a more palatable mission for our foreign allies to take part in," Charlize replied.

"I'm listening," Blair said. "Go on."

The discussion jumped between Blair and Wheeler as they discussed the logistics of recruiting more medical personnel to clinics safely outside the New Frontier with Charlize.

Before long, Lindsey's sat phone rang.

It was the emergency line.

"I'm very sorry, Madam Secretary," Lindsey said. "I've got to take this. You all continue the discussions."

Lindsey stepped out of the conference room.

"Sheriff Plymouth here."

"Lindsey, it's Palmer." His words came out rushed. "I just got word that there's an ongoing attack on a border checkpoint."

"Where?" Lindsey asked.

"Gould Station."

That was one of the northernmost stations just west of Rocky Mountain National Park.

"They're requesting immediate reinforcements," Palmer continued.

"Go help them," Lindsey said. "See if Calvin can keep Estes Park secure with his Steel Runners and get all the Rangers you can to Gould. We cannot afford to lose a border control checkpoint."

"I'm on it, ma'am."

"I'll be up there as soon as I can with Blair," Lindsey said. "We can't let those sick people get past the quarantine zone."

12

CALVIN RODE IN THE FRONT SEAT OF SANDRA SPEARS' car on the way to the Estes Park Refugee Center. He'd thought it would be hard to adjust to a slower pace of life.

But his new mission helping the Refugee Center gave him purpose. It didn't hurt knowing that Maureen and the kids were staying there either.

Even after their scare in Rocky Mountain National Park, he was glad he could keep an eye on them. With more security patrols in the area, he felt a little better.

Plus, Raven was still out there, searching for Eddy and the Rattlesnakes. If anyone could bring that man down, it was Raven.

Calvin kept repeating those thoughts, hoping that it would be enough. That his decision to bring the Gomezes to Colorado hadn't been in vain.

"Are we almost there?" Allie asked from the back seat.

"Almost," Sandra replied.

"Good. I can hardly move."

Calvin chuckled. The girl was packed between boxes of donated clothes and toys. So many people had fled the violence of the New Frontier with only what they had on their backs.

Many of the kind people in the surrounding Estes Park area had been happy to donate some of their gently used items to help those individuals.

"You think you'll stay in Estes Park for a while, then?" Sandra asked Calvin as they turned north on Saint Vrain Avenue headed toward Lake Estes. "Or is somewhere else in Colorado calling your name?"

"I'll be here as long as the Gomezes are." Calvin gazed out at the snowcapped mountains surrounding them. He didn't want to talk too much about what he'd seen in Rocky Mountain National Park in front of Allie, so he stuck to the positives for now. "I could've picked a worse location. In a way, it reminds me of Lake Tahoe."

"Where's that?" Allie piped in.

"It's nestled right in the mountains between California and Nevada," Calvin said. "You know where Nevada is?"

"Nevada? No."

"How about Las Vegas?"

"Yeah," Allie said. "I'm pretty sure Uncle Raven said he wanted to visit there back before the Collapse. He said it had all the best casinos and—"

"All right, Allie," Sandra said.

Calvin wasn't sure what Allie had been about to say, but from what he knew about Raven, it was probably something about his wild past.

He smiled until his radio buzzed.

Reaching down, Calvin plucked off the two-way that Palmer had given him for emergencies.

His mind immediately whirled toward the Refugee Center. He could see it now as Sandra drove down Big Thompson Ave.

"Calvin here," he answered.

"It's Palmer. Where you at?"

"I'm headed to the Refugee Center right now."

"I don't know if you got any Steel Runners that can help, but we're dealing with a border control breach."

"What kind of breach?" Sandra asked.

Calvin held up the radio again.

"I'm calling up all the Rangers in the area," Palmer said. "We're going to have to rely on you to keep an eye on Estes Park in case anyone gets through. Got it?"

"I'll do whatever I can," Calvin said.

He had come here for peace, but after killing the guy on the mountain, and now facing more violence, it seemed peace wasn't meant for Calvin.

His heart hammered as they approached the Refugee Center.

Already a group of six Rangers were gathering in the parking lot around various vehicles. He recognized Thomas and Flannery, two of the lead Rangers assigned to the area.

As Sandra pulled in, Calvin turned to her. "Take Allie inside and stay there. If these raiders get past the border, there's no telling what they might do."

Sandra nodded. "I'll take care of Maureen and the kids. You do what you need to do."

"I will."

Sandra and Allie rushed inside while Calvin marched toward the Rangers. He wanted to go say something to Maureen, but there was no time.

"Thomas, Flannery!" he called. The two Rangers jogged over to him. "Palmer said he was sending you guys up. I need to know where to shore up our defenses. Which patrols are headed to Gould?"

Thomas and Flannery exchanged a glance.

"All of 'em," Thomas said. "We got major forces incoming. Sounds like our guys are strapped."

"Shit, then I won't hold you back. I'll organize my Runners for emergency defensive positions and patrols immediately."

He picked up his radio as he headed back toward the center. "Anna, Ortiz, Boston, Marino, I need you at the entrance to the Refugee Center right now! Bring your weapons!"

As the Rangers hightailed it out of the parking lot, Anna came straight out of the lobby holding Travis's old White Sox cap down while she ran.

"What's going on, Cal?" she asked.

Boston, Ortiz, and Marino showed up shortly after.

Calvin briefed them on everything as fast as he could.

"Holy shit, chief," Boston said. "This is fucked."

Ortiz shook his head, his hands on either one of his holstered revolvers. "We're not going up to help?"

"We're helping here," Calvin said. "Someone has to watch homebase. That's us. Ortiz, I want you to take four Runners and head to the junction of 66 and 36. Boston, you got another four. I want you on 34, right south of Castle Peak. You'll serve as quick reaction forces if anyone makes it through Gould and heads here."

"What about me?" Marino asked.

"Get on top of Deer Mountain with another four. You're our spotters. If you see anyone, I mean anyone, coming toward us from the west, call it out. And Anna, you stay with me. We'll get our last team of three on the roof of the Refugee Center. The Center will serve as our final holdout if shit goes south. Go, people!"

Ortiz, Marino, and Boston started barking orders into their radios, calling out their teams. Calvin took Anna to the roof of the hotel. By the time they were up there, three SUVs were peeling out of the parking lot with the Steel Runners.

"Twenty people to cover all this land," Anna said. "Doesn't seem like enough."

"Nope," Calvin said. "Never will be. Now we really know how the Rangers feel."

When the other three Steel Runners joined them on the roof, he had them post up at different corners with binoculars, ready to identify incoming threats.

Calvin settled in next to Anna facing the west. He had a clear view of the snowcapped mountains and other slopes covered in lush green trees. It all seemed too peaceful up here to be under attack.

Hard to believe that Palmer was dealing with hell just a short drive away.

But at least if everything hit the fan, he was close by to Maureen and the kids. He knew with Sandra here, she would be helping keep them safe.

"See anything?" Calvin asked.

"Nothing yet," Anna replied.

Calvin turned his radio to the channel Palmer and the rest of the Rangers were on. He wanted to hear immediately if any hostiles had made it past the Rangers and were on their way to Estes Park.

"We got shooters at the gates," a Ranger called.

"Nuke, get your ass over here! I need this sniper taken out!"

Gunfire chattered between bouts of static. Yells and curses filled the channel.

"Rogers is moving up! Give him cover fire!"

Calvin could only imagine the chaos.

"This is Nuke!" a voice called. "I got breachers on the south. Near the warehouses! They're trying to flank us."

More gunfire filled the line.

"God," Anna said. "They sound desperate. It's like being on the train again, listening to it all unfold. The gunfire, the screams."

She shivered.

"We're okay," Calvin said. "These guys are good. They know what they're doing."

But he wasn't really sure that was all true. He imagined what would happen if the enemy wasn't stopped. How many hostiles would pour down between the mountains right into Estes Park?

Anna touched the bill of the White Sox cap as if wishing for good luck.

Calvin hoped they got that luck today.

He thought of the Gomezes again. Maybe he thought he was saving them only to deliver them on a silver platter to the hostiles battering Gould.

More gunfire roared over the lines.

Gould was too far for Calvin to hear the actual gunfire, but he could almost feel the battle when he listened to it over the radio. Dark memories reminded him of the smell of cordite and hot metal, the sight of fire and smoke and blood and corpses.

Shit.

He had to hold it together.

"Rogers here!" a voice called. "They're trying to... Oh fuck, they just lit the warehouses on fire! The ammunition, the meds, it's all—"

A boom thudded over the radio, resulting in a stream of static.

Calvin's heart climbed into his throat. He used his binos to scope the road again. He half-expected to see a convoy of vehicles charging into town.

But no one came.

At least not yet.

He and Anna listened to the radio. Watching. Waiting. Worrying.

Sweat beaded down his forehead. He couldn't stop thinking about the Gomezes.

What seemed like an hour later, a panting voice came over the channel. It was Palmer and he finally got his breath. "All clear... hostiles are retreating. I repeat, all clear."

"Palmer," Rogers called. "They left something behind. It's on one of the warehouses."

"What is it?"

"A white buffalo."

———

Raven sat in a dark room that had been fashioned into a prison cell in Mayor Clayton's basement. The air reeked of mold. Slimy black tendrils traced the wall where water dripped from holes in the ceiling. The door was solid wood with a small window eye-level with iron bars. Light shifted in between those bars from the hall.

He had no idea where Jay was. Had the man been killed? Or was he stashed away in another cell somewhere?

Good chance the man had been killed, along with David.

Which meant that once again, Raven was alone.

He paced the cell looking for some way out. Piles of hay lay in one corner. There were two buckets in another. One had water. The other was empty.

He shuddered thinking what the empty one was for.

When he tried pushing on the door, it hardly moved.

He backed away a couple feet then rammed the door with his shoulder.

The wood quivered slightly.

He retreated to the far side of the cramped ten-by-ten space and ran as hard as he could, crashing against the door. The resulting bang shook through the cell.

The door wouldn't budge.

Once more, he reared back and kicked the door. His boot slammed against the wood, shaking it in its hinges.

If only he'd had just one of his hatchets or even a knife... but Clayton's men had taken everything.

No telling what they'd done with his equipment. Or with Jay.

He kicked at the door again and again.

Dust poured from the ceiling. The hinges groaned with each impact.

Then he heard bootsteps echoing against the stone walls outside. A man shadowed in darkness approached.

He pointed a gun at the window. The man smartly kept it far enough on the other side so Raven couldn't simply reach out and wrench it from his hands.

"Step the fuck back," the guard said.

Raven stood his ground.

"I said, step the fuck back. All the way against that wall."

The guard remained where he was. With no chance of grabbing the gun, Raven finally did as ordered.

"Face the wall," the man said

Raven turned toward the damp stone.

All he could think of as he stood there was that Creek was outside the compound, hopefully still near the mining equipment storage building. Alone and probably waiting patiently, wondering when Raven would return.

The pain clenched his heart as he thought about the Akita.

He had no idea how he was going to get out of here and back to his dog. Especially without help coming.

He'd warned Lindsey he might be going radio silent as they stalked Clayton. It could be a couple days before she even suspected anything was wrong.

He hoped not, but there was nothing else he could do.

The door opened behind him.

"Keep your ugly-ass face to the wall," the guard said.

It took every ounce of self-control for Raven not to whirl around and go on the attack.

Then he heard heavy, panicked breathing.

"Let me go!"

It was a woman's voice.

The door closed again with a heavy thud, followed by the mechanical click of the lock.

Raven finally turned.

Lily stood before him.

She wore the same dress she'd had on at the saloon, only it had been torn and shredded. Bruises mottled her arms and face.

"The hell are you doing here?" Raven asked.

Lily clenched her jaw. "You really that dumb?"

She pointed a finger at Raven's chest.

"Some of Clayton's men saw me talking to you and your buddy the other night. Apparently, they put the puzzle pieces together."

"Shit, I'm sorry."

"Your talk with Clayton obviously didn't go well."

"No," Raven admitted. "No, it didn't."

She pressed her palms into her eyes, her voice shaky. "There's no telling what Clayton's going to do to my son now."

She suddenly slapped his face.

"I wouldn't be in this mess if it weren't for you guys!" she snarled.

Raven tried to shield himself, then snatched her wrists, holding her back.

"I'm sorry, I truly am." Raven lowered his voice. "Part of the deal was that I said I'd help your son for the intel you gave us. I still fully intend on keeping that promise."

"How?" she asked. "You're locked in here with me."

"I'll figure out a way."

Her nose was still wrinkled in a snarl. She let out a rough, frustrated laugh, and turned away from him. "Everything's screwed. Everything's screwed because I talked to you two. Especially your smooth-talking friend, Jay. Where the hell is he anyways?"

"I don't know."

"Both of you, against the wall," a voice called from outside.

"Again?" Raven muttered.

They pressed themselves flat against the stone as multiple people stormed in. Rough hands blindfolded Raven and cranked his hands behind his back. Metal cuffs secured his wrists before he was led out of the cell.

He was prodded and pushed up some stairs, then through what he assumed were the halls of the mayor's mansion. Suddenly, a boot kicked against his spine, knocking him down.

His jaw hit the wooden floor with a painful crack.

Someone whipped the blindfold off his face.

Pain throbbed through his jaw. He did his best to pull himself up to his knees before standing and looking around.

Bookshelves lined the room. A massive oak desk was positioned at the end of a red Persian carpet.

Across the desk were stacks of papers and marked-up

maps of Colorado along with open books. Raven wondered if some of that might be the intel he needed on the Rattlesnakes and Eddy.

Mayor Clayton sat behind the desk. Unsurprisingly, all manner of animal heads were mounted on the wall behind him, from pumas to deer to moose and bears.

But they weren't alone.

Between the animals hung the heads of twelve men and women. Each taxidermized head wore a solemn expression that made Raven's insides turn.

He had seen a lot over the years, but nothing like this.

You picked the wrong guy to try and interrogate, Sam, Raven thought.

The monster of a mayor stood from his desk and paced toward Raven.

"I see you're admiring some of my trophies," he said. "Maybe you're picturing your own head up there?"

Raven swallowed hard.

"I'd love to hunt someone like you," Clayton said. "Unfortunately, someone else wants you worse than I do." He sighed. "Shame, really... but I respect my place in the world. That's why I'm still alive. You see, the Collapse gave me an opportunity to live like a king. I get to live like this, do whatever the fuck I want, because of men like Eddy Nez."

Clayton paced again.

"So when Eddy called me up personally and told me to save you and your friend, I said sure, no problem," the mayor continued.

"Jay's still alive?" Raven asked.

"Maybe not for long. Figured it would be best to keep you assholes separate so you can't be scheming."

Clayton paused.

"Not that you'd have much time for scheming. Eddy's on

his way here now," he said. "Sounds like he has his own game to play with you. I wasn't a fan at first. But the more I think about it, the more I can say I'm looking forward to it."

Raven had almost hoped that Clayton would try and hunt him. At least then he had a chance, but if the Rattlesnakes were coming...

Clayton turned back to the wall of human heads. "You and your buddy will look good up there, don't you think?"

"Fuck you," Raven said.

Clayton merely laughed then looked at a guard near the entrance. "Take him back to the cell. I don't want him going anywhere until Eddy gets here."

13

THE STENCH OF BURNING OIL WAS OVERWHELMING AS IT mixed with the charred scent of a smoldering wood. Palmer surveyed the damage around the warehouses and the cabins near the Gould checkpoint.

Two Rangers were dead. Seven wounded.

Palmer could barely keep his mind going. He was exhausted, mentally and physically. Nausea gripped his stomach.

They'd barely stopped the enemy. He couldn't stop thinking about the two guys that had died either—or the seven that had been sent back to Estes Park for medical treatment.

He prayed to God they survived.

In the aftermath, he had directed the twenty-four surviving Rangers defending Gould to gather all the bodies of the hostiles. The nine tattooed men they had killed were now lined up on a tarp next to piles of steaming ash. Every one of these dead bastards had a skull inked on their faces and various other bones tattooed across their bodies.

"Well, these definitely aren't Rattlesnakes," Lindsey said.

She had arrived a few minutes earlier with Blair and was

checking the corpses with Palmer. Nuke and Rogers stood around beside Palmer, each of them covered in dirt and blood. The mess was either from both their own relatively minor wounds or from when they'd done their best to save their downed comrades.

"They left a white buffalo spray-painted on the one surviving warehouse we got," Palmer said. "Why would they do that if they weren't Rattlesnakes?"

"Fuck," Lindsey said. "I wish we had prisoners to confirm that, but... maybe they're one of the groups working for Eddy."

"Sorry, Sheriff," Rogers said. "I tried going after them, but they got on their bikes and..."

Nuke kicked at the ground.

Lindsey leaned down toward one of the dead guys and put on her gloves. Then she moved his head from side to side. Her eyes grazed across his tattoos.

"Nasty fellows," Blair said.

"If these aren't Rattlesnakes exactly, who are they?" Rogers asked. "They got more fucking tats than me."

"These guys are bikers," she said. "A gang we've got on record. They're called the Skulls. We've brought a couple of them in before. In fact, they're rotting in Fort Golden's prison."

"Why would Skulls attack one of our checkpoints?" Rogers asked. "And if they are working for the Rattlesnakes, why?"

"Good questions. I'd love to know how many groups like them are doing Eddy's bidding."

Lindsey stood and stripped off the gloves. Then she jerked her chin for Palmer and the others to follow. They hiked together back up toward the border checkpoint where workers were already patching holes in the fence.

The white quarantine tent thankfully hadn't been damaged. Medical staff moved in and out in PPE, still taking care of patients and refugees.

One of the wooden watchtowers overlooking the area had been hammered by gunfire. Two Rangers were mending it with two-by-fours.

"We need more scouts out here to watch for crap like this," Nuke said. "I can only keep my eye on so much land at once."

"I know," Lindsey said. "We've been forced to fill in all the unmanned defensive spots that the FAC is leaving behind now that they've withdrawn their troops."

"You know we wish we could do more," Blair said.

"If we had more people, maybe the Skulls wouldn't have attacked in the first place," Rogers said. "Then we wouldn't have lost two of our own."

Palmer balled a fist, anger filling him. "We got to get these guys back."

"More than that, if they're connected to the Rattlesnakes, we might be able to use them," Lindsey said. "I haven't heard any recent updates from Raven... and if everything in Ouray falls through, we could use the intel."

"Especially if the Rattlesnakes are planning to send someone to attack like this again," Palmer added.

"I have a feeling if we could track down those guys"—Nuke gestured toward the dead men with skull tattoos—"we could find ourselves a new lead. And even if we don't, I'd like to put the rest of these people six feet under."

"I agree. We need to organize a scouting party." Then she turned to Blair. "I know I'm asking a lot, but is there any way we can get your men to come along?"

"I can come out here to observe and pass on information to my superiors, but I still can't just send my men out at a whim," Blair said. "My team will have to stay behind, especially on an offensive like this."

Palmer understood Blair having to sit this out. The Royal Marines had already been through so much with the Reapers and now the campaign to stop Wild Fire, especially considering the most recent attack on the bridge that nearly got four Marines killed.

"I get it," Lindsey replied. But Palmer could see she was pissed.

Apparently, so could Blair. "Really, I'm terribly sorry, Sheriff."

He walked away and left Palmer with Lindsey.

Nuke and Rogers went off to help a couple of other Rangers repairing the damage to the fences at the checkpoint.

She let out a sigh and looked back to the mountains. "Man, I wish Raven was here..."

"Yeah, he'd be nice to have on the trail," Palmer said with a smile. "When did he check in last?"

"Yesterday..." Lindsey looked worried. "I'll try calling him later, but for now, this is on us. Palmer, I want a group of Rangers. At least fifteen strong. People with the most field experience and military backgrounds if possible. Nuke is decent at tracking, so we'll take him. Rogers can help. You can pick out the rest of the team."

"You got it, ma'am."

Lindsey started to walk away, then pulled out her phone. "Screw it, I'm calling Raven now."

She dialed and then waited.

"Nothing?" Palmer asked.

"Nope," Lindsey said. She tucked the phone away. "He said he might go silent, but I'm really starting to get nervous."

Palmer was used to seeing the sheriff under stress. Usually, she didn't show much emotion, but whenever Raven was in trouble, she had a way of wearing her heart on her sleeve.

"I'm sure he's okay," Palmer said. "Raven can take care of himself."

"What if Jay betrayed him? What if Eddy found them?" Lindsey shook her head. "I want to send someone out looking for him, but with scouts stretched thin and the Skulls..."

"What about the Steel Runners, ma'am?" Palmer asked.

"Good idea." Lindsey called Calvin. She put it on speaker when he answered. After giving Calvin an update on everything, she made her ask. "I can't spare any more men to go look for him, but maybe you could go search around Ouray. Even if he doesn't need our help, it would be good to have people nearby to reinforce him if and when he does make contact with us again. Plus, if he spots Eddy, it'll be good to have a quick reaction force in the area."

There was a long pause over the line before Calvin answered.

"I'm sorry, Sheriff, but I'm not sure that's possible," he finally said.

"What do you mean?" Lindsey asked.

"Look, ma'am, I'm happy to continue helping with security around here. And while I want to help, I want to do it firmly on *this* side of the border. I made a promise to the Gomezes that I intend to keep and after what just happened, I can't just get up and leave."

Lindsey raised a brow and protested, something Palmer wasn't used to seeing. She had let her emotions get the best of her.

"Calvin, we could really use you out there," she continued.

"There are people here that really need me," Calvin replied, almost as firmly.

Lindsey stared at the phone for a moment, then backed down. "Fine. I get it. Palmer, send a group of four recon Rangers. We'll need to pull them off checkpoint duty down south. Send them to the Ouray area immediately. I want them to see if they can find out what happened to Raven and Jay."

Palmer tipped his hat. "Consider it done, ma'am."

"Sheriff," Calvin said. "I do want to be clear about something."

Another cool wind blew over them, kicking up clouds of ash.

"What's that?" Lindsey asked, squinting against the grit.

"I will lay my life down for this place," he said. "I will fight."

"I appreciate that."

"It's just my fight has changed. I'm not protecting cargo anymore. I'm protecting people."

"Understood, Calvin. Thanks for your candidness."

Lindsey ended the call and turned back to Palmer. "We're already losing daylight, so let's get moving."

Palmer suited up in his helmet and body armor. He loaded up into his truck and looked at the destruction one last time at the checkpoint. The shell casings, the bullet holes, the dead bodies.

As he pulled away, he couldn't help but feel he was no longer a cop, but a soldier. And he wondered how many more times he would have to fight until this war was over.

He wasn't sure.

What he did know was that he would never stop fighting. It was going to take a hail of gunfire to cut him down. Until that day, he would do whatever necessary to save his country and the New Frontier.

———

Raven could hardly tell how much time had passed. It could've been hours or it could've been days.

The hall outside his cell remained dark.

Lily hung out in the corner, knees up to her chest, head down. He thought about trying to tell her things were going to be okay, but right now, even Raven didn't believe that. Apologizing wasn't going to do much either.

Why should she forgive him and Jay?

Raven thought of his new ally. He still didn't know where they were keeping him.

Finally, footsteps sounded from outside.

"Turn around and don't fucking move," the guard said.

Lily and Raven did what they were told. The door opened and someone cranked Raven's arms behind his back. He felt the cold steel of a gun barrel at the back of his head.

Before he could turn around, someone forced a rag over his face. His eyes watered and he tried not to breathe in. But the sickly-sweet vapors of chloroform seeped into his nostrils until finally he was forced to suck in a sharp breath.

He fought to retain consciousness.

The fight didn't last long.

When Raven blinked awake again, his head throbbed. Sunlight beat down on him. He held up a hand to shield his burning pupils.

That was when he realized his hands were actually free. He shot up to his feet, fighting dizziness but ready to defend himself.

He blinked again, his vision clearing more.

Someone had placed him next to a creek. Shallow water ran over smooth pebbles. He raised a hand to shield his eyes from the sun, seeing the valley slopes all around him.

Fear jabbed through his gut. He was the prey now.

He tried to turn and take in his surroundings, but something tugged on his left ankle.

Secured just above his bare foot was a pair of metal leg cuffs. One cuff wrapped around his ankle; the other was attached to a second person.

Lily.

She lay on the ground, still unconscious.

"Lily." Raven knelt by her.

She didn't respond.

He could feel eyes on him from the shadows, his heart thrumming against his ribcage.

"Lily, wake up." Raven squeezed her shoulder, but she didn't stir.

He tried a gentle shake.

Her eyelids batted open a sliver.

When her gaze caught his, she sat up. In a panic, she glanced around, then tried to scrabble along the ground away from him. The force of her frightened movement pulled Raven's leg out from under him, and he toppled over the ground.

"Take it easy," he said. "We're chained together."

She sat back down, panting, looking at her legs.

"You have to listen to me, and work with me," Raven said. "Do you understand?"

"I don't want to work with you," Lily said.

"They're awake," a voice called out.

Lily pulled back from Raven as he turned to the woods. About one hundred feet away, in the shadows of several towering pines, stood Mayor Clayton.

He strode toward them with a rifle on his shoulder. Three of his men followed. Raven recognized two of them he'd seen before: the hunters with the birthmark and the limp. Out for revenge, Raven presumed.

"Bring him out," Clayton said.

Another pair of men came out of the woods. They led a third man behind them tied to a rope. The rope was wrapped around the man's wrists.

Jay.

The other two men each had tawny skin and long, dark hair over their shoulders. One was a tall, muscular man with a snake tattoo winding down his arm. The tall man glared at Raven like a hungry wolf stalking a wounded doe. He reeked of violence and brutality.

The man leading Jay, however, was no stranger.

"Raven," Eddy hissed.

Healing wounds covered most of his face. Mangled scar tissue traced over bumps and ridges across his flesh.

"Damn, you look like shit," Raven said. "But still better than all the people you've tortured and killed over the past few weeks."

Eddy walked over leading Jay, who was tied up with a rope. "Ironic you accuse me of something the government you support once did to our people."

Raven considered his next words more carefully than his first. "I understand you want reparations for the past, but this is not the way to lead our people into the future."

"He's right, Eddy," Jay said. "You can't make up for evil with more evil."

"Seems to be working to me, old friend," Eddy said.

He yanked on the rope. Jay fell to his knees on the rocks.

"I once considered you my brother," he said. "I know you still want what's best for the Navajo Nation, don't you?"

"Of course, I do, Eddy. You know that. But—"

"But you don't think my vision for the Navajo Nation is best for our people?" Eddy shook his scarred head wearily. "You might not see it now, but you will soon."

He crouched in front of Jay.

"Due to our past, I'm giving you one last chance to regain your honor and join me," Eddy said. "You do this, or I'll hand you over to Clayton and his boys to do whatever they wish."

The mayor grinned from ear to ear.

"What would you have me do?" Jay asked.

Eddy looked to Raven, and then to Lily.

"Hunt this whore and the wašíču's lapdog," Eddy said. "Regain your honor. The choice is yours."

Raven felt his heart kick. He was right, he was the prey, but not Clayton or Eddy's prey. He was going to be hunted by a man he had considered an ally only minutes ago.

Raven studied Jay, looking for some sign of what the man would choose. But the Navajo detective gave nothing away.

"Need some extra motivation?" Eddy sighed. "I don't like to make threats, but you're out here to hunt me, is that not correct?"

Jay glanced up. "I'm here to stop you. Whatever that takes."

"Stop me? From protecting our people and taking back *our* lands?"

There was anger in Eddy's voice.

Rage.

Hundreds of years' worth of pent-up aggression from his ancestors. Raven understood it well. So did Jay, but this was not the right path in Raven's mind.

"If you refuse, then not only will Clayton get the green light to track you down, but I'll have my own men visit your family back in Window Rock," Eddy said. "I assume you still care about your son and ex-wife. Your brother too."

Jay looked to Raven with a defeated expression but said nothing.

"I'm looking for an answer, Jay," Eddy prodded. "Either

Raven dies or your son just might be tragically killed in a hunting accident soon. Wouldn't that just be terrible?"

Raven hadn't even known Jay had a son. The detective might've been estranged from his family. Maybe it would've been too painful for Jay to admit to Raven. But from the look on Jay's face, his feelings still must have been burning strong.

Jay couldn't meet Eddy's gaze. "You have to leave my son out of this."

Raven knew then the Navajo man had no choice. It was his family's blood or Raven's.

"What's your answer?" Eddy asked.

"I'm sorry, Raven," Jay said.

Fuck me, Raven thought.

"Please don't do this," Lily said.

"She had no part of this," Raven said. "Let her go."

"What's the fun in that?" Clayton asked.

Eddy shot him a glare that wiped the grin off the mayor's face.

Using a knife, Eddy then leaned down to saw through the rope on Jay's bonds.

"Jay, I'm going to let you earn my trust today. We'll follow after, but I'm going to let you do this alone. I don't want you to return to me until you have both Raven's and Lily's heads." Then Eddy gave Raven a diabolical grin. "And, Raven, if you somehow manage to defeat Jay, well, then consider your invitation to join my forces open. We're the ones with the guns and the gold."

"Screw you," Raven hissed. "I will kill you."

Eddy continued grinning. "You won't. You tried before and failed. Now you're nothing. You're just a pathetic man who thinks he's doing the right thing, but you're shooting yourself in the foot."

"Fight me like a man," Raven said. "Don't have Jay do your dirty work."

Eddy's eyes narrowed. "I don't give a rat's ass about you, Raven. You can live or die for all I care." Raven didn't believe Eddy, but the crazed man went on. "Like I said, you're nothing. In fact, you're so weak, so disappointing, we're going to give you a head start. I'll even give you a weapon to make it more fun."

He nodded to one of the guards who tossed Raven a hatchet.

Raven scooped it up, his mind whirling a thousand miles a second, trying to figure out how he would survive with Lily attached to him. Jay was no novice tracker, and he now had a shotgun in hand.

A hatchet against a shotgun was not an even match.

Jay pumped in a shell.

"Time's already ticking," Eddy said. "What the hell are you waiting for, Raven?"

"Come on, Lily," Raven said, turning to run. She tried to keep up, but they tripped almost right out the gate, sprawling into the dirt.

Laughter exploded from Clayton and his men.

Raven got up and looked at her, seeing panic across her features.

"You have to follow my lead," Raven said. "Trust me, you have to."

Holding his hatchet in one hand, he put one arm around Lily's shoulder to stabilize her. They continued, clumsily moving forward through the ferns and brush. Raven tried to guide them into the trees for denser coverage.

He wanted to somehow conceal their tracks, but there simply wasn't any way. Not with their cuffed legs scraping through the dirt.

"We're dead." Tears streamed from Lily's eyes. "I'm never gonna see my son again."

"You think that way and you *will* die," Raven said. "Or you could get your shit together and help me."

She seemed to shake out of it somewhat and trudged alongside him. They were starting to pick up their pace.

Raven glanced at the ridgelines past the trees. He recognized where he was in the valley. By now, he had already lost a good three minutes. He had no hope of outrunning Jay. His hatchet was not going to be enough to fight back against all of them.

But he had one more weapon Clayton and Eddy didn't know about.

He guided them up the slope toward where he thought the old mining equipment storage building was. If Creek was still faithfully carrying out Raven's last command, the dog would be hiding somewhere there.

He was pushing up the slope with Lily, maybe half-a-mile from where he judged the mining equipment storage building was.

That was when he heard the first footsteps from behind.

"No, no, no," Lily said.

"Quiet!" Raven said in a low voice.

But it was too late.

A shape sprinted up from the trees behind them, easily following their trails.

Jay appeared with his shotgun.

Raven held his hatchet up, ready to fling it at Jay.

"Stop!" Jay said.

"Or what?" Raven asked. "You really going to shoot us, Jay? Is that what you want?"

Jay aimed the shotgun at Raven. "Don't take another step, Raven."

"Jay, come on, man," Raven said. "You can't do this. You know you don't want to do it."

He started trying to climb up the slope with Lily. They were so close to the mining equipment building. Creek had to be here somewhere, ready to help.

Jay was still aiming at him, but he hadn't fired yet. Maybe his words were sinking in.

"Raven, I don't want to do this. But I've got to protect my family. I've got to protect my people. You know how it is."

"That's exactly why you need to let me go."

"Raven... He won't stop."

"*I'll* stop him."

Raven saw the look in Jay's eyes. The man desperately didn't want to hurt him. He was looking for an excuse not to, but they both knew what would happen if Raven didn't die during this hunt.

Jay and his family would be punished.

One of them had to die. There was no other way about it.

"Raven, maybe if we get you to surrender, you can convince—"

"It's not going to work that way," Raven said, cranking back his hatchet again. If he had to kill Jay, then he would. The future of the New Frontier might depend on it.

"Please, I—"

A flash of brown fur came from Jay's left. An animal pounced on the man, tearing into his arm. The shotgun went off, the boom exploding in the trees. Time seemed to freeze. Birds took off in fear.

The thunderous blast rang in Raven's ears.

He looked down, expecting to see a hole drilled through his chest or Lily's.

But they were still standing. Still breathing.

Leaves floated down from a splintered tree branch where

the buckshot had hit.

Blood poured all over Jay's arm and into the soil nearby. He'd dropped the shotgun. Now Raven could see clearly what had attacked the man.

Creek.

The loyal dog had listened and hid after all. The dog started biting at Jay's neck, drawing more blood.

Voices yelled out somewhere deeper in the valley.

Jay lay on his back, groaning and pressing his one good hand over the chunks of ragged flesh on his neck. He looked ready to pass out.

"Good God," Lily said. "That animal!"

"He's mine!" Raven said. "Don't worry about him."

Raven led Lily to Jay, who was writhing in pain. He stole the shotgun and aimed back at where Jay had come from. A shadowy figure flitted up toward them between the trees. He squeezed the trigger. A blast erupted through leaves and tore bark. The figure chasing after them dropped.

He didn't know if it was Eddy, another Rattlesnake, or one of Clayton's people. He didn't intend to find out either.

"Creek, come on, boy!" Raven said.

He fired a couple more times for good measure toward where his enemy would be coming from. Just enough to keep them back.

But Raven couldn't stand by and fight with Lily and Creek. They needed to move.

He got the three of them heading back up the slope.

Creek's tail wagged as they fled.

Raven wished he had time to embrace the dog, but he could still hear people rushing up the slope.

They ran as hard as they could together. Raven's lungs felt like they might explode. Lily looked like she could barely breathe. But they never slowed.

Raw survival instinct kept them going.

Not until they'd run a good thirty minutes.

Then he allowed himself to break into a gentler jog.

Shouts echoed from deep within the valley. They were distant.

They would be free soon. That knowledge was all that drove him. He could get back to his Jeep. Escape Ouray. Then get back home to Estes Park.

"Here, stop for a minute," he said.

He used his hatchet to hammer off the chain holding their leg cuffs together.

Finally, he was free.

"What now?" she asked. "Mark's still in the mayor's house. You promised."

Raven looked westward, back toward his escape from this place. Taking a second, he checked the shotgun. He was out of shells. Only a couple options remained for them. He could keep running. He could get back to his Jeep and warn the Rangers where Eddy was.

Mark was an innocent child.

Raven couldn't help picturing the boy's head on the mayor's wall.

Plus, he had a mission. He knew where Eddy was in this moment, sure, but he had no idea what the Rattlesnakes were planning. By the time he made it to his Jeep, Eddy would probably be gone, along with all the intel left in Clayton's office.

Could he really just leave all this behind? Could he really just run to save his own ass, forgetting the promise he'd made to Lily—and even to Lindsey?

He had a mission.

Maybe running was the smart thing to do.

But was it the right thing?

14

Jay was in bad shape when Eddy, Robert, and Kitcheyan found him. Kitcheyan had been waiting in the forest closer to the mayor's house, ready to stop Raven and Lily if they escaped Jay. But Lily and Raven had evidently disappeared. So Kitcheyan had joined Eddy and Robert as they had taken their horses and followed the slope up to a rundown mining facility where the crack of the shotgun had sounded. Clayton met them seconds later with his entourage of three cowboys.

Raven had killed the fourth cowboy who was supposed to be shadowing Jay, keeping an eye on him, Raven, and Lily for Eddy and Clayton. The man had failed his job, and now he wasn't even alive for Eddy to punish him.

"He's not here," Robert said. "Must have escaped with that bitch."

Eddy went back to Jay, who lay groaning on the ground.

"The hell happened?" Eddy asked.

Jay writhed in pain, his arm covered in blood. A piece of flesh seemed to be missing from his neck. He gripped the wound. It looked painful. Bad. But if it were fatal, he'd already be dead.

"Animal," he muttered. "I couldn't... I couldn't stop him."

At first Eddy thought Jay was calling Raven an animal, but then he saw the bite marks. These wounds were from a beast, not a man.

Eddy looked back toward the forest where the footprints of Raven and Lily had gone. Not far away were pawprints.

A dog.

Another few moments of examining the scene helped Eddy come up with a mental image of what had happened. He saw the blast from the shotgun in a tree where Jay must have tried to shoot Raven.

He remembered that damn dog Raven had brought to Montezuma Creek.

Shit.

"Clayton, organize a few of your best hunters to find Raven and Lily," Eddy said. "They couldn't have gotten far."

"Boys, you heard him," Clayton said. "Get the hounds."

Clayton went to follow them, but Eddy grabbed his arm.

"Not you," he said. "I need your militia up north."

"I've already got the vehicles loaded and ready. Even with the hunting teams out, I can send a good twenty men with your Rattlesnakes immediately," Clayton said.

"Twenty men?" Eddy said. "You have *fifty-five* men in your militia. You can afford to send more."

Robert snorted and Kitcheyan stepped forward. The Apache men looked ready to enforce Eddy's request.

"Well, I do need some people to hold back and defend my compound," said the mayor.

"You don't need thirty-five people to defend your shitty castle."

Clayton reared back at that and looked like he was about

to respond until he looked down at Eddy's fingers on the handle of his tomahawk. His eyes then flitted to Kitcheyan and Robert.

"Okay, you're the boss," Clayton said. "You got whatever you need from me."

He whistled for his people to join him and ran off.

Eddy watched them go, resisting the urge to toss his tomahawk into the man's back. He was a coward. Clayton took pleasure in hunting men that stood no chance of fighting back.

Hunting had always been something Eddy did to provide food for his family. Just like it had been for his ancestors. He still remembered hearing stories how trains full of men from the United States were sent west to kill the buffalo. Shooting them from trains and on horses. Gunning them down for nothing more than their tongue and to ensure his people starved.

There were stories about sprawling plains littered with the rotting carcasses of hundreds of massacred buffalo. It filled his heart with anger to think of it now. All of those beasts lying there, wasted.

His people had used every single part of the buffalo for food, shelter, and clothing. Death should never be purposeless or wasteful.

"Let me go after Raven," Robert said. "I don't trust the mayor."

"I'll go with," Kitcheyan said.

"No, not yet. Raven won't get far," Eddy said. "You're too important to waste your time going after one lone tracker, Robert, and we need your men. Now help me get Jay up on my horse."

They picked up the injured man and draped him over Yanaba.

Eddy then hopped up in the saddle, looking down at his

former friend. Jay had failed, but at least he had tried. He wasn't entirely ready to put his trust in Jay, but this was a start. Perhaps there was hope that Jay would see his vision for the white buffalo.

After all, he had some connections back in Window Rock still. But it wouldn't be bad to have another man on his side that also had ties to President Tso. The more, the better for what he had planned.

They made it back to Ouray's main drag a few hours later.

Jay was in bad shape, and unconscious, but his wounds would heal if they got him medicine.

The bustling town came to a stop when they arrived. Residents of Ouray looked at him with a mixture of terror and respect, stepping out of his way long before he got close.

A convoy of trucks and cars were already lined up, ready to go near the western side of town. Near the town's gallows, several rows of prisoner stocks lay.

Ten prisoners were already secured within the heavy timber constructs. They ranged from foreign peacekeepers to UN forces to National Guardsmen and a few other wašíču living in the New Fronter that the Rattlesnakes had suspected of trying to betray them.

"Robert, go make sure the men are ready to move out with Clayton's militia," Eddy said. Robert rode off down the street.

Then he and Kitcheyan got Jay to the makeshift hospital inside an old hardware store.

"Give him the best medicine and make sure he's taken care of," Eddy said to a medic inside the hospital.

Kitcheyan hesitated and looked at the bloodied body of Jay.

"Why are you wasting time?" Eddy asked.

"All due respect, Ahiga, but he failed. Why are we wasting good medicine on him?" Kitcheyan asked.

Eddy glared at the man.

Kitcheyan stepped forward. "We should just kill him."

"No," Eddy said.

"He's a sniveling wreck. A weak man."

A blast of rage took over Eddy before he could stop himself. He grabbed Kitcheyan by the throat. "Jay is far from weak. He shares my blood. There's strength there you can't understand."

He squeezed harder as Kitcheyan's eyes bulged slightly.

Eddy leaned in closer, feeling the blood pumping through Kitcheyan's neck.

"I give the orders, you follow them, and you never fucking question them," Eddy said in a whisper. "Do you understand?"

Kitcheyan managed a nod. Eddy finally released him.

Stumbling backward, Kitcheyan reached up to his neck, his eyes at the ground.

"You think I'm keeping this man alive just because he was once my friend, but that is not the truth," Eddy said. "He worked closely with Tso. He protected Tso. He may be able to help us in more ways than you know, whether he wants to or not."

Robert rode back on his horse toward Eddy and Kitcheyan.

"Clayton told us his men are ready," Robert said. "We can send up the first convoy north right now. They can join the second in a couple hours."

"Good, have the men move out immediately," Eddy said, finally looking away from Kitcheyan.

Robert ran back to the convoy of trucks and cars. Soon the vehicles began snaking out of town and toward the highway. They were filled with a mixture of the militia from Ouray and some of Eddy's Rattlesnakes.

Kitcheyan walked away without another word. For a moment, Eddy watched him go, wondering if he was starting to question Eddy. Maybe he saw through the speech about Tso. Maybe he believed Eddy was weak now for sparing Jay.

Either way, it didn't matter.

If Kitcheyan questioned him again, Eddy wouldn't hesitate putting him down. No one would stand between him and his vision for the New Frontier.

———

Lindsey and her fifteen-man Ranger team had spent the better part of the day following Highway 14 tracking the gang responsible for the attack on Gould. Even as the afternoon threatened to turn to evening, she did not want to give up.

The deaths of the two Rangers at Gould weighed heavily on her mind. She hoped, as the day wore on, the death toll wouldn't grow any higher.

She rode in the front passenger seat of one of the USMARIID Humvees they'd borrowed for the expedition. Rogers drove, and Palmer sat in the back with Nuke. It was odd not having Blair or any of the Royal Marines along, but that was the reality Lindsey had to face.

Three more SUVs carried the other twelve Rangers. They had enough of a fighting force that if Lindsey happened upon the remnants of that attacking Skulls gang, she was sure they could take them on.

The issue was finding them.

They'd spent the better part of the day following a mess of motorcycle tracks on the road.

Thanks to the recent rain, mud had sloshed onto the highways from the slopes. It made tracking their quarry slightly easier than expected. But they still had catching up to do.

As they carried on down the road, following the grooves in the mud, Lindsey's sat phone rang. It was Charlize's number.

She had called the Secretary of Defense earlier to apprise her of everything that had happened. Charlize had said she would see what she could do about helping them.

For all their sakes, Lindsey hoped the secretary had good news.

"Sheriff Plymouth here."

"Lindsey, it's Charlize."

"Good to hear from you again, ma'am."

"Soon enough, you'll be seeing me too."

"What?"

"Diego decided to deploy a platoon of light infantry."

"A whole platoon? Forty men? Holy shit, that is great!" Lindsey nearly shouted.

It must not have been easy for Charlize to convince Diego to agree to sending a fully equipped and well-trained platoon. That was practically a whole army compared to her volunteer force of Rangers who often carried their own personal weapons.

"Thank you," Lindsey continued. "But one question. Why are you coming along?"

"The president likes the idea of me being there personally to remind people we haven't forgotten about the region. Not to mention, it'll show Senator Shelby we're serious about this issue. So my being there serves a few purposes."

"We do appreciate that, ma'am. It couldn't come at a better time. We're headed after the people that attacked Gould right now."

"Right now? Lindsey, be careful." Worry tinged Charlize's voice. "I want to see you tomorrow when I touch down in Denver, understood?"

"That's a promise, ma'am. If we pull this off, we'll have a bunch of new prisoners along with actionable intel."

"Good luck. I'll see you soon."

"See you soon."

Lindsey ended the call with a new sense of hope. She smiled as she told Palmer, Nuke, and Rogers the news.

"Hell yeah," Nuke said. "We're definitely still in this fight."

"Yup, but we can't let our guard down."

"No, ma'am," Rogers said. "Show ain't over until it's over."

"And you've had your chance to wail on the guitar, huh?" Nuke asked.

Rogers grinned. "You're catching on, Nuke. If this platoon helps us clean up the New Frontier, then these dudes will get VIP passes for my future Red Rocks concert."

"Sounds good," Lindsey said. The news from Charlize had momentarily distracted even her from the mission. "But for now, no concerts. I don't want you thinking about groupies right now. The Skulls are the only people we're interested in."

The Rangers all focused on the road. The motorcycle tracks led them north on US-40. Green pines walled in either side of the highway. The normally golden grass was bathed in a vibrant green thanks to the recent rains.

They passed by more abandoned vehicles, then a field of trees charred by a forest fire.

Finally, they slowed, seeing the motorcycle tracks lead north off of 40 toward Steamboat Springs.

"So far, these tracks show our enemy never pulled off the highway until this point," Nuke said, leaning forward and pointing at the road.

Lindsey directed Rogers to park off to the side of the road.

"Assuming they don't have some heavily modified fuel tanks, they couldn't have gone much farther," he continued.

"There's a good chance they made their camp somewhere in Steamboat Springs," Lindsey said. "Lots of shelter. Good spot to post up and set defenses."

"Good point," Palmer said. "If they're in a town north of here, I don't think announcing our presence in the Humvee and vehicles would be a smart move."

"Right, we'll go on foot from here. Stay west of 40 on Quarry Mountain. The mountain will give us a good view of nearly all of Steamboat Springs."

She opened her door and the other Rangers piled out of their vehicles. She handed out orders, sending Palmer with his team to the west.

"Follow the top ridgelines of Quarry Peak. I'll stick closer to half-altitude," she said to Palmer. "Break radio silence only when absolutely necessary. The goal will be to avoid any engagement with the enemy until we find them and come up with a good plan."

Palmer took Nuke with a team of six Rangers. They disappeared into the dense evergreens at the foot of the mountains, heading north and west.

With Rogers behind her, Lindsey led her team of seven into the same forest but followed a different path. They crept through the dense foliage, using the brush and shade of the trees for cover. She had her men split up into three groups to cover each other and watch for any enemy scouts.

After about an hour-and-a-half of hiking, they heard a motorcycle engine in the distance. It whined away, fading into nothing.

The wind took over, whistling through the canopy of dense trees.

As they drew nearer to Steamboat Springs, Lindsey caught a whiff of smoke on the shifting wind. It carried the odor of barbecued meat.

Finally, she came to an overlook with her people. It gave her a vantage of the valley so she could see the southernmost tip of Steamboat Springs. She gestured for her men to stay back as she snuck to the shelter of a boulder.

Lifting her binos, she surveyed the landscape on the other side of the river and highway. Overgrown grass on the ski slopes waved in the wind. Empty chairlifts snaked down toward the town. One entire line had collapsed to the earth below leaving dozens of scattered chairs rusting in the tall grass.

The hotels and restaurants around the resort seemed empty.

Lindsey continued dragging her view down, following a trail of gray smoke. The evening was quickly settling over the town, casting everything in shadows.

But the fire burning outside the rundown Rabbit Ears Motel and its eponymously shaped sign cast an unmissable orange glow.

At least ten men stood around the fire, laughing about something. One tossed logs into it. All had tattoos that she could see even from this distance. The Skulls.

They had a large skewer over the fire with chunks of blackened meat. A variety of bloody knives and saws lay scattered in the nearby grass.

Four men worked on a couple of Harley Davidsons at one corner of the parking lot. One man held a flashlight to help illuminate whatever they were repairing.

A third bike was set up on concrete blocks as one of the men tested the throttle.

The throaty growl of the engine shook up from town.

Lindsey identified six other Skull guards in pairs perched atop the motel and other nearby buildings. The men had hunting rifles equipped with long-range scopes. One on top of the motel used binoculars to sweep the area.

She curled back behind the boulder when his gaze started to turn toward her. Then she crawled over to a new spot in the weeds. Her heart hammered in her chest. She didn't think the man had seen her, but she didn't want to take any chances.

A sudden shrill scream erupted from below.

Lindsey got up and turned her binos to locate the source.

Two Skulls dragged a young woman in her twenties from a copse of Aspens. Another seven prisoners, all women, were tied up to those trees. The women were covered in dirt, their clothes torn and ragged. A couple cried as others appeared to hurl curses at the Skulls.

These women weren't from the checkpoint. They looked as if the Skulls had been hauling them around as prisoners for a while.

The men laughed as the twenty-something-year-old woman tried to claw her way back toward the trees.

Then one took out a knife from his belt. He slashed off the woman's shirt, laughing as she tried to cover herself.

There was no mistaking what these men planned to do.

To think that these disgusting humans had snuck beyond the borders, traipsed through her lands, attacked her people, and now... Lindsey could not bear the thought of letting them go.

She had to destroy these monsters.

Especially if they worked for Eddy.

Their sins were too numerous to count.

She met with the rest of her team, and Palmer's team soon joined them.

The expressions on their faces told her they were equally horrified. Not one man suggested they return to the safety of the border.

"I counted at least twenty hostiles," Lindsey said.

"Are we planning on taking them all prisoners?" Palmer asked.

"Get them to surrender, maybe?" Nuke suggested.

Lindsey shook her head, feeling the heat of anger rise in her chest again. "Our prison at Fort Golden is already full. We only need a few men for intel. The rest, we can take out, so we can free their hostages. We just got to make it into their camp without them seeing us."

Palmer tentatively raised a hand. "I've got an idea. Calvin might not be here, but if we take a page out of the SEALs' book, we can take those assholes down."

"Good," Lindsey said. "Let's hear it."

"You almost got me killed, you asshole," Lily said.

"Quiet," Raven whispered.

He crouched in the darkness-soaked woods with Creek, listening to the sound of people below. He had been observing the remaining guard patrols, looking for the best way out of town.

From on the mountain slope, he watched Ouray with Lily. Already two convoys had left. Fewer guards seemed to be around the town and the mayor's compound.

Those left behind were mostly in the hunting parties Raven had avoided throughout the day.

Using the cover of the streams and mud, he'd even masked his and Lily's scent enough to avoid the hunting dogs.

From the sounds of crunching leaves and sticks, a hunting team was finally drawing close to Raven's position.

"Okay," he whispered. "I need you to be quiet now. If you listen to me, we can do this. We'll be able to get your son back, and I'll get a shot at what I came here for."

He still wondered how wise it was to try infiltrating the

mayor's compound. But his conscience wouldn't let him just run away.

She nodded, her lips pressed closed tightly.

Now might be the best opportunity Raven had to fight back. He signaled for Lily to wait behind the bushes and trees.

Then he walked at a hunch through the trees toward the compound with Creek behind him. His hatchet was secured to his belt.

The bark of a hunting dog erupted from the woods.

Raven directed Creek to hide in a clump of sagebrush.

At the same time, Raven climbed a pine tree. Just twelve feet off the ground, he could see clearly enough through the needles to watch the hunting dog bounding toward his position.

Two men followed carrying rifles.

The dog sniffed around the tree. Its tail wagged as it caught Raven's scent.

One of the men slowly approached the tree while the other roved his rifle around the terrain. Definitely one of Clayton's cowboys.

Just come a couple feet closer.

"Where is he, boy?" The man with the birthmark paused.

The second man walked around the circumference of the tree's branches, his rifle trained on the woods to their east. This man walked with a limp, his gait easily recognizable.

These two had been on the hunt for David Singer and then Raven.

"Another false alarm?" the limping man suggested.

"Shit," the man with the birthmark said.

He started to lower his weapon.

Raven leapt from the tree with the hatchet.

In one fell swoop, he knocked the man to the ground and

slammed the hatchet into his skull. Bone broke with a sickening crack. Blood rushed out.

Raven yanked the hatchet out, then slung it at the other man. It hit the guy square in his shoulder. Bone and tendons snapped. The man cried out as he raised his rifle with one hand.

But Raven was quicker. He snatched the rifle from the first man and swung it like a bat. The heavy wooden stock hit the other guard in the side of the face with a loud crunch.

The man's head twisted violently. Blood flew from his mouth. He lost his grip on his own weapon.

Growling, the hunting dog sprinted at Raven.

"Creek!" Raven called.

The hunting dog latched onto Raven's leg, saliva frothing from its mouth. Pain shocked up from the bite, and Raven kicked the dog off. It went tumbling into the dirt.

As the hunting dog prowled toward Raven again, Creek pounced from the brush. The Akita stood between Raven and the other canine. He let out a vicious growl, the fur raising across his back.

The hunting dog's ears pressed flat against its skull, its tail lowering. For a moment, it looked like it might lunge.

Another growl from Creek sent the hunting dog sprinting off with a whimper.

"Good job, boy."

Raven took one of the hunting rifles, as much ammo as he could find, backpacks, and a pair of knives, then ran low through the woods. With one team down, there was no telling how long before the others noticed.

After running back to where Lily was, he signaled for her to follow him. They snuck through the woods until the compound was in sight.

"I need you to wait here," he whispered. "Don't move. Just

hide. As soon as I'm out, I'll come get you. Understood?"

Lily nodded. "Just don't fuck this up, honey."

"I don't plan to."

In minutes, he and Creek reached the six-foot concrete wall around the compound.

He rushed up to the side of the northern wall, pressing himself against it. After strapping the hunting rifle over his back, he pulled himself to the top of the wall. It was only a foot wide. Just enough for him to perch on.

The men in the guard towers were all looking outward into the valley. They weren't watching the manor grounds.

Perfect.

Raven reached back down, lying flat on the wall.

"Jump, boy," Raven whispered.

Creek launched himself up toward Raven's outstretched arms. Raven caught his front paws and folded him up toward his chest. Together they jumped over the other side.

Raven hid in the lush garden leading to the manor, watching the windows. Candlelight flickered from a single room on the second floor. He could see the mayor surrounded by bookshelves.

The distant barks of the other hunting dogs echoed in the valley. Had they discovered the other runaway dog? Or had they happened on the dead hunters?

Either way, no time to waste.

Raven sprinted through the bushes, flowers, and trees to the mansion, then used a knife to pry open a window, cracking the frame away. He pushed the window up, lifted Creek inside, then snuck in after.

They stalked through a darkened hallway filled with statues and paintings. Panes of moonlight shifted in, slightly illuminating his path to an expansive stairway circling around a taxidermized lion.

He took each step up carefully and quietly.

Based off what he'd seen outside, the mayor's office should be down the corridor to his left.

Raven curled slightly around the corner.

About thirty feet away, two men stood guard in front of a door. Each had a rifle propped against the wall beside them. Hanging lanterns flickered above. They stood with their arms folded, talking quietly.

Raven slipped out the knives he'd stolen from the hunters. He held each in his hand for a second, testing their balance.

He bent around the corner and threw the first knife. The blade cut through the air in a perfect arc. It buried itself into the neck of one guard.

As the guard grasped at the knife, falling to the floor, Raven pitched the second blade. The other guard had more time to react, instinct overriding logic. He held a hand up to block the knife.

It speared through his hand.

While his comrade remained still on the floor, blood pooling out of his fatal wound, the second guard pulled his knifed hand away from his neck. Crimson liquid pumped out of his hand as he fumbled to grab his rifle.

Raven was already sprinting down the hallway with Creek.

The dog reached the guard first. He tore at the man's leg while Raven wrapped his arm around the man's neck. Together they took the guard to the ground.

As the man flailed, desperately trying to throw them off, Raven tightened his grip, holding with all his strength, until the man went still.

Raven let the body fall, then kicked open the door to the mayor's office.

Instead of charging in, he ducked to the side, staying low.

He gestured for Creek to stay back.

Just as he'd feared, a shotgun blast roared from inside. Buckshot tore above Raven's head and into the wall and ceiling. Another pump and click followed before a second deafening blast.

"You bastard!" Clayton's voice rose from inside.

Raven shouldered his hunting rifle as a third shot ripped into the doorframe, splinters flying. He curled around the door, coming in low. The mayor was barely peeking over his big oak desk.

Squeezing the trigger, Raven fired a few wild shots into the desk, hoping one would hit the mayor.

Sure enough, Clayton fell backward with a groan.

Raven sprinted across the room, Creek following, right around the desk under all the taxidermized human and animal heads. He found Clayton sprawled on the floor. The mayor had one hand over his gut as blood stained his shirt and jacket.

"Help... me," Clayton said.

Raven aimed his rifle at Clayton's chest. "Where's the boy?"

"Who...?"

"Lily's boy. Mark. Where is he?"

Pallor washed through Clayton's face. He didn't have much more time in this world. Creek let out a growl.

"Down the hall." His voice grew quieter, and Raven had to lean in close. "The guestroom.... Locked... you..."

Suddenly, Clayton lunged up at Raven. In the hand he had been using to staunch his bleeding, the mayor held a knife. He must've had it hidden inside his jacket.

Raven barely drew back in time. The knife cut across the side of his ribs, ripping fabric. A searing pain cut through Raven's skin. He'd just narrowly avoided a fatal attack.

With Clayton lashing out with the knife again, Raven was forced to leap away. The mayor's injury must've been only a glancing wound. He'd been playing it up to draw Raven close.

"I'll mount you on that wall, boy!" Clayton roared.

He charged. Raven didn't have time to turn his hunting rifle on the mayor. Instead, he let the rifle drop and grabbed Clayton's wrists. Clayton sent a knee into Raven's stomach, then stomped hard on Raven's foot.

Raven pushed past the pain and squeezed on Clayton's wrist until the man dropped the knife. But Clayton wasn't out of the fight yet. He fought with all the desperation of a cornered wolf. He knew the only way out of this was to kill Raven.

With Clayton shoving and kicking, he backed Raven up toward the wall filled with the mounted heads of humans and animals. Creek ran in to help, but the mayor kicked the dog in the ribs, sending him tumbling away with a whine.

Then Clayton stomped hard on Raven's foot again and reached toward Raven's throat. "Die, boy!"

This time, Raven kicked Clayton's kneecap. A splintering crack split the air, and Clayton yowled. With the mayor distracted by fresh agony, Raven picked the man up slightly and swung him hard against the wall.

Right into the antlers of a taxidermied deer.

The antlers pierced the back of the mayor's neck and skull. The man's jaw fell slack, blood drooling out. His eyes bulged until finally they turned glassy.

"Look who's mounted on the wall now, asshole," Raven hissed. He couldn't help himself with all the anger flowing through him.

Creek whined as he joined Raven beside Clayton.

"You okay, buddy?" Raven asked the dog, comforting the animal.

The Akita seemed to be recovering his breathing and a cursory examination revealed no broken bones.

Then Raven turned back to Clayton's hanging body. He patted the corpse down and took out a keyring from a pocket. It had a key marked with the Mercedes Benz logo along with about fifteen others.

He had to save Mark. But that wasn't his only mission.

He scoured Clayton's desk, pulling any papers and maps that looked like they might have useful information. He dumped it all into his pack.

"Mayor, we found the missing team," a man's voice came from a radio sitting on Clayton's desk. "Landes and Ford are both dead."

There was, of course, no answer.

Raven's heart began to pound. He had to leave. Fast.

He raced out of the office, away from the lifeless gazes of the heads on the wall, and down the hall to his right.

"Mark, you in here?" he called.

There were six different rooms. Which was Mark's?

"Find it, Creek," Raven said. "Find the person!"

Creek's tail wagged as the dog sniffed at the floor, winding back and forth between the doors.

From outside, Raven heard yells. The braying of the dogs was growing closer. He thought he heard the smack of horse hooves on the concrete drive.

Suddenly, Creek froze, staring at one of the doors. Raven got out the key ring, ready to unlatch the lock.

But there too many keys to try.

Instead, he leveled his boot back, then slammed it on the door. The doorknob broke off in a spray of wooden chunks. Swinging open, the door thunked back to reveal a room from some twisted moonlit version of *The Great Gatsby*. A zoo full of taxidermy animals hung from the walls. Interspersed between them were more human heads.

A giant four poster bed sat on an intricate rug.

Was this really where Clayton kept the boy?

The clamor outside only increased. More yelling. More barking dogs. A spotlight swept over the front of the house, momentarily shining through the window.

That was when Raven noticed a figure curled in the corner. A skinny child hugged his knees to his chest.

"Mark." Raven lowered his rifle.

"Are you one of the monsters?" the boy asked.

Raven shook his head. "Your mom sent me to help you."

He held out a hand.

Shaking, the boy stood and took a step forward. Shaggy dark hair hung over his face. His pants and shirt hung off him like a windless sail on a mast.

The boy stumbled toward Raven but shied back from Creek.

"He's a friend," Raven said.

Creek wagged his tail playfully.

The boy nodded.

Together they started down the corridor.

Raven figured that he could sneak out over the walls and disappear into the woods again. But this kid looked like he would blow away in a gentle breeze. Even with Lily helping, there was no way Mark could run through the night with Raven. Carrying the boy would only slow them down.

Suddenly, glass exploded from a window down the left corridor. Gunfire lanced through it.

Another window down the opposite hall broke inward. More gunfire forced Raven to duck to the floor with Mark.

Clayton's men must've seen him through a window.

Shit.

Mark cried out and froze, but Raven grabbed him and pulled him away from the broken glass. If they tried running through the gardens, they might get gunned down.

They were out of time.

There was just one more option to escape.

Raven ran through the house and into the garage. A soft beam of moonlight filtered in from a small window. It revealed the old Mercedes he'd seen the other day.

Sure enough, one of the keys he'd stolen from Clayton unlocked it. He got Creek and the boy onto the floor by the back seat. The dog lay protectively over Mark.

"Stay low," Raven said.

Then Raven slipped into the driver's seat and started the ignition. A throaty rumble filled the garage when the engine started.

He flicked on the headlights, illuminating the manually operated garage door. No time to open it.

Instead, he revved the engine and threw the vehicle into drive.

Tires squealed as they grabbed hold, the smell of burning rubber filling the car. The vehicle shot forward, right into the flimsy garage door. The door collapsed over the windshield, part of it sliding away.

Raven twisted the wheel violently to shake the remnants of the door off as he barreled blindly down the drive. Gunshots rang out. One of the bullets connected with a headlight, blowing it out.

Mark cried out again.

"Stay down!" Raven yelled.

Only a lone beam speared out onto the driveway as Raven mashed the pedal. Fortunately, the gate at the end was still open.

The headlight illuminated two figures on horses standing

at the end of the drive. Two of Clayton's men aimed weapons at the vehicle.

"Oh shit," Raven said.

He knew he was screwed now. There was nowhere to go but forward. Right into those guns.

"I'm sorry, kid," Raven said.

He gripped the wheel and kept his foot on the pedal as he watched the riders take aim.

Suddenly, a figure darted toward the horses, waving their hands.

The single headlight illuminated Lily. She was trying to stop the horsemen or maybe even just distract them so Raven could escape with Mark.

That wasn't part of the plan.

"No, no!" Raven shouted.

She turned toward the SUV, locking eyes with Raven just as the guards fired. The bullets punched into her body, knocking her to the ground. Then they began to smack the car, punching into metal. Glass shattered, fragments blasting into the vehicle.

But Lily had given them just enough time.

Raven leaned down, yelling for Mark to do the same.

The vehicle plowed forward, and Raven braced himself for an impact with the horses.

Nothing came.

The gunshots stopped.

When Raven finally looked up, he saw the beasts in the rearview mirror with the men still in the saddle. They twisted to fire, but Raven swerved to the right, tearing down another dirt road.

The last thing he saw was Lily's lifeless body in the dirt.

Her final act was to save her son, and Raven wasn't going to let that go to waste.

Heart pounding, he pushed down on the pedal and raced into the night.

———

A scream pierced the darkness.

Palmer winced as he moved into position. With the enemy watching the terrain from on top of the motels and local businesses, there weren't a lot of ways to get to their camp undetected.

But there was one way. A way that Calvin would have likely used as a SEAL.

Lindsey had agreed to send a five-man team, including Palmer. Nuke and Rogers were two of the men who would wade through the river with Palmer to get past the guards and knock out as many of the enemy as possible. They would clear a route into the camp for Lindsey and the other ten Rangers to come swooping into town.

It all sounded straightforward enough.

But Palmer couldn't help having some second thoughts when he had first slipped into the cold rushing river. That was after hiking about a half-mile north past the enemy camp so they didn't have to fight their way upstream.

While the night air was a comfortable temperature, the water, fed by the snowmelt of the mountains, made his balls climb up into his stomach.

The distant sound of screaming prisoners made him forget about his stupid nuts. He waded with the other four Rangers through the water, wondering how long this gang had been terrorizing people.

The screams haunted Palmer as he waded through the chest-deep water. He used the time to consider something his mom used to say.

A bad man always gets his just desserts when God finally sends them to hell. But sometimes God works too slowly, and the good guys got to help hurry up the whole process.

Tonight, Palmer was going to do the Big Guy a favor.

The only ones he would spare would be used for intel, and after that, Palmer was going to find a way to get rid of them too.

They soon got past the first line of defenses undetected.

The cold seeped into Palmer's bones. He could barely feel his fingers now. The current started to get faster as they made their way toward their ultimate destination.

Palmer signaled for the Rangers to follow him toward the shore.

They quickly got out next to a screen of trees by Yampa Street. Palmer emptied the water from his M4, then pulled the charging handle.

He motioned for Rogers to lead with his partner straight toward the nearest building: a natural foods grocery store. Atop it were two other Skull guards.

As Rogers' team moved toward the building, Palmer took Nuke and the other Ranger toward the camp.

Their goal was the Muddy Creek Motel one block north of the Rabbit Ears Motel. There they would take out the two men on the roof, then use the position to eliminate as many other guards as possible. That would allow Lindsey's force to storm the pedestrian bridge across the river.

The agonized screams of another woman wailed into the night. Men's laughter drifted between the buildings.

Palmer's blood boiled.

He directed Nuke and his partner to follow him into the backdoor of the motel. They cleared the hall and made it up to the rooftop access door without incident. Slowly, Palmer opened the door.

The two Skull guards on the flat roof still had their rifles aimed at the woods across the river.

At Palmer's signal, he and the Rangers rushed the guards as quietly as they could.

The sickening shrieks from below and the laughs and yells of the men helped mask their approach.

In seconds, Palmer was on the first guard. He wrenched the man backward with one hand over the Skull's mouth. With his other, he cranked his arm around the thug's neck and locked it into place.

The man could no longer scream or breathe when Palmer took him to the ground. He tightened his grip, clamping his arm down tighter, and securing the man's kicking legs with his own.

At the same time, Nuke snapped the second guard's neck.

Palmer's target passed out in his arms from the lack of blood flow to his brain. He gently let the guy slump on the roof and checked the man's pulse.

There was none.

He'd never killed a man up close like this before.

Never felt a man's spirit leave his body. But there was no regret in his heart, especially with the screams below.

That was the only motivation he needed to know he had done right by his Creator. Just like his momma had said. Sometimes the good guys had to do bad things.

Quickly, Palmer and the Rangers shouldered their rifles and dropped into shooting positions. Nuke lay prone, sighting up their enemy.

Palmer turned back and used his binos to scope the roof of the grocery store first.

Rogers' team had taken out their marks and were in position. They flashed hand signals confirming they were ready.

Then Palmer directed his rifle at the Rabbit Ears Motel

where another two guards were. While his team would take those ones out, Rogers' team would take out the guards to the north that they'd passed while swimming.

He gave his own hand signal to tell them to get ready.

Then he sighted up the first Skull guard on the roof of the Rabbit Ears Motel. Taking in a breath, he gently squeezed the trigger. The man's head flicked back with a direct hit. He traced his scope over the other man just as rounds from the other Rangers tore into the man.

Shots burst from the grocery store.

Shouts erupted from below in response. Palmer trained his rifle over the side of the motel, sighting up the first Skull near the bonfire in front of the Rabbit Ears Motel. He squeezed the trigger, taking the man down with a burst to the side.

That left another twelve or so in the area, scattered between the trees and vehicles in the parking lot. There might be a few more they hadn't seen in the surrounding buildings.

"Stand down!" Palmer boomed at the men below.

Near the bonfire, there was a woman frozen in fear, two Skulls holding knives above her.

"Put down your weapons!" Palmer screamed again.

A couple of the gang members threw their hands in the air as they dropped to their knees. The two men who'd been about to rape the other woman looked like they were about to do the same thing, but Palmer decided he couldn't let them live.

He sighted up the first one and squeezed off a shot to his chest. Then he moved the rifle and fired at the other guy before he could run.

Both men dropped to the ground, writhing in pain as bullets tore into them from other Rangers that seemed to have the same idea Palmer had.

Lindsey led the other Rangers across the pedestrian bridge. They took positions behind the motorcycles and other abandoned vehicles in the lot.

The woman that had nearly been butchered stood frozen in fear as bullets whizzed past her into the thugs. She looked like a frightened rabbit surrounded by coyotes, no idea where to run.

When there was only a handful of resisting Skulls left, one lunged out of his position behind a sedan and wrapped an arm around the woman's neck as Lindsey's forces advanced.

"Don't move, or I shoot!" He put a pistol to the woman's head.

A couple of the thugs who'd escaped the initial onslaught ran out of sight through town. Palmer signaled for Rogers' team to go after them.

Then he aimed at the Skull holding the woman hostage. He started to backpedal.

"I'll kill her. You know I will!"

Lindsey stalked up toward the man, her pistol steadied with both hands. She snuck toward him. He hadn't noticed her yet.

Palmer looked between the sheriff and the Skull.

By any count, the Rangers had already won this battle. All that hung in the balance was this one poor woman's life.

Either she died as a human shield for the gang member or he stole her away only to force himself on her later until he killed her and left her behind.

Palmer pushed his scope back up to his eye and focused on the man. Lindsey was just behind him now, only a few feet away. Then he must have heard her footstep. He whirled around on her.

But neither he nor Lindsey got off a shot before Palmer did.

He fired at the man's head. The bullet took off the top of his skull.

The woman shrieked as the thug collapsed next to her.

Lindsey waved her Rangers on as they spread through the parking lot. They began securing the surviving prisoners near the thicket of Aspens and handcuffing the two Skulls that had given up.

Palmer left Nuke to hold security.

With their meager numbers, he worried another Skull might try to slip past. But they would do the best they could to hunt the monsters down.

He rushed down the motel stairs and joined Lindsey. She already had the two Skull prisoners on their knees by the campfire.

"Good work, Palmer," she said as he approached. "You saved my ass."

He nodded slightly.

She turned back to the prisoners. "I want you to tell me why I shouldn't just roast you both in that fire."

"You probably will no matter what I say," said one of the men. He had a dark goatee and a torn leather jacket.

"What's your name?" Lindsey asked.

"Hugh O'Donnell, ma'am," he replied politely with a grin.

Palmer grimaced. He wanted to blow that grin right off his face.

"Hugh, want to tell me why you attacked our warehouses in Gould?" Lindsey asked.

"Orders," Hugh said.

"From who?"

Hugh shrugged. "You blew out the brains of the man that gave 'em. Shupert there was our leader."

He looked to the man Palmer had shot in the head a few minutes earlier.

"Shupert, huh?" Lindsey asked. "The leader of your dumbass gang..."

The other guy looked up with an animalistic gaze. "You fucked with the wrong gang, you fucking bitch."

Lindsey backhanded him with enough force he toppled over into the dirt. Then she gave him a kick right in his family jewels followed swiftly by a second.

"You're never breeding again, you piece of shit," she said.

Palmer held back an angry grin as Hugh stared on in what might have been shock.

She turned back to Hugh.

"Get talking, or I'll turn both of those things you call nuts into... how do I put it..." she said. "You know how they make wine?"

Palmer pressed the heel of his palm into his other hand. "First you got to smoosh 'em with your boot."

"Just like that," Lindsey said, raising a boot dangerously close to him.

Hugh laughed. Palmer raised his rifle at Hugh's head. That shut him up.

"Okay, take it easy," Hugh said. "Shupert made a deal with an Indian leader. I never liked it. Most of the other guys didn't either, but it kept us paid, and supplied."

"An Indian? You talking about Eddy Nez?" Palmer asked.

Lindsey glanced back at him.

"Yeah, the ugly dude with a bunch of scars," Hugh said.

"Where were you headed next?" Lindsey asked.

"Somewhere in Medicine Bow-Routt National Park, I think," Hugh said, his words coming out fast. "That's where the Rattlesnakes wanted us next, from what I heard. But I really couldn't say for sure."

"And what were you supposed to do up there?" Lindsey asked.

"I think we were gonna meet some other people working in the Rattlesnake Union. They wanted to strike again like the attack in Gould."

Lindsey stared at the man for a moment longer. Palmer could almost see the calculations running through her mind. Whether she thought this man deserved to live or if she should redeem his one-way ticket to Satan's playground right now.

In the end, she backed away and went back to a group of four Rangers holding security. "Go grab our SUVs, then throw these guys in the back of one and get them to Golden."

The other Rangers continued helping the surviving civilians while Lindsey joined Palmer to talk in private.

"What's in Wyoming?" he asked.

"I really couldn't say," Lindsey said. "All our best-stocked warehouses, the rails, armories, and more are here in Colorado."

"Unless that's exactly what Eddy's after, and he's starting in Wyoming to get 'em."

Lindsey held his gaze. "What are you thinking?"

"Maybe he's massing an army up there to skirt around the borders," Palmer continued. "Maybe he wants to come rampaging down the Front Range, hitting us in Fort Collins, Estes Park, and all those places, then working his way down."

Lindsey looked back to the fresh corpses. "If that's the case, this first attack might have been just to test our defenses. Perhaps to strike fear. It's a perfect way to sap morale before they began an offensive campaign."

Palmer shivered. Not from the cold night air or his soaked uniform.

No, it was because of the frightening realization that this attack on Gould and these Skulls were only a small taste of what Eddy had in store for Colorado.

16

E DDY WOKE FROM A DREAM ABOUT WALKING INTO Clayton's office and finding Raven's head mounted on a wall.

Sitting up, he blinked at the glint of sun on a snowcapped mountain to his east. The dream lingered as the fog of sleep wore off. He wondered if it wasn't a dream, but a vision.

Was Raven dead now?

He would find out soon. His people would contact Clayton shortly to see how their hunt went. There was much to do this morning, and Eddy stood to stretch.

The sun beamed down, warming his scarred face.

All around the shore of the reservoir at Ridgway State Park, hundreds of men from the Rattlesnake Union were scattered. Some were preparing breakfasts of beans and toast over small fires. He noticed Kitcheyan was already up and sharpening his hatchet.

Other men cleaned their rifles on the rocky shore. A few smoked hand-rolled cigarettes by a picnic bench.

Eddy leaned down and secured his sleeping bag. When he was done, he tied it to one of Yanaba's saddlebags. She gave him a happy snort as he rubbed her muzzle. Then he climbed up with a foot in the stirrup and swung his other leg over, settling into the saddle.

From here, he could see the whole camp. Nearly three hundred people, all on the move at his behest. It felt good to have so much power.

Toward their south and east, the mountains formed walls of white and gray. The buzz of insects accompanied him as Yanaba took him along the gravel and dirt paths beside the reservoir's shore.

The prisoners were tied up near the edge of the water where they would drown if they tried to escape in their bonds. Jay was down there now too, patched up, but under watch just in case. Eddy would visit his old friend soon, but first he had a meeting with the leaders of the groups that had rallied to his banner here.

He rode through their camps along the shore. The militias he'd wrangled from Silverton and Ouray were amounting to about forty people. A good sixty Comanche troops led by Williams camped next to the almost one hundred Rattlesnakes from the Navajo Nation and nearly fifty men from the Apache who'd followed Robert. Fifty of the Liberty Militia members, led by Lincoln, were part of the group as well.

And this was just one small slice of the Rattlesnake Union.

Other militias and members of the groups represented here were spread throughout the New Frontier. Many were already congregating in Wyoming, waiting for their next orders. That was where the Skulls were supposed to go too after they finished their mission ransacking the border near Gould.

The Liberty Militia and Comanche leaders were waiting for Eddy at a campfire, drinking coffee and looking agitated.

Eddy dismounted his horse. He approached the leader of the Liberty Militia, Ryan Lincoln.

The conman gave Eddy a wide smile with a cocky confidence. His grin reminded Eddy of a carpetbagging politician.

"Are you all ready for the next phase of this war?" Eddy asked.

"The Liberty Militia is more than ready to roll out," Lincoln said.

The Liberty Militia and their religious zealotry were not a natural fit with the Rattlesnake Union. Their forces at this camp consisted of people who society had forgotten and pushed to the shadows. All had been seeking a feeling of belonging and acceptance, which Lincoln had happily taken advantage of.

Early in the Collapse, they had raided National Guard facilities in New Mexico, securing heavy weapons and explosives invaluable to this war. That was a major reason why Eddy put up with Lincoln's bullshit to have them on his side.

"How have the men from Ouray and Silverton taken to your militia?" Eddy asked.

"It's unfortunate that both of them had such, shall we say, unreliable leaders," Lincoln answered. "But the promise of salvation seems good enough for those people. I think they'll do just fine."

He continued to Leonard Williams, the head of the Comanche. He was built like a linebacker with muscles roping around his bones in gnarled knots.

"And you, Williams?" Eddy asked.

The hulking man nodded with a grunt.

"I'm proud to have you two here to fight with the Rattlesnakes," Eddy said. "As soon as Robert arrives, we'll start talking strategy... In the meantime, there are a couple of new developments."

"Oh?" Lincoln asked.

Williams didn't seem quite as intrigued, merely sipping his coffee.

"We've heard rumors that Senator Shelby is gaining on Diego."

"And why does an election between these ungodly men concern us?" Lincoln asked.

"Because Shelby wants to withdraw all the foreigners from the New Frontier," Eddy said. "He may even be considering eliminating all federal government involvement in the New Frontier."

"Hmm, that's exactly what we want," Lincoln said. "God does work in mysterious ways. I've half a mind to go campaigning for Shelby if that's the case."

"In a manner of speaking, we will be," Eddy said. "My hope is to take advantage of the situation. First, by giving him more fuel for his campaign. Make the New Frontier look like a beast that cannot be tamed. That's where you all come in."

Williams grinned slightly at that. "We will no longer put up with the fed's rule here. But how will you be sure Shelby isn't just another liar looking to trick the citizens and *us*?"

"I'm hoping that with some perseverance, we can open some lines of communication with him."

"How in God's good graces do you propose that?" Lincoln asked. "He's not going to talk to us."

"No, he won't," Eddy said. "But he will talk to the Navajo Nation government."

"I didn't think they were on friendly terms with you."

"Let's just say we've still got people in Window Rock loyal to our cause. In fact, I've been, how do you phrase it, *protecting* some of the family members of certain government officials there. They're bound to cooperate with us, and they'll make it easier for us to get what we want from Shelby."

"What about Tso?" Lincoln asked. "He doesn't seem like a man who would stand for this, even if you can twist the arms of a few Navajo Nation politicians."

"Don't worry about Tso." Eddy waved his hand. "He won't be holding on to power much longer."

"What do you mean?"

Eddy gave him a dismissive wave. "That's all I can say for now. You'll just have to have *faith* in me."

Lincoln considered that for a moment before drinking more of his coffee while they waited for Robert. He searched the crowds behind them for his second-in-command, growing impatient.

Galloping sounded from the shoreline.

Finally, Robert was on his way, racing toward them.

Robert pulled on the reins to slow his horse but didn't dismount.

"Eddy, we need to talk," he said. Sweat beaded down his tanned skin. He held out a radio. "I just got news."

"What?" Lincoln asked.

"News for *Ahiga*," Robert said. "Not you."

"You can't share it with us?" Lincoln asked.

Eddy looked to Robert, sensing something bad had happened.

"Speak," he said.

"But..." Robert protested. A vessel bulged in his forehead.

"Speak," Eddy insisted. "We're in front of allies and friends."

Robert fidgeted in his saddle. "It's the Skulls. The Rangers tracked them down and attacked their camp. Only three Skulls escaped. They made it to the Rattlesnake camp outside Milner."

Eddy felt the chill turn to fire, rage filling his chest.

"Have everyone at Milner head north immediately," he

said. "Tell them to put as much ground as they can between themselves and the Rangers."

"I thought the Rangers were no threat," Williams said in a low, almost menacing voice.

"They aren't," Eddy snapped.

"They wiped out most of the Skulls."

"Maybe you underestimated them," Lincoln said cautiously. "Maybe we should rethink this next attack."

Williams harrumphed in agreement.

Now anger flared sharp in Eddy's gut. These people were so driven by greed and their own selfish ambitions, they feared a fight.

"I never said this would be easy," Eddy said.

Lincoln scoffed. "No, but this is a major setback. I don't much like the Skulls or their sinful ways, but we do need them. Needed, I should say."

"Never let a good tragedy go to waste." Eddy said. "We will turn this into an opportunity."

Lincoln pulled a hand through his slicked-back hair. "You're going to have to explain this one."

Again, Williams grunted.

Eddy got the sense he was standing in front of a crashing tidal wave. The Skulls' defeat was tragic. But what was worse would be if these people started questioning him.

He couldn't allow that.

He glanced southward along the reservoir.

Their prisoners, from Jay to the CVRTF members and USAMRIID, were tied up in long ropes, strung together and chained to the trees.

"Have any of you heard the parable of the spider?" he asked.

The group's momentary confusion was just enough to thwart their collective warpath.

"I'll summarize it for you. An old man was walking through the forest, searching for a great animal to represent his tribe. He was chasing a deer, hoping to take the antlered animal home. He believed it would represent his people's wisdom and strength.

"While he stalked through the woods, he became entangled in a web. Sticky invisible strings wrapped around his body, and a small spider crawled toward him."

Eddy had the group's attention now. They gave him wary looks, as if they thought he was crazy.

Fine, he thought. *Just so long as they listen.*

"The old man told the spider what he was doing and demanded to be released," Eddy continued. "The spider laughed. 'You want the deer to represent your people? An animal afraid of every breaking branch? An animal that will run at the first thought of danger?'

"'A buck does not run,' the old man said. 'A buck stands its ground and fights.' Again, the spider laughed. 'A buck will charge another buck, even if that buck is dead,' the spider said. 'Bucks will charge a *tree* that looks like antlers. How many have gotten their antlers tangled in branches and died? Does a spider do this?'

"The old man was quiet for a moment. The spider answered himself, 'A spider is patient and strategic. If you want wisdom, it is through wisdom that a spider sets its trap. And then the spider doesn't run blindly through the woods. No, the spider waits for all to come to it. Just like you've fallen into my web today. Destiny has brought you here, but *I* have imprisoned you.'"

Eddy had taken some liberties in his storytelling. He hoped the message was clear enough.

"We will be the spiders," Eddy continued. "We will bring the enemy to us. To our traps. We will kill them, yes, but instead of us charging at them blindly like an incensed dumb stag, we will drive them toward our own invisible webs."

From his pocket, he withdrew a small piece of paper and wrote down a short message, along with his sat phone number.

"Robert, take this message and deliver it to someone working for or with the Rangers," Eddy said. "One that's well past the boundaries of the New Frontier. Someone who seems important. If not the sheriff herself, then someone more vulnerable."

"I can take my men if it would be helpful," Robert suggested.

Eddy looked over at Kitcheyan and the other Apache in the neighboring campsite. Kitcheyan was a hazard when he was outside of Eddy's view, even if he wasn't intoxicated.

"No, leave them here with me," Eddy said.

"While you're there, find out as much as you can about the Rangers and their defenses."

Robert nodded but remained in the saddle.

"Is there something else?" Eddy asked.

"Yes. Something for your ears only."

"I'll be back later," Eddy said to the other leaders. He got back into the saddle of his horse and rode away from the fire next to Robert.

"What is it?" Eddy asked.

"Raven," Robert said. "He and that bitch escaped Clayton's men. Then Raven apparently broke into that compound and dispatched the mayor. We think he stole a map and intel on where some of our camps and militias are."

Eddy closed his eyes and took a deep breath, centering his anger.

"Think of this as an opportunity, like you said," Robert said.

"How?"

Eddy focused on the man.

"Raven's still alive for you to kill yourself," Robert went on. "With Clayton gone, you will have full control of his men. No need for the survivors to stay back at that compound. They can join our army too."

The anger remained but subsided enough for Eddy to see this was good news.

"Thank you, Robert," Eddy said. "Excellent idea. Put a bounty on Raven's head. I want him alive. For that matter, let's do the same for his family. We're going to catch him one way or another, and I've got some new ideas if that doesn't work. Do you understand?"

"Yes," Robert said.

"Good. Now go."

Robert kicked his horse in the flanks and took off while Eddy steered his horse toward the mountains. He needed time to think, time to plan.

So much had happened the past day.

As he rode into the forest, he considered what he'd told Williams and Lincoln about Senator Shelby.

If he won the election, Eddy would have fewer people to fight out here.

Perhaps it really was about time to make friends with the enemy. Perhaps it was time to reach beyond the New Frontier.

He'd already laid down the pathway to achieving that. Now it was time to execute.

———

Raven was beat. Mark slept in the passenger seat of Raven's Jeep with his head against the window. Creek had snuggled up next to the boy. The Akita seemed to sense the horrors the boy had endured.

Memories of how Mark's mother had died haunted Raven along the drive. He still had yet to tell the boy what happened and was grateful the child never saw.

Raven let out a sigh.

US Highway 34 took them north past rolling amber hills. Distant mountain peaks rose on either side. Ahead, he saw the shimmering blue water of his destination.

Behind him was a Chevy Tahoe with four Rangers. Apparently, Lindsey had sent them to support his mission in Ouray. Of course, he hadn't made contact with them until he was back to his Jeep and well on his way north.

But all the same, it felt good to have someone watching his back even as he neared his destination.

The drive took him past Shadow Mountain Lake and to the town of Grand Lake. Raven's escort SUV peeled off and started east toward Estes Park as he pulled off the highway and into safety of the town.

A pair of Rangers were blockading Portal Road. He showed his identification to them, and they let Raven through, telling him Lindsey was waiting at the marina.

While the town was only a shadow of its former self, a few people still meandered about the picturesque streets and fished off the docks. Two people even had a rowboat on the lake.

Some of the small grocers and restaurants had also been reopened. Of course all the souvenir shops, ice cream bar, and other businesses intended for tourists had remained shuttered.

A familiar white Bronco, three Ranger SUVs, and an early 1970s Cadillac de Ville were parked near the Grand Lake Marina. It consisted of a two-story brown building that had fallen into disrepair and a roofed dock. Part of the dock had sailboats and pontoon boats tied up to it that looked ready to sail. The rest was filled with half-sunken boats that had been neglected since the Collapse.

Toward where the pier met the land, Raven spotted a handful of people. He could just make out Lindsey, Blair, Palmer, and a few other Rangers guarding the area.

As the Jeep's tires crunched over gravel, Mark woke up.

"Where... where are we?" he asked.

"Somewhere safe," Raven said.

"Is my mom going to meet us here?"

Raven wasn't sure how to answer that even though he had anticipated the question. Maybe he was going to be telling Mark what happened sooner than he thought.

"Not right now," Raven replied after a beat.

"When then?"

"I'm not sure, but for now, you're safe and that's what matters. That's what she wanted... wants."

"Okay."

"I'm going to introduce you to some friends of mine. Is that okay? They're going to take you to a new place for you to stay where it's really fun."

Mark patted Creek and nodded.

Raven's insides felt like they had turned to stone. He felt so terrible for this child. Try as he might, he couldn't get Lily's face out of his mind. If only things had turned out differently.

But he couldn't keep dwelling on what happened. He had to focus on the present.

"Stay here with Creek," Raven said. "I'll be right back."

He parked and got out of the Jeep.

Calvin was already striding over to meet him. To his surprise, the Steel Runner wasn't alone. Lara Lithgow had joined him.

"God, man, you're a sight for sore eyes," Raven said,

meeting Calvin first in a handshake. Then he pulled the man in close for a hug. "It's good to see you up and about. Although I wish it were under better circumstances."

Calvin pulled back, grinning. "Shit, man, don't we all. But I heard about everything you went through. Raven, you got to have a damn good guardian angel."

"Maybe two or three of them. Lindsey told me about California. Mouse's family good?"

"They're adjusting. Hell, I got to say, your sister and Allie have been great, welcoming them all at the Refugee Center." Calvin put a big arm around Lara's shoulder. "Same with our friend Lara. Absolute godsend."

"We've got a good community."

"And I'm fitting to be a long-term part of it. Staying here just as long as y'all will have me."

"There any question about that?" Raven couldn't help smiling. "Lord knows we need more guys like you around." Then his happiness deflated. "Look, I got Mark in the car. He's in a rough spot. Very fragile, you know?"

"I get it." Calvin motioned to Lara. "After what I heard about Mark, I figured we could use some help."

"Calvin told me everything." Lara gave Raven a sympathetic smile. "I'll do all I can to help Mark get adjusted to Estes Park. Just like how you all have helped me."

"Thanks, Lara," Raven said. "Of course, he doesn't have a grandmother like you do. It's going to be much harder for him."

"I'm willing to share mine with him."

Raven put a hand on Lara's shoulder and gave her a gentle squeeze. "I appreciate this very much."

They looked back to Mark, who was holding Creek in the Jeep.

"It wasn't so long since I was in that seat, coming with you from the New Frontier," Lara said. "I'll go talk to him and see if I can coax him out."

"Thanks. I know he's in good hands." Raven watched Lara walk off before speaking to Calvin. "Remarkable how far she's come in such a short period of time."

Calvin brushed a hand over his black, tightly curled hair. "She's been a huge help at the Refugee Center when she and your sister drop by."

"I can only imagine." Raven nodded toward the Cadillac. "Did you get a new ride?"

"Borrowing it from the Refugee Center. Some of the people of Estes Park have been nice enough to loan us vehicles."

"They're good people," Raven said. Then he gestured toward where Lindsey, Blair, and Palmer were talking closer to the marina. "You going to join us?"

Calvin let out a breath. "I'm headed straight to the Refugee Center with Lara as soon as she can convince Mark we're here to help."

"So you're not going to be part of the intel meeting?"

Calvin shook his head. "My calling has changed. Running steel and chasing guys down in the desert is behind me. I want to focus on keeping the families here safe."

"Mouse's family?"

Calvin nodded. "Them, too, of course. Can't leave them again. Especially not after that last attack. Way too close for comfort."

"I hear you." Raven had been through this a thousand times with Sandra and Allie.

"You know I support you, brother, but if some of the Rattlesnake's people come through here again, I won't forgive myself if I'm somewhere far away," Calvin said. "I've got people to protect."

Raven understood and slapped him on the shoulder. "No need to explain."

"We're about ready, Cal!" Lara called from the Jeep.

She was helping Mark down from the vehicle. The boy's eyes still had a wet sheen, but he gave them all a half-hearted smile.

Creek bounded out of the Jeep afterward, his tail wagging.

"I better get going," Calvin said, turning back to Lara and Mark. "Got precious cargo to deliver to Estes Park. Not too different from my Steel Running days after all."

Lara waved at Raven as she led Mark to the Cadillac. She spoke in a soft voice to the boy. Whatever she was saying, it was working.

Raven watched for a moment. The kid was yet another child orphaned by the violence of the New Frontier. All thanks to Eddy's ruthless campaign.

It was time to put an end to this.

He joined Lindsey and the group standing around a picnic table under the shade of the marina's roof.

Lindsey gave Raven a huge grin. "You have no idea how good it is to see you."

She embraced him briefly.

He wanted to hold on to her longer, not realizing until then just how happy he was to see her as well. But he felt Palmer and Blair's eyes on him and pulled back.

"Good to see you, Raven." Palmer shook Raven's hand.

"Lindsey told us you know all about Steamboat Springs and the Skulls," Blair said. "Shall we get down to business?"

"Of course," Raven said. "Sounds like the info you all got was pretty wishy-washy. Hopefully, I can change that."

Raven reached into his pack and drew out a map that he'd stolen from Clayton's manor. He unrolled it on the table.

"There are marked Rattlesnake camps throughout the New Frontier." Dots speckled everywhere from Utah to Colorado. Raven jabbed a finger at Medicine Bow-Routt National Forest. "But since the Skulls said they're going to Medicine Bow, here's the closest camp in the area. Centennial."

Raven grabbed another stack of papers from his pack and deposited them on the table.

"It turned out the mayor kept records on many of the groups working for Eddy," Raven said. "I didn't have time to read these. Mostly just skimmed them over to see what I'd gotten while I was on the road. I think we've got some kind of bank records, inventories, and other stuff. From what Jay and I could tell, Ouray was a central trading post that the Rattlesnakes used to fence goods and deliver supplies to their allies. Those supplies include everything from meds for Wild Fire to ammunition."

Lindsey gestured for Palmer to take all the papers. "Thanks, Raven. This will be very helpful. Secretary Montgomery herself will be arriving later today."

"No shit?" Raven said. "Damn, been a bit since I saw her. Why's she coming?"

"Diego wants her out here," Lindsey said. "Plus, he's sending a platoon."

"Good news, but a platoon... that's nothing compared to Eddy's forces, I'm afraid."

"I know. But at least it's something." Lindsey sighed and looked at her watch. "Anyway, Raven, thanks for your work. Go get some rest. Say hi to Sandra and Allie. I've got to prepare to meet Charlize at Fort Golden. We're going to figure this all out."

"Wait," Raven said.

"Yes?"

"Did you tell Tso what happened with Jay?"

"No, but it's on my list of things. I'm sure the secretary will want to connect with Tso again."

"You think he was playing both sides all along?" Palmer asked. "Jay, I mean."

Raven thought about it but shook his head. "I don't think so. He was given a choice. Kill me, or have his family killed. As much as I hate to admit it, I probably would have done the same thing he did."

17

ONCE BACK AT FORT GOLDEN, LINDSEY BARELY HAD time to freshen up and down a cup of coffee. After last night's operation, the cot in the corner of her office looked almost too inviting. But there was no time to rest.

Taking a deep breath, she thought of what her old mentor, Estes Park Sheriff Marcus Colton, would have said.

Being brave in the face of a monster ain't easy. Being brave when you're surrounded by multiple monsters is nearly impossible. But when everyone's looking at you, you can't afford to piss your pants in fear.

You have to lead.

Lindsey had never appreciated just how true those words were. She leaned back in her office chair and looked out the window.

The peaceful mountains belied the violent reign of the Rattlesnakes and the spreading Wild Fire. Lindsey wasn't too far removed from the ranks of the Rangers to know they were frightened. They could smell the oncoming storm just as well as her.

From her window, she could see the front gate into the

fort. The chain-link barriers were being retracted. Three black SUVs waited outside.

That was her cue.

Secretary of Defense Charlize Montgomery was finally here.

Before she left the office, she took a deep breath and straightened her shirt.

She strode out into the hall past men and women in khaki Rangers uniforms.

After making her way outside, she spotted Palmer. Another six Rangers waited nearby, armed and ready to provide security.

The black SUVs rolled up and parked in front of them. The first and last SUV disgorged four Secret Service agents each, men and women in black suits forming a perimeter around the middle vehicle.

Lindsey made her way to Palmer.

"Lots of security," he remarked.

Finally, the door opened on the middle SUV. Charlize stepped out in jeans and a trim brown leather jacket. While most politicians wore stuffy suits, Charlize preferred dressing like she was *still* serving as a pilot in the Air Force.

Lindsey remembered Charlize for her confidence and poise. The woman commanded attention. She had the air of strength. The kind that exuded off someone who would fight tooth and nail to defend their country.

But Lindsey hadn't seen the secretary in about a year.

Now the woman walking toward her, using a cane to support herself, looked gaunt and pale beyond her years. Her hair was gray. It appeared so dry, it might flake off in the wind.

Lindsey tried not to show any surprise in her expression, but she must've done a poor job hiding her shock.

Charlize smiled as she approached. "I know. I look like

I've aged about thirty years in the past year and a half. You can blame the long-term effects of radiation poisoning for that."

"I'm sorry, ma'am," Lindsey said. "I didn't know."

"It's quite alright. I've got great care, and I'm glad to still be able to serve."

Lindsey offered Charlize a hand to shake. Charlize pulled her into a hug instead.

"It's great to see you, Lindsey." She turned to the deputy. "And you must be Cody Palmer? I've heard so much about you."

After introductions, Lindsey took them back inside Fort Golden to her so-called war room. Blair, Piard, Martinez, and Tiankai were waiting inside, along with Doctor Wheeler.

They settled into the chairs surrounding a central table. Normally filled with the loud voices of the FAC, the room seemed especially quiet today, all eyes on the secretary.

"I want to thank you all for being here today," Charlize said to the FAC. "Not just today, but since the beginning. Without your help, we wouldn't have come as far as we have in the New Frontier."

Blair gave her a stoic nod. "It is an honor, Madam Secretary."

"I understand some of you have reservations about continuing your support." Even in her weakened state, Charlize appeared stern. "I want to assure you, we're going to do what we can to turn more attention on the New Frontier."

"Excuse me for being blunt," Piard said, "but what happens if President Diego loses the election? We heard Senator Shelby wants to send us all home and focus on national rebuilding instead of international aid and relationships."

"You've heard correctly." Charlize's skinny fingers balled

up into a fist on the table. "We cannot allow this to happen. President Diego is currently ahead in this race, but yes, it's gotten much, much closer. However, if Diego wins, he will continue to prioritize the safety of all Americans and those who are willing to help us."

"Is that the only reason you're helping us now?" Piard continued. Of all the FAC members, she was always the most blunt. And the most willing to ask the questions on everyone's mind. "You must know how bad things are, to be here yourself."

"Things are bad, but we can turn them around. I'm here with the explicit mission to support New Frontier security with the resources allocated to us."

Charlize sat up straighter, wincing slightly from some pain.

"I want to cut straight to the chase," she said. "We have limited manpower we can afford to send here. I've got one platoon from 2nd Battalion's 6th Infantry Regiment, the Regulars, being mobilized as we speak."

"Have you heard what you're up against out there?" Martinez asked.

"Yes, Sheriff Plymouth has informed me. While we might be outnumbered, we have critical intel to share." She nodded to Lindsey, who took over.

"We know where the Rattlesnakes are going now with their allies," Lindsey said. "We not only know where, but how many people they have and where their leader is headed."

She set the maps and documents Raven retrieved on the table. The FAC members began poring over them.

"Raven Spears has once again risked his hide to provide this intel," Lindsey said. "We've even got estimates of the inventory of weapons and ammunition they have as well."

Piard looked up from studying one of the intel documents. "Has this been verified?"

"It hasn't been completely verified, but this is from what we believe to be an excellent source."

"Thank you very much, Sheriff," Charlize said. "This intel will be crucial. It will take us a couple days to figure out the best way to neuter Eddy and his forces, but in the meantime, we have other business. Doctor Wheeler, you've been waiting patiently. Go ahead."

The doctor put on his reading glasses and raised a piece of paper. "Good news and bad news. Good news is that the development of the Regeneraid facility is on track. We're beginning our first real production run of Commander now. The bad news is we're already behind, and it's only going to get worse no matter how fast we ramp up to full capacity. With the rate of infected refugees pouring into our quarantine stations at the border, I'd estimate that we're seeing thirty to forty percent community spread out there. We won't be able to keep up with our needs if this continues."

Tiankai shook his head.

"What about the community ambassador program?" Blair asked. "I thought this would help increase New Frontier uptake of the cure."

"It's working," Wheeler said. "Communities are responding more kindly when it's people they know coming back with the cure. But it's too slow to keep up with the Wild Fire spread."

"Christ," Piard said. "We're truly in a bag of *merde*."

"Which brings me to an idea," Charlize said. "We've asked our foreign allies for help. We've scrounged up all we could from within our borders. And now, more than ever, I think it's time we meet with another ally. President Tso from the Navajo Nation indicated he is willing to talk. With him, we might better be able to understand Eddy and how we can defeat him. The Navajo Nation is also willing to support these efforts with manpower."

"That's great news," Lindsey said. "When do we call him?"

"Well, the plan is to do it in person." Charlize got up from the table. "I know I just got here, but time's wasting. Can you organize a trusted security detail for an early departure tomorrow morning?"

Lindsey rose from her seat, eager to get out there. "I'll have some of my best ready to go immediately."

———

Only a day after Charlize arrived in Colorado, Palmer stood beside Lindsey on the dusty makeshift airfield near Window Rock. Majestic, natural golden rock rose like leafless trees around them. A hot wind blew grit across his face. Rangers were unloading aid cargo from a Chinook that had been sent to the Navajo Nation as a goodwill gesture.

Navajo police officers helped stack the crates and boxes onto a pair of flatbed transport trucks. Other vehicles waited near a pair of metal hangars where airfield workers milled about.

Beyond the hangars were some of the brick and stone buildings of Window Rock. They were covered in dust, practically glowing red under the hot sun. In every other direction, it seemed the landscape was nothing but arid desert, rock, and dried vegetation.

Already sweat made Palmer's shirt cling to his back. The M4 strapped over it didn't help. Hell, it seemed to soak up the heat of the sun, adding to the feeling of being baked alive.

While Lindsey spoke with Charlize in hushed voices on the tarmac, Secret Service agents surrounded them.

Palmer's job was to secure the perimeter. He stood in front of a group of twelve Rangers, including Rogers and Nuke.

President Tso had assured them Window Rock was safe, but today, he wasn't taking any chances.

"Rogers, Nuke, take the northwest quadrant," Palmer began. "You'll be Guardian Alpha."

He continued gesturing toward the Rangers and various parts of the airfield.

One by one, he sent them on their way and gave them callsigns.

A Navajo Nation police officer strode toward them from one of the hangars. "President Tso's ready when you are."

The officer led the group—Charlize, Lindsey, the Secret Service Agents, and Palmer—toward one of the hangars. The shade provided welcome relief from the sun.

Between a few Cessnas, other Navajo police officers stood guard. They each carried rifles. By the looks on their faces, they seemed to think Charlize and her group were the enemy. Palmer could feel the eyes of the Navajo men on him, studying him as he walked past.

He felt kind of like an elk that had just wandered into a bear's den.

Only seconds before, he'd thought *he* was the bear.

At the center of the hangar, surrounded by stacks of crates and barrels, there was a single long table. Four more Nation police officers stood near the crates, watching each corner. Two men sat at the table.

One was an older Native American man with gray braids and a face filled with deep wrinkles. He wore a khaki suit and a bolo tie.

The other man looked to be in his mid-forties. He wore a plaid shirt with a leather vest, jeans, and cowboy boots.

Both stood as the group approached.

The older man stepped around the table and extended a hand to Charlize. "Good to meet you in person, Madam Secretary."

"And you, President Tso," Charlize replied. "Thank you for hosting us."

"It's our pleasure." Tso gestured to the other man. "This is Vice President Harrison Bitsui."

"Bitsui?" Charlize asked. "What happened to Vice President Chase?"

A sad look crossed Tso's face. "He had Wild Fire. He passed only a week ago."

"I'm so sorry," Charlize said. "This disease has taken too many already."

Charlize introduced the rest of the group to Tso and Bitsui as they all took their seats again.

Palmer stood a few feet away from the table. He picked a spot by the crates where he could keep an eye on the group.

A few Secret Service Agents spread out behind Charlize and the others. He felt a little better knowing there was so much security, but he couldn't help thinking about the fact Eddy had once been a Navajo Nation police officer.

Palmer scanned the officers around Tso.

Were any of these men still in contact with Eddy? Maybe even believers of his poisonous vision?

No, Palmer thought. *No way Tso picked these people if he couldn't trust them.*

Then again, that didn't matter, because Palmer didn't trust them.

As Charlize began talking about the latest Wild Fire developments and Wheeler's findings, Palmer surveyed the police. Three kept gazing about the room as if watching for danger.

The fourth, a man with a thin beard and muscles pressing against his uniform, seemed to glance at the president and vice president frequently. The nametape on his chest pocket read: KIPP.

Palmer worried he was being paranoid. But Lindsey had once told him it was better to be caught being paranoid than be caught with your pants down.

He brought his radio up for a SITREP.

"All security units, report," Palmer said.

One by one, his teams reported no contacts.

Charlize finished her update on Wild Fire.

"Will you be able to supply us more of the Commander medicine?" Tso asked.

"We will be happy to." Charlize folded her hands together. "I know this comes at a critical juncture for both our governments. We're hoping you'll help us as well."

"No act of goodwill comes without a cost." Tso smiled, his wrinkles deepening. "How do you expect us to repay you?"

"We're looking for information on Eddy Nez," Charlize explained. "Recent intelligence suggests he's staging his Rattlesnakes and his so-called Rattlesnake Union for a major attack. We need help hunting him down and stopping him before he can strike."

Lindsey explained the information they had and even provided maps and intel to Tso.

Tso let out a sigh.

"I feared this day would come, but never believed it would be this fast," he remarked after seeing it all. "It breaks my heart to see how many of our men and women followed Eddy after a Dark Wind took him."

"Dark Wind?" Charlize asked.

"The Navajo believe, when men engage in evil, it's because of a dark wind that fills them with a bad spirit."

Palmer resisted the urge to roll his eyes. Evil men in his book were evil because they were selfish assholes. Saying a spirit was the cause was a copout.

"Eddy wasn't always this way," Tso continued. "I knew him as a young man, but that young man is now gone. He must be stopped."

"Anything else you can tell us about Eddy or the men of the Rattlesnakes could be helpful," Charlize said.

Palmer noticed Kipp shift on his heels.

That caught his attention, and he focused on Kipp.

What if he was a plant sent here by Eddy? Then Eddy would know all the intel they had on him.

Kipp lowered his hand as if he was poised to grab his handgun.

Or maybe this wasn't about intel, but rather an assassination.

Sweat dripped down Palmer's neck. His pulse began to race.

Shoot, was he going crazy? Was he imagining things?

He watched Kipp, who was fixated on Tso and Bitsui.

No, he had to trust his instincts.

A sinking feeling started to pull at his insides.

Maybe he could head this off.

He took a couple steps toward Kipp. The man was too distracted by Tso and Bitsui to notice Palmer.

When he was close enough, he tapped Kipp's shoulder. The man practically jumped, looking toward the deputy.

"Something the—?" Palmer started.

His question was cut off with the deafening crack of gunfire.

Screams erupted in the warehouse. Yells. More gunfire. All of it happened in a kaleidoscopic blur.

Palmer had less than a second to take it in.

Kipp had taken out his handgun. He started to lift it toward Bitsui.

And it was at that moment Palmer saw the vice president also had his own pistol out. It was aimed right at Tso.

Tso was dead.

The president's body was crumpled over the table, blood pooling from his chest. The vice president had killed him.

At least, that was what it looked like. Palmer struggled to believe it.

Bitsui began to wheel his pistol up toward Charlize.

Palmer operated on instinct, turning his weapon on Bitsui and firing. Bullets ripped into Bitsui, knocking him backward.

All the while, a Secret Service agent lunged to throw his body in front of Charlize's. Another pulled her to the floor.

Palmer scanned the carnage, ready to fire again. Two of the Navajo officers were now trying to staunch the bleeding in Tso's chest.

Kipp had his handgun out, pointed where Bitsui lay on the floor.

Secret Service agents flooded around Charlize, lifting her to her feet and whisking her away. They formed a huddle around Charlize as they escorted her out toward the chopper.

Palmer ran over to find Lindsey had flecks of blood across her chest.

"Sheriff!" Palmer yelled.

His heart raced faster until he realized it wasn't her blood.

Navajo police officers swarmed the warehouse, their voices calling out in a clamor.

"All units fall back to guard Eagle One," Palmer said over his radio, using Charlize's callsign. With his ears still ringing, he couldn't hear if there were any replies. He could only hope the Rangers and the Secret Service were doing what they were supposed to.

Amid the chaos of policemen gesturing wildly and screaming things that Palmer could only just begin to hear. He kept his eyes on Kipp as he pushed past a couple of panicked officers.

When Palmer reached Kipp, he grabbed him by the shoulders, but Kipp shrugged out of his grip. Lindsey snatched the man's wrist, squeezing until Palmer could disarm Kipp.

A few of the nearby policemen looked bewildered, their eyes darting between Lindsey and Palmer and the bodies of Bitsui and Tso.

Palmer's ears were ringing, but he could make out the officers' voices now.

Some demanded to know what happened. Others called hopelessly into their radios for medical aid.

"Let me go," Kipp said.

"Stop resisting then," Palmer said.

Kipp loosened up, and Palmer let him stand.

He stared hard at Palmer, anger radiating from his eyes.

"What the hell did you do?" Kipp asked.

"Me? I saw that look in your eyes! Then Bitsui... he shot Tso and was about to hit Charlize. You looked like you were going to shoot Tso too."

"I was going to *save* the president." Kipp pushed Palmer away and rushed over to the officers hovering around Tso's still form. Some of them looked up and stared daggers at Lindsey and Palmer. "I could've prevented this. But you stopped me."

Palmer's brain was finally catching up to everything he had seen.

The wild urgent nerve impulses from the flagging adrenaline gave way to rational thought.

"How'd you know he was going to shoot Tso?" Lindsey asked.

"I didn't." Kipp's nose scrunched into a snarl. "I just got a really bad feeling. Cop instinct, you know? Or maybe you wouldn't..."

"I was just trying to protect—" Palmer began.

"Convenient timing," another man said. He had been one of the policemen trying desperately to save Tso. Blood covered his hands and the front of his shirt. His nametape read: Summerhill. "You wanted this. Your government wanted this. Maybe Eddy was right."

"That is evil talk about an evil man possessed by a powerful dark spirit," Kipp said. Then he pointed at Palmer. "But this man is wrong. This man..."

Kipp looked ready to explode, pulled between both sides. Palmer finally took a second to count the other officers in the warehouse. There were about fifteen of them. And all were looking at Lindsey and Palmer.

Palmer got a rotten feeling in his gut.

These guys were mad. They wanted someone to blame. He didn't fault them for it. Not after Tso had just been assassinated.

There was bound to be a lengthy investigation to get to the bottom of this later. But right now, tempers and emotions were flying high. These men wanted blood.

And if Palmer put himself in their shoes, he could see why they might suspect he was as much a part of this as Bitsui.

He put his gun back in its holster and held up his hands defensively, taking a step back. "Look, I'm really sorry, fellas, but I honest to God was just here to protect Charlize.

I saw what I thought was an assassination about to happen and—"

"And you helped it along," Summerhill said.

"He did no such thing," Lindsey said. She lowered her tone. "I'm sorry about President Tso. Truly I am."

A voice chimed in over Palmer's earpiece. "Rangers One and Two, this is Archangel Alpha." It was the head of Charlize's Secret Service personnel. "We need to take off. Now."

"We're on our way," Palmer said.

"Look, we have to get our Secretary of Defense to safety," Lindsey said.

"Get off our land," Kipp said. "You've brought enough destruction. Go."

Palmer noticed at least another four policemen with their hands on their holstered pistols. A couple had already drawn weapons. They weren't pointing them at Lindsey and Palmer.

Yet.

Lindsey and Palmer exited the warehouse as fast they could and headed toward the chopper.

Another six Navajo officers were near the Chinook, yelling and making wild gestures at the Secret Service agents near the open rear ramp. Palmer and Lindsey had to shove their way past and into the chopper as the Secret Service agents held back the Navajo men.

As soon as the agents retreated inside, a crew chief began closing the rear ramp. The whine of the engines and thump of the rotors grew louder.

Almost immediately, the Chinook took to the air.

Palmer barely had time to find a jump seat. Across from him was Charlize, her head in her hands, blood still matted across her face and clothes.

"What in God's name happened?" she asked him.

He told her everything.

"My God," she said. "This is a disaster."

She brushed a hand through her thin hair, smearing some of the blood on her fingers. "This is going to set back our relationship with the Navajo Nation a hundred years."

"I think this might be the end of it," Lindsey said.

Charlize used her sleeve to wipe the blood from her head. "I fear you're right, but even more, I fear the survivors back there will rally to Eddy. It reeks of a false flag operation."

"You think..." Palmer started to say.

"That Eddy planned this from the start?" The secretary sighed. "I have no doubt. Not only did he want Tso dead, but he wanted me out of the picture as well. Two birds, one stone."

"Three birds if you count the people that will rally to his banner now," Palmer said.

"Well, he's only got one bird so far," Lindsey said. "You're still alive, and if we can get the truth out about what Eddy did, then his plan will backfire. He'll have the entire Navajo Nation after his ass."

18

CALVIN WALKED DOWN THE CORRIDOR OF THE ESTES Park Refugee Center. Night had fallen.

With limited electricity, most of the passages were lit by a combination of candles and kerosene lanterns. It gave the place an eerie, haunted feeling. He couldn't help thinking he might run into a wandering spirit.

Of course, the only lost spirits here were the refugees seeking salvation from the Badlands. And they were whispering rumors of what happened at Window Rock.

Calvin approached two Rangers on guard that were discussing what had happened. He recognized them in the dim lighting as Fawn and... no that wasn't right.

Flannery and Thomas.

While volunteering at the Refugee Center and working to help organize guard patrols in the area, Calvin had made it his mission to get to better know the security teams around here.

After what he'd seen in Gould, he had to make sure they were ready for the evil in the New Frontier.

Of course, Estes Park was a large territory to defend. No matter how Calvin tried to help organize the Rangers' patrol routes, there was always some area that had to be left unguarded.

The Rangers spoke quietly about the events that had left President Tso dead. Calvin still wasn't exactly sure what had happened.

"Sorry to butt in," Calvin said.

The Rangers looked at him skeptically. He'd been getting a lot of that. He thought they would be happy to have his help and that of the other Steel Runners, but some didn't exactly seem to trust outsiders.

Not that he blamed them.

"Yeah?" Flannery asked.

"Do you know when the sheriff will be back?" Calvin asked.

"Not sure," Thomas said.

"But she's okay, I take it? Along with everyone else on our side?"

Flannery and Thomas both went silent. Thomas shrugged.

"Okay, I understand," Calvin said. "I know I'm not a Ranger, but I do care."

"Look, we think the sheriff and company are all good, but things have been messy and confusing," Flannery said. "Then they have you Steel Runners coming in here trying to do our job and... well, it's a lot for us to deal with."

"I'm not trying to take anyone's job," Calvin said. "Trust me, I wouldn't dream of replacing you guys. Just trying to help out best as I can is all."

Flannery seemed to soften up. "Well, truthfully, I appreciate that. It's just a little hard with all this backstabbing. Someone in Tso's own administration gunned him down. Someone he trusted. Gets you thinking that maybe it could happen here. You know?"

"I know," Calvin said.

Thomas was still quiet.

"Well, I guess just let me know if you guys need anything from me. I'm going to continue my rounds."

Calvin started down the opposite way, headed to check on Mark.

The boy had been assigned a cot in one of the rooms full of New Frontier orphans. He approached the room cautiously. Most of the children should be sleeping by now.

But as he neared the room, he heard children giggling.

The door was cracked slightly, letting out the flicker from a lamp.

Calvin nudged open the door wider.

Inside were ten boys and girls, all under the age of ten, sitting in a semicircle. Lara Lithgow stood in front of them, her hands outstretched as she told a story.

"That's when the great big bear said, 'Hey, that's *my* tail.'"

Again, the children erupted into laughter. Raquel and Frankie were amongst the smiling kids.

Calvin searched the faces to find Mark sitting on the edge of a cot. Allie Spears was next to the boy, holding his hand. Sandra was in the room watching over them all, seated beside Mark and Allie.

The Spears family never ceased to amaze Calvin. They'd done more for this community than people probably realized.

"You know what the mouse said?" Lara asked, looking around animatedly at the children. "*My* tail is better anyway! You take yours back, you big hairy monster!"

The children roared in glee.

Mark didn't clutch his belly and laugh like the others, but a slight smile at least cracked across his face. It would probably be a long time before he could really laugh.

Sandra turned her head just enough to catch Calvin's

eyes. She stood and snuck out around the entranced children as Lara continued her story.

"I know they should be sleeping," she whispered.

"I'm not judging," Calvin said. "Kids need a little laughter."

Sandra smiled as the children devolved into another giggling fit.

"It always amazes me just how resilient kids are," she said. "We all could use some happiness like that."

"Someday," Calvin said. He took a step back. "So, how is Mark?"

"He's in bad shape. He's malnourished and definitely dealing with a good amount of psychological trauma."

"Damn," Calvin whispered.

"Raven told me he doesn't know his mother died yet."

She explained what had happened to Calvin when Raven broke the boy out of the compound. He hadn't heard the full details of Mark's rescue up to this point.

"Jesus," Calvin said.

"Yeah... she was a brave woman, and Mark is alive because of her, but I can't imagine what she went through in those final moments of horror."

Sandra let out a sad sigh. In the flicker of candlelight, Calvin saw the exhaustion burning in the dark circles under her eyes. She was a resilient woman, hard-working, and tirelessly doing her best to improve the lives of others, just like her brother.

"Maybe you should go home," he suggested. "Get some rest. You'll be better for it."

"I have some more work to do," Sandra said. "What about you?"

"Same. I'm going back outside to make my rounds. Have a good night, Sandra."

"Thanks, Calvin."

He went to leave, but she reached out and touched his arm.

"Yeah?" he asked.

"It's good to have you here," she said. "Thank you for coming back. We're lucky to have you. I know Raven feels the same."

"I'm the lucky one." He dipped his head and then walked away, listening to the sound of laughter.

When he got outside, he was feeling rejuvenated by the joy from the children. He walked across the parking lot to the edge of the woods. The trees whispered in the breeze.

Maybe he would have heard the footsteps coming from around one of those trees if his guard wasn't down. But the children's happiness had distracted him.

He froze when he felt the unmistakable cold press of a steel gun barrel against the back of his neck.

"Don't turn around. Don't say a thing. Or I put a bullet through your skull," a man's gravelly voice said. His breath stank of onions and meat. "Then, I go in there and kill those families you've been watching."

"Who are you?" Calvin asked.

"Doesn't matter who I am. What matters is what you're going to do."

"What do you want?"

"For you to deliver a message to the sheriff of the Rangers," he said.

While keeping the gun pressed to Calvin's neck, the man stuffed a piece of paper into the Steel Runner's pants pocket.

"Make sure she gets it, or I'll come back for them kids," the man said.

Calvin fought back the anger burning through his chest. He wanted so badly to turn around and rip this bastard to pieces. But he didn't know if this guy had other allies waiting in the forest. Other men who might shoot him, then raid the hotel as he'd promised.

As much as it pained him to do so, he stood frozen. Not for himself, but for the Gomezes and all those innocent children.

"Do not turn around for five minutes," the man said. "Walk straight back into the hotel. If I see you look back, if I see you do anything I don't like, I will kill you. And then, well, I've already told you what I'll do next."

Calvin's fingers curled into fists. The hand closest to his holstered sidearm could just brush the metal. But by the time he pulled it out, a bullet would be lodged in his skull.

"You understand?" the man asked.

Calvin gave a nod.

The gun barrel left the back of his neck. The man, whoever he was, retreated so quietly, so carefully, that Calvin wasn't sure he'd even left at all.

The only sign that the man had departed was the lack of his stinking breath wafting up Calvin's nostrils.

Forcing himself to look straight ahead, Calvin walked across the parking lot. The eerie sensation he was being watched never let up.

Finally, when he entered the hotel and judged his five minutes had passed, he found cover behind a window. Then he looked back out toward the woods, seeing nothing moving in the tree line. Hands trembling slightly, he slipped the note from his pocket.

It said simply: "Eddy wants to talk to Sheriff Plymouth." The message was followed by a phone number.

Calvin's heart climbed into his throat. Eddy's people had penetrated the security in Estes Park. Gotten close enough to get a gun to Calvin's head.

And if they could do that to him, they could do that to anyone.

_____

Bonfires shimmered around the small town of Encampment, Wyoming. Eddy rode through the town on Yanaba. He held his head high. Men and women's excited voices filtered between the Great Divide Restaurant & Lounge and the humble Presbyterian Church. Lincoln, Williams, and Hayden had turned those buildings into their temporary camps.

But a simple night's rest stop had turned into a celebration when news of the most recent success reached the group.

Yanaba took Eddy down the gravel street. Some smaller groups of men and women hung around the vacant houses and storefronts, drinking and smoking.

When they saw Eddy approach, they cheered and clapped or raised their fists. He returned the greetings with nothing more than a humble nod. He didn't want to be seen as some grandiose leader full of his own bullshit. He wanted them to see him as one of their own. A man of the people.

That was one reason he didn't have a massive security entourage trailing him around.

Not like Secretary of Defense Montgomery or President Tso.

Eddy couldn't help but smile to himself. How well did that work out for Tso anyway?

The sounds of laughter reached his ears. What was that about?

Yanaba whinnied as Eddy stopped her, then hopped off. He tied her up on a porch post and walked alone around the corner of a dilapidated barn.

The barn was the Union's temporary prison. Most of the

prisoners—ranging from the USAMRIID personnel to foreign aid workers and some Colorado Rangers—were locked up inside.

Two prisoners were tied up to the cottonwood trees in front of the barn. Ropes wrapped around their chest and limbs, pressing them to the trunk.

Kitcheyan was throwing knives at them with a group of three other Rattlesnakes. Blades thunked into the bark above the frightened prisoners' heads.

"You want to take a stab at it?" Kitcheyan asked, holding out a knife.

The other men laughed, but Eddy stared at Kitcheyan.

That shut the other three up, and they bowed their heads like scolded dogs.

"Our prisoners are worth more alive than dead," he said.

"These men are some of the dissidents from Silverton," Kitcheyan said. "We don't *intend* to kill them."

"Silverton, huh?" Eddy asked. "They're still loyal to that belligerent sheriff we had to kill."

"They're cowards and traitors." Kitcheyan directed his knife blade in their direction.

"Maybe so, but I decide who lives and who dies, got it?"

Eddy got close enough to see if he could smell alcohol on Kitcheyan's breath. But instead of responding, Kitcheyan simply nodded. They had a momentary stare down before Kitcheyan withdrew.

Then Eddy strode past the men. He passed another couple of guards beside the six horses tied up outside the barn, then went inside. Lanterns hanging from the rafters lit the space.

The glimmer of light and warmth over his scars evoked angry memories. He tried to keep a stone face as approached Jay.

His old friend was in the back of the barn, tied to a post alone. Dried blood stained his tattered clothes. Bandages covered the bite wounds on his flesh.

Eddy knelt in front of him and pushed his chin up.

"I've got news," Eddy said.

Jay's eyes burned into Eddy's, full of hatred. "I heard the celebrating. Who did you massacre now?"

"Someone that betrayed me and you."

He let those words hang in the air for a moment.

Jay remained quiet.

"Tso," Eddy said.

"What?" Jay squinted. "What did you do, Eddy?"

"I got rid of a problem. A problem that even *you* complained about."

"What the fuck did you do?"

"I ridded the Navajo of a weak leader, a man that bent over backwards to appease the wašíču."

Jay suddenly leaned against his restraints. "You evil bastard!"

Eddy felt the spittle hit his face. He wiped it away as Jay squirmed and winced from his injuries. When he finally seemed to relax, Eddy leaned back down.

"Do you remember Bitsui?"

Jay cursed and spat on the ground.

"He was loyal to me and *our* people," Eddy said. "As I set out with the Rattlesnakes, he was one of the few I left behind in Window Rock. I mean, I did keep one of his kids under our protection, sure. You know, just to keep him motivated. So like any good warrior, he was ready to strike when an opportunity presented itself. Tso always held Bitsui in high regard."

Eddy explained in excruciating detail the events leading up to the moment when Secretary Montgomery came to visit Window Rock. How Bitsui had given his life to stop Tso, and while he'd failed to kill Montgomery, the fallout had been better than Eddy had expected.

Now from the insiders Eddy still had in Window Rock, he heard more and more people suspected the US Federal Government was responsible for Tso's death. They believed that was the most likely explanation of how Montgomery and her ilk hadn't died. The conspiracies had taken almost no time to take root.

Eddy watched the color drain from Jay's features.

"More of our brothers and sisters will join us now." Eddy stood. "I only hope you'll be one of them."

Jay said nothing. That was okay with Eddy. He would let Jay think on this new journey.

He left the barn without another word and jumped back on Yanaba. As they approached Encampment's main street again, the drifting songs of a piano coming from the bar and celebratory voices swallowed him.

Eddy dismounted Yanaba outside the so-called Grand Encampment Opera House. The white and red-trimmed building was lit up by a couple of bonfires out front. He pushed through the front doors to the smell of mildew and kerosene.

He focused on the table at the middle. It sat in front of a small stage.

Williams and Lincoln had a lantern between them on the table as they talked in hushed voices. Orange light flared over their features. Each had a glass of what looked like beer.

When they noticed Eddy approaching, Lincoln stood and smiled. "I was wondering when our esteemed chief would arrive."

"Don't call me that," Eddy said, trying not to snarl.

Lincoln held out one hand defensively. "No offense meant. Just glad to partake in this glorious day."

"Two steps ahead of your enemies," Williams said, raising a mug in his bear paw of a hand. "Nicely done with Tso."

Eddy lowered himself into an empty chair. He had plans far more extensive than what had happened at Window Rock, but these were not the people to share them with. At least not yet.

He couldn't trust them with much intel.

Their job was to fight when the time came.

"The time is approaching for battle," Eddy said.

William took a swig, set his drink down, then rubbed his hands together.

"I've got the perfect role for you and the Comanches," Eddy said. "About four hours ago, Robert made contact with someone working with the Colorado Rangers. I'm awaiting the sheriff's call, but soon we'll set our trap. Then we can prepare to launch the first of our attacks on northern Colorado. I'm keeping the locations secret for now. Fewer people know, the better off we'll be. But I'll need the Comanche with me, Williams, for the first step."

"We cannot wait."

"Good." Then Eddy turned to Lincoln. "After we our first attack from the north, we'll launch our second to the south, beyond Estes Park and Fort Collins. Williams and I will meet you later for this one, but I want you to start preparing now."

"We will," Lincoln said.

"You'll be like the spiders, making your webs as I distract our enemy. You've got a major role in bring the white buffalo's promise to life."

"God willing, we'll be ready." Lincoln leaned back in his seat, showing a bit of anxiety.

Not that Eddy was surprised. Conmen usually got nervous before a real fight. But Eddy wasn't worried about Lincoln. Regardless of their leader's bravery, his people, all true believers in the Rattlesnake's cause, would do what needed to be done.

The doors to the Grand Opera House slammed open. A figure stood in the doorway, silhouetted by the bonfires behind him.

Eddy reached instinctively for his sidearm but then saw it was Robert. He had returned from his task in Estes Park.

"Eddy!" he called. "We got a problem with the prisoners."

Eddy hurried after Robert to the barn. When they got there, Eddy heard groaning. His eyes went to the prisoner tied up on a cottonwood. The man had a knife sticking out of his gut. Blood drizzled out of the wound.

Kitcheyan wasn't wearing a grin, which helped ease Eddy's anger, but did not forgive the man for breaking orders.

"This way," Robert said. "Kitcheyan, you come with."

To his surprise, he waved Eddy and Kitcheyan past the dying prisoner. They went into the barn where he noticed that instead of six horses, there were only five tied up outside. One was missing.

Then he spotted the empty post on the far side. Torn ropes had been left behind where Jay had been only half-an-hour or so ago.

"What the hell happened?" Eddy screamed. He whirled toward the Apache.

"I was distracted. I'm sorry..."

Eddy took a step closer.

"He won't get far," Robert said. "We already have scouts on the trail."

"I was told the same thing about Raven," Eddy said. He kept his gaze on Kitcheyan, anger filling his muscles, threatening to take over his body. "But Jay stole a horse, didn't he?"

Kitcheyan's hesitation was answer enough. "I'll find him myself. I will."

"You've been a disappointment and a failure." Eddy stomped forward. "You disobey my orders and now *this*."

Eddy swung his tomahawk down in a brutal swing at Kitcheyan. It struck him in the side of the neck with a gruesome, slurping thunk.

A guttural scream of horror escaped Kitcheyan's throat.

Eddy yanked the blade free, showered by a geyser of blood. Kitcheyan dropped to the ground on his back, holding his neck with one hand and holding up his other.

"No!" Kitcheyan screeched.

Eddy let out his own scream as he pounced on him. "This is one failure too many. You're just as bad as Raven or Jay. A traitor to our cause!"

He brought the blade down again, this time on Kitcheyan's chest. Prying it free was harder when the edge got stuck on a rib.

Kitcheyan yelled again in agony.

The third and fourth strikes hit him in the face with crunches and splattering blood. One of his eyes bulged out as he fought for air.

Eddy lost track of his strikes as he mutilated Kitcheyan. The other men did nothing to stop him.

Gripped by rage, Eddy struck again and again.

Standing, chest heaving, and drenched in blood, Eddy looked upon his work. He no longer recognized the mess that had been Kitcheyan.

Then he stumbled away. He raised his tomahawk and pointed it at the other men.

"What the fuck you waiting around for," he growled. "Go find Jay!"

19

Lindsey racked her brain as she walked outside the halls of Fort Golden's prison. After everything that happened in Window Rock, she worried about a failure in her own security protocols. After all, it hadn't been all that long ago when a UN representative on the FAC betrayed her people.

So she had spent the day going over security procedures with her Rangers. If a threat was going to come from within, she figured one of those weak spots might be the crowded prisoners.

She could hear yelling and chanting from behind the security doors. Peering through a window down into the cells, she spotted faces pressed up against the bars, cranked up to look at her.

Withdrawing from the window, she started back down the hall.

Everything seemed secure enough. She had people in place that she trusted.

But then again, Tso had probably thought the same.

Footsteps came pounding down the hall from where she'd

just been. She turned to see Rogers running toward her, holding an envelope in his right hand as he waved it at her.

"Sheriff!"

Lindsey froze. "What's going on?"

"Calvin Jackson from the Steel Runners called. I wrote down the message we got from him."

Lindsey took the envelope and peeled it open. It contained a note that said she should call Eddy, along with a phone number. "Is this... Is this for real?"

"Calvin says so," Rogers said. "He told me a guy pointed a gun at his head and told him to make sure this message got to you. He never saw the guy but was certain it was a Rattlesnake."

"This Rattlesnake just snuck up on *Calvin*?"

"That's what he said."

Lindsey tried to slow down her swirling thoughts. She was exhausted, which didn't help, but the fact a Rattlesnake had snuck past her defenses in Estes, and put a gun to Calvin's head, had her on edge.

More than on edge.

Calvin was a former SEAL.

Whoever had snuck up on him had to be good. One of Eddy's best.

"Make sure you tell everyone to be on the lookout," she remarked to Rogers. "In the meantime, I'm taking this to Charlize."

"On it," Rogers said before running off.

Lindsey put a call in to Palmer and told him to meet her at Charlize's office.

In minutes, the two of them stood outside of a door where four Secret Service agents stood guard.

After showing their credentials, the men let them pass.

Inside, Charlize sat behind a desk. The room still had

dusty old paintings and prints from one of the previous prisoner administrators that had used it before the Collapse. Charlize hadn't even bothered to remove the family photos on a bookshelf. The only changes she'd made were the two laptops and a pair of sat phones on the desk.

She was on one of those phones now in a heated conversation.

"It's a mess," she said. "I know that... I told you I know."

Judging by the purple bags under her eyes, she hadn't slept either. The only sign that she'd taken even a short break was that she had changed to a different jacket from the blood-stained one she'd worn in Window Rock.

She waved Lindsey and Palmer forward and then hung up the phone.

"Christ, things keep getting worse," Charlize said. "I asked President Diego to reach out personally to Window Rock. He did. Right now, there's a debate over who is in charge of the Nation and whether they believe our people did indeed have a hand in the assassination."

"It's that bad, huh?" Lindsey said.

Charlize shook her head wearily. "I hope you have some good news."

Lindsey stiffened. "Not exactly."

"What is it?" Charlize asked, immediately appearing alarmed.

"One of Eddy's people made it past my guards in Estes and gave a note to Calvin Jackson," Lindsey said. "The note was for me."

"What's it say?"

"It says to call Eddy. It's got a number."

"Eddy wants you to call him?"

"Yes." She handed the note over. "I thought you should know."

"Have you called him yet?" Charlize asked.

"No."

"Good. Let's do it now."

"Here?"

"Yes, I'd like to join in. Let's see what this jackass wants after all this chaos."

Lindsey and Palmer exchanged a glance.

"That okay?" Charlize asked.

"Of course," Lindsey said.

"I think it goes without saying that his request to make contact must be tied to a trap," Charlize said.

"Agreed," Lindsey agreed. "And I don't really like spending time talking to terrorists."

"No doubt," Palmer said.

"All understandable," Charlize said. "But I'd like to see if we can't gain something out of this. Maybe this is his desperate attempt to get us to leave him alone. Maybe he's already lost too many men. Or maybe he thinks he can scare us. All the same, I want intel. This is as good of a chance as any."

Charlize pushed one of the sat phones across the desk to her.

"Let's see what this asshole has to say," Charlize said.

Lindsey put the phone on speaker and dialed the number.

The phone buzzed. She wondered if Eddy would ignore the call. Maybe return it on his own time later.

But to her surprise, he picked up after only a few seconds.

"Sheriff Plymouth, I hope," he answered. His voice was calm.

"This is her," Lindsey said.

"Ah, glad you got my message," Eddy said. "I was surprised how easily it got through your people, to be honest."

Lindsey saw Palmer tense up. She motioned for him to stay quiet.

"What do you want, Eddy?" Lindsey asked.

"As you probably guessed, I want to negotiate," he said. "You know by now I've built an army, and I'm preparing to take back the New Frontier."

Lindsey looked to Charlize, who narrowed her eyes.

"Eddy, this is Secretary of Defense Charlize Montgomery," she said. "You won't succeed in taking the New Frontier."

"Wow, I didn't realize you were on the line," Eddy replied. "Is there anyone else I should be aware of. Perhaps President Diego has been conferenced in."

"Deputy Palmer of the Colorado Rangers," Palmer said. "Nice to meet you, asshole."

Eddy laughed. "And you as well."

"Get to the point," Lindsey said.

"Fair enough." Eddy paused. "You're short on manpower. Rumor has it your foreign helpers are leaving. With the election coming up, I doubt Diego will send much more in the way of personnel... if I'm right, and I think you all know I am, then you stand no chance of stopping me."

Lindsey looked to Charlize.

"You won't take the New Frontier," said the secretary. "It will never happen."

"But it will," Eddy said. "I'm giving you a chance to avoid bloodshed. Pull back your troops, remove the USAMRIID members, Rangers, and everyone else. Leave the New Frontier to me and I'll leave you alone."

"You attacked my people, killed hundreds, and want us to just leave?" Lindsey asked. "How about this, how about you lay down your weapons, or I will hunt you down and kill you myself."

Eddy let out a soft laugh. "You are quick with the threats, Sheriff."

"It's not a threat. It's a promise. A foregone reality."

"I want peace," Eddy said. "Peace with the Rangers."

This time, Lindsey laughed. "You've shown nothing but brutal violence, so it's pretty hard to believe you."

"It's your people, you wašíču that want violence. You subjugated us in the first place. But that's history. Our future can be brighter without you."

"Before we even talk about peace, you let my people go and release all of your prisoners."

"I will if you agree to leave."

Charlize and Lindsey shared a glance.

"I also want all the foreigners out of our lands. Just like Senator Shelby does," Eddy continued. "You don't have to answer now, but I do want an answer soon, and I want it in person where I can look someone in the eye to make sure whatever deal we make will be upheld."

"So you can assassinate us like you did Tso?" Lindsey said.

"Why do you think *I* had anything to do with that?"

"You know I'm smarter than that."

Eddy snorted. "I'm not asking Secretary Montgomery to be there personally. Or if you're too frightened, not even you, Sheriff."

Lindsey bit back a retort. "Then who?"

"I'd like it to be Raven Spears."

Again, Lindsey looked up at Palmer and Charlize. They all took a second in silence, before Charlize grimaced and waved her hand for Lindsey to continue.

"I'll see what he says," Lindsey finally said.

"I'm sure he will agree when he understands what is at

stake," Eddy said. "Let me know, and I'll tell you where to meet. Talk soon."

He hung up before anyone could say another word.

"You know if we send Raven, Eddy will try to kill him," Lindsey said. "Eddy put a bounty out on him."

"Most definitely," Charlize said. "But it's also an opportunity. If he really does meet Raven, this is a chance for us to learn more about him. Perhaps we can figure out exactly where his forces are in Medicine Bow, and we may have a chance to pay him back for what he did to Tso."

"If we can get him to come out from the woodwork, we could track him back to whatever hole he crawled out of. Maybe we can even stop his plans in Wyoming before they get started."

"That is my hope. I'll flesh out some of the details with my people and get back to Diego. I just need you to get the last lynchpin in this plan together so we can move forward. You know what that means."

Lindsey nodded. "I'll talk to Raven immediately."

———

Raven pictured Lily in his mind. He saw her again rushing out and waving at the mounted riders, giving him and Mark the opening they needed to escape. Then watching her turn and look right at him before her body was riddled with bullets. He winced at the memory.

"Earth to Raven, you still there, brother?" Sandra asked.

Raven shook the painful images away. He needed to stay in the present. To focus on moments like this. Because only God knew how many opportunities they would have to continue enjoying the comfort of friends and family.

The morning sun warmed Raven's face. He sat at a folding table set up in Sandra's front yard eating food. Lara Lithgow was helping Allie construct a new bow for herself. Allie wasn't alone in the project. Raquel and Frankie Gomez were building their own bows, absolutely enthralled by Lara's lessons.

Even Mark was here. He never seemed to leave Creek's side. The dog wagged his tail when Lara pulled back the bow. The children crowded around to watch.

At the table, Calvin sat next to Joanne Lithgow and Maureen Gomez, talking in quiet voices as they glanced up at Lara and the children.

"Sorry," Raven said, finally responding to Sandra. "I've got a lot on my mind."

"I get it," she replied. "I can definitely relate."

He knew that. When she wasn't busy taking care of patients at the clinic, she was at the Refugee Center. All while trying to be a mom.

"You're both doing a great job," Calvin said.

"Thanks," Sandra said.

Raven nodded. "Did I tell you how good it is to have you out here with us, Cal?"

"Sure beats the rails," Calvin said.

"Beats San Diego too," Maureen said. "Fewer people. Fewer riots. Not a bad thing, in my book. Safer all around."

Calvin and Raven exchanged a glance. He had told Raven about the Rattlesnake sneaking into Estes, and Raven had been on guard ever since. He scanned the trees now, discreetly as he could so he didn't worry Sandra.

"You've been awfully quiet," Sandra said to Raven. "Something you want to talk about?"

"Just really tired," Raven lied.

Sandra frowned. She got up and went inside to get some

more food. Maureen followed, leaving Calvin and Raven alone.

Calvin grinned at Raven.

"What?" Raven asked.

"You're a shitty liar," Calvin said. "Your sis knows it, I know it, *Maureen* knows it."

"Yeah, and you can play shrink, then, I suppose."

"Hell, nah, man. I don't have the time to listen to your shit. Got my own problems to deal with." Calvin gave him a grin to let him know he was kidding.

Raven chuckled. "I mean, we both had the plague and got the shit beat out of us a couple weeks ago. I was hunted by someone I thought might be a friend." He shrugged. "Guess I'm not too worried about a few bags under my eyes."

"Honestly, man, I hear that." Calvin leaned over the table toward him, making sure the kids couldn't hear him. "This crap in the New Frontier, it keeps me up at night. I got Anna, Boston, Ortiz, Marino and all the other Runners still dealing with the trauma of losing all our damn friends."

"Thought neither of us were playing shrink."

"I ain't playing nothing. I'm here as a friend. I consider you one of mine too. So I just want you to know, you got my back, I got yours. And if that means you got something on your mind you feel like you can't tell your sister, I'm here for it, man."

Raven smiled. "Thanks, brother. I appreciate that. The kind of shit that's on my mind is the kind of shit you usually leave overseas, you know what I mean?"

"The battlefield stuff," Calvin said. "Trust me, man, I know what you mean. I left more of that crap to rot in the sands of Iraq than an elephant shits in its lifetime."

"Not going to lie, it's good to have someone around that understands." Raven paused.

The crunch of gravel sounded before a white Bronco turned up his drive.

Raven's stomach sank. "Oh, man. Lindsey just doesn't show up unless there's bad news."

Maureen and Sandra came out to see what the fuss was about. The kids all came rushing over, excited to greet this new visitor. Except for Mark of course. He clung to Lara like she was the last floating board of a shipwreck and he was a desperate sailor.

"Hey, someone mind grabbing the kids?" Raven said. "I have a feeling Lindsey didn't expect the whole entourage when she came to see me."

"You got it," Maureen said, ushering the kids back to the archery range with Lara.

Lindsey got out of the Bronco, dipping her hat at Maureen. She strode right over to Raven, Calvin, and Sandra.

"Guess I missed the invite," she said.

"And yet somehow you showed up anyway." Raven gave her a playful smirk. The expression quickly disappeared. "But I'm guessing you didn't come all the way here just to shoot the shit."

"Mind if I..." Lindsey gestured to an empty spot at their table. She didn't wait for Raven to respond before sitting down. "We just talked to Eddy."

Raven's heart thudded heavily against his ribs. Calvin raised his brow, and Sandra cocked her head, confused.

"You're going to have to explain," Raven said, "because you just told me you spoke to the most wanted terrorist in the New Frontier. What in the hell is going on?"

Lindsey summarized her call with Eddy, along with his demands that they leave the New Frontier to his people.

"He wants to negotiate further," she said, "but he's only willing to speak with you. Face to face, unfortunately."

"Bullshit," Raven said.

"I know it sounds insane."

"You know it's a trap, right?" Calvin asked. "You remember what he did to us last time?"

"Yeah, man. I don't forget."

Sandra shook her head and scoffed. "No way are you going out there, brother."

"Raven won't be alone," Lindsey said. "This is our best chance to capture or kill Eddy. Charlize has already authorized two drones for surveillance and monitoring."

"That's it?" Sandra asked. "Two drones?"

"It's all we could cobble together from the supply stores. Most that have been repaired are being used in other cities. But it's not just drones. We'll have Rangers staked out throughout the woods. Snipers providing cover fire. Plus, we've got Charlize's new platoon. They'll have soldiers ready to provide backup. I'll be there personally."

"I still don't like it," Sandra said. "You're asking him to risk his life."

"I wouldn't ask if it wasn't important. Besides snagging Eddy, we also have the chance to follow his men—because you know he's going to have others out there—back to their camps or bases or wherever they're hiding nowadays. We've decided, if we can't stop Eddy right there and then, we're going to launch a full-scale attack on his camp. We'll cut apart his militia before they have a chance at attacking any of our checkpoints or towns again. This will be the end."

Raven scratched at his chin. He wanted to see Eddy dead and gone. But Lindsey was asking him to walk right in front of a loaded gun to do it.

The calculus was clear. One life risked to potentially save thousands. Maybe tens or hundreds of thousands.

"With Eddy and the Rattlesnakes gone, you could ramp up your campaign to stop Wild Fire," Raven said.

Lindsey nodded. "So long as he's out there twisting people's minds, we can't get to those suffering with the plague cure. They're just going to keep dying and spreading Wild Fire. For that matter"—she paused and looked at Sandra—"we all know the cost on this side of the border."

"Wild Fire's hit some of our communities," Sandra said. "Clinics are constantly full. If it gets worse..."

Lindsey bowed her head. "We need to stop the Wild Fire at its source. Which means we need to stop the Rattlesnakes."

"Isn't there a better idea?" Sandra asked. "An alternative to sending Raven to talk to this clown?"

"I feel like there aren't any good ideas left," Raven lamented. "Everything we try to do here, from delivering medicine to just trying to secure our borders, goes to shit."

"Sure, it does," Calvin said. "But on the other hand, I guess we've got to keep trying. What's the alternative? Give up?"

"You saying I should talk to Eddy?" Raven asked.

"Look, brother, I don't want to tell you what to do. All I know is that I'm staying here to watch over Estes Park. This is where I'm needed. Where I can have the most impact. You, though, you're at home in the woods and the mountains. Maybe Lindsey's right. If you can get Eddy out in our sights, if you can make him think we're falling for his trap, then we can pull a fast one on him. Just like that trickster spirit you told me about before."

"Iktomi?" Raven asked.

"Exactly. But, again, man, I'm not telling you what you *should* do. Because like you said, the whole world is raining shit on us." He pointed at Lara and the kids near Maureen. "Right now, those are the most important things in my life. The kids are the ones that have a chance of escaping this shitstorm and living in a future where the US isn't still mired in an apocalypse. So I say you do whatever you think is mostly likely to make that happen."

"By staying here with us," Sandra said. "Right, Raven?"

Lindsey said nothing, merely observing the conversation.

Creek barked as Mark tossed a stick. The Akita kicked up dirt as he sprinted for the stick, picked it up, and came galloping back to the young boy. Mark smiled and hugged the dog, pressing his face into the canine's fluffy coat.

Raven thought on Lindsey, Calvin, and Sandra's words, quiet for a moment. They all had made their points. Calvin sounded a hell of a lot like Lindsey. And Charlize had been in agreement.

"A lone wolf might survive another day by running from a bear hunting it," Raven said, "but if that wolf never joins his pack so they can kill the bear together, the bear won't ever stop hunting the wolves."

"Do bears really hunt wolves?" Calvin asked, brow raised.

"Nah, man, but it's a saying. You know?"

"Raven, you know your wolf pack needs you," Lindsey said. "I need you."

"I know," he replied.

A sad look crossed Sandra's face. "You're going to do it. You're going to meet with Eddy."

"I have to. When are we going to have a better chance at getting close to him?"

"What about us?" Sandra asked.

"Stopping Eddy keeps you all safe," Raven said.

"They've already hit us once in Gould," Calvin added. "I've been working with the Steel Runners to bolster our patrols around Estes Park, but like Raven said, if we can't stop

Eddy soon, I'm not sure how well a few Rangers and my Runners can hold off another attack."

"Charlize is going to join us up here later today," Lindsey said, looking between Calvin and Raven now. "We're going to start staging our troops for the offensive operation. Raven, if you're ready, we can prepare you for negotiations with Eddy. Calvin, it might be nice to have you along. We could use your input."

"I'll be there," Raven said.

Lindsey checked her watch. "I've got to get going to finish prep work. We'll be meeting up at the Stanley Hotel Administration Office. I hope to see you both there."

She got back into her Bronco and took off, leaving Raven to his thoughts.

Calvin turned to him. "I'd be glad to tag along. I want to see what they're going to do about defending Estes Park while they march on Eddy. Because if things look bad up here, we need to start considering alternatives."

"What do you mean?" Sandra asked.

"We got to think about getting you all somewhere away from the New Frontier like Raven suggested," Calvin said, gesturing to Sandra then Maureen and the kids. "Somewhere safer."

"Like Fort Collins?" Sandra asked.

Raven glanced at the kids. "I'd feel a lot better if you were even further south."

"Denver, maybe," Calvin added. "With Fort Golden and the Regeneraid facility down there, the city is better guarded."

"You want us all just to run away?" Sandra asked.

"Not run away," Raven said. "Just head to somewhere safer until this Eddy business is behind us."

"What about all the other residents of Estes Park? What about the clinics and the Refugee Center?"

"I'll start working with the Steel Runners to shore up our defenses," Calvin said. "But for people who can't defend themselves, we should at least get some potential evacuation routes set up. This will take some time, but I think it's worth it."

The children were giggling about something Lara said as she showed her homemade bow to them.

"It seems like every hour, we get more refugees in the center," Calvin continued. "We're going to reach capacity in a few days anyway. From what those refugees say, the number of Wild Fire patients in the New Frontier is growing exponentially. Starting some regular transport convoys south is going to be important, whether the Rattlesnakes show up here or not."

"Our clinics are filling up fast, sure," Sandra said. "And we're already short-staffed. I can't run away."

"See?" Raven said. "You're willing to put yourself in danger to help your patients. If you're willing to risk your own safety, why shouldn't I? I'm not a doctor. I'm not a nurse. I don't have many skills that are helpful in Estes Park. I've got to use my skills where they're needed. My decision's made. I'm going to help Lindsey bring Eddy out."

"Raven, why do we always have this fight?" Sandra asked. "Why do I always have to tell you to think about being like Calvin? Protect us over here? Stay where I can see you. Where I can help you if you're hurt."

"One way or another, Estes Park is going to be overrun if we don't do something to stop Eddy. Maybe it'll be from Wild Fire patients. Maybe from the Rattlesnakes. Either way, we can't make any progress until Eddy's gone."

Sandra sighed.

"I should've made sure Eddy was dead when we left Montezuma Creek," Raven said to Calvin.

"Yeah, but you can't spend your time dealing with regrets," Calvin said. "What matters is what we do now."

"I'll trust you to take care of the families."

Raven watched as Creek played with Mark. The young boy was another who suffered because of no fault of his own. His mother had been destroyed by what had become of the New Frontier.

Just like Lara.

How many more children would lose their parents before this war was over? How many families would be ripped apart?

All he knew was that he couldn't let Allie and Sandra become another.

"I'll take care of Eddy this time," Raven said. "One way or another, he's going to die."

20

Calvin sat in the passenger seat of Raven's Jeep as they drove through Estes Park. Creek sat in the back, tongue lolling out of his mouth.

Walls of mountains surrounded them. Calvin could smell the crisp air through the open windows.

Nature like this gave him a sense of peace he'd never known growing up in Baltimore. It was why he'd been building his cabin in Lake Tahoe. While those plans had changed dramatically, he was glad Estes Park seemed like a fine place to make his home.

So long as they could defend it from the monsters dead-set on destroying it.

They wound up Streamer Parkway toward the blackened ruins of what once had been the Stanley Hotel. Calvin had heard the story of how arsonists destroyed it early in the Collapse.

"So that was where *The Shining* took place?" Calvin asked.

"Yup," Raven said.

"Wish I could have seen it in its prime."

"Yeah, I feel the same way about DC," Raven said. "I never made it out there, but always wanted to after the Marines. See the monuments, the museums, the cherry blossom trees. But from what I hear, it's just a giant crater in the ground."

"Not exactly, but it sure ain't as pretty as it once was."

Raven took a turn up a drive, passing by sporadic cabins and tall pine trees.

"There are a lot of things I wish I would have seen, but I count myself lucky to be seeing anything at all today, if we're being honest," he said.

Calvin glanced over. "I feel you."

"So many of my brothers died before the Collapse in war, and I've lost a lot of friends since." Raven shook his head. "A mountain of dead haunt my dreams."

"I hear that too, man. Every time I close my eyes, I see the Angel Line on fire. All my people just... God."

"Yeah. Don't suppose that's ever gonna change, but I'm trying to focus on the living." Raven smiled. "I see you're doing the same. That's why you came back with Mouse's fam, right?"

Calvin nodded. "Mouse was the closest thing to a real brother I had. Maureen and the kids are basically family."

"Well, if you stick around, you'll have a lot more."

He slowed the Jeep as they crested the drive.

Ahead, transport trucks, SUVs, Humvees, and other vehicles were parking in the lot right in front of the charred skeletal remains of the hotel.

They got out into a throng of Colorado Rangers, US Army soldiers, foreign peacekeepers, and more.

Seeing all these people gathered, ready to bring Eddy down, had Calvin feeling a little better about Estes Park's odds of surviving the Rattlesnakes. He knew Raven had to meet with the guy. That it was the smart thing to do. Any of the brass would push for a move like this. Sending just one guy to potentially turn the tide of war?

It was a no-brainer.

Still, Raven wasn't just one guy to Calvin. He was a brother. They'd fought and bled together.

"You sure you want to do this?" Calvin said.

Raven glanced at him. "Do what?"

"Face Eddy. I know I laid it on thick, and I'm going to feel real guilty if you go out there on account of me."

"I don't want to, man. I have to."

"Yeah, but... You don't. You can choose not to go."

"You know the score. I know the score. If we're going to protect our families, new and old, I got to go out there."

Raven put a hand on Calvin's shoulder.

"I'm doing of this of my own volition. Don't think you're so persuasive that you can boss me around." Raven smirked.

Calvin laughed. "Fine, man. Then after you do this shit, I look forward to another barbecue. Maybe this time at my place."

"You got a place out here?"

"I'll be looking. We just need to make sure no Rattlesnakes are going to come burn it down, you hear me?"

They marched past the charcoaled fallen beams and ashy remnants of the hotel to the rebuilt administrative offices. Fresh paint covered the two-story white square structure. From the outside, it looked more like an old school Craftsman house than any kind of office building.

Inside, they were hit with a bustle of activity. The entire open floor was covered in tables with Toughbook laptops, phones, and radios. Rangers, foreign peacekeepers, and Army personnel worked side-by-side at these temporary desks, their hushed voices filling the place.

Lindsey, Charlize, and Blair were at one table with some other men and women that Calvin believed were representatives from the Foreign Advisory Council.

When Lindsey saw Calvin and Raven enter, she gestured for them to join their conversation.

"Just in time," Charlize said. "Just so everyone knows, this is Calvin Jackson, a former Iron Lead in the Steel Runners, and Estes Park-based tracker, Raven Spears. They're responsible for bringing down the Reapers with Sheriff Plymouth and Lieutenant Blair."

Charlize introduced the other members of the Foreign Advisory Council Calvin hadn't met before. He shook hands with Tiankai, Piard, and Martinez before Charlize continued.

"Finally, this is Lieutenant Shane Abbott, the platoon leader Diego sent," Charlize said.

Abbott had a tan face etched in tightly drawn lines and vibrant green eyes. "Good to meet you all. I'm looking forward to leading Spartan Platoon in the fight against the Rattlesnakes."

"Thank you, Lieutenant," Charlize said. "By all accounts, we know Eddy will have something planned when Raven goes to meet with him. We're hoping to secure the area with the strategic placement of snipers and reserve forces, should they become necessary. We'll use a squad from Spartan and a contingent of twenty Rangers to accomplish that. In addition, I've gotten clearance for the use of two RQ-7 Shadow drones. They aren't much, but they're what we have on hand. We'll use them to track Eddy's people following the meeting with Raven."

"What's the goal when I talk to Eddy?" Raven asked.

"He wants to meet you in a densely wooded section of Pinkham Mountain. Draw him away if possible. Ideally, take him here." She pointed at a map on the table. "This pond off Colorado Road 49 would be best."

"You get him out there, then we'll have much better sight-lines," Lindsey said. "I don't want the trees ruining any of our snipers' shots."

"The numbers you're talking about taking on this mission..." Calvin began. "Well, it sounds an awful lot like you aren't leaving many people behind in Estes Park."

"We're not." Charlize gestured to Calvin, then addressed the rest of the people assembled there. "Calvin and his Steel Runners will remain in Estes Park to protect the city."

Blair nodded. "Ma'am, so long as it's not an offensive oper-ation, I can have my Marines standing by in case they're needed as well. I can't put them on the front lines, but they could help in escort or reserve roles."

"Thank you, Lieutenant," Charlize said. "We'll figure out a way to—"

Voices rose near the entrance as the doors opened. Everyone turned around as two Rangers hauled a man into the space, practically carrying him.

Calvin could see the guy was in bad shape with a bruised face, tattered clothes, and bloody bandages on his limbs and neck. His head lolled like he was barely staying awake.

"What in the hell is this?" Martinez asked.

"Is that... that's Jay," Raven said.

"What's going on, Nuke?" Lindsey asked the Ranger who had brought Jay in.

"He came in over the border at Gould," Nuke replied. "Says he needed to speak to Raven and Sheriff Plymouth. Says he was sent with Raven to gather intel on Eddy but got captured."

"Bring him over," Charlize said, then turned to an Army

officer at a nearby desk. "And go get some medics. He looks like he needs help."

Nuke carefully deposited Jay into a seat.

"Does he have weapons?" Raven asked.

"Already searched him," Nuke said. "He's got nothing."

Still, Raven pulled out his pistol. "Guy tried to kill me, so I'm not taking chances."

Lindsey and Palmer crowded around.

"What happened to you, Jay?" Lindsey asked. "After you tried to kill Raven."

Jay glared, looking at them in turn.

"Eddy took me prisoner," he started. Then he locked eyes with Raven. "You know I had no choice."

Jay reached out to Raven, and for a moment, Calvin worried Raven might shoot him right here. Instead, he lowered the gun.

"Yeah, I told everyone what happened, but you got a lot more explaining to do," Raven said.

"Damn right. First off, why are you here?" Lindsey asked.

"I escaped and came to help you," Jay said. "To help you take down Eddy... he killed Tso. He's hurt my people."

Jay seemed sincere. His injuries were real and his story checked out as he went on about how he made it back here using a stolen horse to reach the border checkpoint at Gould. But Calvin wasn't sure if this was part of Eddy's ruse. Judging by Raven's suspicious glance at Jay, he wasn't either.

"Where were you held?" Lindsey asked.

"I was in Encampment, Wyoming. I overheard something his guards were saying about setting up in Medicine Bow in a couple days and then... then... maybe they were going to try to attack right after that. They had what looked to be a couple hundred people with them, but I heard they have other forces spread out in the New Frontier, ready to strike in four, maybe five days..."

"To strike where?" Raven asked.

Jay groaned. He looked like he might pass out. Medics rushed in through the front door, and immediately began examining Jay.

"I think they mentioned a two-pronged attack." Jay took a deep breath. "They want to come in from somewhere around Cheyenne and work their way south. Maybe Fort Collins. Maybe Estes Park. I couldn't really tell from their conversations."

"Anything else you can tell us?" Lindsey asked.

Jay shook his head. "You have to stop him..."

"We're going to." Charlize motioned to the Rangers. "Take him to rest and recover. I want to have him ready to move back down to Fort Golden so we can keep him close."

The medics offered to take him out in a stretcher, but Jay waved them off. He walked out, leaning on one of them.

After the door was shut again, Charlize looked to Raven. "You believe him?"

"Yeah," Raven said. "He really doesn't like Eddy."

"He just corroborated a few things for us too," Lindsey said. "He's also given us Eddy's current location. Plus, we now have a very, very rough timeline of when we might expect an attack on northern Colorado and some numbers on the Rattlesnake forces in Encampment."

"That timeline at least gives us a deadline to act," Charlize said. "Earlier intel suggests that Eddy was headed toward Centennial, but at this point, we really don't know if Eddy's changed his plans, especially since he'll know we might have prior information thanks to Jay and Raven. I really don't want to send all our troops to an empty town only to have Eddy attack us from somewhere else."

The FAC members and Abbott nodded along.

"When Raven meets with Eddy, we'll use our drones to track him and whoever else is tagging along to their main forces. We'll see if they're still in Encampment or if they're moving somewhere else. We can scope out the precise area, their exact numbers, and ensure we aren't blindly committing troops and resources."

"Good," Lindsey said. "Then we can stop Eddy before he begins either of these attacks Jay was talking about."

Tiankai scratched at his chin. "I'm still dubious about an offensive effort. It is not that I think it won't be effective. It's just that we've lost too many people already. Even if we win, I'll have a hard time convincing my own commanding officers to commit troops. Like Blair suggested, we could provide security and vehicles for any evacuation routes you set up in case the offensive doesn't go as planned."

"I'm okay with that," Charlize said. "I'd prefer to have some help there rather than none."

"I'm in the same boat," Piard said. "Canada's patience is wearing thin. We can provide evacuation relief as necessary."

"Mexico too," Martinez added.

Charlize looked at Calvin. "We're going to need most of the Rangers on the front lines. Do you think your Steel Runners can help hold on to Estes Park? It's a small but important community, given its access to the mountains and community beyond."

"I can handle the responsibility, ma'am," Calvin replied.

"Good. As of now, we'll be putting you in charge of coordinating defensive operations in Estes Park with the handful of local Rangers staying behind. I will be organizing the federal government's involvement from Fort Golden."

She looked over at Blair and the FAC. "I understand that you and your teams can't go on the offensive. Lieutenant

Tiankai, your suggestion of helping with any evacuations and security on the safe side of the border isn't a bad idea."

"Thank you," Tiankai said. "I want to reiterate that we would be happy to still help our allies. We just can't obligate ourselves to any offensive operations."

"That's understood," Charlize went on. "If the Rattlesnakes do launch a two-pronged attack, I'd like most of the FAC's peacekeeping forces in the area available to provide emergency support as you suggested. Buckley AFB will serve as a staging area for your equipment, vehicles, and personnel so you can respond swiftly to anywhere we might need help. Would that be amenable to all of you?"

Tiankai did not hesitate. "We can handle that."

Martinez scratched at his chin. "That should be doable."

"I agree," Piard said.

Blair hesitated before answering. "If everyone else is staging at Buckley, I'd like to request that the Royal Marines stay north. We can assist with evacuations around Pinkham if it's necessary. We have perhaps the best vehicles suitable for the mountains." Then he looked at Lindsey. "I truly don't want to leave you high and dry."

"It would be damned nice knowing we have Royal Marines watching our backs, even if you can't engage on the offensive front," Abbott said.

"Agreed," Lindsey said. Then she looked at her deputy. "Palmer, you'll stay at Golden with the secretary. In case I'm preoccupied, I need someone to be the decision-maker at home."

Palmer nodded. "Yes, Sheriff."

"Very good," Charlize said. "Raven doesn't meet with Eddy until tomorrow. If Jay is correct, we have only a small window to launch a preemptive strike. Lieutenant Abbott, you can begin staging in Livermore tonight. We'll plan on launching our attack in two days' time at the latest. So let's get to it, people. The timeline has been moved forward, which means we're going to stop this madness even sooner than expected."

———

A day after the meeting with Montgomery, Raven rode in Lindsey's Bronco. Creek lay on the backseat, panting heavily. They drove up the narrow road to Pinkham Mountain where Raven was set to meet the leader of the Rattlesnakes.

With the windows open, the fragrant scent of ponderosa pines drifted in. Behind them trailed four SUVs with Rangers. Somewhere above flew one of the two drones that Montgomery had requisitioned for them. The other was already circling north of the area.

Two fireteams from a Spartan squad were spread out in the trees on the southside of the mountain, ready to move into position if Raven needed help. Lindsey had assured him that another six Rangers snipers had various viewpoints over the mountain.

All the same, he didn't feel that much better.

Everyone knew they were walking into a trap. The question was whether Eddy would realize his trap was leading straight to his own demise.

No matter how he spun it, Raven was the bait.

Yet he had no choice if they wanted to drag Eddy out into the open and take him down before he could unleash a full-scale war.

"We're getting close," Lindsey said. Dense forest filled their view on all sides. "If you need anything, you call."

"You got it," Raven replied. "And if he won't leave the forest?"

"We'll call off the meeting. But Eddy won't let us do that."

The wind whipped into the vehicle, tousling Raven's hair. "How can you be so sure?"

"Eddy has a big ego. I mean, the guy thinks he represents the coming of this white buffalo, right?"

"Something like that."

"Well, a guy who thinks he's a messenger of the gods... Look, Raven, I've dated a few guys that think they're a *gift* from the gods."

Raven forced a smile. "I hope I'm not on that list."

"Some days not so much." Lindsey laughed. "In all seriousness, guys like Eddy have the same flaw. He needs his ego stroked like a wolf needs to hunt. He's not going to want to have wasted all his time coming out here just for us to say, 'never mind.'"

They took a turn left, tires crunching over gravel. The peak of the forested mountain came into view.

Raven checked over a map of the area. "Looks like we're about two miles from the meeting point. Better let me out here."

"Make the exit quick," she replied.

The plan was that Raven would disappear into the woods. Lindsey and the Rangers would continue driving closer to the agreed-upon meeting spot.

If Eddy had anyone watching for the vehicles—which they were sure he would—then they would hopefully be distracted by the small convoy. That would give Raven and Creek a chance to patrol the area quietly and discretely.

Best case scenario, Raven could get the drop on Eddy.

Lindsey reached out to Raven.

She squeezed his hand. "You get back alive, and maybe we can have that dinner we talked about."

For just a moment, Raven relished the spark from her touch. "Promise?"

"Yes."

"Then I'll be back."

Lindsey stopped, and he leapt out with Creek following. He darted straight for the cover of the trees.

Raven watched Lindsey and the Rangers drive on, the rumble of their engines echoing against the mountain slopes.

"Come on, boy. Just you and me now."

He climbed the incline toward where he was supposed to meet Eddy.

Sure enough, after only a half-mile of quiet padding and clinging to the shadows, Creek froze. The dog's tail stuck straight out, and his nose pointed toward the northeast.

He had a scent.

Raven lowered himself into the shelter of a pine and drew out his binos. He scoped the area Creek had indicated.

A single man with a rifle gazed to the south. The man had a khaki jacket with a yellow Rattlesnake patch on the sleeve.

No mistaking who he worked for.

Avoiding the man, Raven advanced methodically through the woods with Creek. They identified four more guards.

So far, none of those guards had noticed Raven.

After another thirty minutes of prowling, he finally made it about one hundred feet from the peak of Pinkham Mountain, where Eddy was supposed to be waiting.

The trees and brush were extremely dense. Raven had to watch his step so as not to crack the loose branches and twigs around his feet.

Creek's tail went straight, his body going rigid after only a few seconds.

Raven peered between the trees to get a better view.

In the shadows of the trees, he saw a person.

Eddy?

Raven took out his crossbow, sneaking closer. He almost had a clean shot. He just needed to get a good shot.

Inch by inch, he advanced. He signaled for Creek to take a wider berth, flanking Eddy in case Raven needed assistance.

But as he grew nearer, now only about fifteen yards away, he noticed something strange.

The man had darker skin and black hair. He wore a khaki jacket like the other Rattlesnakes, but the man hadn't moved the entire time.

Raven's heart began to climb into his throat.

A chill shot down his spine.

The man, Raven realized, had his hands tied behind his back. A rope at his waist kept him secured to the tree he was standing in front of. A cloth was tied around his mouth as a gag.

All of it had been difficult to see in the shadows, but now, Raven realized, this man was part of the bait.

Shit, shit, shit. Where's Eddy?

As he studied the area beyond where the man was, he saw the silhouettes of more people. Eight that he could see.

They were on their knees. Barely visible between the ferns and bushes, cloaked in the darkness of the tree canopy.

A couple of the prisoners wore Colorado Rangers uniforms. Another appeared to be from the CVRTF. Others were members of the Chinese peacekeeping forces, the United Nations, and even a USAMRIID servicewoman judging by their clothes.

This hadn't been part of the plan.

"Raven," a voice called out.

A familiar voice.

Raven's stomach twisted in a painful knot.

He curled around the tree trunk and saw Eddy step out

from between a few pine trees. Enough sunlight pierced the branches to illuminate his scarred face. His hairline was uneven where the fire had blistered his skin. While some of his face was covered in knotted, pink tissue, other parts had already started to form whiter scar tissue.

He wasn't alone.

In one hand, he clutched the arm of a young woman in scrubs. She had a USAMRIID patch on her shoulder.

The Rattlesnake had a pistol pressed to her temple.

"Come on, Raven." Eddy looked around. "I can smell your dog. And I'm not the only one. I heard the birds go quiet just to my southeast. That's where you commanded your dog to go, right?"

Raven said nothing. He wanted to see if he could get a clear shot on Eddy. Creek trotted over next to Raven, but he motioned the animal back.

"All I want to do is talk," Eddy said. "I know it seems like we're trying to outfox each other here, but I'm just ensuring my own safety. No one has to get hurt if you just come out."

"Fat chance," Raven said, still behind the cover of the tree. At the sound of his voice, Eddy spun, facing his direction.

"You want to talk, you let these innocent people go," Raven said. He walked around the tree with Creek behind him. "Let's get somewhere you don't have all your guards waiting to gun me down—unless you're too much of a coward."

Eddy let out a harsh laugh. "A lot of good they did. You have surprised me, and for that, you should be proud."

"I don't give a shit about surprising you," Raven said. "I care about ending this. I care about peace in the New Frontier. The people deserve it."

"Your people?"

"All people."

"That's where I don't see eye to eye with you and Jay or Tso... *our* people are what matters. Getting our land back, being free is what matters."

"That will never happen if you continue doing what you're doing. Killing does not change the past. It only darkens the future."

"I can see where this is going... I thought by talking to you face to face, I might have a chance of changing your mind. Of having you join our cause."

"So that's why I'm here? To join your crusade? You had to know that isn't going to work."

"Why?" Eddy took a step forward. "Why not consider an offer to join a new tribe. A tribe that will take back the New Frontier and build something different. Something for the First Nation men and women."

Raven considered something. Maybe playing along would buy Lindsey and her people time to swoop in and take Eddy down.

"What are you going to build?" Raven asked.

"A new home for us."

"Then you have to stop killing, let these people go."

Eddy scoffed. "How about you take out your radio and tell the sheriff to back off. Tell them to get the hell out of here or I start killing these prisoners."

Raven froze.

"Fine, then. Every minute they're still in position, I shoot one prisoner, and when all of these people are dead, I've got another thirty prisoners waiting with gun barrels pointed straight at their heads miles from here. If your people move in and I die, all my prisoners die. You want that blood on your hands?"

A hot anger furnaced through Raven's insides. He wanted to strangle Eddy, to light him on fire again.

A gunshot cracked through the woods. Birds flew, squawking.

The man strung up on the tree slumped against the rope. His head lolled on his shoulders, blood soaking through his jacket.

"No!" Raven shouted. "Eddy, stop. You have to stop the killing."

Eddy pointed his pistol at the young woman's head again. She let out a muffled squeal in his arms, eyes bulging with terror. The other prisoners were pressing against their own binds. Some sobbed. Others screamed into their gags.

"Now that I've got your attention, tell your people to get back," Eddy said, "Tell them they have to withdraw from the area."

Raven hesitated a single moment.

Eddy shot another prisoner. A USAMRIID worker slumped forward, collapsing into the leaves and branches.

Sweat trickled down Raven's forehead as he watched the woman squirm in Eddy's grip. Creek growled, ready to attack.

"You've been corrupted, Raven," Eddy said. "Just like Jay. Just like your family and all the people you love back in Estes Park. Your sister. Your niece."

Raven said nothing.

"Oh, yes, we sent our people to follow Jay and see where he went. It's nice of your sister and her daughter to work at that Refugee Center. Your friend, Calvin Jackson, and that family he seems so close to. All of them trying to help people as if it matters."

Now Raven's blood ran cold. How many of the Rattlesnakes had been sneaking around behind the borders?

If they'd followed Jay right into Estes Park, they might even know what Lindsey and the others were planning.

This was turning into a disaster very quickly.

"Call them back or she dies," Eddy said.

Raven pulled his radio out and did as ordered.

"Good," Eddy said. "Now I'm going to give you a choice like I did Jay. One last chance. Join me or die."

"You know I can't," Raven said. "But I can tell you, if you carry on like this, it doesn't end in the white buffalo's appearance. It ends in your death. You won't succeed. You won't help your people. You will only hurt them."

"That's where you're wrong, and if you can't see that, then there is nothing left for you in this world."

Eddy pushed the woman away and pulled out a small metal canister from his utility belt with his free hand. It took Raven only a blink to realize it was a grenade.

"You left me to die on fire!" Eddy yelled. "I think it's only fair I return the favor."

Raven had only a second to leap away after Eddy pulled the pin and pitched it toward him and Creek. The grenade clunked against a tree, bouncing away from Raven as he flattened himself into the dry soil and branches, dragging Creek down with him.

The grenade burst into a ball of hot flames.

White-hot fire roiled up through the branches of the nearby trees. Almost instantaneously, that inferno enveloped the trees between Raven and Eddy. Gray smoke billowed above them as Eddy sprinted northward, throwing his hostage to the ground. Raven twisted up his M4 and took a few shots as the Rattlesnake dodged between trees. Bullets splintered the bark but didn't seem to have hit Eddy.

Dry as the forest was, the fire was already leaping across the branches and trees, creating a wall of fire and smoke.

Raven was already losing sight of Eddy. He knew he should go after the man, but the conflagration was burning straight toward the young woman and the other hostages Eddy had left tied up.

If Raven went after the Rattlesnake, they would die a horrific death.

Raven immediately put in a call on his radio as he ran toward the hostages, smoke scratching at his eyes.

"Lindsey, Eddy's getting away, headed north. Tail him!"

"I got Nuke and Rogers on it," Lindsey called back, worry tinging her voice.

Raven pushed through the smoke. Quickly as he could, he used his knife to saw through the ropes binding the hostages. When one was free, he gave another knife to that man. The freed prisoner helped cut through more ropes. In minutes, the smoke had engulfed them, but all the surviving hostages were free.

"Come on!" Raven shouted.

They followed him, coughing through the dense smoke. Fire raged around the group. Raven pulled up his shirt over his mouth, but it was too much. His eyes burned and watered as he pushed on, trying to find a way out.

"I'll find you!" Raven screamed. "I'll find you and kill you, Eddy!"

The flames licked higher as he led the freed hostages toward safety. For a moment, he worried all their efforts had amounted to nothing.

But soon Lindsey called back over the radio.

"It worked, Raven," she said between breaths. "We have one of Charlize's drones following Eddy's people. We'll follow them back to their lair—and then we'll exterminate them."

They may not have gotten Eddy today. But their preparations had gotten what they needed.

So long as the drones remained on the Rattlesnake's trail, they would end the enemy's evil conquest.

21

CALVIN STOOD ATOP THE ROOF OF THE ESTES PARK Refugee Center with an M4 strapped over his back. By his side was Anna. She was serving as a lookout with a pair of binoculars and a radio. Boston, Ortiz, and Marino were watching the northern, southern, and eastern approaches to the Center.

Using the intel Jay had shared, Calvin had organized a round-the-clock defensive effort in conjunction with the Rangers to keep Estes Park safe.

"We've got the rest of the Steel Runners—all twenty of the healthiest ones—spread around town," Anna said. "If hostiles slip past the Rangers somehow, they won't slip by our people."

Calvin hoped that was true, but the park and the city was a lot of ground to cover. If someone really wanted to sneak in, it wouldn't be all that hard. The best they could do was block off the streets from vehicles.

Two Steel Runner teams with five men each were stationed at checkpoints, Alpha and Bravo, to the northwest on Highway 36 and southwest on Highway 34, respectively.

Closer to downtown, another five-person team was at the blockade they'd put together at the critical junction of Highways 34 and 36.

Calvin could barely see it from where he stood. There were a few abandoned trucks and cars that they'd pushed to block off the main street between the restaurants and shops.

Flannery and Thomas were among the ten Rangers left to help Estes Park. They were positioned near the clinic just south of downtown. The Rangers also had four scouts spread between the Steel Runner positions to the west to watch the mountains.

And then there was the reserve force. Twenty-four civilians had volunteered to protect their town if all hell broke loose. They were using the old cabinlike building of the Estes Park Visitor Center just east of downtown as their headquarters and staging area.

If any position was looking weak during an attack, they would immediately respond.

"I hate all this waiting," Anna said as she scoped the town again with her binos. "It reminds me of being on the trains."

"I hear that," Calvin said.

"At least on the damn train, we were always moving," Boston said. "I like moving. It means we're getting away from the assholes trying to shoot us. Up here, we're just sitting ducks."

"Yeah, man," Ortiz said. "But with you here, I know we're safe."

"Oh yeah? My shooting's gotten wicked good."

Ortiz laughed. "Nah. It's more like you're so damn loud, when the enemy attacks, they'll all be targeting you instead of us."

Marino chuckled. "He's not wrong. It's kind of like how you protect yourself from bears."

"How's that?" Boston asked.

"Well, you bring a buddy along," Marino said. "Someone you know is slower than you. That way, while the bear's eating your buddy, you escape."

"Ah, come on, Boston ain't that bad," Calvin said. "At least he knows when to shut up."

"Oh yeah, when's that, brother?" Ortiz asked.

Calvin grinned. "When he sleeps."

Marino laughed. "I don't think so. The guy *talks* in his sleep."

Calvin appreciated the playful banter. Everyone still had their eyes on the roads, making sure no one caught them unaware. But for a second, it was like they were back on the trains again.

The good parts of the train. When they were perched in the nests, talking shit and enjoying the comradery.

"Marino, you think you'll still travel the world someday?" Anna asked after a beat of silence.

Marino looked out over the horizon. "I hope so. I want to. But I'm not leaving this country until it's in a better place. I'd feel too guilty."

"Yeah," Anna said, almost dreamily. "It'd be nice to get away from all this. I'd love to settle down with my nieces and sister back up in New York, but like you said, there's work that needs to be done."

"Amen, you guys," Boston said. "'Course I got a lot of sins to make up for. I'll be on the rails or keeping watch at refugee centers for the rest of my life. Only way I can live with myself, know what I mean?"

Ortiz dipped his cowboy hat at Boston. "Hombre, you know I give you a lot of shit, but you've done your time. You don't owe anyone anything."

"Wicked nice of you to say, bro, but I like this life better than my old one. I'm clean, I got purpose, and I'm not hanging around a bunch of losers—I mean, besides you guys."

Calvin laughed. "Losers or not, I'm still proud to have you on the team, Boston."

Their banter faded, and Calvin was left with his thoughts again. He wondered where the Rattlesnakes might hit first.

He checked his watch.

By now, Raven should be meeting with Eddy. He was starting to grow anxious.

But while he worried for these others, he had a job to do.

"Checkpoint Alpha, status?" Calvin called.

"All clear," a Steel Runner replied.

"Checkpoint Bravo, status?" Calvin called.

There was no response.

"Checkpoint Bravo, Sierra Lead here. Respond immediately."

Again, no response.

Calvin's stomach sank, adrenaline already chomping at the bit. Anna gave him a worried look.

"Blockade, status?" Calvin asked.

"All accounted for."

Calvin immediately placed a call to the Rangers.

"Romeos One and Two," he said, referring to Thomas and Flannery, "Checkpoint Bravo is MIA. Do you have recon in the area?"

"One moment," Thomas replied.

There was silence over the line. Calvin imagined they were calling their available scouts to check in on the area.

After a few tense beats, Thomas called back. "Recon One and Two are not responding, either. We can't reach anyone near Checkpoint Bravo."

Now Calvin's heart thudded hard enough he feared it would break his ribs.

Thomas went on. "We're sending scouts there now, but—"

A gunshot rang out from the southwest.

"All teams, on high alert," Calvin called into the radio. "We believe hostiles are on their approach from the southwest. Reserve Forces, prepare for deployment."

"Sierra Lead, this is Romeo One," Thomas called. "We're headed to reinforce the blockade."

"Copy that," Calvin said.

He kept his binos aimed toward the road leading to downtown. Too many buildings blocked his sightline to see what was coming.

A storm of gunshots sounded, booming louder and closer.

Thomas's voice came back over the radio. "I've got reports civilians are fighting back, but it's not working."

"Shit," Calvin muttered to himself. "Reserve forces, head to the blockade immediately. Fall into defensive shooting positions."

The Steel Runners and the Rangers had rehearsed this with the civilian volunteers. They would head to spots along downtown in the restaurants and stores that had been barricaded and turned into improvised bunkers.

If all worked as planned, downtown Estes Park would be like a shooting gallery for the defensive forces. They would cut down the attackers as they were funneled into the kill zones there.

"Guys, get ready," Calvin said to the others on the roof. "If this doesn't work, we are the last line of defense."

More gunshots erupted closer to town.

And then Calvin got his first glimpse of the enemy.

A man in a khaki jacket rode down out of the woods of Prospect Mountain on a black-and-white stallion. He had a rifle in one hand and a Molotov cocktail in the other.

With a cry, he tossed the incendiary weapon at a small coffee shop.

Orange flames rolled up from the breaking glass and splashing liquid.

Behind him rode another twenty men launching Molotov cocktails at the buildings along the street.

A hellish scene unfolded in seconds as even more men broke out of the surrounding woods on horses.

Then he counted another five, ten, twenty, then thirty men on horses galloping down 36. Some carried rifles and handguns. Others had Molotov cocktails, lit and ready to throw.

"Blockade, I got maybe fifty hostiles all headed your way," Calvin said.

The enemy voices echoed through the town between gunshots.

The horsemen charged straight toward downtown. All at once, the Steel Runners and civilian response forces stationed there began firing. The first few Rattlesnakes went down in the hail of bullets, their bodies tumbling from the horses and skidding across asphalt.

But then the hostiles spread out. They started launching Molotov cocktails toward the blockade and the buildings around it. Fires licked up from storefronts, and black smoke began funneling down the street, creating a wall of haze.

"Shit, I'm losing visuals," Calvin said.

Gunshots cracked, echoing from the main drag.

"We're engaging now!" Thomas called over the radio. "Romeos are flanking and—"

Suddenly, static sounded over the radio.

"What the fuck is going on?" Boston asked.

Then Calvin heard shrill war cries echoing up between the gunfire. More clouds of black smoke clogged the town.

"Thomas is down!" Flannery came over the radio. "They had another team of, I don't know, twenty men and... We're taking casualties. We're losing ground!"

Fires were quickly leaping between the buildings downtown. The screen of black smoke engulfed most of Calvin's view.

"Checkpoint Alpha, status?" Calvin asked.

"Still clear here," the Steel Runner lead there replied. "Should we fall back?"

Calvin thought hard. If they left their post, that might be where the next leg of Rattlesnake reinforcements would attack.

"No, hold tight," Calvin said.

Between the gunshots and screams over the radio, he could tell the killing zone they'd intended to defeat any invaders was instead a slaughter for their own people.

"Chief!" Boston yelled. He was pointing to the south.

More fires were being lit, devouring houses and stores. Even in the woods and on the mountain slopes where cabins and individual homes lay between the trees, smoke began rising.

The Rattlesnakes were laying waste to the town.

Calvin couldn't help thinking of Eddy's grudge against Raven. Was this all some massive stroke of revenge?

If so, Calvin was caught in the middle with the Gomezes and his Steel Runners.

"We can't hold them!" Flannery called over the radio. "They're everywhere and the smoke... we can't see anything!"

"Fall back!" Calvin yelled into the radio. "All reserve forces, all Romeos and Sierras, fall back to the Refugee Center immediately!"

Flames leapt from building to building. The dense wall of smoke rolled down the road toward them. A couple of civilian reserve volunteers burst from the smoke, fleeing down Lake Estes Trail along the water toward the Center.

Then came a trickle of Steel Runners and Rangers. Ash marred their uniforms. Some held their arms or sides where they'd been wounded. Calvin spotted a man helping a woman who was limping along.

"Hurry, hurry, hurry," Anna muttered under her breath.

Ortiz was praying. Marino had her rifle shouldered, facing down the trail. Boston was pacing.

"As soon as the enemy is in range, start firing!" Calvin said. Then he placed a call to the Refugee Center staff, warning them to open the doors to receive the defenders in the lobby.

More and more Steel Runners, Rangers, and civilian volunteers rushed toward them. Calvin counted about twenty-five or thirty that had made it from the deluge of smoke. Gunshots boomed from behind them in the acrid fog.

Calvin spotted Flannery running among the survivors. She was waving her hands to encourage the men and women around her to hurry.

The first few people were only a hundred yards or so from the Refugee Center.

"Here we go!" Calvin said. "We have to hold this Center!"

And that was when a Rattlesnake emerged from the smoke. Wearing a black jacket and streaks of warpaint across his face, he looked like a spirit released from hell. Flames and smoke swirled behind him.

In one hand, he carried a pistol. In his other, he had a tomahawk.

The rider raced toward a Ranger at the rear of the retreating defensive forces. Running with a limp, the Ranger looked back, terrified.

"Open fire!" Calvin yelled. "We cannot let a single hostile into this building!"

More Rattlesnakes rode out of the smoke, firing and shrieking.

All around Calvin, his comrades squeezed off calculated bursts.

Calvin sighted up the hostile in the black jacket and squeezed the trigger. One of the bullets lanced into the enemy's shoulder, nearly knocking him off the horse. Somehow, he still managed to sling his tomahawk at the fleeing Ranger, hitting him right in the back.

Roving his rifle, Calvin saw the Ranger hit the asphalt. He moved the scope back to the rider, but the man had already turned his horse and was galloping out of range.

A wave of wild gunshots erupted from the other approaching riders. Calvin ejected his spent magazine, counting at least thirty riders now chasing down their beleaguered defensive forces while he reloaded.

Below, the first few Rangers and Steel Runners finally made it to the parking lot of the Refugee Center.

Calvin brought up his rifle and fired again and again.

All the while, the Rattlesnakes continued their own vicious salvos, closing in on the building. Rounds slammed against the side of the Refugee Center. Others smashed into the side of the roof, shrapnel flying from the impacts. Some rounds seared through the air past Calvin's head.

Even as Rattlesnakes went down in the return fire, they continued to slaughter the defensive forces fleeing. Calvin lost count of the bodies spread on the trail.

Emotion and anger threatened to overwhelm him.

He held on to a single phrase Mouse had instilled in him: *It's just a mind game.*

Focus. Focus. Focus.

He had to keep his cool. Every squeeze of the trigger became more and more important as enemy fighters closed in on the Refugee Center.

Some of the warriors lit fresh Molotov cocktails.

"Take out the hostiles with the Molotovs!" Calvin yelled over the din of gunfire.

A couple of the Rattlesnakes collapsed off their horses. The bottles they'd been carrying cracked against the ground, fire exploding where they hit.

But one of the many Rattlesnakes left still had his Molotov cocktail in hand. Calvin tried to adjust his aim, firing just as the soldier launched the cocktail into the air.

Flames suddenly erupted from the window the Rattlesnake had thrown it through one floor beneath Calvin. The enemy must've already shot out the glass. Which meant there was an active fire where people were supposed to be sheltering.

"Ortiz, Boston," Calvin yelled. "Put that fire out!"

The two Steel Runners immediately ran through the open roof access door.

Calvin continued firing on the Rattlesnakes with Marino and Anna. But nearly a dozen men made it past them—and under the roof of the lobby.

They were going to get inside. The Gomezes, the Spears, the Lithgows... all were in danger.

"Marino, keep watch," Calvin said. "Anna, on me!"

Cradling his rifle, Calvin ran to the door, his heart climbing in his throat. All he could think about were the Gomezes and their room on the second floor.

Anna followed him down the stairs to head off the invaders. In seconds, they were on the first floor near the lobby.

A couple of Rangers had posted up at a desk at the entry.

Bodies lay sprawled over the floor—a couple Rattlesnakes and a handful of defenders. Steel Runners and civilian forces tried to keep the hostiles pinned down in the lobby, but Calvin could hear gunfire cracking in other areas.

There were more Rattlesnakes somewhere in this building.

With the attackers in the lobby pinned down, he turned to his left, studying the hallway. It was filled with other Steel Runners, Rangers, and civilian defenders, many of whom were injured. Most were holding their arms, sides, or legs, groaning from gunshot wounds.

No Rattlesnakes there.

Calvin's blood turned to ice.

Near the lobby entrance was another stairwell. The door had been opened, leading to the second floor with the sheltering refugees—and the Gomezes.

"Upstairs!" Calvin said to Anna.

The two of them bounded right back up the stairs to the second floor. To their left and right was a corridor lined in doorways. Calvin heard screams and cries inside the rooms from frightened civilians, but saw no Rattlesnakes.

He gestured for Anna to follow and they sprinted down the hall to the next corner. Calvin paused there, hearing voices in the next hallway. He snuck a glance, seeing two Rattlesnakes were at one of the open doorways aiming their weapons inside. They were holding their fire, thankfully. That told him they were trying to take hostages or were looking for someone specific.

He indicated to Anna there were two hostiles and to cover him. She nodded back.

Calvin strode into the hallway, blasting the first Rattlesnake. The man jerked from each impact before crashing sideways.

The second man started to turn Calvin's way. He began firing immediately, bullets slashing past Calvin. Rounds hit the wall and ceiling.

From behind, gunshots cracked from Anna's rifle.

The man slumped forward, dropping his weapon and gripping a chest wound pumping blood.

Calvin's ears rang from all the close quarters gunfire, but even so, he could hear a strange calm. The gunshots from downstairs were no longer resonating through the floor.

"Lobby is clear," someone called over the radio.

"Outside is clear," Marino added next.

There was a pause before Ortiz came on the line. "Fire's under control."

"Second floor is clear," Calvin said.

Flannery called next. "No sign of more hostiles coming from town. Recon teams report hostiles fleeing back westward."

Calvin started to stand, signaling for Anna to follow.

But after he took the first few steps, he realized she hadn't taken a step. He turned.

Anna was leaning heavily against the corner. She started to slide down it. Blood streaked the wall as she did.

"Oh, shit, no!" Calvin shouted. "Medic! I need a medic!"

He turned back to Anna.

"Cal..." she managed.

He knelt beside her and held her hand as she leaned against him. Blood dribbled from a hole in her shirt. Calvin felt his own heart kick when he saw it was right where her heart was located.

"Cal..." she whispered.

Footsteps rushed up from behind him.

"Calvin, let me help." It was Sandra. He pulled back to let

her work, but it was clear right away there was nothing she could do.

Calvin held Anna's hand as she bled out. Within seconds, he felt her strength in his grip fading.

"No," he whispered. "Anna, please, fight..."

Anna took in another breath of air, her lips opening one last time. He thought she was trying to say something, but instead, Anna smiled at him.

Then she was gone.

Calvin held her hand in shock, watching as Sandra tried to revive Anna to no avail.

The New Frontier had claimed another soul.

Anna would never make it back East. Her nieces would be without their aunt, her sister now missing a sibling.

Time seemed to slow around Calvin. He heard shouting, crying, and then a familiar voice.

He turned to find Maureen standing in the hallway with her arms around both kids. Calvin finally let go of Anna's hand and stood.

She had died to protect them, to protect all of the civilians that were flooding out of the rooms. Calvin walked over toward Maureen when he saw the White Sox cap that had belonged to Travis. Anna had lost it when she was shot.

He bent down and picked it up, finding flecks of fresh blood on its bill. Tucking it into his shirt, he then went and hugged Maureen and her kids.

"It's okay, the fighting is over," Calvin told them soothingly.

For now, he thought.

22

PALMER STRODE DOWN THE HALLS OF FORT GOLDEN with a radio pressed to his ear. He could still barely believe all the chaotic news. Especially the updates from Estes Park and the horrific attack by the Rattlesnakes.

But there was more.

"Eddy got away," Lindsey said, sounding exhausted. She was still up north. Palmer judged she wouldn't have made it far from Pinkham yet. "That son of a bitch had a bunch of hostages. We managed to free them thanks to Eddy, and we're going to send them your way for protection."

"Okay," Palmer replied. "I'll take care of them. What about the rest of the Rattlesnakes?"

"We're searching for them, and thankfully, the drones we set up helped us pick up the trail of some other Rattlesnakes leaving the area. They're headed north to Medicine Bow like we thought. Only instead of going to Centennial, they're headed to Albany."

"I should be up there, ma'am. I should be up there with you. I want to see Eddy dead."

"We all do, but we all have our roles, and yours is in

Golden. Abbott's Spartan platoon is ready, and we've got the rest of the Rangers. I'm going to see if I can even convince Blair to support me on this one. These are desperate times."

Palmer dodged past a couple of Rangers escorting a prisoner down the hall. Yet another lawbreaker to add to the increasingly stuffed cells.

"All the more reason to have me up there," he said. "My pa always said, 'What good is a hound dog if you don't take it hunting?'"

"Some days, a guard dog is more important than a hunting dog." Lindsey paused and sighed on the other line. "Look, I'm not great with words, Palmer."

"That makes two of us, Sheriff."

"Point is, I've got to deal with the north. You keep Fort Golden secure. That means the prisons, the Secretary of Defense, the Foreign Advisory Council, and the refugees."

"What about the people of Estes?"

"They are in bad shape. Everyone that's survived has either run off to nearby towns or they're bunkered down at the Refugee Center. We want to get them to safety, but we're still trying to organize *how* we're getting them out of there."

Palmer racked his brain for a second. Then he thought about the prisons. "Ma'am, I've got an idea. You focus on Eddy. I'll get everyone from Estes Park safely evacuated with our prison buses. Drop off those hostages you rescued in Estes Park too, so you don't have to waste your own vehicles bringing people south. They can board with the refugees. Shoot, I can even have some of our FAC's peacekeepers escort the buses for safety, just like they said they would. How's that?"

"It's risky, but..."

"They're safer here. No way Golden is attacked. Eddy

knows it would be too devastating to his forces, but he could return to Estes Park to finish the job."

"True... okay, get it done. I got to go."

"Good luck, Sheriff."

"And to you. Thanks, Cody."

As Palmer navigated the corridors, he made some calls to get the ball running on deploying resources to Estes Park. Once he confirmed they had the vehicles and personnel, he called Calvin.

"Get your people ready to move," Palmer said. "We're bringing you to Golden."

"When?" Calvin asked.

"Our convoy is leaving shortly. They'll be there in just about an hour and a half. Be ready as you can be."

"On it." Calvin's voice sounded gravelly and hoarse. "Thank you, Deputy Palmer."

"You doing okay?" Palmer asked.

Calvin paused. "Nah, man. I'm pretty far from okay. I just lost... I just lost another four Steel Runners. Watched seven Rangers bite it, and a handful of civilians. I only got twelve Steel Runners still able to even fight—and even some of those men and women are wounded. We're in sorry fucking shape."

"I'm so sorry, Calvin," Palmer said. "Lindsey's going to make this right. She's going to get Eddy."

"Getting Eddy ain't going to make this right. No amount of death is going to make this right. I just want to make sure these civilians—Raven's family, the Gomezes, all these refugees and people who just watched their homes burn—I want to make sure they make it through this madness."

"Me too. You all get on those buses and get down here. We'll keep them safe together."

Palmer ended the call.

After nearly an hour of making arrangements and

ensuring the convoy was ready to go north to help those in Estes Park, he walked out from the building. He started his way around the metal catwalks set up behind the two-story concrete walls. Toward the western side of Fort Golden, spotlights shone through the darkening evening sky from the two guard towers overlooking the steel gate doors.

Making good on his word to Lindsey and everyone else, he wanted to ensure every detail of the defenses was taken care of.

From his vantage, he could see the silhouettes of machine guns poking out from the guard towers. Rangers were positioned across the wall.

As he patrolled around, checking in with the Rangers, the last prison buses left Fort Golden's gates with an escort of two SUVs filled with Canadian and Mexican peacekeepers. He was glad the FAC finally had a role they could play to help.

God knew they needed it around here. He just wished the other hundred peacekeepers and aid workers stationed at Buckley could actually be on the front lines, watching for Eddy, instead of waiting in the wings.

The gates closed as the buses chugged away down the street. He watched for a moment, still wishing he was going.

Voices distracted him from his thoughts and Palmer turned toward a group of ten people moving out through a parking lot below. He certainly hadn't assigned all ten to stand in that one position. Not when they needed men and women patrolling the foothills and city around Fort Golden.

He started toward the group, walking along the reinforced concrete walls. As he drew nearer, he realized that most of the group wore black suits.

Secret Service agents.

At the center was Secretary of Defense Charlize Montgomery.

Palmer took a walkway down to the parking lot.

"Madam Secretary," Palmer said as he approached, surprised to see her outside like this. "What are you doing out here?"

"Deputy Palmer." The secretary waved away a couple of her Secret Service agents so Palmer could join her. She leaned on a cane. Her radiation-poisoned bones must have been getting to her tonight. "I'm not the type of leader content with pushing papers around a desk. I'd rather see what my people are up to."

Then she paused, closing her eyes and inhaling.

"Besides, I needed a good breath of fresh air," she continued. "Especially after hearing about what happened in Estes Park."

From where they stood, Palmer could just see the tops of the dark foothills in the distance to see where the buses would be driving with the convoy. Only the moonlight shone out there. No fires. No electricity.

"Breaks my heart to think about that town burning after everything it's been through," Charlize said. "I'm just glad to hear the refugees and civilians are okay. It would have been a slaughter if Calvin and his Steel Runners weren't there."

Palmer nodded and snorted.

"Sorry," he said.

She glanced over. "For what?"

"Just don't understand people like Eddy."

"I've known many of them in my day," Charlize said. "Fenix comes to mind."

Palmer remembered the neo-Nazi leader that had risen up after the Collapse. He was the one that killed Charlize's brother, a pilot named Nathan Sardetti.

"The war allowed a lot of evil men and women to rise up in the ashes," Charlize said. "It's up to men and women like you and me to stop them, and that's what we're going to do with Eddy. You have my word."

"Yes, ma'am."

The rumble of engines faded in the distance.

After Charlize said her goodbyes and went back inside, and Palmer climbed back up to the walls for a view.

Although he wanted to leave and join the real fight, he had a job to do here with the refugees coming from Estes Park. They needed protection once they arrived.

And Lindsey was perfectly capable of taking care of herself up north. He had to trust her to carry out her mission as he carried out his.

————

The convoy returning from Pinkham had a view of the smoke billowing from Estes Park long before they got up the mountain passes. Lindsey drove her Bronco after a pair of Spartan MRAP APCs. The rest of Abbott's Spartan Platoon was preparing in Livermore.

Raven and Creek rode with her. He gazed out the window.

As they turned toward Estes Park, she called the two Spartan APCs on the radio.

"Have all your men head up to Livermore immediately," she said. "We need to start preparations for the attack. The timeline may have moved forward."

"Understood, Sheriff," one of the Spartan drivers replied.

The two APCs peeled off and headed north.

She knew the hot feeling of anger rising in her gut. She'd also felt the iciness of raw terror plunge through her vessels plenty of times. And she had been stricken by the utter defeat of watching loved ones die during the Collapse more often than she wished to count.

Turbulent emotions were no stranger to her.

So when she drove into town and saw the smoldering remains, she knew what to expect. She knew how her body would tighten, her muscles coiling. Knew what the sensation of adrenaline would feel like preparing her for a fight.

Yet as she neared Estes Park, she felt something different this time.

She eyed the broken windows of the nearby general store. Embers glowed around the support beams that had collapsed inside.

Black smoke plumed off the raging fire still burning from a motel. Restaurants and souvenir-shops-turned general stores were all consumed by flames. The smoky air made Lindsey's eyes water.

"This is worse than I imagined," Raven said. His voice came out in a rasp as if he still couldn't believe this was reality.

Creek whined, nudging his head against Raven's leg.

Lindsey sighed mournfully. "He sent people behind our lines... one small raiding party on horseback did all this..."

"We just don't have enough people. How in the hell are you and your Rangers supposed to watch every inch of the Rocky Mountains?"

Raven looked up at the night sky like the answers were somewhere behind the smoke-choked stars.

"Eddy's horsemen must've taken the mountain paths, away from the highways, then cut through somewhere further along," Raven said. "These bastards knew our weak points."

Lindsey still felt shell-shocked as they drove down the street and saw the first of the bodies lying where they had been gunned down.

"God," she whispered.

"I should have seen this coming," Raven said.

He cursed and hit the side of the door with his fist.

Lindsey had only seen him like this once, years ago. Not that she blamed him. She was full of rage just as much as she was full of sadness.

"Eddy baited me so he could do this," Raven said. "I'm going to make sure he pays."

Lindsey tried to find the right words to reassure him but failed. Nothing she could say would make this right.

Only actions spoke now.

They stared at the corpses that had been left behind in the slaughter. It would take days to clean up the wreckage. Days to figure out who had died and whose families needed to be told about the sacrifice or the needless murder of their loved ones.

She finally stopped at the Refugee Center. Already the prison buses and the FAC SUVs and APCs had made it. A twenty-person group of Mexican, Canadian, and a few Chinese peacekeepers had formed a perimeter around the parking lot.

Calvin was outside with his rifle cradled, waiting, next to another set of twelve Steel Runners. They were ushering the civilians from the entrance of the Refugee Center and onto the buses in an orderly fashion.

Raven and Creek hopped out of Lindsey's Bronco as soon as she stopped. "Got to find my family."

When Lindsey stepped out, a couple of Ranger SUVs pulled up, disgorging officers. Among them were Nuke and Rogers. They helped organize a defensive perimeter to watch over the refugees. Another pair of Rangers escorted the hostages they'd rescued from Pinkham to the refugee buses.

"Keep your eyes open," Lindsey ordered, flashing hand signals.

She turned back to the civilians making their way to the prison buses in single file lines. Raven had found Sandra and Allie. He was holding them both.

Lindsey made sure security was in place before joining them.

"You can't leave us," Sandra said. "Raven, you know this is it. You know if you go after Eddy, you won't come back."

Allie was crying and Sandra had tears in her eyes. She directed her gaze at Lindsey.

"Sheriff, you have the army with you now," Sandra said. "You don't need my brother."

Raven whispered something to Sandra that made her pull back.

"No," she sobbed. "You always say that, Sam."

"This is personal," Raven said.

"And that is what makes it all the more dangerous."

"Raven, if you want to stay behind, I understand," Lindsey said.

Sandra and Allie both looked to Raven. Even Creek did.

"You will never be safe if Eddy's alive," Raven said, a sad expression directed at Sandra. "He tried to kill you and everyone I love. I have to make sure he goes down. I'm sorry, Sis."

He kissed her on the cheek, then leaned down to hug Allie. She reached up into his embrace, then Creek joined them, nestling against the girl.

Raven stood and helped Sandra and Allie toward a bus.

"You'll be safe in Golden," Raven said, "and I'll be there as soon as I can. I promise."

Sandra looked at Lindsey with a defeated, sad gaze that made her nearly melt.

"I won't let anything happen to him," Lindsey said.

For another moment, the two women held eye contact. Sandra didn't seem like she believed Lindsey. But before she could protest, she turned and helped Allie up into the bus.

The last people to head to the buses were the Steel Runners.

Lindsey grabbed Calvin's arm before he could load up. He turned to her, his eyes full of iron and fire.

"We're going to make this right, Calvin. We're going to do something about your Steel Runners. I promise. Their deaths won't be in vain."

He gave her a solid nod. "I'm going to get these people to safety. That's all that matters right now. Then, if we all live through his hell, we can talk about the dead later."

Calvin loaded up.

Before the Rangers could leave, another small convoy rolled toward them. Blair and his reserve force of Royal Marines had arrived.

Blair's Royal Marines had three Land Rover Wolfs lined up. They also had two MRZR lightweight vehicles that looked like souped-up dune buggies with mounted machine guns both on top and on a passenger-side swing arm. Those vehicles would make quick work of the mountainous terrain and the woods.

As Blair got out of one of the Wolfs, the convoy with the refugees began to take off.

"This is a bloody mess," Blair said, heading toward Lindsey and Raven.

A vessel bulged in his forehead, and his cheeks radiated crimson. He seethed with more anger than Lindsey had ever seen from him.

"Eddy cannot be allowed to get away with this," Blair continued.

"No shit," Raven replied. Creek barked as if in support.

Lindsey was silent for just a moment. "This terror needs to end tonight."

"What are you saying?" Raven asked.

"We hit Eddy now," Lindsey said. "We don't give him a chance to regroup or reorganize. We stop him right *fucking* now."

Blair's brow furrowed as he gazed back at his Marines.

"I know," she said. "You can't be a part of this. I get it."

"No," Blair said. "No, that's not quite right. I told my CO about the attack on Estes Park. I told them that you all were staging an assault to stop the Rattlesnakes."

Blair gestured back at the vehicles.

"My CO told me, if I got volunteers, I could send a small party with yours. He seemed to understand the importance of this mission. And so did twenty-five of my men."

"You're kidding?" Raven asked.

"I'm as serious as the bloody plague, mate."

"I assume you told them the assault was tomorrow," Lindsey said. "Are you clear to go tonight?"

Blair nodded. "Most certainly."

It didn't take long to load back up in their vehicles and begin their journey north. As soon as they were back on the road, Lindsey called Lieutenant Abbott in Livermore.

"I'd like to press the attack for tonight," she said. "But ultimately, you're in charge. I can be there in about ninety minutes, with twenty-five Royal Marines and forty Rangers. What do you think?"

"Sheriff, after I heard about Estes Park, I thought you'd never ask. We can have the Spartans ready for the assault before you even get to Livermore. Then it's just an hour drive to go take those motherfucking Rattlesnakes down."

Soon enough, they had left the destruction of Estes Park

behind and made it to Livermore. The small town was little more than an abandoned saloon, a rotting church, and a defunct gas station.

But already it was a hive of activity.

Abbott had already organized his platoon for the attack.

Their three APCs and four Humvees were idling and ready to go.

She and Raven stepped out of her Bronco as soon as it was parked. Creek tagged along on the way to find Abbott standing in front of a Humvee. He had a map spread out on the hood. One of his enlisted officers shone a flashlight at it. Blair joined them there.

Abbott faced them and nodded. "We finished all our preparations, and we know where Eddy's people are."

"Hell yes," Raven said. "Where?"

Lindsey looked at the map as Abbott used his finger to point.

"Both drones still have his people pinned down here in Albany on the southwestern edge of Medicine Bow-Routt National Forest," Abbott said. "Before we get into the strategy, I want you to understand this is a military operation now. I'm here on personal orders from the President of the United States. Understand?"

Lindsey had expected this and was glad to have the support of this platoon. As long as he didn't do anything stupid, she would listen. "Yes, sir."

"Good. Now what do you know about Albany?" Abbott asked.

"It's heavily wooded and full of muddy roads, homes, warehouses, and a couple of small lodges," Lindsey said. "At least, that's what it was before the Collapse. Far as I know, it was abandoned."

"Until Eddy's people took it," Raven said.

Abbott nodded. "Without knowing how much time they've had to dig in, I can't say whether they've just used this as a temporary staging area or set it up as a fortified base. The longer they've been there, the more defensive measures I imagine they've prepared. Worst case scenario, this looks like it's going to be our Fallujah."

"Urban combat?" Lindsey asked.

Raven nodded. "Fighting block by block was an absolute hell. Booby traps, gunmen behind every blind corner. IEDs. A real fucking nightmare."

"We're going to need to approach with the utmost caution," Abbott said. "Bad news is that our drones are going to be running on fumes soon. They'll only be with us for another two hours. Just enough time to monitor the enemy on our approach, but not enough to keep surveillance up during the attack."

"In that case, I'm going to propose I go ahead," Raven said. "Let me scout out the terrain. They're going to have their own patrols throughout the woods. I can track them. Find us a way in."

"I'm glad you volunteered, because otherwise, I was going to order it," Abbott said. "I want some recon forces that know those woods. We can use them to identify and even eliminate as many hostile scouts and guards as possible before we make our approach."

"I can assign some of my best," Lindsey said.

"Perfect. They'll be critical to the first stage of the attack. We obviously want to get as close as we can without them noticing."

"Knowing Eddy's people, it's going to be unlikely we make it all the way in completely unnoticed," Raven said. "I'm better off on my own with Creek."

"If we had the luxury of time, I'd agree with you," Abbott

said. "But tonight, time is not on our side. You can't cover that much ground on your own."

Raven looked like he was about to argue, but Lindsey shook her head

"Lieutenant Blair, divide your team up to take the north and south sides," Abbott said. "You'll have the advantage of the mountain slopes, so the higher ground will allow you to trap the Rattlesnake forces in. The rest of the Rangers and the Spartans can advance on the road via the eastern approach. We'll be the hammer that crushes them when you have them pinned down. Our goal is to converge on Eddy and to take him out."

Abbott pointed at a spot on the map of Albany.

"This is Sawmill Lodge," Abbott explained. "We never got a positive ID on Eddy, but since tracking his forces up there, the most activity seems to be in and out of that lodge. It's the central nervous system of their operations in Albany, I'd guess. So if Eddy's up there, I'd bet this is where we find him."

Then Abbott locked eyes with Raven.

"In case we somehow miss him, part of your job on recon is positively identifying Eddy," Abbott said. "I don't want him to run or get past our lines. You see him, you let us know."

"You want him dead or alive?" Raven asked.

"Our goal tonight is to end the Rattlesnakes by killing Eddy," Abbott said. "We remove him, take down his closest allies, and all these groups working for him will leave."

Lindsey nodded. "He may have an army, but they're bought and paid for. Take away their funds, and they will scatter like leaves in the wind."

23

JUST A COUPLE OF HOURS AFTER RECONVENING WITH THE forces in Livermore, Raven found himself navigating the hilly terrain of Medicine Bow. He had his suppressed M4 strapped over his back, two hatchets in sheaths on his utility belt, and extra magazines secured in both his tac vest and his pack. The ceramic plates and ballistic inserts in his body armor helped protect his vitals.

Lieutenant Abbott had even ensured he had two fragmentation grenades, a smoke grenade, and a flash grenade in his tac vest. Similarly, he and the Rangers had all been outfitted with NVGs.

For the first time since the Collapse, Raven was truly well-equipped. He almost felt like a Recon Marine again.

Of course, the crossbow he cradled wasn't exactly standard issue for a Marine. But he'd already used it to send four bolts through armed men he'd seen in the woods.

From the sporadic reports from the other Ranger Recon teams, they'd had equal success.

The chilly mountain air curled between the trees as

Raven walked at a hunch. Creek prowled along right beside him.

Harsh voices echoed through the woods and up the rocky slopes.

Between the trees about a hundred yards ahead, shapes moved around in the darkness. They ran between warehouses and cabins carrying weapons and ammunition crates.

Raven whispered into his encrypted comms. Another gift from Abbott.

"Hammer Alpha-One," he said, using Abbott's callsign. "Recon Alpha. I have eyes on the target location. They must've seen or heard your vehicles, judging by the panic around Albany."

"Copy that," Abbott voice came back over the radio. "All Recon teams, SITREP."

One by one, the others called in. All teams were accounted for. They had successfully formed a perimeter.

"Anvil Alpha and Bravo, begin advance," Abbott said, addressing the two Marine teams that would come in from the north and south respectively.

"Wilco," Blair's smooth voice answered.

"All Hammer teams, wait for my signal," Abbott continued, referring to the mix of Spartans and Rangers that would come in from the east.

While the Marines had the cover of the trees, the Hammer teams would have no such advantage. Their sole goal would be to come in hard and fast after the Anvil teams had already sowed chaos in the Rattlesnake's ranks.

"Recon teams, hold positions and provide fire support for Hammer teams," Lindsey finished.

Raven settled into his cover behind a tree. While he was invisible to the enemy forces, the infrared tag on his NVGs would alert the Royal Marines to his position, ensuring he didn't become a victim of friendly fire.

Soon enough, he heard the whine of engines. Flashing infrared lights broke between the trees and over the tops of the hills to Raven's south.

He pivoted to look out over the town again to see the same infrared lights coming in from the north.

Blair and his small group of Marines were making their charge. Raven respected him and his men for volunteering to join this battle.

He turned back toward the town.

More panic filled the Rattlesnake Union ranks as shouts filled the air. Armed warriors started flooding into the buildings or finding shooting positions behind berms and vehicles parked along the muddy road.

As they did, Raven and the other Recon teams reported every enemy position they spotted.

For the first time, Raven felt like they actually had a chance.

They were no longer tracking and hunting an enemy that was two steps ahead. This time, he and his allies were the ones who had caught their enemy unaware.

Raven stowed his crossbow and took out his suppressed M4. The first of the Marines' MRZRs was just fifty or so yards away.

As it tore down the slope, winding between trees, Raven turned his attention back to the enemy. One of the Rattlesnakes poked up from behind a truck where he was hiding with two other contacts. He appeared to be ready to throw something.

A grenade, Raven guessed.

He aimed at the man, then fired a burst into the hostile's chest.

The man fell backward and disappeared behind the vehicle. The two warriors who had been hiding beside him began to sprint away from the truck.

Not a second later, an explosion tore from the dead man. The blast lifted the truck up, glass shattering in a spray of diamondlike pellets.

The pressure wave and shrapnel tore apart the two men who had been trying to escape. Flames licked up through the interior of the vehicle, and a second explosion shredded its gas tank.

"The cavalry has arrived," Blair said over the comms.

The MRZR raced past Raven. The gunners on the top- and side-mounted machine guns opened up. Tracer fire tore through the woods and into the Rattlesnakes' positions.

All the men who thought they'd been hidden behind the cars and other vehicles parked along the road were forced to scatter. The Marines hammered the positions Raven and the other Recon teams had provided.

Windows to the warehouses and general store closest to Raven burst into flying shards of broken glass under the onslaught. Screams rang out as hostiles were turned to bloody ribbons by the fusillade.

The MRZR barreled to the edge of town, crunching to a stop beside a dirt road. Right behind it came an armored Land Rover Wolf. The vehicle disgorged a team of four Marines.

A quick scan along the edge of town revealed the other Wolfs and MRZR hitting their own targets. Gunfire flared from nearly every direction as the battle erupted over the town.

"Contact with hostiles," Blair said, his voice urgent now. "Anvil teams have established perimeter positions. Requesting Hammer support immediately."

"Hammer teams, advance!" Abbott roared over the comms.

The gunfire continued for several minutes as the Marines suppressed the Rattlesnake positions. Raven crept closer to the edge of town with Creek following. He did his best not to draw any attention.

As much as he wanted to assist his comrades, he had a singular goal now: find Eddy.

The roar of the Humvees and APCs from the east reverberated through town.

From Raven's position, he couldn't get a good view of them. But the sound of more gunfire and shouts told him that the Rattlesnakes now must have realized they were surrounded.

"Recon Alpha," Abbott's voice came in over the channel. "You are clear to engage target."

"Copy," Raven called back. Then he motioned for Creek. The dog let out a low growl as if he understood what was at stake.

As the Marines nearest Raven's position pressed the advance, clearing first a parking lot and then infiltrating a storage shed, Raven snuck eastward.

He used the cover of the trees and bushes to move. His NVGs revealed a stark landscape devoid of life.

The pervasive gunfire was working, forcing Eddy's forces to shrink back into town, thoroughly pinning them down.

Raven slipped between a trailer home and an auto repair shop. The big doors of the repair shop were open, revealing four different trucks and SUVs on the lifts. Tools were scattered around the shop as if they had been recently used.

No lights shone from inside the mobile home. Not that Raven expected any with the attack taking hold of the town.

He started prowling through the long grass next to the trailer.

Something about the home irked him.

Maybe a sixth sense of sorts.

He expected to see gunmen in defensive positions nearby. There must be someone inside the trailer home, but he hadn't seen movement.

Why would they leave their flank open to attack like this?

He searched between the overgrown blades of grass, wondering if there was someone waiting nearby. Listening for footsteps. Looking out for movement.

Then he saw it.

A thin filament so light, he nearly missed it. Probably would have had he not worn NVGs.

A fishing line.

Gesturing for Creek to stay put, Raven knelt and crept toward it.

Sure enough, the fishing line stretched from a pole in the autoshop's parking lot straight across to the trailer home.

He followed the line to see that it led to what appeared to be an improvised explosive device at the foot of the trailer home. Sniffing at the air, he also detected the scent of gasoline.

Using his NVGs, he peered down the length of the trailer home to see a couple of gas canisters with their caps left open.

Good God.

If he hadn't noticed the line, he would've set off the IED. Then the gas tanks would've erupted into expanding balls of fire, finishing him off if the explosive hadn't.

"All teams, be aware, I just identified an IED on a fishing line trigger," Raven said. "Keep your eyes open."

He plucked his multitool then snipped the fishing line, letting it drift gently to the ground.

Then he continued, his heart pounding wildly. He had come so close to death. He couldn't just charge ahead into town like he'd hoped.

If this was any indication, then this whole sector was probably mired in traps just like Abbott had warned. The advance to Eddy's position wouldn't be nearly as fast as he hoped.

Gunfire intensified with a cacophonous fury.

"Anvil Alpha, requesting additional fire support," a Royal Marine called over the radio. "Meeting heavy resistance near the gas station."

"Recon Bravo here. We're seeing Rattlesnake movement from the southwestern warehouse. More headed your way, Anvil Alpha. Will try to cut them off, but we count at least twenty hostiles. Too many for us to handle alone from our current position."

The frantic radio calls continued. More of the Rattlesnakes seemed to be emerging from the buildings, maneuvering to reinforce their defensive positions.

Tremoring thuds from grenade blasts erupted from all directions. Then came a quaking blast that sounded to Raven like an IED had been set off.

A ball of fire rolled into the dark sky to his northwest.

"Heavy resistance on the eastern approach!" Lieutenant Abbott reported. "Our advance has stalled. Enemy is firmly entrenched."

From the reports, it sounded to Raven like the attack was quickly coming to a stalemate. It would soon devolve into a lengthy battle of attrition as both sides hunkered into shooting positions.

That made Raven's role even more important.

He had to be like a cruise missile, ignoring the chafe and

distractions, headed straight toward a target that would debilitate the enemy.

If he could make it to Eddy, he could end this battle before there was more bloodshed.

At a hunch, he stalked around the end of another trailer home.

Down the road, he could see other trucks and SUVs parked along a road. A barn stood alongside the eastern length of the road after a line of one-story cabins. Silhouettes moved inside several of the six cabins, visible through the windows.

From studying the map of Albany, Raven knew the Sawmill Lodge where Eddy's headquarters were should be just beyond the cabins and the barn.

Just to his west, a good hundred yards or so from the cabins, the flash of gunfire, roaring fire, and shouts revealed where the battle between the Marines and the Rattlesnakes was fiercest.

Another blast tore into the air to his right, to the east. Blinding fire reached into the sky like a demon tearing up from the bowels of hell almost three hundred yards away.

"Help!" a voice called over the radio. "Hammer Team Delta requesting medical assistance! Six down, I repeat, six down!"

"We're sending Armored Personnel Carrier One straight toward the Sawmill Lodge," Abbott said. "Move, move, move!"

The throaty wallop of the APC engine echoed up through the wooded town between the incessant crack of gunfire.

Raven began his advance between the cabins, headed toward the cover of the barn, sticking close to the trees behind them. He continually glanced up at the windows, then down at the ground looking for more booby traps.

Another length of fishing line was strung between the trunks ahead.

He studied the woods, spotting three more IEDs. He took out his multitool, snipping through two. Then he headed to the third.

As he stepped toward the last one, his boot suddenly seemed to pierce the soft ground. The leaves and branches at his feet fell away, and he nearly lurched forward into nothingness.

He threw himself backward instinctually.

Camouflage netting crumpled into a pit. It fell in around sharpened metal poles at the bottom of what must have been an eight-foot-deep hole.

A punji stick trap.

Raven took a deep breath and flashed a hand signal to Creek to stay back. After skirting around the pit, Raven went and clipped the last fishing line.

With the booby traps dismantled, he motioned for his dog. They trekked toward the end of the cabins, identifying another punji stick trap about halfway there.

Raven moved around it and finally made it to the side of the barn. He heard muffled voices inside barking orders.

While he couldn't quite make out the words, it was clear they were preparing some kind of defensive action. Raven made his way alongside the barn to the easternmost side.

Now he could see farther down the road.

A line of trees fenced in a pair of cabins right next to the two-story Sawmill Lodge where Eddy should be. On the front of the lodge, the unmistakable form of a white buffalo was spray-painted, visible in Raven's NVGs.

The rumble of the APC sounded closer. Raven could just start to see it cresting up the road.

Gunfire from the cabins pinged against the armored vehicle.

Those gunmen stood no chance against it.

Maybe the APC would even be enough cover to get Raven closer to the lodge.

Before he could make a move, an explosion tore in front of the APC. Soil geysered around it. The vehicle withstood the blast, barreling up the slope toward the lodge.

It looked like the Spartans would in fact finish the job, striking at the center of Albany before the other teams could.

As the APC began to slow as it neared the lodge, Raven heard the crack of a wooden door sliding open. He looked up to see the door to the hayloft pulled back.

A man knelt there with an NLAW rocket launcher. This was military hardware. It sent a chill up his spine.

Fire bloomed from the launcher as a rocket speared out at the APC.

The blinding explosion cleaved through the armor. Metal peeled and protested as the wheels splayed. The APC ground to a sickening halt, its ruptured hull plowing through the dirt road. Screams came from within the vehicle.

At the same time, the Rattlesnakes in the barn began firing on the few soldiers spilling from the inferno raging from the shredded APC.

All Raven's hopes that this battle would be over in a matter of minutes were destroyed as quickly as the APC's armor had been.

24

THE HEAT OF THE BLAST TORE ACROSS THE DIRT AND washed over Lindsey. She took cover behind the Spartans' second APC next to Abbott. Gunfire rattled against its armor, pinging and ricocheting relentlessly.

Lindsey's personal squad of six Rangers, callsign Hammer Charlie, were stacked up behind the shelter of a couple burned-out cars stalled in the street just about five yards from her position. Nuke and Rogers were both on the team.

Already they had lost three Rangers to IEDs. Gunfire had injured at least four more. From the radio, Lindsey knew an additional three Royal Marines had been injured. Potentially one KIA.

Now one whole squad of Spartans had been decimated by a rocket. The fact that the Rattlesnakes had NLAW rocket launchers told Lindsey they were up against far more than they anticipated.

The blinding flash of muzzle fire seemed to be coming from every direction at once. Explosive blasts boomed between the staccato bark of gunshots. Most of her allies seemed to be pinned down by the sheer volume of violence.

Eddy's troops weren't well-trained military members like most of Lindsey's attack force. What they lacked in skill, they made up for in numbers.

Every time Lindsey killed one, it seemed two more sprouted from the earth, taking shooting positions and raining lead on them.

Sawmill Lodge was located near the top of the hill. In between it and Lindsey's position were two warehouses. Past the warehouses and the lodge was a barn where the NLAW seemed to have been fired from. Just beyond it was a line of six cabins. Those buildings were all filled with hostiles, according to Raven and the other recon teams.

Trying to get the Marines to drive in with their weaker vehicles from the west to support Hammer teams' advance would be a deathtrap.

Lindsey eyed the two large warehouses standing sentinel on either side of the road leading up to the lodge again. No gunmen had emerged from them, but Lindsey didn't like how quiet they seemed.

Neither did Lieutenant Abbott apparently. He was still crouched down behind the APC beside Lindsey.

"We need to clear those warehouses before we risk sending this APC up," he said. "I don't want to lose another vehicle trying to charge ahead if they've got more unexpected weaponry."

Rounds rattled from the roof mounted M240 on the APC. Rounds blasted into the barn, sending splinters flying.

Back down the road behind them, the rest of the Humvees and the Hammer teams waited. Lindsey could see the IR tags of her Rangers and the Spartans scattered between burned out Rattlesnake cars and trucks or peeking out from the ditches alongside the road.

"I'll take the north warehouse," Abbott said. "Can you handle the south?"

Lindsey nodded.

"Good. Call when you clear it. Then we'll move the APC up closer to cover Sawmill."

Abbott peered around the side of the APC.

Rounds sparked overhead in response.

"We're going to lay down cover fire," Abbott said. "Then move on my mark."

Lindsey shot a hand signal to the rest of Hammer Charlie. She gestured toward the warehouse and relayed the plan over their comms.

"Ready," Abbott said. "Ready... Go!"

The APC's machine gun let out another teeth-chattering burst.

Tracer fire slashed through the night, blasting into the barn and the cabins behind it. Wood chips erupted with every impact of the 7.62 mm rounds. Spartans crouching in the ditches followed suit with an equally devastating salvo.

Lindsey sprinted as hard as she could for the side of the warehouse. All six of her Rangers made it, stacking up on the single door leading inside.

She plucked a flash grenade from her vest.

At her signal, Rogers positioned himself at the door, aiming his shotgun at the locking mechanism. Sweat beaded off his forehead, and she noted his Adam's apple bobbing. The guy was nervous. She didn't blame him.

A couple years ago, he'd been just a professional musician volunteering for the Rangers on the side.

Now he was in an all-out gunfight for survival.

She took a deep breath, centering her thoughts.

Just like a drug bust, she thought to herself. *Nothing more than a casual raid. We got this.*

She tried to believe those thoughts when she counted down.

Three.

Two.

One.

Rogers blew the lock away with a single blast. He kicked the door open, and Lindsey tossed the flash grenade inside. Her Rangers all turned away until they heard the telltale pop of the grenade going off. The flash of light pierced even her closed eyelids beneath her NVGs.

"Go, go, go!" she yelled.

Rogers pushed into the warehouse. Nuke and one other Ranger followed, and Lindsey went behind them before the last couple of soldiers entered.

In a blink, she took in her surroundings.

Adrenaline made it seem as if time was slowing. She first saw the chest-high rows of crates near the door they'd entered. Just around the crates were two vehicles. Transport trucks, parked side-by-side.

She counted at least eight men around the trucks, recoiling from the effects of the flash grenade. A couple blindly waved their rifles around.

Near the center, in front of the trucks, two men had another NLAW. Another hostile stood near the controls to the motorized front doors. They appeared to have been setting up an ambush just like she'd suspected.

As Rogers started to move around the crates, a sudden gun blast exploded from above.

Rogers went down in a spray of blood. He was somehow still alive, clutching his chest and gasping. Blood poured out of messy wounds in his shoulder and neck.

"No!" Nuke yelled.

It took Lindsey a moment to understand what had

happened. He'd been routed right into another of the Rattlesnake's traps. A tripwire had been rigged at the end of the crates attached to a sawed-off shotgun.

Even with his bulletproof vest, the pellets from the blast had torn through Rogers's unprotected flesh. She pulled him to safety around a stack of crates and issued a warning to the rest of her team.

Nuke immediately searched for other tripwires on the other end of the row of crates.

Sure enough, they found one, disabling it.

All the while, the Rattlesnakes were struggling to recover. One man in a leather vest turned his AK-variant toward the door, blinking like he was still blinded.

Lindsey lifted her rifle, aiming at his chest. A squeeze of the trigger sent rounds spearing through his ribs. He crumpled backward, and his rifle clattered over the floor.

Her men joined in the assault. Bullets lanced through the disoriented Rattlesnakes. Gun blasts filled the warehouse with an ear-shattering din.

One Rattlesnake in full camo fired back with his assault rifle, blindly spraying rounds their direction. Lindsey was forced to duck as bullets ripped into the crates and pounded the metal wall behind her.

She looked down at Rogers. He was gasping for air, blood bursting from his mouth.

"Hang on," she said. "We're going to get you out of here."

Rogers's face contorted in a wave of pain.

"Think about that concert at Red Rock," she said. "You got to shred on your guitar, okay?"

Rogers managed a weak nod, and Lindsey did her best to steel herself.

Nuke joined her to help.

"Help him," she ordered before rising and firing another burst.

Then she ran at a hunch behind the crates to a new position at the end of the line. She sighted up the two hostiles with the NLAW. One was a hulking man, all hard muscle. The other was a lanky man with tattoos snaking up and down his bare arms.

She pulled the trigger twice. Didn't matter what they looked like.

They both went down like sacks of meat, thumping against the floor.

Her ears ringing, she signaled for her men to head to the rear of the warehouse where the trucks were. They spread out into combat intervals, leapfrogging down the length of the trucks, clearing the cabs, then the beds.

Nearly breathless, Lindsey finally paused when they reached the end of the warehouse.

"Hammer Alpha, this is Hammer Charlie, we're clear," she called.

Machine gun chatter nearly drowned out her comms when Abbott replied.

"Our warehouse is clear," he said. "Took out two antiarmor weapon setups."

Traps upon traps, ambushes upon ambushes.

Eddy was making them bleed for every inch of ground they took.

Lindsey retreated to the crates where Rogers had been hit. Two men were now applying hemostatic gauze and coagulants to his wound. The gauze had already soaked through.

"Medics, we need immediate assistance in the southern warehouse," Lindsey said.

She returned and knelt next to Nuke. The Ranger was

holding Rogers's hand. He looked up at Lindsey with a sad expression and simply shook his head.

Lindsey cursed.

"Cancel my last," she said after a pause.

She leaned down and shut Rogers's eyes.

"I'm sorry," she whispered.

He would never again play his guitar or regale her with his love of music. And she would need to tell his brother and sister back in Denver their beloved sibling would no longer have a chance to play the concert he'd promised them all. Even if it was just in the guy's dreams, those dreams no longer existed.

She wanted to scream and yell. But for now, other lives depended on her. She clamped down on that storm of emotions.

Eddy needed to die.

With new urgency, she guided Nuke and the rest of her unit back outside and toward the rear of the APC. The rest of her men stacked up behind it, taking shelter as the bullets flew from the cabins and the barn ahead. There was no cover between this position and the lodge, except for the vehicle.

"Anvil Alpha-One, this is Hammer Charlie-One, what's your position?" she called over the comms to Blair.

"Hammer Charlie-One, this is Anvil Alpha-One," Blair replied. "The hostiles in the cabins are holding us back. Multiple contacts have antiarmor weaponry. We lost one of our Wolfs and an MRZR."

"Recon Alpha, position?" Lindsey tried.

Raven replied, "I'm hunkered down near the barn. Can't move without getting their attention. Too many IEDs and crap everywhere to make a run for it."

The easiest way to disable the rest of the enemies' defenses would be to run the APC right up the street, gunning for the Rattlesnake Union goons entrenched in the lodge and the cabins.

But with their luck, they'd crash the vehicle right into more IEDs, or worse, another NLAW rocket.

"How do we get past them?" Lindsey asked.

"We've got to draw them out of those positions!" Abbott shouted between sporadic bouts of gunfire.

"They've got to know they're trapped. They're eventually going to lose."

"You'd think," Abbott said. "But... but not if they've got reinforcements coming. Maybe they know they just have to stand their ground long enough."

"Maybe," Lindsey said. "Or maybe they're just stubborn."

"Either way, so long as we got them surrounded, they aren't going anywhere."

That sparked an idea. One that was risky but might be a way to end the stalemate.

"Look, if they got reinforcements coming, we don't have time to waste," Lindsey said. "We need to stop them quickly."

She wiped the sweat and dirt from her face, taking a moment to think.

"We give them an opening," she said. "If they don't have reinforcements, they'll try running. If they do have reinforcements coming, maybe they'll try to retreat so they can encircle *us*."

"I see where you're going with this."

Another blast of sustained gunfire erupted from the APC, putting a pause on their planning.

When it ceased, Lindsey shouted to be heard over the battle again. "We can have Anvil Teams retreat. In fact, send Anvil Bravo all the way back up the side of the mountain. Anvil Alpha can follow, but then go completely dark. Right at the edge of the woods. Make it seem like we're giving the enemy an exit."

"Then crush them when they try to escape," Abbott said.

"Most of the Rattlesnake Union isn't really loyal to Eddy. They're just glorified mercenaries. After all they've seen, why would they stand around and fight? Only the most loyal ones will. The ones bunkered up with him in his headquarters."

"You should have been a soldier," Abbott said.

"Today, I am," Lindsey said.

"Hell, everyone out here is today. Good plan."

He relayed the orders to the other units, then gave the command.

"Executing now!" Blair called back.

The roar of the Marines' vehicles' engines carried into the night, echoing over the mountainside. Lindsey watched the IR tags from their forces travel up the side of the hill overlooking Albany. Most disappeared completely beyond the slope.

The other half hunkered down in the woods.

"Now we wait and see," Abbott said.

Lindsey hated waiting. Especially when it meant waiting for vengeance. Waiting to get back at the Rattlesnakes for what they'd done to her people and to her state.

She hoped the enemy would take the bait. Because she couldn't wait much longer to get into that lodge and take Eddy Nez down.

———

With his M4 strapped over his back, Calvin knelt next to Maureen, Frankie, and Raquel in the library of Fort Golden's prison. The library was securely locked down from the rest of the dormitory-style inmate housing areas.

But Calvin still didn't like the fact that he could hear the prisoners' voices rising from their cells, past the security gates and bulletproof windows. Everyone was already exhausted. The dark early morning hours weren't making it any easier, and he doubted anyone could fall asleep now.

All the same, there weren't many better places to lay low.

And Calvin was just glad to be somewhere with far more security. He had been lucky that Ortiz, Boston, and Marino made it too.

But there were still four others who were gone. The rest were receiving medical care, their fates still uncertain.

At least behind the guarded walls of Fort Golden, Calvin figured his crew and the refugees had a better chance at making it through whatever Eddy and the Rattlesnakes might have planned. He pressed his fingers against the jacket pocket where the White Sox cap was, wishing it would bring him better luck to survive the night than it had Anna or Travis.

"Are we going to be okay?" Frankie asked, looking up at Calvin.

"I won't let anyone hurt you," Calvin promised.

"Were those men trying to hurt us back in Estes Park?" Raquel asked.

"Not you kids," Calvin lied.

In all honesty, he wasn't sure what would have happened had the Refugee Center fallen into enemy hands.

Maureen snuggled closer with the children as they nestled against a wall.

Most of the bookshelves had been pushed to the sides of the room allowing for blankets to be spread out for the many families and individuals.

From what Calvin knew, the recreation facilities, mess hall, multipurpose rooms, and even the storage closets were full of others sheltered down here until they were given the all-clear.

Of course, no one really knew when things would be clear, much less what was happening outside.

Coughs and quiet sobbing filled the library along with the murmur of soft, worried voices.

Calvin scanned the frightened faces.

His eyes locked with Sandra's. She sat against a bookshelf a couple feet away with Allie in her lap. Lara Lithgow was also here with her grandmother. Between them was Mark. The boy was white as a sheet.

Sitting down here was not doing Calvin any good. He decided to head topside to check with Palmer on what was happening and perhaps see how his Steel Runners might be able to help.

"Maureen," he said softly as he could.

She looked over.

"I'm going to go see if I can get an update, okay?"

Maureen nodded. She was trying to be strong, he could tell, but there was no doubt she was scared. Calvin felt guilty for that. He had promised them they would be safe in Estes Park.

He walked over to Sandra on his way out to check on her.

"Hey," he said. "Are you okay?"

"Good as I can be, considering my brother is out there in the chaos," Sandra said. "Are you... are you okay? I mean after Anna and the others..."

"Don't worry about me."

Sandra shot him a look of concern. "Just let me know if there's anything else we can do down here. I made a couple rounds to make sure no one needs any more medical attention. If there's a need for nurses somewhere else, I'll be there."

"If everything goes well tonight, hopefully, we won't."

"Even if we hold Eddy's people back, Wild Fire isn't going away," Sandra said. "With so many people packed into

Fort Golden, the risk of disease spread is going to increase. I know it's not top priority, but it might be worth mentioning."

Calvin had almost forgotten all about that due to the turmoil. He looked around, growing uneasy.

Shit, you might have brought Mouse's family into an even worse situation....

He shook the thought away, trying to stay positive.

They were safe down here.

He forced a sympathetic smile before departing the library. The corridors were filled with Rangers. Many ushered refugees to various shelters within the facility. Others carried weapons and ammunition outside.

He jogged his way up a set of stairs to the command center of Fort Golden. The three Rangers and two Secret Service agents guarding the room made way when they saw him approach. Palmer had already given them explicit permission to let Calvin in whenever he needed.

Inside, Secretary of Defense Montgomery stood behind a desk, leaning on her cane, behind two communications officers. Palmer was busy talking with three Rangers at another corner of the room, poring over a map of Fort Golden and the surrounding area hanging on a wall.

The FAC members, Martinez, Tiankai, and Piard, were talking with their own respective personnel, relaying frantic orders to their peacekeeping forces around Colorado. It sounded like a Wall Street trading room in the middle of a sudden economic collapse.

All around the room, staff huddled near computers showing live CIC camera feeds, maps, and more. Tension hung in the area as radio chatter from Albany kept them all updated on the bloody battle.

Calvin made his way to Palmer.

"Deputy," he said.

"Calvin, how you doing? How are the kids?"

"We're okay," Calvin said. "How about up here?"

Palmer looked toward Charlize and her staff.

"It's a mess," Palmer said. "Our people are bogged down bad in Albany."

Calvin wasn't sure what to say. "Just got to have hope."

"Hope won't save them, but reinforcements might," Palmer said. "All due respect, and all."

Calvin didn't mind his tone. He knew exactly what Palmer was going through. "Nope, I get it. How do you think I felt in Estes Park? Or hell, all those times running Steel when shit looked dark?"

"Shoot, I was so wrapped up in my crap... yeah, you know what it's like."

"I do. And I want to let you know I've got twelve Steel Runners willing to help. They're watching over the civilians right now in the library, but you just say the word, and we can be where you need us."

"Thanks," Palmer replied. "I'll let you know if—"

"We might have a problem," announced a Ranger, a middle-aged woman at a computer. Her nametape read Bollinger.

Palmer went over to her. "What is it?"

Calvin joined them, trying to make sense of what he was seeing.

Bollinger was monitoring black-and-white security cameras from a manufacturing facility. Huge flames billowed out the front of it.

In the grainy view, Calvin could see what appeared to be gunmen rushing into the building's loading docks.

"That's the Regeneraid facility," Palmer said. "What the hell is going on?"

"Looks like an attack," Bollinger said.

"Get Wheeler on the horn."

Calvin huddled behind them as more staff moved over to see what was happening. Charlize made her way through, asking for a SITREP.

"I'm trying to reach Doctor Wheeler," Bollinger explained. "He isn't answering. No one is. The facility seems to be under attack."

Calvin's heart began to climb up into his throat. His vision tunneled on the scene of carnage.

Some of the gunmen were exiting the building with scientists and technicians in tow. They began stuffing their new hostages into all manners of vehicles waiting in the parking lot.

Others, they simply executed. Bodies began to fill the asphalt between the cars.

Calvin's blood boiled at the unfolding massacre.

Bollinger suddenly shot up at her desk. "I tapped into the comms, and a man named Lincoln from Liberty Militia claims to have taken over the facility. All the security forces there have been defeated."

"Lincoln and the Liberty Militia," Charlize said. "That mean anything to you, Palmer?"

"No, I don't think so."

"Is that Wheeler?" someone asked, pointing at the screen.

"Oh God," Palmer said. He leaned down and confirmed it was indeed the doctor being shoved into one of the vans.

"We need to get backup out there immediately," Palmer said. "We cannot let Regeneraid fall. Maybe we can call in the FAC reserve forces."

Calvin knew that it was too late for that. By the time they got to the facility, this Liberty Militia would be long gone. The ride to Centennial from here would be a minimum of thirty minutes.

Charlize seemed to know the truth too. She ran a hand through her thin hair and said exactly what Calvin was thinking.

"The facility is compromised," she said. "It's done."

"So what do we do?" Palmer asked.

Everyone seemed to look to the Secretary of Defense for an answer. Before she could respond, a distant boom sounded outside.

The first low thud was followed by a second and third.

Then the sound of gunfire.

Calvin felt his muscles tense.

All the emotions that had been flooding through him a second ago vanished.

It was clear what had to be done.

The enemy had come to them. The Gomezes and the rest of the refugees were in danger. For that matter, if this stronghold fell, all of Colorado was at risk.

Calvin unslung his M4, pulling back the charging handle. He touched the White Sox cap in his pocket solemnly, thinking of those he'd lost. The time for deliberation and careful consideration of their defenses was over.

It was time to fight.

"I'm going to go get my Runners," he said.

25

RAVEN WAITED NEAR A CHARCOALED OLD VOLKSWAGEN near the barn in Albany.

Through his NVGs, he watched at least twenty white shapes flee out of the barn and the neighboring cabins. They ran down the dirt road to the west.

The enemy was taking the bait, leaving their entrenched positions.

Abbott wasted no time giving the orders to gun down anyone and everyone trying to retreat.

"No prisoners," he called over the comms.

The harshness of those words echoed through the comms struck a chord of fear in Raven. It wasn't that he didn't agree with it, though. Not after what the Rattlesnakes and their Union had cost the Rangers, and everyone else in the New Frontier.

Anyone that escaped tonight was an enemy they would have to fight another day. And anyway, they weren't interested in taking prisoners. They had to stay focused on their ultimate goal: stopping Eddy.

Dealing with prisoners would get in the way of their ultimate goal: stopping Eddy.

Raven stayed crouched with Creek by his side.

To the west, a sudden salvo of gunfire boomed. Muzzle flashes flared near the IR tags of all the Anvil Team forces that had been waiting to ambush the fleeing Rattlesnake Union forces.

Raven watched the battle rage for only a few seconds.

"Hostiles neutralized," Blair reported drily.

"Copy, advance to the cabins," Abbott ordered.

The IR tags representing the Anvil teams filtered in from the west. At the same time, the engines of the APC and the rest of Hammer Teams' vehicles echoed through the town from the east.

A few sporadic gunshots burst from the cabins, but the booming return fire from the machine guns atop the APC was enough to stop the defenders.

Abbott's forces closed in down the road, decimating the final stubborn resistance with concerted gunfire.

Finally, their forces began to converge near Sawmill.

"All teams, we need a perimeter around Sawmill now," Abbott said. "Leave reserve forces throughout town to clean up the rest of the Rattlesnakes and prepare for our final assault."

Raven took the cue to make his advance, sticking close to the shelter of trees.

Even with the main contingent of defenders eliminated, sporadic gunfire popped around the town. It seemed that the enemy had a hard time learning when to stay down.

Those fighters that were still out there would keep at it until the last of them were dead.

Calls over the radio sent members of the Anvil and Hammer Teams in different directions to root out the remaining enemy soldiers.

Raven stopped when he was nearly at Sawmill Lodge. The two-story building was only about thirty yards away now. Gunmen were poking out of the windows on the second floor and first floor. He guessed the lodge held more booby traps to slow down the attackers.

A balcony wrapped around the second floor. Only two windows and a screen door led inside from the balcony. A truck with a rigid camper shell was parked beneath.

"Hammer Charlie-One," Raven called to Lindsey. "I think we can make our way up to the second floor. Maybe attack from the top on the western side. There's a truck parked close enough that we can climb up and make our way in."

"Copy that," Lindsey said. "Anvil Alpha One, meet me on Raven's position."

Abbott chimed in next. "I'll send additional Rangers and Spartans to clear the ground floor. Hammer Charlie will clear the second floor with Recon Alpha and all available Anvil teams."

"Copy, on my way," Blair said.

While the attacking forces surrounded Sawmill, Raven calculated a concealed path through the woods.

By sticking close to the underbrush, he thought they stood a chance of making it to the truck unseen. Then they could quietly climb up to the balcony, almost completely out of eyesight from anyone inside the building.

Crunching came from the woods behind Raven. He turned to see IR tags of three Royal Marines who'd made it through the carnage.

Blair led them. Raven gave him a silent nod as the Marines broke into combat intervals, posting up in the woods.

They hunkered down and monitored the lodge for another couple minutes as the fighting raged on elsewhere.

More crunching sounded through the woods to their east. IR tags followed, bobbing between the trees.

Lindsey's team of five Rangers joined Raven and the Marines.

The sheriff signaled that she had two more squads of Rangers and Spartan soldiers standing by, ready to infiltrate the lodge from the street. They were stationed behind the single functional APC working its way around the smoking wreckage of the first.

Raven and Creek took point through the forest toward the truck with the camper shell. He kept low, prowling through the tall dry grass. Their enemy would have a hard time seeing them sneaking through the foliage without their own NVGs.

Once the group was only a couple yards away from the truck, he snuck toward it alone after motioning for Creek to return to the woods.

The dog would be a liability in close quarters combat, and he couldn't easily lift the canine up to the balcony either. Creek whined, but followed the command, slinking back to the forest.

With the Akita safely hidden again, Raven climbed over the truck's camper shell until he reached the balcony.

Stretching up on his toes, he got his fingers around the edge of the balcony. He pulled himself up, his muscles straining as he listened for voices through the open windows above.

He heard whispers, but so far, it didn't sound like anyone had heard him.

Slowly, he hoisted himself over the railing then pressed himself flat against the wall.

Then, with a hand signal, he let the others know the path was clear. One by one, the Rangers and Marines silently climbed the truck.

The staccato rattle of gunfire throughout the town helped conceal the rustle of their equipment and their bootsteps on the wooden balcony. The two Marines made it up first, helping Blair climb up. Lindsey and her five Rangers followed.

The Marines each took position under a window.

Raven, Lindsey, and the Rangers stacked up outside the screen door.

Plucking his flash grenade off his chest, Raven then used his other hand to pull out his buck knife and cut through the screen.

Lindsey began the countdown, holding up three fingers.

Somewhere to their west, an explosion roared.

Screams rose in the distance.

Lindsey counted down to two.

At the same time, the APC pushed up the dirt road, closing in.

The rumble from its engine shook through the lodge's wall. Gunfire blasted out from the bottom floor. The smack of bullets against the APC's armor rang out in a shower of sparks, followed by the buzzsaw screech of a machine gun unleashing hell.

The countdown went to one.

Raven pulled the ring on the flashbang.

Lindsey curled down her last finger.

Go-time.

Raven pitched the flashbang through the hole in the screen. It clunked inside on the old plank flooring. A mere second later, the grenade burst with a ringing pop and a supernova of brilliant light. The NVGs automatically responded by temporarily flicking dark to protect Raven's eyes.

That was the signal to move.

"All teams, go!" Lindsey said.

Bootsteps pounded from below. Abbott's Spartans and the other teams that had used the APC to advance would be breaking through the ground floor now.

Raven kicked open the screen door and pushed into the darkness.

As he did, the Marines infiltrated through the windows to either side of the door. Raven went into a corridor with doors on each side, stretching about thirty feet until it ended in a T-intersection. Two hostiles were in the hall, trying to take cover behind an overturned cleaning cart.

Raven unleashed a burst that sent the first man sprawling to the floor. Lindsey, surging in behind him, fired another salvo that lanced through the second man.

On both sides of the hall were the guestrooms. Judging from the sounds of gunshots in the first two, Raven guessed the Marines had successfully entered through the windows. They would now be clearing those rooms.

The Rangers behind Lindsey covered Raven as he pushed down the hall. Lindsey signaled them to take the next room on the right.

Again, Raven opened the door, rifle ready. His muzzle swept over what appeared to be an empty living space. Just a bed and another open door leading to a bathroom.

He and Lindsey started to walk at a hunch toward the bathroom.

As they made it around the bed, Raven saw the glint of a fishing line. Yet another trap. When he bent and began to cut it, a shape leapt up from the other side of the bed.

Lindsey swiveled and started to fire. But her ambusher, a Rattlesnake with a tomahawk, leapt over the bed, then bent her wrists back so her rifle was aimed at the ceiling.

With one hand, he kept her muzzle aimed at the ceiling. With the other, he started to slice down with his tomahawk.

Raven still had his multitool in hand from cutting the IED wire.

He flicked the knife blade out of it and threw it straight at the attacker in one fluid motion. The small blade punched into the side of the man's neck, causing him to recoil.

It wasn't enough to kill him, but it bought Lindsey time. She stepped back, dodging his swinging tomahawk.

Raven closed the distance in a single lunging step. Then he swung his M4 up, catching his foe in the stomach with the gun barrel. He squeezed the trigger, sending bullets tearing through his guts and into the wall behind. More blood popped out of the man's mouth in bubbles as he crashed to the ground.

Gunfire and screams sounded from the hallway.

"Raven!" Lindsey yelled.

They rushed out to find two of the Rangers already down at the end of the hallway where they had come. A Rattlesnake stood above them with a shotgun, smoke whisking out of the barrel.

He aimed it at Lindsey and fired just as Raven yanked her back into the room.

Raven then dove out into the corridor and fired a burst at the warrior pumping in another shell. The bullets caught him in the jaw, blowing off half his face.

Angry shouts came from the opposite end of the hallway where Blair and his two Marines had been searching. Raven twisted around their direction.

One of the Marines was on the floor, gripping a chest wound. His head jerked back as gunfire blasted his skull. The shooter came out of another door, holding a pistol.

The enemy warrior aimed his pistol at Raven and started

firing. The first couple shots slammed into the wall as Raven ducked back. Drywall and dust burst out from each impact.

But then the bullets stopped coming, which hopefully meant he was out of ammo.

Raven cautiously moved from his cover to fire. As soon as he got a better look at the enemy, he recognized the tall, muscular Apache.

Robert Cosey.

"Raven! I've been waiting for you!" he shouted. The man took out a stone ball club from his belt and rushed forward.

Gunshots spewed from another doorway to Raven's right. A Rattlesnake tumbled out in a spray of blood. Blair strode out after him, covered in crimson. The Royal Marine had his rifle aimed at the Rattlesnake's chest and fired again.

At the sound of those shots, Robert whipped his club at Blair. The club slammed into the side of Blair's face, knocking him backward. Blood flecked from a new cut along his cheek, and his fingers splayed, dropping the rifle.

Raven traced his aim back toward Robert. But before he could get a bead on him, three more hostiles emerged from the doorway where Raven had shot the first man in the face.

Rounds exploded in Raven's direction. They crashed into the doorway and wall, sending sprays of woodchips and splinters.

He was forced to retreat into the cover of his room again, blocking Lindsey from exiting. She still had a flashbang on her vest.

It gave Raven an idea.

Yanking off the flashbang, he threw it around the corner at the three hostiles advancing toward them. Then he ducked back, covering his ears. The resulting high-pitched blast and blinding flash of light tore through the hallway, making Raven's ears ring.

He waited two seconds before moving back out. Somewhere in the chaos, Robert had descended on Blair. They were on the ground, struggling in a vicious fight. Fists flew as they cursed and yelled. Raven couldn't get a clear shot and turned back to the three disoriented Rattlesnakes in the opposite direction.

With his rifle shouldered, Raven blasted the closest Rattlesnake in the chest. He roved his rifle to the guy on the left, ending his life with a burst to the head. Blood and bone flecked the wall as the man slid against it, leaving a crimson streak.

When Raven sighted up the third man, the bolt clicked, his magazine empty.

"Lindsey, help Blair!" he shouted.

Raven let his rifle fall on its strap and pulled out his knife, running for the last of his targets. The disoriented Rattlesnake was still stumbling around, holding his hands over his ears and blinking rapidly.

Just as he prepared to pounce, the dazed man raised his rifle and began firing wildly. Most of the bullets lanced into the ceiling and walls, but one round hit Raven square in the chest. It felt like a brick had slammed into his ribs at a hundred miles per hour.

The air wheezed from his lungs. Darkness clouded his vision as pain flooded his system. He couldn't breathe and stumbled, hitting the wall. Then he slid to the floor.

He landed on his back, struggling for air.

Lindsey wrapped an arm around Robert's neck, trying to peel him off of Blair. The Apache warrior surged to his feet and slammed her into a wall. Cracks spread through the drywall as Robert recovered his stone ball club and started swinging it at Blair and Lindsey.

Raven twisted back to the Rattlesnake that had shot him.

Agony clouded Raven's vision, but he could see his enemy was regaining his composure. The man was fumbling with a new magazine for his rifle.

There were only seconds to act.

Raven gripped his chest. He tried to inhale. His ribs felt like they were on fire, and he started to slide back down.

A voice called his name in the distance.

Or maybe it was close.

Was it Lindsey?

Raven got up to his knees just as the Rattlesnake palmed in another magazine and raised his rifle.

This was it, the end.

Creek wasn't coming to save him, and there was no time to fight back.

Still, Raven tried to bring up his hand to shield himself from the bullet. Like that would actually do anything. The futile gesture was pure animal instinct, desperation before death.

Then something slammed into his shoulder with a heaving impact. But it wasn't a bullet tearing through flesh. It was the weight of a body.

He crashed back to the floor under the corpse of his would-be killer. Lindsey had abandoned Robert and stood several feet away from the dead man, her pistol in hand.

As his vision slowly returned to normal, Raven saw blood pooling into a river of red from the corpses. There were so many of them.

Two Rangers. Two Marines. Four Rattlesnakes.

The corridor had become a death trap.

Gunfire was still sounding in other rooms, along with the clash of hand-to-hand combat.

Screams came from Blair as Robert beat him. Lindsey turned back to him and Robert.

Raven blinked. It was already too late. The lieutenant slumped with his back against the wall. Half his face was a pulpy mess, gore and broken bone. The Royal Marine tried to push himself up as Robert coiled back his club for a killing blow.

"No!" Lindsey yelled, bring her pistol to bear on Robert.

Instead of hitting Blair, Robert swung his blood-drenched club at Lindsey, knocking her pistol away. She fell to the ground, and Robert continued his arc with the club. It struck Blair right in the neck. The sickening crunch of cartilage was followed by a hissing gasp from Blair.

His trachea was broken.

Pushing at the ground, Raven tried to get up, but between his injury and the weight of the dead man on top of him, he was pinned down.

Robert jerked his club back, and Blair slumped over sideways. Then Robert strode toward Lindsey, club held high.

She had a knife out, but he easily swiped it away with the club. The knife flew, pinging across the blood-soaked floor.

Again, Raven tried to get up. He could still barely breathe. The weight of the body was too much. Lindsey, meanwhile, dodged two violent swings of the club.

She couldn't avoid the third.

Robert hit her in the stomach with enough force to slam her into the wall.

She fell to her knees, spitting blood.

No, no, no!

Raven used all of his strength to finally buck the corpse off and roll out.

"Stop!" Raven wheezed.

Turning, Robert looked at him and grinned.

"She means something to you?" he called out.

"Let... let her go..." Raven stammered, stumbling forward. "Fight me."

Again, Robert smiled. He kicked Lindsey in the chest. Her body crashed backward into the wall again, and she hit the floor with a heaving thud.

Raven lurched toward Robert, arms outstretched, ready to avenge Lindsey.

But the sheriff wasn't done yet.

She scrambled toward Robert with another knife in hand. She slashed at Robert's ankle, slicing through his left Achilles' tendon. A gut-wrenching snap sounded from the severed tendon.

Screaming out in pain, he collapsed to the floor in a heap and dropped his club.

Panting for air, Lindsey snatched it up, then smashed Robert in the nose. Cartilage and bone crunched and gave way. She hit him again. His orbital bone shattered. A slurping pop sounded as his eye escaped its socket.

Robert fell to his stomach, then pushed himself up, incapable of surrendering to the agony.

"Where..." Lindsey choked out. "Where is Eddy?"

Blood gushing from his nose, palming the ground on his knees, Robert looked up at her. She stood above him with the club, ready to deliver another devastating blow.

"Where is he?" Lindsey asked.

Robert spat blood on the floor. "You don't find... you don't find Eddy. He'll... he'll find you..."

Lindsey brought the club up. A fire burned in her eyes as she let out a baleful cry.

Raven had never seen the sheriff filled with so much rage. Any modicum of mercy left in her had been destroyed by Blair's death.

She brought the club down on Robert's head like a

lumberjack pounding a stake into the ground. His skull burst in a violent, nauseating crack.

-26-

Palmer had wanted to travel north to join the fight, but the fight had come to him. Still, though, he wasn't out there engaged in battle. He was inside the CIC with the other leaders, trying to keep everyone alive.

It seemed that was going to be impossible with the enemy descending upon Fort Golden. Their base was under a relentless assault by an unknown number of forces.

Another boom thudded through Fort Golden followed by the staccato rattle of gunfire.

"They're hitting the southside hard," Bollinger reported from her comms station desk.

Palmer took stock of the room.

Charlize was still monitoring the attack up north with her team. Rangers watched monitors piping in security camera views or listened to radios filled with reports of hostile sightings.

The FAC members were huddled around their own table, contacting their reserve forces at Buckley.

Palmer watched a monitor streaming a view of the front gate. He was having a hard time standing around and not being out there fighting like his Rangers, Calvin, and a shit ton of other people, but he was needed here to lead.

Fires roared up around hostiles vehicles that seemed to have been sent straight at the walls like explosive suicide drones.

Flashes of gunfire sparked from the abandoned neighborhoods to their south. It seemed like the main enemy force was using the cover of the old houses to advance.

"How many hostiles have already made it to the walls?" Palmer asked Bollinger.

"Reports range between ten and thirty, Deputy," she said, her voice hitched in panic. "It's hard to say. They're using the cover of the fire and smoke to conceal their movements."

"They're trying to breach the southern wall *and* the main gate," another officer cried.

"Send Reserve Forces Alpha through Charlie there immediately," Palmer said.

"Deputy!" Montgomery called from her station. "I need you here *now*."

Immediately, Palmer rushed to join her.

"What's going on, ma'am?" Palmer asked.

"We're receiving word that the fighting in Albany is not going as planned," Charlize said. Her lips tightened into a grimace. "We've taken some casualties. Lieutenant Blair... is KIA... and there's no sign of Eddy."

That hit Palmer like a punch to the throat.

The lieutenant had been a staunch ally, a major force in the Foreign Advisory Council, and even a close confidante to Lindsey. He couldn't imagine what the lieutenant's loss meant for their war efforts. Much less for how the United Kingdom would view its obligation to help secure the New Frontier.

Of course, none of that mattered if they couldn't keep Fort Golden secure tonight.

He had to hope that Lindsey could still pull off a victory and take Eddy down. Assuming he was up there.

But at this point, Palmer feared that Albany had just been another of Eddy's distractions. He wouldn't be surprised if the asshole was one of the people trying to tear through Fort Golden's front door.

"We need to get you out of here, ma'am," said a Secret Service agent. "If we wait much longer, we won't be able to get a chopper in here."

Palmer looked around the room in what seemed like slow motion. On each of the security cameras, more attackers were hitting different areas of the fort.

One by one, his people on the walls were being picked off. This was a coordinated, planned attack that he didn't know if he could stop.

"Go now while you still can, Secretary Montgomery," Palmer said.

She waved him off like she had her agents.

"The cancer from my radiation is going to finish me off soon, and I'm not one to cut and run," she said. "I'm staying right here with you all."

Palmer wanted to argue. But he knew better. This noble woman had made her choice. She wanted to stay and fight and, God forbid, maybe even die beside her people.

Seeing her bravery, Palmer vowed it wouldn't come to that.

"If you're not going to leave, we've got to at least get you to safety. This room is liable to be targeted by—"

Without warning, the lights went dark.

Most of the computers flicked off save for a couple hooked up to external backup batteries. A battery-powered red emergency light illuminated the exit nearby.

"Oh shit, external power is gone," Palmer said. "They must've severed the lines."

The automatic generators kicked in a few seconds later. Lights flickered back on, and the hum of rebooting computers filled the room.

Another dull thud echoed outside followed by the incessant chatter of gunfire.

"We've got people trying to get rope ladders up on the north wall now!" Bollinger shouted. "They've gotten Molotov cocktails in both guard towers. We've lost our machine gun nests."

"Send Reserve Forces Delta and Echo to the parking lot," Palmer said. "Prepare for a possible breach."

"On it," Bollinger replied.

Palmer had to think fast. "Right now, we've got the civilians spread out in facilities around the building and near the prison." His stomach flipped at that thought. "Good Lord, we've locked up so many outlaws... Maybe that's their goal. Maybe the enemy wants to rebuild their army with all those prisoners."

Charlize's face went pale. "How many prisoners do you have here?"

"Capacity is 1500 people, ma'am," Palmer said. "We reached that months ago. I think we're near 1700 now."

"We're sitting on a time bomb," she said. "If those generators get cut, and Eddy's people make it into the prison, then..."

Palmer tried to think like Eddy, to figure out what the Rattlesnakes had planned. No doubt the enemy would come straight to this room to take down Fort Golden's leadership. At the rate things were going, Palmer feared that would happen before any reinforcements could help.

So he was going to have to play a little hide-and-seek with the Rattlesnakes.

If the main parking lot was taken over, there was one potential emergency exit. One way he could get people out of Fort Golden without sending them through a blender of gunfire and explosions.

First, he needed to get the civilians down to the laundry

facilities and storage rooms of the prison. The huge, rein-forced doors blocking off the industrial-sized laundry machines and food stores could withstand a tremendous amount of abuse. Not to mention, the storage facility was directly connected to a secure loading dock.

He double-checked the security cameras to ensure that part of Fort Golden had not been breached. Most of the enemy forces were still focused on the main defensive threats at the front gate.

Palmer raised his radio and shouted for everyone in the room to hear. "Listen up!"

When Piard, Martinez, Tiankai, and everyone else were looking at him, he continued.

"We're moving command and heading to the laundry and storage facilities," he said. "Start packing up and get ready to go."

The staff began to load up their equipment while he brought up his radio. "Calvin, do you copy?"

"Copy," he grunted back.

"What's your position."

"We're holding security with the civilians."

"Okay, listen closely. We're moving to the laundry and storage area of the prison. I need you to get everyone ready to move. I'm coming that way shortly."

"Is it that bad?" he asked.

Palmer couldn't lie. "Get ready for anything, brother."

"Understood."

"Okay, let's move out!" Palmer shouted.

The staff followed him out into the hall. Rangers rushed from the command center, splitting into groups. Palmer had to slow as Charlize leaned heavily on a couple of her agents, unable to keep up with the brisk pace.

More booms echoed outside. Screams and the sounds of gunfire penetrated the building.

A radio transmission crackled, making Palmer stop in his tracks.

"Front gate has been breached," called a Ranger. "Rattlesnakes have taken the north wall."

"Shit," Palmer muttered. He stood in place, knowing he needed to move, but trying to think at the same time.

At this point, anyone staying out there was just waiting for death. They would be isolated from the rest of the defensive forces if they tried to maintain their positions.

He brought the radio to his lips and gave an order he never thought would be necessary. "Everyone, fall back to the main building. Abandon the walls."

The group came up on the medical facility next. It was already being evacuated. The chief physician, a man named Samson, ran over.

"We need more time," he said. "We've got too many patients to move."

"We're out of time," Palmer said. "Grab the supplies you need and get everyone that can move downstairs."

Nurses and other doctors were scattered throughout the ward, dealing with patients that had already been hospitalized and new ones suffering trauma wounds from the unfolding battle.

"Hurry, y'all have to clear out!" Palmer shouted.

Palmer noticed Jay Wauneka limping in a hospital gown. He staggered over to Palmer.

"Give me a weapon," he said. "I can fight."

"Hell no," Palmer said. "Stay out of the way."

He didn't trust the guy for shit and didn't have time for this.

"Fine. I'll use my fists," Jay said. His bruised features contorted into anger. "But I'm not going to just sit and hide."

Palmer ignored him, turning around, but then felt a hand on his shoulder.

"If Eddy's people make it in here, they will kill everyone," Jay said.

That sent a chill up Palmer's back.

"Then we better hope they don't make it in," Palmer said. He shook out of Jay's grip and hurried from the room.

From there, they headed for the library. Halfway there, another shocking call sounded over the radio.

"Hostiles have breached Fort Golden from the northern wall. Repeat, hostiles inside..."

No, no, no, Palmer thought.

His heart raced in concert with the pounding feet echoing down the hall. They were almost to the library. Almost to where Calvin and the civilians were located.

Just as he entered the corridor to the library, the lights went out again.

This time, they didn't turn back on.

"They cut the generators!" a voice called over the radio.

Darkness bathed the hall.

Only the malevolent crimson glow of emergency lights guided their path.

When he opened the doors to the library, he was greeted first by shrieks and screams. Flashlight beams hit the faces of the frightened civilians.

"It's okay! It's me, Deputy Palmer," he called out. "We need to get you all moved to a safer location."

Calvin pushed his way to the front of the group. He had a group of Steel Runners behind him. A handful had bandages over their arms or legs. But all were armed, and Palmer could see they meant business.

"Stay calm, don't push, and follow the person in front of you," Calvin said in a booming voice.

Holding the door open, Palmer waved for the refugees to exit down the hall. They began filing down the corridor after the Rangers using flashlights to guide them.

Charlize and the Secret Service agents stayed with him as the last of the refugees exited.

The last of the civilians began to leave the library. Raven's sister, Sandra, came out holding the hand of a younger girl that must've been her daughter. He knew the Gomezes from California of course and the Lithgows from his time visiting the Estes Park Refugee Center.

"Is that everyone?" he asked.

"That's it," Sandra replied.

"Good. We need to keep on moving."

The Secret Service agents remained on rearguard as they advanced down the corridor. Charlize was growing slower, her face paler. Gunfire echoed in the distance.

Palmer tensed up.

The fighting was now inside the facility for sure.

Panic took hold and people started running ahead.

At the same time, Palmer heard heavy footsteps rushing their direction.

They began running down the shadowy corridor, passing by multipurpose rooms and offices, then started down a set of stairs.

As soon as they reached the bottom, Palmer heard the clash of boots against the stairs. He turned as a group of three gunmen rushed out of the stairwell behind him.

These weren't Rangers or security personnel. A few wore the unmistakable khaki jackets of the Rattlesnakes.

Running was no longer going to save the group. Charlize was moving too slowly to outrace the enemy.

It was finally time to get into this fight. He signaled for a couple Rangers to post up with him.

"Keep going!" he said to Charlize and the Secret Service agents. "We'll slow them down!"

Palmer raised his rifle, aimed at the enemy, and held down the trigger. The shots tore into the lead Rattlesnake warrior just as he raised his rifle. His body jerked from the impacts. One of the other men pulled him out of the way while the third aimed at Palmer.

"Not today, asshole," he said as he squeezed off another burst.

The bullets caught the man in the face, blowing out the back of his head. The third man fired at Palmer. Rounds drilled into the wall nearby or hit the floor, sending up fragments of tile. Palmer was forced back. One of his Rangers moved around the corner to fire before Palmer could stop him.

Bullets ripped into the man, dropping him where he stood. Blood pumped from a neck wound and soaked through his shirt. By the time Palmer dragged him to cover, he was already dead.

"Fuck," Palmer said.

He waited a beat, then whipped around the corner to fire another burst. It was just enough to force the third hostile back. The brief reprieve gave him time to move from his cover as the Rattlesnake retreated into the stairwell.

"Palmer!" Calvin shouted from deeper down the hall.

Palmer put down another burst to keep the third hostile back.

"Go!" he screamed back to Calvin. "There are still civilians around the base. You've got to help them and get them down here too!"

"On it!"

Calvin ushered the others through the heavy metal door

at the end of the hall, the Steel Runners guarding them. When the last of the civilians was through, the Steel Runners ran up another set of stairs near the door.

Palmer reloaded his magazine and checked around the corner again, making sure no one would follow them. He signaled for his remaining Ranger to go join the civilians.

Loud voices called out from the stairwell where the third Rattlesnake had vanished. The open doorway beyond was dark. The shadows concealed whether or not if someone was lurking inside.

He maintained his aim at the opening, his finger on the trigger. Three enemies started to emerge from the dark, and Palmer fired. Rounds lanced into the first of the men, sending the guy sprawling, his rifle clattered over the floor.

Return fire exploded his direction.

He pulled back fast, but not fast enough to avoid a bullet glancing across the side of his neck. He stumbled around the corner to safety, bringing a hand up to feel warm, sticky blood. But it wasn't gushing out. The wound didn't feel deep. He must've just been clipped. The pain was like a sting from an angry wasp, but he didn't care.

He had been lucky.

"You got this, Cody," he said. "Chill and focus."

There were civilians relying on him to hold this corner. He had to keep these men from rampaging past him and massacring all those innocents. If he didn't keep it together, all those people could be slaughtered.

He knew he was risking his life. He knew this could be a losing battle. But shoot, three hundred Spartans had held off a hundred thousand Persians at the Battle of Thermopylae. Why couldn't he hold off some of Eddy's vermin for just a few minutes?

Sure, the Spartans fell. But their sacrifice had not been in vain.

Just like his wouldn't be.

He raised his rifle, held a breath in his chest, said a prayer, and prepared to meet his Maker.

———

Eddy walked down the Fort Golden corridor with his rifle, stepping over the bodies of people that had died to protect this place. Many were braver than he thought. They would have made good soldiers. Better than some of these mercenaries he had working for him.

But in the end, his mercenaries and allies had gotten it done.

Eight of his most trusted warriors followed him. They were hunting down the final wašíču that had fled in fear. There weren't many left now. Most of the Rangers and defenders were either dead, captured, or hiding.

There was only one that seemed to be giving his people a particular amount of trouble.

Deputy Cody Palmer, according to a scout that had seen the man. He had gunned down four Rattlesnakes before escaping after a group of civilians. Eddy reached those four dead warriors a few minutes later. Their bodies lay inside an open stairwell where they had fallen. Blood pooled around their bullet-filled bodies.

"We hurt him," said one of his soldiers accompanying Eddy. The man's name was Niyol—or wind.

Judging from the blood stains the man pointed to, it wasn't a fatal wound to Palmer.

The deputy was very much still a threat.

But soon he too would be eliminated.

Thanks to intel from his scouts, Eddy knew Palmer and a ragtag group of fighters had taken the refugees to the laundry and storage area in the next corridor. He wasn't sure how many civilians were down here, but he guessed there were hundreds of refugees.

Eddy didn't want to kill them like the government had once killed his own people. He thought of the Long Walk.

Now, finally, after over one hundred and fifty years, he would get his revenge.

Soon he would have his spoils of war—Raven's family.

His men had spotted them first in Estes Park. Then scouts had seen them escape here with the other refugees.

And even better, Secretary of Defense Charlize Montgomery was here.

Never before had the opportunity to realize the white buffalo's promise been so close. If he took the secretary alive, then there would no limit to his demands to free the New Frontier. But he had to do it fast, for reinforcements were no doubt on the way. Thirty minutes had already passed since they started their attack. He wanted to be long gone in another thirty. He had no intention of giving any incoming soldiers, Rangers, or whoever might be responding to this crisis time to follow.

As soon as he had Charlize and once he dispatched Raven's loved ones, he would vanish into the wilderness where he would use the secretary as a bargaining chip. The federal government didn't want to listen to him before, but they would now.

Before the invasion of Fort Golden, they probably thought they had won the day. From the last transmissions Eddy had received in Wyoming, he knew Robert was likely dead as were most of his forces there. But his enemies hadn't realized that Albany was just bait. A distraction. He hadn't planned on losing in Albany, but fate often worked in mysterious ways.

In any case, it was a necessary sacrifice to win the real prize.

Fort Golden and Charlize.

Eddy marched on with eight of his men through the corridor, their rifles pressed to their shoulders. He slung his and pulled out his tomahawk.

"The last of their resistance isn't far," said Niyol. He looked ready to live up to his namesake, prepared to blow away his enemy in a violent blast.

Eddy followed his men into a connecting hallway that led to a large doorway that sealed off the corridor leading to the laundry and storage area of the prison. On the floor were two dead Secret Service Agents, and two dead Rangers, illuminated by the glow of the red emergency lights.

"Can't get through this, Ahiga," Niyol said. "But that's where the wašíču went."

"Get Williams down here," Eddy said. "Tell him to bring some explosives. Fast."

They waited a few minutes for the big man to arrive. A sheath of grenades hung over his barreled chest, along with a bandolier of shotgun shells.

He carried a tactical shotgun with a door-breaching barrel.

Blood drooled from under a ripped-off sleeve that had been wrapped around his upper arm.

Two of his comrades followed into the corridor toward the door. The red glow gave his men demonic visages as they advanced. The light also reminded Eddy of the flames that had scarred his face. Memories of the fires licking his flesh at Montezuma Creek erupted in nightmarish fury, threatening to fill him with rage.

He clenched his teeth, ready to break into the room and take these wašíču down.

A voice suddenly crackled over his radio. It was Lincoln. He had made his way back here from Centennial and taken the command room center.

"We've disengaged the locks on prison cells for the prisoners that have agreed to fight for us," he said. "Your army is growing, Ahiga."

Eddy smiled then turned to his men.

"I want Charlize alive," he hissed. "The same with Raven's family. Take them all hostage. Anyone with weapons, kill them."

Nods all around.

"Do your thing, Williams," Eddy said.

Williams set a small block of C4 on the door's hinges and locking mechanism. He retreated with his men around the corner. Eddy put his tomahawk away and unstrapped his rifle.

Holding a detonator, Williams smiled for the first time since Eddy had met him. A deafening explosion followed, sending grit and debris around the corner in a wave of dust and smoke.

Niyol swiveled around the corner first with his rifle. Before he could get a shot off, a blast tore into his face. Niyol collapsed backward. What was left of his skull was nothing but a grisly mess of red and white. He had been pulverized by a shotgun blast.

The rest of Eddy's men fired back, forcing whoever had killed Niyol into hiding.

"Take them down!" Eddy said.

He followed his group inside as they took cover in the dark room. He took in the scene quickly, using the flashlight beams from his comrades and his rifle's tactical light.

They had entered a large rectangular room filled with

shelves of canned goods and boxes. The space was truly cavernous, with plenty of hiding spots.

Whoever had killed Niyol was already gone in the network of shelves.

Gunfire cracked from behind a row of crates across the room. Gunfire slashed into two of his men. One of the men's head flicked backward, then crumpled into a shelf. The other soldier writhed in pain, holding his gut.

Eddy fired at the barrels and stacks of boxes the shooter had hidden behind. Canned goods exploded on impact. Grain and rice sprayed from big plastic bags. Someone behind those shelves dashed away. But an agonized groan told him that someone else hadn't been so lucky.

"One Ranger down!" one of his men said.

Williams advanced with his two men on the left. They moved down a row of shelves full of cleaning supplies.

Eddy directed his light down his aisle and searched for movement. He thought he saw someone moving behind a stack of crates.

Screams and cracking wood sounded to his left where Williams and his men were. Eddy turned just as shelves crashed onto all three of them.

Machine gun fire ripped into the pinned men trapped under the shelves. Eddy searched for the shooter, firing a blast through the shelves farther down. A silhouette rushed past his glancing rifle light. The shooter was gone again.

He ran over to Williams. The big man pushed up one of the shelves. Blood dripped from lacerations in his face and arms. His two men remained flat against the floor. Blood soaked the floor around their body.

"Keep moving," Williams growled. "Let's kill this motherfucker."

As the rest of the Rattlesnakes advanced, they were again hit by a hidden gunman.

Eddy sighted up the enemy's muzzle flash across the room and let off a wild spray. Bullets shredded cardboard boxes and sent another stack of aluminum cans tumbling and leaking over the floor. He fired a second burst, aimed at the boxes at the bottom shelf. Whoever was behind it escaped again.

Eddy was starting to wonder if the shooter was just one man.

One man that killed five of mine, he thought.

Was it really this Deputy Palmer that Niyol had told him about?

Eddy flashed advance signals to his fighters, who continued onward, their lights raking over the shelves and boxes.

"Palmer, can you hear me?" Eddy called out, his voice echoing. "There's no escape. Surrender and save your life."

"Fuck you!" a voice called back.

Eddy looked to Williams and the other men.

"Find him and kill him," Eddy snarled.

He stepped through the middle aisle of shelves. Two of his men went to the right side and another two to the left. Eddy picked up the sound of footsteps.

He heard rustling between some of the shelves behind him.

Instinctively, he threw himself to the ground.

Gunshots roared above him from behind, the sound blasting the enclosing space. Rolling to his back, he fired randomly into the darkness.

But nothing was there.

Eddy got up and found cover, breathing heavily.

This Ranger, Palmer, was toying with him.

"*Mai-coh*," he whispered. Mai-coh meant both wolf and

witch.

Williams waited ahead, looking at Eddy as if to see if he was hurt.

"Keep going," Eddy said.

A slight icy tingle trickled up inside him.

Fear.

He buried it, sublimating the emotion to fuel his movements instead of making him freeze. Together, with three of his remaining men, they advanced across the room. Williams was on point now, his shotgun up and ready to take off the face of this witch wolf.

They were almost across the room when he heard footsteps coming from behind again. Palmer was once more trying to flank them.

Eddy whirled with his rifle. He expected to see a Ranger. Instead, he was met with a man in a hospital gown.

Not just any man.

Jay.

The shock of seeing the Navajo detective made Eddy freeze for just a second.

That wasted second cost him the chance to shoot Jay dead.

Fists pounded the side of Eddy's face, breaking old wounds.

He dropped his rifle so he could grab the man's wrists. Then he sent a knee straight into his groin. Jay let out a cry of pain, and Eddy pushed him backward, slamming him into a shelf.

Eddy pulled out his tomahawk and prepared to bring it down on Jay. Before he could, gunfire exploded at the end of the room. Eddy instinctively ducked as rounds peppered his remaining men.

The last of his Rattlesnakes hit the ground. All except for

Williams, who dove behind the cover of a crate with a heaving grunt.

The shooter finally appeared, standing from behind a crate. He was silhouetted in the darkness against the red glow of emergency lights. He moved around the crate. Eddy assumed he was trying to get a clear vantage to shoot at Williams.

The man wore a cowboy hat and Rangers' shirt. On his shirt, a deputy badge gleamed with the emergency lights.

Definitely Palmer, Eddy realized.

But Palmer wouldn't get the shot he was looking for. Eddy moved away from Jay just for a second, freeing a hand from his tomahawk and pulling out his pistol. He needed to save Williams from the deputy.

Eddy fired wildly at Palmer. Rounds crashed into the shelves, forcing Palmer to duck. Williams used the moment to lunge up and around the crate, wrenching the pistol from Palmer's grip. Then he tossed the deputy backward into a stack of cardboard boxes.

In the few seconds that passed, Jay recovered and lunged at Eddy. He sank his teeth into Eddy's scarred nose.

Eddy let out a scream of agony and tried to push Jay off. It wasn't until he slashed Jay with the tomahawk that the incensed man let go.

Water streamed from his eyes in response to the intense pain. Eddy blinked, trying to clear his eyes. Jay spit out a chunk of flesh, snarling like a wild animal. Then he lunged again.

This time, Eddy was ready. He grabbed Jay's shoulder and used his momentum to slam him into the toppled canned goods. His skull cracked against the concrete floor.

To his surprise, Jay went limp, fingers loose. Blood dripped from his skull.

Eddy searched for his rifle in his blurred vision. The tactical light beamed across the floor, revealing it was resting under a shelf. He scooped it up and aimed it at Williams and Palmer.

Palmer now had a knife out. He thrust it into Williams' stomach over and over. The massive man had blood pouring from multiple wounds. He still fought like a bear, grunting and yelling. Eddy couldn't get a clear shot on Palmer, but he could tell Williams was done for and Eddy squeezed off a burst.

Palmer pulled Williams in front him to block the bullets. The big man jerked and roared in agony.

Eddy fired until the bolt locked back on his rifle. Empty.

Palmer let go of Williams and turned to run. The big corpse hit the ground with a thud.

Eddy pulled out his tomahawk, cocked his arm, and let it fly.

The blade whirled through the air and cleaved a chunk of flesh behind Palmer's shoulder blade. The Ranger tumbled to the ground, yelling in pain. He collapsed right in front of another metal door at the back of the storage room. The doorway, Eddy assumed, where the civilians must be hiding behind.

Blood oozing down his face and eyes streaming tears, Eddy stumbled. He took a moment to wipe off his face. The wound stung like hell and his stomach lurched when he realized how much of his nose was missing.

But adrenaline kept him moving.

As he walked toward Palmer, he took out some gauze from his pack. He did his best to staunch the bleeding from his destroyed nose. He spat as he passed Jay's limp body. The traitor deserved his ignoble death.

Footsteps pounded near the entryway. Eddy raised his

rifle and palmed in a fresh magazine, ready to blast whoever it was.

He was relieved to see four more Rattlesnakes surge toward him. He gestured toward the door to the next room.

"The civilians are back there," Eddy said. He could picture the frightened faces on the other side of the door.

Sandra and her daughter came to mind.

And, of course, Charlize.

Soon he would have her as a prisoner. He would be on the final path to victory. But first he had to finish off Palmer.

The deputy lay on his side, groaning and staring at Eddy.

"Don't hurt the others," he said as Eddy marched over to him "They're innocent."

Eddy pulled out his knife and leaned down. He was going to make Palmer hurt before he killed him.

"I'm taking your scalp, mai-coh," Eddy said.

He swatted off Palmer's hat, then pulled the man up by his hair.

"This is for Robert," Eddy said.

Palmer's face paled, his chest heaving. His expression contorted in agony as mucus dripped from his nose and blood dribbled out from a cut lip.

"Asshole..." Palmer said.

Eddy placed his knife up to Palmer's scalp. He started to slice into it, drawing beads of crimson.

A voice suddenly called out behind him.

"Stop and drop your weapons!"

Eddy dropped his knife, raised his rifle, and spun in time to see a person glowing in the emergency lights near the storage room entrance. Another familiar face.

He remembered it suddenly.

Back in Montezuma Creek. This was one of the men with Raven.

27

CALVIN KEPT HIS RIFLE AIMED AT EDDY NEZ BUT HELD his fire. Palmer was on the ground, writhing in pain, a tomahawk sticking out of his back. If Calvin made too rash of a move, Eddy would slaughter Palmer. Behind the two of them, near a door to a second storage room, stood four Rattlesnakes with weapons raised back at Calvin.

Ortiz, Marino, Boston, and two more of his Runners had joined him after getting another group of civilians to safety in a nearby storage room.

"Put your weapons down," Calvin said. "My people got you surrounded."

Calvin and the Steel Runners had taken up shooting positions among the toppled crates and shelves in the room.

Eddy seemed to take them in with a sweep of his eyes in the darkness. Blood dripped from a makeshift bandage on his nose. The guy looked like he was considering his chances at coming out of this alive.

They weren't good.

The Steel Runners outnumbered the Rattlesnakes six to four, and they were all behind cover.

"You can either leave this room alive or dead," Calvin said. "Your choice. But you have three seconds to decide."

These next few seconds would also decide if more Steel Runners died under Calvin's watch.

Eddy angled his gun at Palmer. "Is he your friend?"

Calvin swallowed hard, hoping the enemy couldn't see his features go tight.

"How about this," Eddy said. "Drop your weapons, or he dies."

"Don't do it, bro," Boston said. "The criminal's a fucking liar."

"He'll kill Palmer and us no matter what we do," added Ortiz.

Palmer groaned. "Listen to them. Kill this asshole."

"I just want the Secretary of Defense," Eddy said. "Give her to me, and then you can all live. Even this filth."

"Don't," Palmer said again more urgently.

Eddy kicked him in the jaw, silencing him momentarily.

Calvin took a couple more steps toward Eddy. The Rattlesnake was about twenty feet from his position. The rest of his men looked between their leader and Calvin's team. He could practically feel the hot thread of tension drawing them all together.

How was he going to pull this off? Even with the help of the other Steel Runners, what could he do? What was his next move?

"I just want Charlize," Eddy said. "Give her to me and—"

"I said no!" Palmer shouted.

The deputy pulled out a knife and swiped at Eddy's leg.

Gunfire rang out, flashing in a blinding wave.

Screams erupted across the room.

Calvin held his trigger down. Bullets lanced at Eddy. The Navajo warrior dove to the ground, firing.

Three of the Rattlesnakes rushed for better cover positions under the onslaught. One collapsed in a bloody heap, sprawling over the concrete.

Calvin rushed forward to a new position behind a crate, shooting as he moved. In the chaos, he spotted Palmer crawling away.

But before Calvin could reach them, Eddy grabbed the tomahawk sticking out of Palmer's back and yanked it out.

Palmer's scream rose above the gunfire.

"NO!" Calvin shouted.

Eddy brought the blade down into the back of Palmer's head. Then he raised his rifle and fired off a wild burst.

Calvin dodged to his left, then slammed into Eddy, knocking him to the ground. The rifle flew out of his hand, but Eddy swung the tomahawk with his other.

Jumping back, Calvin narrowly missed having his gut opened by the blade. He used his rifle to parry another blow. Eddy fought his way up to his feet. Blood poured from his nose where the bandage had fallen away.

Calvin tried to bash his rifle stock right into it, but Eddy ducked and then swiped a leg out. Eddy's boot cracked against Calvin's knee.

Pain shot up from the impact. Calvin stumbled but took a step back to recover his balance.

The tomahawk came swinging at Calvin again. He moved back, losing his balance and falling, just as someone else surged past Calvin and slammed into Eddy.

Two of Calvin's Steel Runners lay nearby on the floor, reaching out toward him. One was Ortiz. A revolver lay a couple feet from him as he desperately tried to reach it. The other was Marino, her face screwed up in agony, clutching a wound in her side.

If Calvin stood any chance of helping them, he had to make sure Eddy and his surviving men were dead first.

Pushing himself up, he directed his rifle at Eddy and his attacker.

To Calvin's surprise, it was a guy in a hospital gown covered in bandages and bruises.

His shock only increased when he realized it was Jay Wauneka.

The two Navajo men tumbled across the ground.

Eddy lost control of his tomahawk, and Calvin scooped it up. The Rattlesnake shoved Jay off him. Jay went rolling across the floor.

At the same time, Calvin brought the tomahawk down on Eddy. The Navajo man kicked at Calvin, knocking him back. As Eddy pushed himself up, Calvin swung again with the blood-soaked blade right at Eddy's butchered nose.

Eddy brought his hand up, catching the blade with his wrist. He howled as the sharp metal cleaved through flesh and into bone.

He pulled his arm back, staring at Calvin like a horrified, wounded animal. Then he whipped out a knife with his other hand, slashing it at Calvin and forcing the SEAL backward. Then Eddy planted a leg into Calvin's stomach, knocking him over. Pain rocketed up Calvin's bad back, making him howl.

Screams sounded behind him.

Calvin briefly turned, eyes watering, to see three more Rattlesnakes pouring into the room. Boston was pinned down, firing at the three men, trying to force them back.

When Calvin recovered to take on Eddy, he realized the Rattlesnake was gone, disappeared into the shadows. He crouched behind a crate to change his magazine, watching the Rattlesnakes as Boston released a hailstorm assault on their position.

But instead of surging into the room, the Rattlesnakes backed away, holding their position near the entrance.

Calvin saw why a second later.

Eddy darted through the exit, escaping.

"Hold here!" Calvin shouted to the other two remaining Steel Runners. "Boston, let him be!"

The Steel Runners both took cover behind the shelves. As much as Calvin wanted to finish Eddy, he couldn't risk going after him and leaving the door to the civilians unguarded.

"Close that," Calvin said to Boston. "Barricade it, and don't let anyone through!"

Boston carried out his orders, Calvin turned to check on Marino and Ortiz. The sheer amount of blood around their bodies told him everything he needed to know.

Marino would never finish seeing the country, much less the world.

Ortiz wouldn't live to see New Mexico cleaned up and safe again.

Rage and sadness clashed in Calvin's mind. He went to Palmer next, hoping that somehow the deputy had survived.

On the way over, Jay got up on his knees, holding his head with one hand.

"Where's Eddy?" Jay asked.

"Escaped."

Jay stood and started toward the exit where Boston was working to secure the door. Calvin felt a hand on his leg, flinching at the touch. He looked back down to see it belonged to Deputy Palmer.

"Palmer," he stuttered. He leaned down to help.

But Calvin could tell there was no saving him.

Palmer mouthed something that Calvin couldn't quite hear. He bent down closer.

"Tell... tell Lindsey I'll miss..." He stopped to swallow. "Miss working with her."

"I will," Calvin said, grabbing the deputy's hand. "But you just hold on, brother, and you can talk to her yourself."

"Are the others... Charlize... are they... safe?"

Calvin looked over his shoulder at the metal door.

"Yeah," he said. "You saved them."

Palmer smiled. Or at least Calvin thought he did. The final bit of life clinging to the deputy drifted away. His fingers went slack, slipping from Calvin's.

He waited there for a few moments to make sure Palmer was really gone, not wanting to leave his side. Calvin closed his eyes. That tide of emotions was only growing stronger.

But his mission wasn't over yet.

After a minute, he stood and knocked on the door where the civilians were hidden.

"It's Calvin Jackson, Steel Runner," he said. "Open up."

The massive door scraped across the ground. The first person Calvin saw was Sandra Spears. She looked down at Palmer, then across the room. A tear slipped from the corner of her eye.

"Is it over?" Lara Lithgow asked, peeking out from behind her.

"I'm not sure if it's really over," Calvin said, "but I think we're safe for now."

————

"Faster," Raven said.

"I'm going as fast as I can," Lindsey said.

Raven sat in the passenger seat of her Bronco with Creek nestled up beside him. They were among the convoy of vehicles racing south toward Fort Golden and Denver. A light blue glow had begun to push back the blanket of darkness to their west as they raced down the highway, still an hour from reaching Golden.

Robert Cosey was dead, as were most of the Rattlesnake Union forces in Albany. They'd taken only a couple prisoner, stashed away in one of the Humvees with Lieutenant Abbott's soldiers.

Blair and the rest of the dead were still back there with a small crew that was working on gently preparing them to be moved for their last rites.

Raven had thought the death and destruction they had seen in Albany would be the end of it. He had been wrong. That had only been the beginning.

Eddy's forces had skirted down south while they were mired down in their offensive operations up north. Every step of the way, since the very beginning, this had been one big deception set by the Rattlesnake.

Abbott's voice called over the radio. "Lindsey, do you read?"

"Copy," she replied.

"I've got word from the FAC reserves forces," he said. "They've just made it to Fort Golden. No more sign of the enemy in the surrounding area, but they're reporting heavy casualties outside. I've told them to form a perimeter and keep the place safe for our arrival."

In the distance, with the sun's first rays, tall black columns of smoke clawed into the sky far beyond Denver's skyline. Raven guessed it was coming from the Regeneraid facility.

Lindsey tried them on the comms, and once again, no one answered. She tried Fort Golden next, also getting no answer.

Raven had never seen her so worried, so panicked. He felt the same way.

His insides were shriveling up and turning to stone. All he

could think about was Sandra and Allie tucked away some-where in Fort Golden beside all the other civilians like Mark and Maureen and the kids.

If Eddy found them... God, he didn't want to think what would happen.

"This is worse than I could have imagined," Lindsey said. "Regeneraid is gone. No more Commander pills to stop Wild Fire. And Fort Golden... I can't reach anyone."

She pounded the steering wheel out of frustration.

They continued onward.

Raven tried to reassure himself that it would be okay. Calvin was at Fort Golden.

The Steel Runner was a hell of a man. Hell of a warrior. If anyone could stop Eddy, it would be him. Calvin would know how to protect everyone.

Right?

Creek whined, and Raven petted the dog's neck. The Akita seemed to sense his worry.

Raven couldn't pry his eyes off the smoke.

Lindsey raced on in silence the entire hour until they finally made it to Fort Golden. The main gates had been broken and twisted, leaving a wide gap into the parking lot.

The Ranger and Army vehicles from their convoy spread out between the blackened husks of other vehicles. Some still burned. Smoke plumed from the guard towers, and Raven spotted rope ladders hanging from the walls.

Mexican, Canadian, Chinese, and other UN peace-keepers were now helping the injured or manning the damaged walls, keeping an eye on the foothills.

Bodies of men and women, both the enemy's and theirs, lay scattered in the parking lot.

Lindsey, Raven, and Creek got out of the Bronco, watching civilians filing out through the parking lot. Many were crying. Parents shielded their children's eyes from the death and destruction. Colorado Rangers ushered them out of Fort Golden and toward four idling buses.

Raven wasn't sure where those buses would take the people. Presumably to wherever the government thought was safe right now.

But he couldn't imagine anywhere in Colorado truly was safe anymore.

"God have mercy on us," Lindsey said.

Raven reached out to her and squeezed her hand. She took his as they watched the people stream by.

Fort Golden had once been a monument to the United States' recovery. Raven had visited several times to see Lindsey in the past. It had always looked formidable and impenetrable. Some belligerent forces had assaulted it before, but the Rangers had always dispersed the attackers with relative ease.

Now the place was a ruined mess.

Raven's gut turned over as more civilians came out of the main building and into the parking lot.

His heart began to race as he waited for the two faces he most yearned to see: Sandra and Allie.

He waited to see if they would come out on stretchers or covered in bandages.

Practically holding his breath in anticipation, he studied every survivor streaming out.

To Raven's surprise, Jay came out on a stretcher, escorted by a couple of soldiers. He looked in worse shape than the last time Raven had seen him. Another group of soldiers and Secret Service agents exited, all closely surrounding Charlize. Then came Calvin Jackson and a few of his Steel Runners escorting the Gomezes and the Lithgows.

And behind them came Sandra and Allie.

Raven ran to them, Creek bounding after. He scooped Allie up in his arms and pulled Sandra in tight. "I'm so happy to see you both."

Raven felt her hot tears soak into his shirt. Allie tightened her grip around his neck like she was trying to hold on to a light post in the middle of a tornado.

"Really, you have no idea how glad I am to see you," he said, unable to stop his own tears of joy. "I thought for a second... well, it doesn't matter now. I love you both so much."

"Raven," Sandra said, barely able to conjure words. "We love you too."

When Raven set Allie down, he looked back to see Calvin and Charlize were talking with Lindsey now in hushed voices. Charlize held Lindsey's hand, and Calvin put a hand on her shoulder, both their faces filled with sorrow.

Raven thought he overhead something Calvin said about Palmer being a hero and how thankful they were for what he did. Calvin caught Raven's eye and came over. Raven offered Calvin a hand. They shook before Raven pulled him into a hug.

"Thank you, brother," Raven said. "Thank you for standing guard."

"It wasn't just me," Calvin said. His eyes were red, and a tear rolled down his cheek. "You've got a whole bunch of people to thank. Palmer, my Runners, the Rangers... God rest their souls."

Calvin glanced back at the Gomezes. They were huddled together with the Lithgows.

"This is far from over," Charlize said. "We have very difficult work in the days ahead to take down Eddy and his army. I'm not leaving the New Frontier until they are defeated."

28

LINDSEY STOOD AT A TEMPORARY PODIUM SET UP IN White Ranch Park a full week after the Fort Golden disaster. The rolling green slopes overlooking Denver were filled with lush trees. This was the largest park in Jefferson County.

But right now, it felt far too small.

She looked out over a crowd of over three hundred people who'd gathered to grieve together. Military, Rangers, and civilian vehicles filled the parking lot, overflowing along the gravel road leading into the park.

Near the parking lot was a pavilion and an old cabin that used to be an open-air museum piece. Now it was the center of the memorial she had created for the lives lost in last week's battles. The rolling slopes offered eternal respite to all those buried here.

Lindsey looked out over the crowd that had gathered. Civilians, soldiers, Rangers, and politicians had made it.

After Fort Golden, they still hadn't seen any sign of Eddy, his Rattlesnakes, or his purported Operation White Buffalo. There had been no more attacks on border checkpoints or cities and towns on what used to be called the "safe" side of Colorado.

It was like the enemy had vanished into the mountains.

But she knew they would return. Stronger than before.

She would too, but for now, her concern was honoring the people who had made the ultimate sacrifice. Men like Blair and Palmer.

Charlize sat in the front row, looking up at her. Raven stood around the edge of the crowd among the hundred or so other people who had no seats. Calvin was next to him, along with the Lithgows, Gomezes, and Sandra and her daughter. One of the Steel Runners Lindsey recognized, a guy named Boston, was there.

Tiankai, Piard, and Martinez were there among the crowd. The FAC had yet again gotten smaller.

Standing to one side of the audience were the Royal Marines, all donning their dress uniforms.

Blair's body and the four of his Marines that had perished in the fighting were in caskets, ready to be shipped back to the UK. Everyone else was already in the freshly dug graves on the gentle slope.

Without adequate power, they didn't have enough functioning morgues to hold all the bodies. No cold storage space was big enough. With the hot late summer days washing over the Front Range, their only choice had been to bury the bodies as fast as they could.

It was not what these people deserved, but it was all Lindsey's depleted forces could handle.

Taking a deep breath, she started her speech.

"I'm not one for words, but today, I will do my best," she began. "We lost a lot of our friends and family over the past few weeks. Over time, I hope we will have a fitting memorial to honor each and every soul who lost their life defending our beloved state and the ideals we hold dear."

All eyes were on Lindsey. She hated this. Hated being behind a podium. She felt like a politician giving a stump speech.

"Their sacrifices were not in vain," she continued. "For now, we lay them to rest here on this slope, looking out to the east. Every morning, they will watch the sun rise over Colorado. A new day, promising new hope."

There was silence in the crowd. A few encouraging nods from people like Raven. Something just didn't feel right.

Sure, she'd rewritten this speech a dozen times, trying to convey her emotion. But she wasn't a master orator. This wasn't why she'd taken the helm of the Colorado Rangers.

This wasn't working.

Leaving the written speech behind, she stepped out from behind the podium, off the improvised stage, and toward the crowd.

"I'm sorry," she said, letting her voice boom over the audience. She didn't need a microphone. "I'm not a speech writer. Whatever words I came up with just don't do these people justice."

She faced the crowd.

"We are here to honor the dead, but I'm also going to explain how we win the fight so that their sacrifices weren't in vain." Lindsey pointed to the mountains. "The enemy is still out there. Eddy Nez and his band of murderers will strike again. We must be ready."

Her chest heaved as she went on. She could feel the tension in the audience, people leaning forward in their seats, shocked by the change in her demeanor.

"I promise you all one thing," Lindsey said. "I promise all

of you, until the day I die, I'm fighting for the New Frontier. We will never give it up to the enemy."

With that, she walked back to her seat near Charlize. Scattered applause sounded from the crowd. She didn't care if she'd left some of them bewildered by her anger. No doubt most expected her to give the same tired discourse people had heard so many times since the Collapse.

The governor got up to give a speech, but she tuned it out mostly. Because all those words might sound nice, but she was still missing chunks of her heart. Even if the United States recovered, Palmer wouldn't be here to see it. Blair would never get to see that his help had been worth it after everything.

So many other men and women were missing parents and brothers and sisters and spouses today who would never get to see the America that Diego promised.

Other notable people had a chance to share their thoughts and condolences with the crowd. Mostly politicians.

Lindsey tried to pay attention. Tried to respect their lip service.

Eventually, the speeches died down and people began to disperse down the trails and roads back toward Denver and Golden.

Lindsey lingered, walking alone over to the rows and rows of graves. Each was marked with a simple wooden board, carved with the occupant's name.

She stopped by one.

Deputy Cody Palmer.

She knelt and traced her fingers over the etched letters.

Footsteps sounded behind her followed by a friendly voice.

"He was a good man," Charlize said. "One of the best. I've

recommended him for the Public Safety Officer Medal of Valor to President Diego. Without hesitation, he already said yes. We didn't want to take from today's focus on honoring all the other victims, so we thought it best to hold off until we can have a memorial specific to the deputy."

Lindsey stood. "Thank you, he deserves it."

Charlize gave a warm, sympathetic smile, but then sighed.

"I wanted to wait until after the ceremonies to tell you," she said. "Thing is, we're running out of time."

"What?"

Charlize looked over her shoulder toward where Tiankai, Piard, and Martinez were speaking. "Your Foreign Advisory Council is being retracted. Every member organization and country is withdrawing from the New Frontier region."

"I figured."

"Between Eddy and Wild Fire, our allies are fleeing. They're saying this is *our* fight."

"Looks like both Eddy and Senator Shelby got what they wanted, then."

"Here maybe, but Shelby wants our foreign allies completely out of the country. He wants to shirk their help. You know as well as I do that we cannot afford that."

Lindsey lifted her hat, then brushed a hand through her hair. "What's this mean for Commander treatments?"

"Right now, I've got the UK agreeing to take up the manufacture of the Commander treatments. It's going to take at least twice as long as Wheeler had projected for their efforts in Regeneraid, but at least someone's able to pick up the mantle safely out of Eddy's reach."

"How soon can they start shipping meds our way? Our current supplies aren't going to last more than a couple weeks."

Charlize again sighed. "They've only just begun converting a manufacturing plant to increase their production capacity. They have some small stores of it, but it's going to be several weeks before they produce the first new batch."

"My God..." Lindsey said. "That makes it all the more important we keep people around the New Frontier. We need more security to keep the Wild Fire locked down inside those borders."

"We're going to try, but Shelby's fiery campaign is hell-bent on painting our efforts in the New Frontier as a complete waste. He's claiming that if we keep spending money on it, we won't have the resources to rebuild the parts of the country that we do have left. Just today, he released a statement asking Americans what's the point of sacrificing themselves to secure a place that doesn't want to be part of the US anyway."

"Because it *is* part of the United States." Lindsey felt the heat rise behind her face. "We haven't given up so much to just surrender. I didn't just promise these people we'd continue fighting for nothing."

"I know, and I'm going to make sure that doesn't happen."

"Thank you."

Charlize nodded, and they parted ways. Lindsey walked back to the few people that were left. To no surprise, Raven was there with Sandra and Allie. Calvin was talking with the Gomezes, and even the Lithgows were nearby with Mark.

Raven walked over and put a hand on Lindsey's arm. They stood side by side as they looked over the graves. They didn't need to make any promises or say another word at all. Deep down, they both knew what was going to happen next.

They would be heading into the mountains soon, tracking Eddy. None of them would give up until the New Frontier was free of his terror.

New Frontier book 3: Wild Warriors, coming January 2023!
Preorder your copy now.

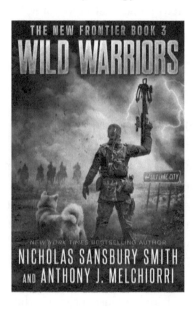

-ABOUT THE AUTHORS-

Anthony J Melchiorri is a scientist with a PhD in bioengineering. He used to develop cellular therapies and 3D-printable artificial organs. Now, he writes apocalyptic, medical, and science-fiction thrillers that blend real-world research with other-worldly possibility. When he isn't at the keyboard, he spends his time running, reading, hiking, and traveling in search of new story ideas.

Read more at https://anthonyjmelchiorri.com/ and sign up for his mailing list at http://bit.ly/ajmlist for free books and to hear about his latest releases.

Nicholas Sansbury Smith is the *New York Times* and *USA Today* bestselling author of the Hell Divers series, the Orbs series, the Trackers series, the Extinction Cycle series, the Sons of war Series, and the new E-Day Series. He worked for Iowa Homeland Security and Emergency Management in disaster mitigation before switching careers to focus on story-telling. When he isn't writing or daydreaming about the apocalypse, he enjoys running, biking, spending time with his family, and traveling the world. He is an Ironman triathlete and lives in Iowa with his wife, daughter, and their dogs.

Made in United States
Troutdale, OR
07/13/2023

11227016R10268